Why couldn't she come here even after she joined the church? What harm was there in helping the seniors with their craft projects? She enjoyed them and they seemed to like her just fine. Why did she have to choose between the church and them?

Zach.

How long could she pretend that every day she didn't like him more?

"Lorie?"

She shook herself from her thoughts, realizing that everyone had put away their crafts and were preparing to go to lunch. "Sorry." She stood and made her way to where they were waiting.

It was the truth. Every day she liked Zach more. At this rate she would be completely in love with him before the end of the summer. And where would that leave her? Joining the church and living in Wells Landing while her heart was in Tulsa with Zach. How would she survive that?

Books by Amy Lillard

CAROLINE'S SECRET

COURTING EMILY

LORIE'S HEART

Published by Kensington Publishing Corporation

LORIE'S HEART

AMY LILLARD

ZEBRA BOOKS
KENSINGTON PUBLISHING CORP.
http://www.kensingtonbooks.com

All Kensington titles, imprints and distributed lines are available at special quantity discounts for bulk purchases for sales promotion, premiums, fund-raising, educational or institutional use.

Special book excerpts or customized printings can also be created to fit specific needs. For details, write or phone the office of the Kensington Sales Manager. Attn.: Sales Department. Kensington Publishing Corp., 119 West 40th Street, New York, NY 10018. Phone: 1-800-221-2647.

Zebra and the Z logo Reg. U.S. Pat. & TM Off.

First Printing: August 2015
ISBN-13: 978-1-4201-3457-5
ISBN-10: 1-4201-3457-4

eISBN-13: 978-1-4201-3458-2
eISBN-10: 1-4201-3458-2

10 9 8 7 6 5 4 3 2 1

Printed in the United States of America

*To everyone who has ever questioned
if they made the right decision.
To everyone who has ever wondered
if things could be different . . . should be different.
Life can be hard and confusing, but it's beautiful.
Live it to the fullest.*

ACKNOWLEDGMENTS

Once again I have more people to thank than there's paper in the world, but I'll give it a try and be as brief as possible.

Thanks abound to the good Lord for giving me the important "what if . . . ?" question and the imagination to see it through. Even more important, He puts people into my path who help me in ways I would have never dreamed possible.

Thank you, Stacey Barbalace, for holding my hand and telling me it wasn't terrible when I'm sure you wanted to roll your eyes and do anything other than prop up my tender ego. Lorie's story could not have been told if not for your beautiful friendship.

As always, I owe a big thanks to my family for putting up with my slightly crazed "deadline" self who stumbles around at all hours of the day and night, constantly points out to anyone within earshot that "I have a book due," and is sometimes a bit, shall we say, disheveled. Your love means more to me than you will ever know!

Thanks to the team behind the book: my agent, Mary Sue Seymour; my editor, John Scognamiglio; and the entire Kensington team. I could not ask for better people to support my work.

Many, many thanks to my friends in Lancaster who allow me to run ideas by them and assist me when the right Dutch word is out of my grasp. Your help is invaluable; your friendship even more so.

And thanks to the readers who support my work. Without you, none of this would be possible.

Chapter One

Lorie Kauffman's black walking shoes squeaked against the overly waxed tile floor as she made her way down the long corridor. One arm was wrapped around her stepmother, Maddie. Her *mamm* pulled her close, neither one of them ready for the task before them. In truth, Lorie wanted nothing more than to turn and run from the coroner's office as fast as she could. As far as her feet would carry her.

The doctor walked in front of them, slower than she wanted, faster than she could take. He didn't say a word as he led them into the cold, sterile room. It was so different than anything Lorie had ever seen. Stainless steel and buzzing lights.

Only the squeak of their shoes could be heard as he led them to a wall that appeared to be a large filing-type cabinet. It was a little like the one her father kept in his office at the restaurant, except this one took up the entire wall.

She randomly wondered how the doctor knew which drawer to pull out. But he did.

The drawer opened, the body inside covered with a plain white sheet.

Mamm squeezed Lorie's hand so hard her fingers started to tingle. Her heart pounded in her chest as she watched the doctor fold back the sheet to reveal the lifeless face of her father.

With a gasp, *Mamm* turned away, only briefly looking at the man she had been married to for as long as Lorie could remember. But Lorie herself couldn't tear her gaze away. Her eyes were transfixed, as if by staring at him long enough she could somehow bring him back to life. She took in his wavy brown hair, normally so carefree, now pushed unnaturally back from his face. His beard matched in color, with only a few streaks of gray in the chest-length strands. Gone was the sweet smile that graced his lips. His eyes, normally the color of the afternoon sky, were closed, still behind their lids.

A cut slashed across his temple, the skin surrounding it dark. It was the only mark to testify that he'd been in an accident. A freak injury, they called it, that caused his brain to die when his body was still able to function. One tiny cut that ended his life.

"I'm sorry, ma'am," the coroner said. Lorie wondered how he did it. How he worked day in and day out with crying, grieving families.

Beside her, Lorie heard *Mamm* stifle a sob. Typical Amish, *Mamm* tried to hide her feelings. The only emotion she readily shared was her displeasure. Lorie pushed away the uncharitable thought. She would pray about it later, but for now all she could do was ignore the twinge in her gut and focus on what remained of her father.

"*Jah*," *Mamm* finally said. "That is my husband."

From the corner of her eye Lorie saw the man nod, then he started to pull the sheet back over her father's face.

Her hand flew up of its own accord to stop him. She wasn't ready yet. She wasn't ready to say good-bye, to have him covered and locked away from her forever.

A tickle twinged at her cheeks, and she wiped at it with her fingers, surprised to find them damp with tears.

"Lorie?" *Mamm* asked.

"Not yet," Lorie whispered in return. "Just a little while longer." She had to look all she could. What if she forgot his face as time passed? That happened with her own *mamm*. Her mother had died and over the years Lorie had forgotten her face. Since photographs were against the *Ordnung,* there were none to remind her. She couldn't let that happen to her *dat* as well.

"Lorie." *Mamm* tugged on her hand, but Lorie resisted. She needed to get one last look at him to hold in her heart. The strong slant of his jaw, the straight line of his nose, the mark just above his heart.

She blinked. It couldn't be. It went against everything the *Ordnung* stood for, the Bible, and all that God wanted for his people. Yet there it was, penned just above where his heart once beat. Another heart. This one had wings on each side and a name in such intricate letters she almost couldn't make it out. May not have been able to had the name not been as familiar to her as her own. Belinda.

That was her mother's name. Her mother who had died so long ago.

"*Kumm.*" *Mamm* tugged on her hand, pulling Lorie away from her father as the doctor covered him again. But it didn't change anything. The mark was still there. The heart, the wings, the name.

Her father had a tattoo.

In the days that followed Lorie didn't have much time to think about the tattoo, yet it was never far from her thoughts. There were preparations to be made. A coffin to be bought, a funeral to be planned. A father and husband to be laid to rest. A life to go on living.

The police had given them a box of things that had been found in her father's car. How did her father have a car? He was Amish!

When they arrived back in Wells Landing, *Mamm* had taken the box to the storage room above the restaurant. She taped the box shut and dusted her hands as if a dirty job had been completed. Lorie itched to climb the stairs and go through the box. What other secrets were hiding there?

She scanned the dining area of the restaurant. They had closed today in honor of her father. Maddie had wanted everyone to gather there to pay their last respects, eat, and otherwise spend time talking about Henry Kauffman. More than half the town had shown up to say good-bye to her father. He was nothing if not loved and admired by his community.

But there were too many people. More than Lorie could easily handle. Of course some of the mourners were *Englischers* that her father had worked with over the years. They didn't know a person needed to be invited to the funeral and had just shown up instead. Thankfully there was enough food to go around. But not enough room in the restaurant for the crowd and her own grief.

She glanced over to where her stepmother sat, tissue in hand as she talked with Helen Ebersol, the bishop's wife. The few remaining people at Kauffman's were starting to clean up the mess left behind from the wake. Paper cups and plates were tossed in the trash. Empty aluminum casserole pans disposed of as well. So much needed to be done that Lorie was overwhelmed with the prospect of doing anything at all.

"Lorie?" Emily Riehl grabbed Lorie's hand and squeezed.

Lorie shot her a watery smile and returned the reassuring clasp. She and Emily had been friends for as long as Lorie could remember, though so much had changed over the last couple of years. Their other close friend, Caroline Fitch, just had a new baby, a sweet baby boy they named Hollis after Caroline's father. Emily herself had just last fall married Elam Riehl. Now this.

"You want to talk about it?" Emily asked.

She shook her head. There wasn't anything left to talk about.

Emily glanced over to where Lorie's *mamm* talked with her own mother. "Not your *vatter*," she whispered. "But whatever else is bothering you."

Lorie attempted another smile. "Why would something else be bothering me?"

"You and I have been friends ever since first grade. Do you honestly believe that I cannot tell when something is on your mind?"

Lorie thought about protesting again, but Emily was tenacious as a bulldog. If she felt something needed to be done, she held on until it was complete. Lorie had no cause to believe that this would be any different.

She cast another glance back toward her stepmother and hooked her arm through Emily's. "Can you walk to the park with me?" She needed some fresh air, a new perspective, her father back.

"*Jah.* Of course."

Lorie didn't bother to tell *Mamm* where she was going. She just pushed out of the restaurant with Emily close behind.

"Where's Elam?" Lorie asked once they were out on the sidewalk. The fresh air didn't help. She still felt as bereft as she had before. This time maybe more so since the bright, cheery sun seemed to mock her very being.

"I sent him home, so we could talk. I had a feeling . . ."

Lorie nodded as they crossed the street to sit in the park directly across from Esther's bakery. Had it only been two years ago since she had sat here with her friends enjoying the beautiful spring day when Andrew Fitch pulled up on his uncle's tractor? It seemed like yesterday and forever ago at the same time.

They sat on the swings, pushing themselves with their feet. The wind stirred the untied strings on her prayer *kapp*.

Lorie pushed them over her shoulders wishing for the umpteenth time that she could just cut them off. But that was a sign of rebellion, and Emily's father, Bishop Cephas Ebersol, would never allow that in his district. The last thing she needed right now was trouble with the bishop. Not after . . .

"My father has . . . *had* a tattoo." Would she ever stop referring to him in present tense?

"He what?" To Emily's credit she didn't raise her voice, didn't drop her chin in surprise or any of the other shocked reactions that Lorie had been expecting.

"I saw it when we went to the coroner's office to, uh, you know."

Emily nodded. "Are you sure?"

There was nothing else it could be. "I'm sure."

They sat there in the warm summer sun, not speaking, just being.

Then Emily said, "We all make mistakes, Lorie."

"I know," she whispered in return.

"Do you want me to talk to my *dat?* Maybe he can give you some peace about the matter."

But it wasn't peace she needed. Answers, that was what she wanted. "I'm not worried about his soul, if that's what you mean." And most people would be.

"Maybe he did this on his *rumspringa.*"

That had been Lorie's first thought, too. But she had heard the story of how her parents had met and fallen in love. Though her father had never come right out and said that it was after he joined the church, she knew he had been well past his run-around years.

"It's a heart," she said. "With an angel's wings. And my mother's name."

"He must have loved her very much," Emily said.

Lorie nodded. Her father had never said as much to her, but any time she asked him a question about her mother, his eyes would light up, *Mamm*'s frown would grow a little deeper, and things around the Kauffman household would become tense. "I know he did." She stared off into the distance. "I don't think Maddie ever forgave him for that."

"For loving your *mamm?*" Emily asked.

"I know it sounds dumb, but it's just a feeling, you know?"

"Sometimes there is only one love in a lifetime," Emily said.

Lorie smiled at her friend. If anyone knew about the unpredictability of love, it was Emily Riehl. She had loved Luke Lambright her entire life, only to realize the love wasn't real. Luke left the Amish to join the fast-paced world of stockcar racing while Emily had stayed behind in Wells Landing and fallen truly in love with Elam Riehl. "Maybe," she said. "But—"

"But what?" Emily asked.

"I think he got the tattoo after my *mamm* died. He would have been around thirty years old."

"What does that matter truly?" Emily shrugged. "That is between him and God, don't you think?"

"*Jah,*" Lorie said, pleating her fingers in the material of her apron. She was already tired of wearing black. "But what if there's more to it than that?"

A frown pulled at Emily's brow. "What do you mean?"

"I feel like there's so much of his life that I didn't know about." More than the cook who ran a tight kitchen, who made regular trips through the restaurant greeting his guests and checking on their meals. More than the man who loved his family and always had a smile on his face no matter what the day handed him.

"Of course there is," Emily exclaimed. "Are you sure you just haven't realized that your father was a person aside from being your father?"

Lorie shook her head. "It's more than that. I don't know how I know, but—"

Emily took Lorie's hand into her own, stopping the gentle sway of their swings. "Listen to me," she started, her voice soft, but threaded with steel. "Give yourself time to grieve before you do anything."

"I'm fine," she lied. What else could she say?

"Lorie." At Emily's stern tone, Lorie turned to face her friend. "You've got that look in your eyes."

"I just want to know," she whispered. "How could Maddie have not seen it?" She had called her *Mamm* for the last twenty years, but now there was a chasm between them, bigger than before. She and her stepmother had never been very close, but this tore the fragile trust apart.

Emily sighed. "Okay," she finally said. "She had to know it was there."

"Then they were both keeping secrets." Lorie studied her fingernails. She couldn't bring herself to tell her friend the rest, about the box of his possessions hidden away in the storeroom. About the car the police found and claimed belonged to her father. "Why?"

"I wish I had an answer for you."

The birds in the trees chirped to one another even though they were in the middle of town. From the street came the clop of horse hooves against the pavement, the purr of the car engines as they drove by. That was Wells Landing, a perfect blend of city and country, of Amish and *Englisch*. One of the reasons she loved it so much.

But everything seemed a little dim today, dull, as if the sparkle had gone out of the world. Was that just the pain of losing her father? Or did it have more to do with the secrets he kept?

"Promise me," Emily said. "Promise me you won't do anything for a while. Give yourself a chance to heal before you start digging around. There may be truths that you don't want to know."

That was exactly what she was afraid of, but now that she knew what she did, how could she ever go back?

"Can I talk to you for a bit?" Lorie slid into the booth opposite her *mamm*. It had been nearly a week since the funeral. A week of sleepless nights and exhausting days of learning to get along without her father.

She reached for the stack of napkins. In the restaurant business, there was no such thing as downtime. Something always needed to be done. Lorie started rolling the flatware in the paper napkins like she had been taught when she was eight years old.

"*Jah,* of course," *Mamm* said. Her mouth turned up at the corners, but still managed to look more like a frown than a smile.

Lorie stopped rolling silverware and instead started to tear little pieces from the napkin in her hands. "I think we should talk about the tattoo."

Mamm shook her head. "I don't."

"So you did know it was there." A small part of her had hoped that by some miracle, her *mamm* didn't know about the mark on her father's chest.

Maddie shot her a look, but continued to roll the silverware.

"Did you ever ask him about it?"

Mamm took a deep breath, Lorie was sure to remind her that she had said she didn't want to talk about the tattoo. Instead she slowly released it. "*Jah.* He told me he got it during his *rumspringa.*"

Lorie shook her head before Maddie even finished. "That's impossible, and you and I both know it. He owned a car, *Mamm.* A car."

Maddie slammed the last rolled bundle of flatware into the large gray tub they used for storage. Her lips were pressed even tighter than usual, her eyes shooting sparks like the firecrackers on July Fourth. "He got the tattoo on his *rumspringa,* and that's all there is to say about it." Maddie's words held such conviction Lorie wondered if she was trying to convince Lorie or herself.

"But—"

Maddie stood, towering over Lorie, a frowning menace in head-to-toe black. "We will not speak of this again." She picked up the tray of utensils and marched toward the waitress station.

Lorie watched her go, feeling defeated and worn. So many unanswered questions floated around in her head. So many secrets kept for so many years.

"What did you say to *Mamm?*" Melanie slid into the booth opposite Lorie, her blue eyes searching.

"Nothing. It's just hard right now." She did her best to smile at her sister. In all actuality Melanie Kauffman was her half sister, though Lorie had never felt that way before. What was happening to her?

Grief, Emily would say. She was probably right.

"I know," Melanie said with a nod. "It's hard when I miss him so."

Lorie blinked back the tears welling in her eyes and squeezed Melanie's hand. Their father's death had been hard on them all. *Mamm* wanted Melanie to postpone her wedding since she was now in mourning. Melanie was heartbroken over the decision, but Lorie knew she wouldn't go against their *mudder's* wishes.

She looked over to where her half sister Cora Ann brewed fresh tea for the afternoon crowd. At twelve, Cora Ann was still in school, working on the weekends and every time they needed an extra hand. Sadie was in the kitchen, most likely preparing food for the supper crowd. She was actually Lorie's stepsister, but since she had been an infant when Maddie married *Dat,* he was the only father she had ever known.

Six-year-old Daniel sat at the table by the kitchen coloring a picture. His tongue was stuck in the corner of his mouth, his eyes nearly crossed behind his glasses as he concentrated on his work. He was so special, their Daniel. Of all of them, Lorie knew he was the most confused. He didn't understand why his *vatter* was never coming back.

They had all been devastated by his untimely death. So why was she the only one with all these questions?

She stood and smoothed her hands down her black dress. She felt antsy, like her skin was too small and itchy from the inside out.

"Where are you going?" Melanie asked.

Lorie shrugged, another lie she would have to pray about. "Nowhere."

"*Mamm* won't like it if you're not here when the dinner crowd starts coming in."

She didn't like a lot of things too, Lorie thought. Then she pushed the hateful thought away. Grief, that was all it was. "I'll be back before then. I just need to . . ."

Her legs were stiff, and her heart pounding as she walked away.

She just needed to get some answers. She needed peace, understanding. As if her father's death wasn't enough, there was a tattoo and a car. And a stepmother who wanted to ignore it all.

The bell on the door dinged behind her as she stepped out into the overcast day. She could almost smell the rain in the air and hoped the clouds didn't produce a storm. They bothered Daniel like nothing else. He had been through so much lately she didn't know if he could handle any more right now.

Slowly she walked around the building as if she was out for nothing more than a casual stroll. Once she was out of sight to anyone looking out the window at Kauffman's, she removed the key she'd tucked into the waistband of her apron. Sneaking around was not the best way to handle this, but she didn't have many options.

She eased up the staircase to the storeroom above the restaurant. It held a little of everything from extra to-go lids and spare chairs to the paintings she hid there where no one could find them.

And the box of things given to Maddie by the police.

Her *mamm* might want to push everything aside and forget it, but Lorie couldn't. The box was sitting just inside the door, as if *Mamm* didn't want to spend any more time on it than was necessary.

Lorie looked at the box. She took a deep breath. She knelt on the floor. But she didn't touch it.

What if what she found in there changed everything? Emily was right: she couldn't un-see whatever the box contained. Yet she couldn't un-see her father lying there in the morgue.

Her hands were sweaty, and she wiped them down the front of her dress skirt.

She had to know. No matter how bad she felt about disobeying her *mamm* and opening the box, she had to know.

Her hands trembled as she reached for the length of tape sealing the box shut tight. She pulled on it, wincing. A little of the cardboard tore as she stripped it away. There was no going back.

She folded down the flaps, and tears sprang to her eyes. All that was left of her father was in this box. All the stuff collected by the police. It seemed pathetic, such meager remains from a full and happy life.

His black felt hat lay on top. She lifted it out and set it in her lap, her fingers trailing around the brim.

She hadn't asked what had happened to his clothing. She supposed they had removed it at the hospital. She wasn't sure she wanted that anyway.

She wasn't sure she wanted the box in front of her.

She moved the hat to one side and took out a set of keys she had never seen. The ring held five keys, none of them marked. Perhaps they went to the restaurant. At least that was what she wanted to believe, even though in her heart she knew it was more than that.

A denim vest was the next thing she pulled out. It was so unlike anything her father ever wore, but when she held it close to her face, it smelled of him. The soap he used and the tangy scent of the restaurant.

In the very bottom of the box was a leather wallet.

Her heart pounded in her throat as she removed it. It wasn't the one he usually carried, the one she had seen too many times to count over the years.

Somehow she knew this was it. As much as she wanted to put it back inside the box, tape the thing up, and pretend it didn't exist, something inside her could not let it go.

She opened the wallet, and her gaze fell upon an *Englisch* driver's license. Her father's face smiled back at her from the tiny picture. There was no mistaking it was him. But the name . . .

Henry Mathis.

Her father's name wasn't Henry Mathis. His name was Henry Kauffman.

Yet it was his picture.

She ran her fingers across the plastic holder. The birthday was right: June sixteenth. And his eye and hair color. He was an organ donor, though she didn't even know what that meant.

The address was in Tulsa, not Wells Landing. How could this be right?

She pinched the bridge of her nose where a headache was starting to throb. How could this be?

But there it was, right in her hands. No matter how she looked at it, only one conclusion came to mind. Her father had been living a double life.

Chapter Two

"Jonah," Lorie started, then stopped to take a breath and gather her courage before continuing, "Can I talk to you about something?"

He turned from hitching up his horse and buggy and gave her a long, steady look. "What's wrong, Lorie?"

That was Jonah, always aware and concerned about those around him. It was one of the reasons why she loved him. But she hadn't told anyone about the stuff she'd found in the storeroom in the week since she had snuck up there and opened the box. Not even to her *mamm* who knew what was inside. Or did she? *Mamm* could have simply put the box away, unconcerned with the secrets it held. She certainly wasn't interested in discussing Lorie's father's tattoo.

"You've had something on your mind for days now," Jonah said.

That was the truth.

"I just—" She just what? Had begun to doubt everything she knew to be good and true? Had started wondering what other secrets her father had kept from her? Worried now that her entire life was a lie? "I found out some things about my father. Things I never imagined could be true."

Jonah shook his head. "We don't speak of the dead, Lorie."

He turned back toward his task as if their talk was over. But Lorie had so many unanswered questions, so many thoughts in her head. She had to get them out or she might go crazy. "He had a tattoo, Jonah." She spoke the words quietly, but they seemed to echo between them.

He stopped again. "Like an *Englisch* tattoo?"

"There certainly aren't any Amish ones."

Jonah shook his head. "You've been through so much lately. I think maybe you're overreacting. He could have done something like that on his *rumspringa*."

"*Nay.* He got this long after he joined the church, after he and *mamm* were married."

Jonah dropped all pretense of hitching the horses and grabbed her hand in his own. "*Kumm,* let's sit down and talk this through." He led her over to the porch and the rockers that waited there. He let go of her only long enough to settle himself next to her. Then he scooped it up again touching her fingers one by one in that special way of his. The familiarity was soothing.

Lorie closed her eyes, basking in the attention, then she opened them again.

"I know how close you and your father were, and I've been trying to give you time, but . . . it seems you have more on your mind than I imagined."

She nodded as tears spilled down her cheeks. As if losing her father wasn't bad enough. All these secrets, it was like losing him all over again. "The police gave *Mamm* a box of *Dat*'s things."

"*Jah,*" Jonah said by way of encouragement.

She went on to describe the items in the box. "And he had an *Englisch* driver's license. But the name on it was different. It wasn't Kauffman. He lied to me."

"You don't know that. Kauffman could be his real name and the other the fake one."

She hadn't thought of it that way. So many questions and

no answers in sight. She stared at their intertwined fingers until her vision turned blurry.

"Lorie?"

"Hmmm?" She switched her gaze to his.

"Maybe you should let it go."

"Let it go?" She blinked, trying to pull everything into focus once again.

"Just forget about it," he explained.

"How can you say that?"

"This is causing you so much pain. I can see it in your eyes. You've had enough hurt for a while."

Lorie pulled her hands from his and stalked toward the porch railing. She wrapped her arms around her middle and stared out at the yard before her. Across the road were stalks of corn growing taller by the day. Hidden there in the cornfields was the pond where they all went swimming every summer. Except there seemed to be less and less time for such activities these days. Was it because everyone was growing up or were they growing apart?

"There's just something wrong with the whole thing, Jonah. I don't know what, but something isn't right." Yet it was more than a feeling. It was a box of goods that shouldn't have belonged to an Amish man. It was a car impounded by the police, the denim vest, and the current driver's license with a Tulsa address. It was the name of Mathis and the tattoo that no one seemed to want to talk about. "I can't let it go," she cried. "Can't you see that?" The situation was tearing her apart. She felt lost in her own skin, unable to grieve and move on with her life as long as these questions hung over her head, over her heart.

He stood and made his way to her side. She breathed in the clean scent of him, sunshine and detergent mixed with the smell of hay and freshly turned field. "I know that you have to do what you have to do," he said on a sigh. "Just promise me one thing. Promise me you won't do anything rash. Give yourself some time before you decide. Things may look different in a couple of weeks."

Lorie nodded. "*Jah,* okay. Fine," she said. "I promise."

But nothing changed in the two weeks she watched crawl past. Every day she grew more and more anxious to know the truth behind the mysteries.

"Are you sure?" Emily asked as they sat at the picnic table in the park like they had so many times before.

Caroline nodded as she propped her baby at her shoulder and gently patted his back. Emma played in the sand not so far away.

Around them the town bustled in the way that only Wells Landing could. Buggies rattled by, cars purred down the road. Across the street Esther worked in the bakery and next door Lorie's family's restaurant geared up for the early lunch crowd.

And tomorrow the auction started, launching the beginning of the market season. The whole town would be crawling with *Englischers* who had come to bid on quilts and other goods. Even workdays would be put up for the bidding. Lorie would attend the tent the restaurant sponsored each year, serving drinks and food to the visiting *Englischers.*

"It's not that I don't want to be supportive," Emily said. "I just worry about you. You've been through so much."

How many times had she heard that since they had buried her father? Too many to count. She had been through a lot, and that was exactly why she needed to find out the truth.

"Hush," Caroline said, shooting Emily a stern look. "Lorie, if you want to go to Tulsa and see where that address is, then I say you should."

"But what if it leads her to something terrible?" Normally, Emily was a positive person, but having recently found out that she was pregnant with her first child, she seemed a little more worrisome than normal.

"And what if it leads to something wonderful?" Caroline countered.

"Please." Lorie looked at each one of them in turn. "Don't argue. My mind's made up anyway."

Her friends fell silent as they both contemplated the meaning of her words.

"How will you get there?" Caroline asked.

"I don't know. I just don't want *Mamm* to know." She didn't have to add that her stepmother would try to stop her. The three of them had been over it enough to know that Maddie Kauffman would not approve of her digging into the matter.

"If you hire a Mennonite driver, it'll be all over the district within the hour."

"I know." That was the problem with small communities. Secrets had a way of working to the surface no matter how deep they were buried.

Lorie folded her fingers in the skirt of her black dress. Her father would have hated everyone going around in such solemn clothing. He would have rather seen everyone wear blue in his honor, but tradition and the *Ordnung* dictated that the family wear black for a year. Eleven more months . . .

"I could call Luke and see if he could maybe take you there," Emily said. Luke Lambright, Emily's once-upon-a-time beau, had left Wells Landing behind in order to drive race cars in the *Englisch* world. Not long after, he had sustained a terrible injury, but in the year since, he had regained his ability to walk and drive once again.

"You would do that for me?" Lorie asked, her eyes wide.

"Of course, I would. It's not that I want to keep you from finding out. I just want to make sure you understand what you're getting into."

Lorie shook her head. "I can't say that I know, but only that I have to. Does that make sense?"

"Absolutely," Caroline said.

"But only because we know you so well," Emily added.

Lorie scanned their faces, first one and then the other. These were her friends. The two people in the world she could always depend on, always trust.

"Don't do it," Caroline said as tears welled in Lorie's eyes.

"You'll get us all started," Emily added.

Lorie chuckled and wiped away the moisture. "I just appreciate you both so much."

Emily gave her a watery smile in return. "That's what friends are for."

Half an hour later Lorie made her way back into the restaurant, thoughts of traveling to Tulsa lightening her steps and weighing them down all at the same time. Thankfully there were no tourist buses in town and business was filled with the typical lunch crowd. This gave her plenty of time to think about other things, her father, what she might find at the mysterious address, and keeping secrets.

She knew that she would have to tell her *mamm* eventually about her planned trip to Tulsa, but just because she was planning it didn't mean she had to confess just yet. It would certainly be more informative to tell *Mamm* after she had gone and come back. That way she would have something to report. Found nothing or ran across . . . but she wasn't able to finish that sentence. She had no idea what she would find. She had no idea how it would change her. She only knew she had to do it. She had to go see what only her father knew.

"*Dochder.*"

She stopped wiping down the last table bussed and waited for her *mamm* to draw closer. "*Jah?*" she asked.

"I have something I need to talk to you about."

Lorie's heart skipped a beat. Did *Mamm* know about the box? Had she somehow found out about all the plans Lorie had made to go to Tulsa? She mentally shook away the thought. There was no way *Mamm* could know, not unless she had started seeing other people's thoughts. Lorie was being ridiculous and oversensitive.

"*Kumm.* Sit." *Mamm* motioned toward the table where they sat in the afternoons and rolled the clean flatware up into napkins to be placed on the tables for the customers.

Lorie slid into the booth and waited for her stepmother to join her.

Maddie slipped in across from her and clasped her hands together on the table in front of her.

Lorie couldn't say her *mamm* was a loving woman. In her own way, Lorie supposed Maddie was, but she also had a bitter air, as if life had somehow dealt her a blow that she had yet to recover from. Lorie supposed that being a young widow could do that. But that had been a long time ago. One would think that the lines bracketing *Mamm*'s mouth would have subsided by now, but in the month since they buried Henry Kauffman, they had only gotten worse.

"Bishop Treger is starting baptism classes next week." That was one thing about Maddie: she didn't mince words. "It's time, Lorie."

Lorie bit back a sigh. In all honesty, the time for her to join the church had long since come. But instead of being excited, the thought of ten church weeks of classes filled her with dread. Or maybe it had something to do with the doubts that had filled her heart lately. The uncertainty that plagued her.

"Well?"

She met her *mamm*'s hard and steady gaze. There was no getting out of this one. She had waited long enough. All of her friends had joined the church. Even Jonah had bent his knee the year before. If they were to be married, she would have to become a member as well. "*Jah*," she said. "Of course." She tried to muster up a smile of excitement, but her lips felt like they had been pulled into a grimace.

"*Gut, gut.*" Maddie gave a stern nod of approval. "It is what your *vatter* would have wanted."

Not for the first time, Lorie wondered how this frowning woman had captured the heart of her easygoing father. But that was a mystery that might not ever be solved.

Lorie looked out over the sea of *Englisch* faces that waited under and around the Kauffman Family Restaurant's tent. It seemed to stretch to the end of the block and beyond. She braced the back of one hand at the small of her back and chanced a brief stretch. This day had gone by in a flash, but seemed to be dragging all at the same time. A couple more hours and surely she would have time for a break. Even if it was only five minutes to rest her feet and drink a bottle of cool water.

"What all comes with the chicken finger dinner?"

Lorie turned her attention back to the customers and sucked in a quick breath. Before her stood the most handsome *Englisch* boy she had ever seen. Well, *boy* wasn't the best word she could use to describe him. He was about her age, though with *Englischers* it was hard to tell. With their worldly air, they looked so much older than Amish. Whatever his age, his presence captivated her. His hair was the color of strong black coffee but his eyes were the pale blue of a new spring sky.

"Miss?"

And something about him was just so . . . so . . . or maybe she was just tired.

"Miss?" he repeated.

"Huh?"

"The chicken finger dinner. What's the difference in it and the chicken finger basket?"

She laughed nervously. Thankfully the heat from the day masked the flush she felt creeping into her cheeks. "What are chicken fingers anyway?"

He smiled a little indulgently, and Lorie knew she was embarrassing herself.

"Bread and slaw," she finally said. "That's the only difference."

He looked first one way and then the next as if he was about to ask something he wanted no one else to hear. "And how's the slaw?"

"*Appeditilch,*" she said.

"That good, huh?"

She smiled. "I made it myself."

"Then I guess I'd better go with the dinner."

She smiled and wrote his order on the notepad where they tracked the food.

"Two of them."

She couldn't account for the pitch in her stomach. It wasn't like she knew this man. But somehow she felt like she'd taken one lick of an ice-cream cone, then dropped it in the sand. Ridiculous.

"Two finger dinners," she called over her shoulder to Cora Ann who was scooping the food into white Styrofoam containers. "Would you like drinks?" she asked the handsome *Englischer.*

"Two waters," he said.

"Sixteen dollars, please."

He took out his wallet and thumbed through the bills, pulling out the correct amount. He handed her the bills and took the containers. "Thanks."

"Have a *gut* day."

He smiled at her words, but she knew he wasn't laughing at her. With a quick nod, he disappeared into the crowd.

"He was cute."

Lorie jumped. "Sadie! You scared half the life out of me."

Her sister smiled. "I didn't mean to. Maybe if you hadn't been off in dreamland."

Lorie shook her head. "It's just the heat."

"Uh-huh." Sadie gave her a knowing look, then sauntered off to restock the ice in the coolers.

"It is," she called toward her back, but Lorie knew she wasn't fooling anyone. Not even herself.

As ridiculous as it was, Zach Calhoun found himself back at the food tents. His mother was at the quilt auction—her reason for coming out to visit the Amish today—and he found time on his hands. The only problem was he found his feet carrying him back to the tent where he'd bought their lunches. He just wanted to catch sight of the brown-eyed girl who had helped him.

He stepped around the stakes and ropes that held the tent in place and shook his head at his fanciful thoughts. Once he found her, then what? It wasn't like he could ask her out. Well, he supposed he *could,* but she'd probably slap his face. Wait. Weren't the Amish pacifists? Okay, so she might not hit him, but she would surely laugh in his face.

Time to get out while the getting was good. He turned to go back the way he came and ran smack into a soft, sweet-smelling form. Instinctively he reached out to steady the girl as something cold trickled between them. Something liquid and filled with ice. And clear. Hopefully water.

"I'm sorry," he said.

"It's *allrecht.*" She pulled away from his grasp.

He knew that voice. He lifted his gaze and met deep brown

eyes. "Here," he said, both glad and remorseful that he had found her. "Let me buy you another drink."

"It's fine, really."

"I insist."

She shook her head, but he persisted.

"It's the least I can do after spilling it all over you."

"It is only water."

"Please." What was wrong with him? Maybe he had been out in the sun too long, but the day was pleasantly cool for mid-May, a perfect day to be out and about.

She hesitated a split second, then nodded her head. He bit back his smile of joy and nodded toward the tent. "Something from here?"

"I'll get it."

"If I let you get it, how is that me buying you another drink?"

She smiled at him again, and it seemed as if the sun was coming from inside her. Oh, brother. He'd better get himself under control and fast. Any sappier and they could bottle it and pour it over pancakes. "My family owns the restaurant," she said. "It would be my pleasure to buy you something to drink."

She disappeared into the back of the tent and came out a few seconds later carrying two to-go cups. "Sweet tea?" she asked, handing him one.

"Perfect." He took a sip. "Really good. Did you make this, too?"

"My sister Cora Ann did."

They automatically started walking through the tents. Zach let her lead the way.

"Isn't there a park just a little ways from here?" he asked.

"*Jah,* but—" She bit her lip and stopped.

He took two more steps before he realized she wasn't at his side. He doubled back. "But what?"

The wind stirred the untied strings of the funny little hat

she wore. He had noticed since he'd been in Wells Landing that all the Amish women wore one.

She chewed on her bottom lip some more. He was making her uncomfortable. What a jerk he was. She hadn't wanted to come with him, but he had insisted. But only because he wanted to spend a little time with her. All he had done was make her nervous. She wasn't a regular girl like he normally dated. She lived by a different set of rules that had her dressing like a matron and covering her pale blond hair to the point almost none of it showed.

"I'm sorry," he said, taking a step closer to her and then one back. "I didn't mean to make you uncomfortable."

"It's okay," she said.

She smelled of lavender and fried chicken. That should have been weird, but somehow it wasn't.

He was working too hard. Yep, that was it. He'd been studying like crazy these last couple of weeks. And studying for his college finals was exactly where he should be at this very moment. But his mom had wanted to buy an Amish quilt for her bed and a wall hanging for the common area at the retirement center where they worked.

"I think I should go."

"No!" He tempered his voice. "You don't have to. I mean, I don't even know your name."

"Lorie. Lorie Kauffman."

"Hi, Lorie, I'm Zach. With an *h*." Gah! Could he have said anything lamer?

"Nice to meet you, Zach with an *h*. Enjoy the rest of the auction."

Before he could say another word, she turned on her heel and disappeared into the crowd.

"Do you have something you want to tell me?" Sadie asked that night as they washed the family's supper dishes.

Lorie shot a glance at her sister. She was really too tired for such games. Where Sadie got all the energy was anyone's guess. "About?"

"I saw you walking with that handsome *Englisch bu* this afternoon."

She shrugged as if it were no big thing and kept on with the task at hand. "It was nothing." How many times had she said that to herself since she walked away from Zach? She hadn't even found out his last name. It didn't matter. It wasn't like she was ever going to see him again.

"I'm glad," Sadie continued. "You know how *Mamm* would feel about you talking to a guy like that."

Lorie bit back an exasperated sigh. "I said it was nothing."

Sadie raised a brow. "It didn't look that way to me."

"I'll probably never see him again," Lorie said. "There's no telling where he lives." Not to mention he bought two dinners. A boy that good-looking had to have a girlfriend.

What was she thinking? He was *Englisch*. She was Amish. There was no future in that. Plus she had Jonah. As soon as she finished her baptism classes they would be married. Stress was doing weird things to her head. Losing her father, finding out he had secrets he'd kept for years. It was a lot to take in.

"You're vulnerable right now," Sadie said. "Just be careful, okay?"

"*Jah.*" Lorie wiped her hands on a dishtowel as she and Sadie finished their chore. But being careful wasn't really the issue. She would never see Zach with an *h* again.

Chapter Three

The following days were spent working in the restaurant and otherwise learning to live with the questions knocking around inside her head. Every night Lorie prayed for understanding and wisdom. She prayed that it be God's will to have all of her questions answered. She prayed that she was making the right decision in starting baptism classes in the next over district.

But that decision had always been in question. Not that her father or Maddie knew of the secrets she herself had kept. All the paintings in the second-story storeroom. It was vain and arrogant to think that others would want to see the art she had created. But how was she supposed to live with the pictures in her head calling out for a canvas? Not even Jonah knew of the many paintings she had created and carefully hidden in the storeroom. Only Caroline and Emily knew that she painted when no one was looking, then hid her work out of guilt.

The bell on the restaurant door dinged out a warning as Lorie wiped down the plastic-covered menus.

"Hi." Emily Riehl waved from the door and made her way over to the waitress station where Lorie stood. "Are you getting off soon?"

It was three in the afternoon, the time they worked to catch up from the lunch rush and prepare for the dinner crowd.

"In an hour or so," Lorie said. Then her shift would be over and she could go home for the day. But she almost wanted to stay. At least at the restaurant the questions that haunted her had to make way for the work she had to accomplish. Still, it was her job to feed her siblings and get them into bed before Maddie came home in the evenings.

Emily glanced from side to side, then dropped her voice to just above a whisper. "I talked to Luke."

Lorie's heart fell into her stomach at the words. It was what she had been hoping for and dreading all at the same time. "Oh, *jah?*"

"Maybe when you're done here you can come down to the bakery for a while."

"*Jah.*" She nodded, her mouth suddenly dry. "I'll be there in a bit."

Just over an hour later she entered Esther's bakery at the end of the block. Esther Lapp had started the bakery after her husband had died and ran it for many years all by herself. Then she had taken Caroline Hostetler under her wing and helped her young friend raise her daughter and get back on her feet. But that was years ago. Now Caroline was married to Andrew Fitch and had a baby boy to add to their growing family. Esther had married Abe Fitch, Andrew's absent-minded uncle.

The two women plus Emily were seated in the corner booth, a plate of cookies in front of them. Esther was always trying out new recipes, and Lorie wondered what today's experiment would bring.

"I told Esther," Caroline said with a small grimace. "I hope you don't mind."

Lorie slid into the booth next to the woman and tried to smile. She really didn't mind Esther knowing. What she did mind was so many people being involved in her deceit. She didn't want her friends having to carry around her secrets.

But Esther had kept Caroline's secret. She had been alone and pregnant when she arrived in Wells Landing. Everyone had assumed that she was a young widow when the truth of the matter was she was running away from her district carrying the baby of an *Englischer*. Emma's father, Trey Rycroft, had wanted to marry Caroline and give their baby his name, but once he saw how much Andrew loved Caroline, he forever stepped aside. He never came to see his daughter, that had been part of their agreement, but Lorie knew that Caroline took photographs of the child and sent them to Trey on a regular basis.

"It's all set," Emily said. "Luke will come pick you up on Thursday."

Caroline reached across the table and covered Lorie's hand with her own. "Are you sure you want to do this?"

"I have to."

Esther shook her head. "Some secrets are better left as secrets."

Wasn't that exactly what the bishop had told Caroline?

"How can I look in the mirror every day and not know the truth?" Her father had been her world. Yes, he had started a new family here after her mother had died, but to Lorie he had been everything. She loved her stepmother and her brother and sisters, but she and her father had a special bond, as if they had been through tragedy and survived. She supposed that the death of her mother would qualify even if she had been really too young to remember much.

"We only want to make certain that you're sure about this," Emily said. "There's still time to say no."

"*Nay.*" Lorie shook her head to emphasize her words. "Tell Luke I'll be ready to go on Thursday."

* * *

"Do you have any special plans for today?" *Mamm* asked over breakfast Thursday morning. It was the one day other than Sunday when Lorie was off from the restaurant. And today was a special day off indeed.

Lorie jumped, startled at the words. "*Nay* . . . no, not really. Jonah and I were talking about going fishing." It wasn't much of a lie. She was going on a fishing expedition of sorts, and she had asked Jonah to go with her, but he wanted no part in her explorations in the *Englisch* world.

"It's just the one time," she'd told him, but he refused, saying he was taking the day to go fishing with his cousin before the weather turned too hot.

Still she would add the falsehood to her prayer list. The lies seemed to be coming more easily as time went on. The fact shamed her.

"Just make sure you're here when the bus brings Daniel home at four."

"I asked Sadie if she would be here then." Her sister could meet the bus and seemed happy to do so. "She said she would," Lorie added.

Mamm stopped stirring the big bowl of pancake batter and turned back to Lorie. "Thursday is your day to be here for him and bring him into the restaurant."

"I know, but this is the only time I can go with Jonah."

A frown burrowed into *Mamm*'s brow. "I know this has been hard on all of us, but I never thought you'd be the one shirking your responsibilities."

"I'm not shirking anything." Lorie wanted to rise to her feet and stamp one in frustration. Never before had she been this upset over nothing. But it wasn't nothing. She was about to find out the truth. Had her father been lying to her—to them all—all these years?

"I can't imagine what else you would call it."

Lorie slouched back in her seat and stopped cutting the

tops off the strawberries. "I just need a little time away, that's all."

Maddie's voice softened, though her expression remained stern. "We all do."

Lorie slowly exhaled and started trimming the berries once again. Now all she had to do was get out of the house and in the car with Luke Lambright without any of her family seeing her. Oh, how many lies would she end up telling in order to discover the truth?

Lorie was shaking by the time she got everyone out of the house. *Mamm,* Sadie, and Melanie headed to the restaurant while Cora Ann went off to school. The bus stopped by shortly after that and picked up Daniel for his day at his special school.

She peered at herself in the mirror above the bathroom sink and tried to tell herself she was doing the right thing. She had to know the truth. She needed to know. *Mamm* might want to forget about it and bury her head in the dirt like the ostriches Lorie had read about in school, but Lorie couldn't let it go. And frankly she found Maddie's attitude confusing. The woman had been married to Henry Kauffman for nearly twenty years, how could she not want to know about the car the police had told them about or the address on the driver's license?

The sound of a car engine floated in through the window. Luke was here.

As if to prove her words, she heard a car door, followed by a knock.

"Coming," she called, smoothing her hands down her black dress. She had wanted to wear something different, maybe the pale purple one she had worn to Emily and Elam's wedding. But tradition dictated the immediate family should wear black for the year following a loved one's passing.

Black dress, black apron, black walking shoes. Was this what she would wear to face her destiny?

She shook her head. She was being overly dramatic. She was only going to one place: the address on her father's driver's license. After that, she would return home and continue her life as normal. Well, as normal as it could be after losing her *vatter*. But it wasn't like this visit was going to change anything. She would still be the same old Lorie no matter what she found out.

She stuck her tongue out at her reflection, but even that didn't ease her nerves. Without another look she whirled on her heel and headed for the door.

Luke Lambright stood on the other side of the threshold. He smiled at her in that carefree way of his and suddenly he reminded her so much of her father that tears sprang into her eyes.

"Lorie, what's wrong?" He stepped into the house, his cane banging against the floor as he took her hands into his own. Living in the *Englisch* world had done that to him, made him less restricted with touches and words.

"Nothing. Just nerves, I guess."

He nodded. If anyone understood it was Luke. He had left the district a couple of years ago to join the fast-paced world of *Englisch* race-car driving. But a terrible racing accident had left him nearly paralyzed. Lorie didn't know if he would ever drive race cars again, but he still had made a living from the track. He had learned the trade of mechanic as he was taught to walk again. Of course it didn't hurt that his *Englisch* girlfriend, Sissy, was the daughter of one of the sponsors. But Lorie could tell that despite his limitations, Luke was happier in the *Englisch* world than he had ever been among the Amish.

He peered at her closely, then gave another nod. "If you're sure. You don't have to do this, you know."

"I know," she said. But she did. Just add that one to her growing list of lies. She had to go into Tulsa and to the address on the license as surely as she needed her next breath. She didn't understand this drive inside her, only that it was there and needed to be assuaged.

"Are you ready?" he asked.

She took a deep breath and attempted a smile. She could tell by the one she received in return that her efforts were lacking. "As I'll ever be," she said, and started out the door toward Luke's car.

"Are you sure this is right?" she asked nearly forty minutes later.

Luke stopped the car and turned off the engine. "Pretty sure." He held out a hand toward her. "Let me look at the license again."

Lorie handed over the small rectangle of plastic and studied his face as he doubled-checked the addresses.

"Yep. This is it."

He handed the license back to her. "Now what?"

Lorie stared at the flat-roofed brick building in front of them. "I . . . I don't understand. What is this place?"

"It's an assisted living center."

She shot him a look.

"The *Englisch* don't take care of their elderly like the Amish do," he explained. "This place is where old *Englisch* people go when they can no longer live by themselves."

That sounded outright cruel, but Lorie didn't say so. She had more important things on her mind. "Why would my father use this place as his address?"

Luke shrugged. "Maybe he knows someone who lives here or even works here."

She didn't know whether to be grateful that the address on

the license wasn't a house with a whole other family living inside or shocked that it led to this home for the elderly.

"There's only one way to find out." Luke nodded his dark head toward the large double doors of the building.

Lorie sucked in a deep, steadying breath, but nothing could slow the pounding of her heart. "Will you go in with me?"

Luke smiled. "You know I will."

They received a few looks as they entered the facility. Lorie had never felt so self-conscious before. Maybe because Amish folk were all over Wells Landing. But here in Tulsa, her manner of dress was so very different than everyone around her. Most gave her kind smiles while others pinned her with curious stares.

Luke seemed to sense her hesitation and walked toward the large circular desk and the two women seated behind it. One woman was plump and blond and to Lorie looked like some of the grandmothers who came into the restaurant. Though this woman looked very properly *Englisch* with her short-sleeved turtleneck sweater and brown-and-gold scarf.

The younger woman was thin, with dark hair and deep red lipstick. She looked like the newsperson Lorie had seen one time on the television displayed at Walmart.

"Hi," Luke said, flashing the pair his most charming smile. "My friend here is looking for some information."

The dark-haired woman returned his smile with a dazzling one of her own and looked at each of them in turn. Surprise flashed in her eyes. Lorie supposed they were an odd-looking couple, she in her Plain mourning attire and Luke dressed like every other *Englisch* man in town. "I'll do what I can."

He motioned for Lorie to join him at the desk. "Where's the license?"

She handed it to him, then studied the scuffed toes of her

shoes. It was better than trying to meet the confused looks of the two women.

"Do either of you ladies know Henry Kauffman?"

They shook their heads, and Lorie's hopes splintered into a hundred pieces.

Luke tapped the plastic license on the counter and then showed it to the ladies. "This man," he said.

"That's Henry Mathis," the brunette said after a careful look at the license. "But I haven't seen him in a while. Why do you ask?" She looked from Luke to Lorie and back again. "Is he in trouble?"

"Actually, he passed away a few weeks ago."

The words stabbed at Lorie's heart. She lifted her gaze to look at the women behind the desk. "He was my father."

"Oh, my," the blond-haired woman said. "I'm so sorry for your loss."

"*Danki.*" Lorie nodded her head, hating the tickling sensation of her prayer *kapp* strings against her bare neck. Or maybe her emotions were so raw she couldn't take any more sensations.

Her father had come here. These women knew him as Henry Mathis, not Kauffman. Her knees started to tremble. "Why?" she whispered, her words directed at no one in particular.

"Are you all right?" Luke laid his hand on top of hers.

"*Jah.* No. I don't know." She shook her head. "Why did he come here, Luke?" She focused all of her attention on him. He was the one steady and familiar thing in her world at that moment, and she couldn't take her gaze from him and remain upright.

"You say you're his daughter?" the blonde asked.

"How could you not know why he came here?" The brunette searched their faces.

Lorie took a shuddering breath, trying to calm her nerves

and set her thoughts back to rights. "It seems my father kept some secrets." She did her best to keep her voice steady, but it trembled even more than her knees. "No one . . . no one in my family knew that my father came here. At least not until now. *Danki* . . . thank you for your time." She turned on her heel and started for the door. She couldn't stand there any longer. She had to go somewhere and get her swirling thoughts in order before they exploded inside her head.

She heard Luke's uneven footsteps behind her, the clink of his cane as it met with the waxed tiles of the foyer. Their voices sounded behind her, but she kept walking, kept going toward the door.

"Miss?"

Her steps remained steady though her heart pounded.

"Miss?"

"Lorie." Luke caught her arm and halted her escape. "The ladies at the desk want to talk to you again."

"*Nay,*" she whispered.

"I know it's a lot to take in, but just hear them out, okay?"

His sea-colored eyes were so earnest, she stilled. She had waited for this moment for so long, too long to let it slip away. But all of the advice she had received in the days since her father died knocked around inside her head, while her need for answers filled her heart. "Okay." Her chin bobbed in consent, and she allowed him to lead her back to the two ladies and the circular desk.

They shared a look as she and Luke approached. Then the blond-haired lady stood, smoothing the wrinkles from her lap as if she was as nervous as Lorie was.

"Your father," she started, quickly glancing at Luke as if he could confirm this as truth, "he came here to visit his mother."

"His mother?" Lorie repeated.

"Betty Mathis." The brunette nodded.

Her father had a mother? That would make her Lorie's grandmother. She had a grandmother? She tried to remember anything her father had told her about his parents. Only that they "were gone."

"Can I see her?"

The women exchanged another look.

"It's not exactly allowed," the blonde said. "Not without proper identification."

Luke drummed his fingers against the desk and flashed the pair of them a charming smile. At least it took the sting from his words. "She's Amish, you know. It's not like she has a driver's license."

Like being Plain had stopped her father.

"I'm Luke," he said, like it made a difference. "And she's Lorie."

The women exchanged another look.

"I'm Carol," the blond woman said.

"Amber." The dark-haired woman stood and flashed them another smile. "Follow me."

Chapter Four

Lorie's breathing turned shallow as she and Luke followed the woman down the carpeted hallway. The place was clean, brightly lit, and smelled like pine cleaner and cinnamon.

Not a bad place to be, but confusing to Lorie all the same. Why would her father keep his mother here? Why didn't she live with the family in Wells Landing? But she knew the answer. Because her newly discovered grandmother was *Englisch*.

"So everyone who lives here is older?" Lorie asked Luke as they followed the brunette.

Luke shrugged. "Some of them could be people like . . . like James Riehl."

"Elam's father?"

Luke nodded.

James had been kicked in the head by one of his milk cows a couple of years back. The injury had left him with the mind of a child. He could function fairly well on his own, but Lorie knew that his family felt the need to make sure he had supervision in case he had a dizzy spell or a memory lapse.

"Did my grandmother get kicked in the head by a milk cow?"

Amber gave her a patient smile. It was a look Lorie was

used to seeing as it was a favorite of the *Englisch* to bestow upon their Plain neighbors. "Not exactly. But she does suffer from some dementia and possible early stages of Alzheimer's."

"I don't know what that means." She looked to Luke for answers. Oh, how she wished Jonah had come with her today. She needed his steady and quiet strength. But she was grateful Luke was there. He had a knowledge of the *Englisch* that neither she nor Jonah possessed. Yet it seemed this one was out of his range of knowledge.

He shrugged, then turned to the woman for the answer.

"She has trouble remembering things. Sometimes she even thinks it's a different time."

"Like time to go to bed when it's time for breakfast?" Lorie asked.

"Like it's 1972 when it's . . . not."

"Is this a good idea?" A frown of worry puckered Luke's normally smooth brow. He was as easygoing as anyone could be and his concern was almost as unnerving as the surprises she'd faced the last few weeks.

Amber smiled. "All our tenants love having visitors. Just don't bring up your father unless she does. And don't tell her about his passing. I'll inform the therapist who comes in once a week. He can work with her on accepting that, okay?"

"*Jah*. Yes." Lorie nodded, doubts flooding her. Emily had tried to warn her. Jonah, too. Was this worth all the risk?

Before she could decide, the woman knocked on the door in front of them.

"Come in," a sweet voice called out.

Amber opened the door and peeked inside. "Miss Betty, you have visitors. Are you up for company?"

"Company?" the sweet voice asked.

She pushed the door open a little farther and stepped back so they could enter the room.

Lorie's mouth went dry, and her palms grew sweaty as she eased inside.

"Hello, dear. Come sit down. Would you like for me to have Pearl bring us some iced tea?"

"Now, Miss Betty," Amber said, stepping into the room. "Pearl no longer works for you."

"Oh, that's right." Betty Mathis patted her cap of soft white curls. "I had forgotten."

"No worries, Miss Betty. This is Lorie . . ."

"Kauffman," Lorie said.

Amber gave her an approving nod as if she had given a false name in order to protect her grandmother's delicate mind. But it was the only name Lorie had ever known.

"And this is Luke . . ."

"Lambright," he supplied.

"My, what an interesting name." Miss Betty set her knitting off to one side. "I'm so glad you came to visit today. Won't you sit down?"

Lorie cautiously inched into the room and perched on the edge of a wooden rocking chair. To say the situation was awkward was a pitiful attempt to describe it, but Lorie could tell that even Luke was a bit uncomfortable. Neither one of them had expected to find a long-lost grandmother tucked away in an *Englisch* retirement home. Yet here they were.

Luke came farther into the room and took up a place in the stuffed armchair, while Amber hovered by the door. She seemed as if she didn't know whether she should stay or go. Lorie supposed it wasn't every day she found herself in this place, related strangers meeting for the first time. Or maybe her presence was to protect Miss Betty. The thought warmed her. Her father might have left his mother here, but he had placed her with people who obviously cared a great deal about the people in their care.

"You can take off your hat, dear," Miss Betty said with a quick nod toward Lorie's prayer *kapp*.

Lorie's hand flew to her head to protect the sacred garment. "Oh, no." She shook her head.

A small frown puckered Miss Betty's brow, then she smoothed it away with a smile. "I don't get many visitors," she said. "Would you like some cookies? I don't know where that Pearl has gotten off to." The frown returned. "Really, dear, it's not very ladylike to wear a hat inside."

Lorie looked to Luke who shrugged. Had this woman ever seen an Amish person? Or maybe this was one of those memory problems Amber had told them about. "It's a prayer *kapp*," Lorie explained. "Not a hat and I'm not allowed to take it off until I go to bed at night." That wasn't entirely true, but explaining the many rules that directed how to wear a *kapp* and when, Lorie figured this was as good an explanation as any.

"Well, I've never heard of such a thing." Two bright spots of pink rose to her wrinkled cheeks.

"I'm Amish, you see." It was a terrible explanation but it was the only one she could give.

"Amish?" Miss Betty frowned again. "How can this be? Pearl didn't say anything about that." She turned accusing eyes toward the doorway where Amber still stood. "There you are, Pearl. Why didn't you tell me this girl here is Amish?"

"I'm sorry." Amber gave her an indulgent smile. "It must have slipped my mind."

"We can't have this," Miss Betty fretted. "This will never do." Then tears filled her eyes. "How can you be Amish? How?"

"Okay, visit over." Amber motioned them to get out of the room.

Lorie gladly stood and hurried on stiff legs toward the

hallway. "It was nice to meet you, Miss Betty." But she wasn't sure the woman could hear her, sobbing as she was.

Luke followed her out into the hall.

"She's not always this bad. In fact, most days are pretty good for her. I'm sorry."

Luke muttered something that sounded like, "That's all right."

"Can you find your way back to the front desk?" Amber asked.

They nodded.

Amber smiled, then ducked back into the room. As they turned to leave, Lorie heard her soothing voice promising that everything was going to be all right.

Lorie stopped and leaned against the wall. The entire situation was bizarre, heartbreaking, and she was having trouble taking it all in. She had just met her grandmother, a woman she hadn't known existed before today. Did Betty Mathis know about her? How would she ever know? Her head thunked against the wall.

"Are you okay?"

She closed her eyes. "It's just a lot, you know?"

"Yeah." She felt him draw nearer, then his warm hand on her shoulder.

What would her father say to her now? *Time to buck up, baby girl. Life goes on. Meet each day ready for the wonders it holds.* Except she hadn't been ready for this. Not at all.

She took a deep breath, opened her eyes, and straightened her spine. "I'm *allrecht* now."

The look on Luke's face was doubtful, but he didn't contradict her. He merely gave a small nod and together they continued toward the front desk.

Carol spotted them and stood, her mouth pulled into a small wince. "It didn't go well?"

"No," Luke said.

"It's not uncommon for family members to have trouble dealing with a loved one's memory loss."

But that wasn't the problem. Something about her being Amish had upset Betty. Maybe since her son had left her here and gone to live among the Plain people, she blamed them for her being alone.

"Listen," Carol started. "I know today didn't go well, but don't let it scare you off from ever coming back. Henry was her only visitor with the exception of the volunteers."

"He was?" she asked, even though she knew it to be true. Who else would visit her? Her father was an only child. Or at least that's what he told her.

Stop. You can't go around doubting everything he ever said.

"Maybe you should give her a couple of days, maybe even a week, and try again. I hate to see you find her only to never see her again."

"I'll think about it," Lorie said, but how could she come back? She lived miles away, and she couldn't get a driver every week without raising suspicions all over Wells Landing. "*Danki* for letting me see her. I hope we didn't cause too much trouble."

Carol gave her a kindly smile. "It was no trouble at all."

"Lorie?"

She turned at the sound of her name. Zach, the *Englisch bu* from the auction, walked toward her, surprise and something that looked like joy lighting his expression. "Hi."

She dropped her gaze to her feet. This day was turning out to be even more than she expected.

She could feel Luke's questioning eyes on her as Zach approached. But he wasn't the only one. Carol and Amber watched with undisguised curiosity as he drew near.

"What are you doing here?" he asked, coming to a stop just in front of her.

She lifted her gaze to his and felt the bottom drop out of her stomach. His eyes were just so beautiful.

"Do you know someone living here?" Confusion puckered his brow.

"Sort of."

"I never expected to see you again." His voice rose in what she thought was excitement. But her thoughts were spinning so she couldn't focus on more than one at a time.

"I need to go," she whispered. She couldn't stay there a minute longer, not even for sky-blue eyes and a smile like the sun.

Zach glanced from her to Luke, then back again. His confusion so apparent. As if it hadn't been before. "Oh, okay. Well, maybe I'll see you around."

"*Jah,*" she murmured.

"You want to tell me what that was all about?" Luke asked as they continued out into the warm Oklahoma sunshine.

She could feel Zach's eyes on them as they left. He must have stood there in the hallway and watched until they disappeared out the door.

"It's nothing," Lorie said.

"Uh-huh."

"What?"

Luke shook his head. "You want to get something to eat?"

Her thoughts were tumbling over each other, every one pushing to be the one she settled on. Her father, her grandmother, Zach . . . "What? No. Sure. I mean, I guess."

Luke chuckled at her indecision and unlocked the car doors. "Food it is."

Half an hour later Lorie found herself seated in a booth in a pizza restaurant staring at Luke across the table. "I just don't understand how he could keep that from me." She punched down the ice in her soda and took another drink, but so far she hadn't been able to touch the loaded pizza in front of them.

"Maybe he was trying to protect her. You saw how confused she was when she saw us."

"I guess." Lorie picked off a piece of bell pepper and popped it into her mouth.

"Or maybe he was trying to keep you safe?"

"Me? What would he need to protect me from?"

"I dunno."

"I think you've been watching too many *Englisch* spy movies."

Luke quirked a brow in her direction. "And how would you know if you haven't been watching them yourself?"

"*Mamm* wants me to go to baptism classes."

"I thought they weren't being held until next year."

"She wants me to go to Bishop Treger's district so I can join this year."

"Oh." The one word spoke in bulk. "She must really be ready for you to join."

"*Jah.* I suppose."

"How do you feel about that?"

Lorie shrugged one shoulder. "I don't know how I feel. I've been so confused since *Dat* died and now this." She stared out the window next to them, but no answers waited in the parking lot or beyond.

"Are you thinking about not joining at all?"

"I'm not sure how *Mamm* would take that." She snorted, then sat back in her seat. "Who am I trying to fool? She would be devastated and angry." And a bunch of other negative emotions. So many that Lorie couldn't think of them all in one sitting.

"So go to the classes."

Lorie nodded.

"And you and Jonah?" Luke fished.

"He wants me to join, of course," she said, snagging another topping off her otherwise untouched slice.

"Have y'all been getting along better?"

"I suppose." His frown of consternation appeared in her mind. "He didn't want me to come today."

"I suppose not."

"What does that mean?"

"Well, anytime you start poking around in the *Englisch* world Plain folks get a bit upset."

"*Jah.*"

"Jonah's already joined the church. If you don't join, then the two of you can't get married. He's not going to turn his back on the church now and risk a shunning."

"I guess I hadn't thought about it like that." Jonah was close to his family and wanted to carry on with his father's farm. Like any Amish boy in *rumspringa* he'd gone out and tasted the world. But that was all he wanted, just the experience before he settled down. He hadn't understood her reluctance to join up when he had. But she hadn't been ready at the time. Didn't know if she was ready yet. But she was twenty-three years old and the decision was at hand.

"He loves you," Luke said, bringing Lorie out of her thoughts.

"I know." She pushed her plate away and tried to make sense of it all. But it seemed as if one decision and one decision alone had to be made. "I guess I should just go back home and forget all of this ever happened."

"Are you okay with that?"

"Does it matter?"

"I think so. Just because you're in baptism classes doesn't mean that you can't come to Tulsa from time to time and visit your grandmother."

Hearing him say those words was weird beyond anything she had ever heard. Her grandmother.

"What if *Mamm* finds out?" she asked. And it would

surely matter to the bishop if he happened to find out she was coming to Tulsa. Later, maybe that would be okay, but this summer? Secretive trips to visit *Englisch* relations could ruin joining the church for her.

"Not to sound harsh, but she can either accept it or not. You said she knew about your father's tattoo, right?"

"*Jah.*"

"Then what's to say she doesn't already know about this?"

Lorie sat back, her thoughts spinning. Could *Mamm* know about her grandmother in Tulsa? The thought was too bizarre to comprehend. "But what about *Dat?* If everyone knows that his mother is *Englisch* . . ."

"That doesn't mean that she wasn't Amish before. Maybe that was why she acted so strongly toward your prayer *kapp.*"

"Maybe," she murmured.

"And with her memory problems how are any of us to know the truth?"

He was right about that as well. The only other person who could definitely tell the story was her father, and he was gone.

"Are you kidding me?" Luke walked around the car, his aluminum cane clicking with each step. "This is your father's car?"

"That's what the police said." She looked at the faded orange car and shook her head. It was the kind where the top would come off. A convertible, she thought they called them, but she wasn't sure.

Her father had kept it in a storage building. She had found the papers for the place in his wallet, and the key on the chain the police had given *Mamm.* It wasn't hard to find, and now there it was, another reminder that her *dat* wasn't at all who she thought.

"This is a '62 Karmann Ghia."

"It is?" she asked. "What does that mean?"

"It's a neat car." Luke smiled. "What are you going to do with it?"

"Sell it, I guess." Too many decisions. "I don't know. I guess I should talk to *Mamm* about it." Like that conversation would go well.

"You can leave it at my place until you decide."

"Thanks, Luke." What would she do without her friends?

"I'll get one of my buddies to come over here with me and drive it back."

Lorie nodded and handed him the keys to the funny little car. She had never seen anything like it. There certainly wasn't one in Wells Landing, but it seemed to fit her father. It was different and edgy, just like him. Only she hadn't realized it while he was alive. He had just been her father. She hadn't thought about the way he talked and the little things he did that weren't big enough to catch the attention of the bishop but not traditionally Amish either. Had the answer been right under her nose all along, but she had been too close to see?

"So are you going to tell me about this guy from the assisted living home?"

"There's nothing to tell." Lorie got into Luke's car and waited patiently for him to join her.

"Didn't look that way to me." He slid into the driver's seat and started the engine. "That man had his eyes all over you."

Lorie scoffed. There was no way she had captured the attention of the handsome *Englischer*. He could probably have any girl he wanted. It was downright crazy to think he wanted anything more than friendship with her. "Maybe he needs a friend."

Luke shot her a look.

"Look at me." She ran a hand down the black apron. "If *Englisch* men thought dressing like this was attractive, then the *Englisch* women would be dressed Plain."

"You don't think *Englisch* guys can see past all of that?"

"I . . ." She sputtered to a stop. She hadn't really thought about it before. She had just assumed that *Englisch* men were into looks and the way women were dressed. And she was ashamed of herself. It was unfair to put that shallow label on all *Englisch* men. "Whatever," she finally managed. "Just because he said hi to me doesn't mean he's anything more than polite."

A small chuckle escaped Luke. "You just keep telling yourself that."

This was the last thing she should be doing. She knew how the church felt about paintings and such. It was a sin to be prideful of one's creativity.

But she had to. Last night she had lain in bed and tried to bring her father's face into mind. And she had failed. He had only been gone a few weeks and already his memory was starting to fade. She had to do something to keep that from happening. She just had to. So she had snuck away to the storage room above the restaurant and dragged out her paints.

Lorie stared at the blank canvas. That was the thing about art. It just *was*. She had no other way to describe it. The painting was already on the canvas. It might look blank to others, but she could see the picture there, already painted in the vivid colors she preferred. Her father's dark hair flopped across his forehead, black hat like a halo around his head. Twinkling blue eyes. His favorite blue shirt, black suspenders, yellow background as if the sun shone just for him.

She had too many feelings, too much emotion filling her to keep it all in. She had to paint. She just had to. She took a deep breath to steady her nerves and her hands, then she dipped her brush into the paint and touched it to the white.

Chapter Five

"You seem miles away, Lorie. Are you *allrecht?*" Jonah asked.

"Huh?" Lorie visibly started, then turned her focus toward him.

"I knew you weren't listening to me." He tried not to sound hurt, but it had been this way far too long. Lorie seemed to walk around in a daze lately, staring off into nothing as if she had too many thoughts inside her head to pay attention to anything else.

"I'm sorry." She placed one hand on his arm where it lay atop the rocking chair's armrest. "What did you say?"

They had been sitting on the porch of his house enjoying the beautiful afternoon. Soon summer would hit and the heat and humidity would make lounging around outside uncomfortable at best.

"I asked how the classes were going."

"Baptism . . . *Jah* . . . *gut*. I mean, for baptism classes." She smiled at her own little joke. She was so pretty when she smiled, like the sun came directly from her heart. But these days, the gesture didn't reach her eyes. And as the weeks passed he got more and more worried about her. Sure, she had lost her father, but it seemed like more than that was bothering her.

"Is this about the tattoo?" He had tried to be supportive, but it was near impossible to know what to do or say in such a situation. Things like this didn't happen often and surely not in little districts like Wells Landing.

"No," she said. "Well, sort of . . ." She pleated her fingers in the black folds of her apron and sighed as she stared off toward the cornfield. "There's a lot of things. I went to Tulsa the other day. To the address on his driver's license."

He hid his shock as best he could. She had gone to Tulsa without him, without telling him. That wasn't like her at all.

"I thought we agreed to let this go."

Her head whipped around, and her gaze sought his. A deep frown burrowed its way into her smooth brow. "I never agreed to anything."

Her mood change was confusing, but he was here to be supportive and that was exactly what he planned to be. "I thought we said it would be better if you gave yourself some time."

"I did," she cried. "And all I got was more questions."

"What was at the address?" he asked, though he was a little afraid of the answer. He'd heard once about an *Englisch* man who had two families, two houses, two everything, though neither wife knew they were sharing him with the other. It seemed too bizarre to be the truth, but now, he was starting to wonder. . . .

"It was a home for older people. His mother lives there."

"Wow." The word was so much less than he wanted to say. No wonder she had been walking around like her mind was filled to the brim.

She went on to explain her visit with her grandmother and how Betty Mathis couldn't remember the smallest things and was confused by Lorie's Amish dress.

"That settles it then." He sat back in his seat as his

breathing returned to normal. Everything was going to be *allrecht*. "If she can't remember you and you upset her by visiting, then you shouldn't go back."

She bit her lip as tears filled her eyes. "You're right, I suppose."

He patted her hand reassuringly. "I know I am. You need to just concentrate on your articles for baptism and joining the church. Everything else will fall into place."

"You think so?"

He flashed her his best smile. "I know so."

Zach let his gaze wander around the rec room searching for that one sweet face. He shook his head at his unlikely thoughts. What did he think? She was just going to show up out of the blue?

Well, yeah, that was exactly what he thought. It was kismet or fate or something that brought her here to begin with. Surely it would bring her back.

"Hey, Dream Boy." Tori Ann snapped her fingers in front of his face to bring his attention around. "Table eight needs your help." Unlike Zach, Tori Ann volunteered at the Sundale Retirement and Assisted Living Center. The residents loved her sassy ways and bright smile, though today her brassy attitude grated his nerves. "They asked for you specifically."

"Right. Sorry." Time to quit spacing out over a girl he would never see again and get back to work. He turned toward the table, making note that Betty Mathis was among the seniors seated there. He smiled. She was one of his favorites. There was just something about her smile and the innocent light in her eyes. She had memory problems and was easily confused, but she didn't let that stop her. He admired her spunk.

"Johnathan," she said as he approached the table.

"Zach," he gently corrected.

"Oh, yes, of course." She patted her hair and smiled as if she had meant to call him Zach all along. "Will you help us with these airplane kits? We have the instructions, but I still can't tell where the wings are supposed to go."

"Of course." He pulled out a chair and studied the instructions. Then he showed Betty and the rest of table eight how to attach the wings.

"We're sending these over to the children's hospital," Betty said, examining her plane from all angles. Normally she preferred knitting to the craft of the day, but the thought of making a balsa wood airplane must have appealed to her.

"The VA hospital," Stan Marley corrected. Stan was a retired shoe salesman from back in the days where the reps took the shoes around to the stores. Zach loved hearing him talk about traveling and carrying a sample case. It seemed everyone had lost the human touch these days. Maybe that was why so many people were angry all the time.

"Of course," Betty said, her brow puckering, then smoothing itself out as if she had gotten it right from the beginning.

"That's a great idea." As Zach spoke his gaze drifted toward the entrance to the rec room.

"That's the fifth time you've looked at the door," Eugene Horton boomed. His voice was huge, but his body didn't match. He was a short man, barely five foot, with a thin build and long, slender fingers. The odd combination of his small frame and his over-loud voice was enough to bring a smile to Zach's face, though he hid it so the man wouldn't think he was laughing at him. "You waiting on someone?"

Zach shook his head. "No," he lied.

"Is it a girl?" Linda, Eugene's sister, asked. She was the opposite of Eugene in every way—tall, rounded, and quiet-spoken. Zach had heard the rumor that the two of them were twins, but he'd not found an opportunity to ask them.

"No." A heat rose in his face to belie his words.

"I saw a girl leaving your room the other day, Betty." Fern,

Betty's next-door "neighbor," grabbed the page of stickers and started to place them on her plane.

"If you do the stickers first, you'll ruin them when you start to paint," Eugene said.

"Hush." Linda smacked his hand. "It's her plane, and she can decorate it in any order she wants."

Betty handed the red paint to Zach for him to uncap. He removed the lid and handed the small tub back to her. "I don't recall a girl," Betty said.

"Thursday," Fern explained as she carefully removed one sticker to reposition it on the unpainted wing.

"She must have been visiting someone else," Betty continued, not looking up as she carefully painted the underside of her plane's wings. "I never have visitors."

"What about your son?" Eugene asked.

Betty looked up, her eyes squinted in confusion. "No," she said slowly. "That must be someone else too. I never have visitors."

"She was a pretty thing, even in that heavy black dress she was wearing," Fern said. "I think she was Amish."

They were talking about Lorie! Excitement rose inside him. She had been there visiting Betty Mathis. Maybe he should ask Carol and Amber up front if she had said anything to them. As a matter of fact, he wondered why he hadn't asked them already. Surely Lorie stopped at the circulation desk before heading to Betty's room.

"There!" Stan said triumphantly. "You looked at the door again."

Zach smiled and shook his head. "Sorry."

He had two more finals to take and then it was on to the real world. Hopefully Lorie would come back to the living center again before he found his "real" job. After all, he loved the residents at the home, but there were only so many balsa wood airplanes a guy could make.

* * *

Lorie eased up the staircase and into the second-floor storeroom. It seemed these days she spent every spare minute she had there. Painting.

She had almost talked herself out of ever painting again, but that was before her father's death and all the secrets she'd uncovered. Too many emotions filled her up and spilled out onto the canvases. It wasn't like she was any good, not like the artists who filled museums and galleries. This was just her way of expressing herself and dealing with her swirling emotions.

She let herself into the stuffy room and turned on the fan she had snuck up there the week before. She wished she could open a couple of windows and let the breeze come through, but she was afraid it might alert someone to her presence. Then *Mamm* would find out and that would never do.

She covered herself in the overlarge shirt she used to protect her clothes and opened the box where she'd stashed her paints. It was hard and messy painting in secret, but right now she had no choice. She was going through baptism instruction and one slipup could keep her out of the church. She should shut the box, put away the canvas, and head back down the stairs, but she couldn't stop painting any easier than she could stop breathing. The time she took away from painting only stored up the feelings. She found they were there waiting for her when she returned.

It wasn't like she was showing them to people. They were just for her. She gave a quick nod at her justification. She wasn't going to sell the paintings, or try to put them in a show. They were simply her way of coping. Surely Bishop Ebersol couldn't find fault with that.

She had finished the painting of her father. She wasn't the kind of painter who painted exact replicas of the subject. Nor could she be called abstract like the paintings of Jackson Pollock she had looked at in that big library reference book. No, her efforts fell somewhere in between. Anyone looking at the painting could tell what it was of, but she tried to capture the spirit of the person, the glow that seemed to come from within.

She set up her easel and uncovered the half-finished painting she had started a couple of days before. She had started off with the inspiration to paint a picture of the car that she had left with Luke. It was the biggest thing she had from her father and represented the dual life he'd been living. But somehow when she started painting it wasn't the cute little orange car but the handsome face of the *Englischer* Zach. She studied it now with critical eyes. She should have never started the painting. It was wrong of her to paint a portrait of another man when she was practically engaged to Jonah. Not that he would ever know about it unless she made the point to tell him. Still, it seemed wrong somehow.

With a shake of her head she put it aside and took out her last blank canvas. She set it up on the easel and stared at it for a moment. Then she closed her eyes and imagined what needed to be painted there.

Over the years she had painted almost everyone she knew and the people who had come into her life—Caroline, Andrew, and Emma. She had even painted one of Caroline's parents who had moved to Wells Landing from the very conservative Swartzentruber district in Ethridge, Tennessee. With the exception of Caroline and Emily, none of these people knew she had painted their picture. And it was a secret she would forever keep.

She opened her eyes and the purple paint beckoned. She answered by squeezing a large dollop on the cutting board she had turned into a paint station. She dipped her brush into the oil paint and ran it across the canvas.

"Come walk with me." Caroline Fitch ran her arm through Lorie's and didn't give her much choice in the matter as she led her out of the house and into the yard.

They had all gathered at Caroline and Andrew's for a summertime get-together. She and Jonah. Emily and Elam. Even Andrew's cousin Danny and his wife, Julie. Lorie was glad for the diversion, but still she felt as if her every step was weighted by secrets and lies.

"What's wrong?" Lorie asked as they tromped across the yard. The others had settled in to playing a rousing game of Scrabble. She was glad for Caroline's demand to walk with her. Lorie couldn't concentrate long enough to form more than a three-letter word.

"That's my question." Caroline led her toward the barn where her husband housed his newest horses for his budding breeding business. Andrew had taken over his uncle's house and land when his *onkle* Abe had married Esther Lapp and moved into town. Now Andrew leased part of the farm to horse trainers and other breeders while he used the other part to support his own business. Abe's shop sat to the other side of the yard where he came out and made the furniture pieces too big to build in the backroom at his shop in town.

"Do I look like something's wrong?" She had been so careful of late, smiling when she didn't feel like it and trying to keep going when so many questions ate at her very being.

"*Nay.*" Caroline led them over to the fence where the horses munched on the grass and released Lorie's arm. "But that's the problem. You look like nothing is wrong and I know better."

Lorie shook her head. How could she tell her friend when she didn't understand everything herself?

"There's just a lot going on right now."

"And?" Caroline urged.

"I just need some time to adjust."

"Uh-huh. What about your trip to Tulsa?"

It had only been a week since Lorie had returned from Tulsa and her discovery that she had a grandmother tucked away in a home there. Seven days of thinking about the new relative who didn't know Lorie existed. About the car she'd left at Luke's and the handsome *Englischer* she'd run into again. Seven days of wondering if she should tell her *mamm* or do as Emily and Jonah suggested and "just let it go."

One thing was certain, she wouldn't be able to move forward without talking it out with someone. It wasn't the Amish way, to share feelings so readily, but she felt as if she might explode from all her swirling and churning emotions.

"I started painting again," she said, staring out over the green pasture.

"Really?"

"*Jah.*" Though Caroline knew of her secret painting, Lorie had never let anyone—not even her closest friends—see her efforts.

"Of course, you have." Caroline patted her shoulder reassuringly. "You've been through so much."

"I have a grandmother living in Tulsa." The words escaped her like the bubbles of a shaken soda. She turned as Caroline blinked, her eyes widening. Her *freind* was normally calm and collected, but Lorie could tell even this surprised her. "My father had a tattoo, a car, and a mother he never told me about."

"Oh, Lorie." The warm weight of Caroline's arm settled around her. Lorie leaned her head onto her friend's shoulder, needing that moment of comfort. "What are you going to do?" Caroline's words hummed through her.

"I don't know." She straightened and fought back the tears of frustration and helplessness that seemed so close to the surface these days. "She's got some problems with her memory. Sometimes she doesn't remember where she is. I don't think she will be able to tell me anything about my father."

"Maybe that's God's way of telling you that it's time to concentrate on the future."

"Maybe," Lorie murmured in return. The future . . . joining

the church, marrying Jonah, learning to live with all the secrets her father kept.

But how was she supposed to look forward when it seemed as if the past kept calling to her?

Lorie swayed with the horse's steady gait as she rode next to Jonah on the way home. He was quiet and had been since they started on their drive, but she could tell that he had something on his mind.

"Everyone's talking about you going to Tulsa with Luke."

Lorie whipped around to stare at him. Jonah's gaze was glued to the road ahead.

"How does anyone even know about this?"

He shrugged one shoulder. "Some ex-Amish who knows Luke said something to someone in Bishop Treger's district. You know how these things get around."

She did. For all the talk on the sins of gossip, it seemed to be a popular pastime in Wells Landing. "Do they know why I went?"

"I haven't heard for sure, but I don't think so."

Lorie wilted in relief. The last thing she needed was for everyone in town to know about her *Englisch* grandmother. It was only a hop and a jump from there to her father's deception. She couldn't allow her father's memory to be tainted.

"You've got to be more careful," Jonah admonished.

Lorie couldn't find fault in his criticism. This was an important summer for her. The district would be watching everything she did. Especially since she wasn't attending her own church's baptism instruction. One mess-up and it could ruin her chances of joining the church this summer.

"I'm not going back," she said. Until that moment she hadn't made the decision. But Caroline was right—everyone was right. It was time to look to the future. "I'm sorry. I know I've been hard to understand lately."

"It's *allrecht*." Jonah cast a small look her way, a smile tugging at his lips. It was the first smile she had seen from him in weeks. Her trials had taken their toll on him as well. It was time to straighten up, fly right as the *Englisch* said, and get down to the business of going forward.

Chapter Six

But the questions remained, just below the surface like a crafty fish—almost invisible, but there all the same.

As much as Lorie wanted to forget all about it and move forward, these many unanswered questions dragged at her, holding her prisoner until they were answered. Even painting didn't help. Or maybe it seemed not to because it was one more secret she kept.

"I'm heading to the market," Sadie said, taking off her cooking apron and replacing it with a clean one. "We're going to need a few more tomatoes before tomorrow's truck gets here. I thought I'd go down and see if anyone has any."

Escape. "I'll go." Lorie patted her sister's hand. "You rest your feet."

Sadie smiled. "You just want to get outside on this beautiful day."

"Can you blame me?" The sun was shining and temperatures were on the rise, but for now it was a perfect Oklahoma day.

"Not at all." Sadie took a ten-dollar bill from the petty cash box and handed it to Lorie. "Just don't dally too long in the sun."

Lorie smiled. "I'll try not to." She left the restaurant as

Sadie slid into the employees' booth and started wrapping
silverware.

Outside, the day was even more beautiful than it looked to
be through the plate-glass windows. Lorie closed her eyes
and raised her face toward the sun.

She stood there for a second, thankful to be out of the
restaurant, out in the open air, just out. Inside it seemed as if
the walls were closing in on her. Every day they seemed
closer as if they had moved during the night to make her
uncomfortable. It was a ridiculous thought, but it was how
she felt all the same. Everything seemed too small these
days, from the black dresses she was required to wear to her
own skin. And she didn't know how to make it comfortable
again. Didn't know if it ever would be.

"Excuse me."

She opened her eyes, realizing she was taking up the
middle of the sidewalk. People were having to walk around
her as she stood there and basked in the sun when she needed
to be making her way to the marketplace.

Two blocks down and three blocks over was the empty
parking lot where the Amish of Wells Landing set up a market
each spring and summer. The farmers and crafters, jelly
makers and pickle canners all set up shop to sell their wares
to Amish and *Englisch* alike.

Lorie always enjoyed the market, perhaps because the
restaurant kept their family so busy that they didn't have time
to spend on what most considered the traditional Amish pur-
suits. They didn't farm or can goods for the winter. They
didn't keep milk cows or goats. They didn't make their own
cheese and butter. But the restaurant had been her father's
dream and the entire Kauffman clan gladly embraced it with
him. As much as Lorie enjoyed the fresh produce and goods
available at the market, she couldn't imagine her life any
other way.

Eustace Chupp, an Amish-turned-Mennonite farmer,

usually had the best tomatoes and Lorie went straightaway to
his stand.

She bartered for a crate, arranged to have them carted to
the restaurant, then wandered through the market for a few
minutes, looking for treats for Daniel and Cora Ann.

"Lorie!" Emily waved her over to the table where she
and her father-in-law, James, sat tending the milk they had
for sale.

She made her way toward her friend, glad for the opportunity to take a little more time at the market. She wasn't
ready to go back to the restaurant.

"I didn't expect to see you today," Lorie said as she approached their booth.

"I didn't expect to be here today. But Becky needed a day
off for a youth meeting."

Becky, Elam's oldest sister, had recently joined the church.
She and Billy Beiler were quite close and everyone was waiting for the two of them to announce their intentions to get
married. Lorie envied the young girl in knowing what she
wanted at such a young age. It seemed to be the way among
Amish youth. They knew what they wanted and made it
happen. So why was she so confused?

James smiled at Lorie, then wrinkled his nose as he took
in her dress. "Do you have a purple *frack?*"

"*Dat.*" Emily's tone took on a chastising edge. "Lorie is
in mourning, remember? Her father passed a few weeks
ago."

"That's right. I'm sorry." His brow puckered into a frown.
"Sorry about your *vatter* and sorry you can only wear black."

Me and you both. "It's okay." Lorie smiled at James to
reinforce her words. James was a kind soul who'd been
rendered childlike in ways and mannerisms after being
kicked in the head by a cantankerous milk cow.

Most would say that it was God's will. But Lorie had a
hard time believing God would want a strong and capable

man like James Riehl reduced to less than he had been born to be.

Yet, Emily had brought him far when she and Elam were courting. Emily had been responsible for checking his medication and seeing that it might be doing him more harm than good. Emily was the one who encouraged him to go to church and get back into the act of living. Because of Emily, James and Joy now had a sweet baby girl James insisted on naming Lavender. Despite his injury, he had a new start to his old life.

And Emily could help her, too.

"Emily," she said her name where only her friend could hear. "Will you call Luke for me again?" She hadn't meant to ask the question. She had told Jonah that she was done with trips to Tulsa and all the secrets they revealed. But she couldn't stop the words.

"Of course. *Jah.*"

One more time. Just one more trip to the assisted living center. One more visit with the ladies at the front desk and the woman who was her grandmother but didn't even know her name. Just one more trip to answer a few more of the questions haunting her, then she was done with this for good.

"You what?"

"Jonah, I don't appreciate your tone. Now please sit back down and stop yelling at me."

Jonah threw himself into the swing beside her. "I'm not yelling. Amish men don't yell."

"Don't raise your voice then." She knew he was going to be angry with her. That was the exact reason why she chose to tell him in the park. He couldn't raise too much of a fuss in the center of town.

"You said you weren't going back there, Lorie. I don't understand why you've changed your mind."

How could she explain it where he could understand? "These secrets," she started, hoping he could see her point of view. "They're like a cancer eating up my insides. The only way I can stop it is to know the truth."

"You know the truth." Jonah's tawny-colored eyes begged her to let it drop. She would do almost anything for him, but this was something she had to do for herself.

"My father wasn't who he said he was. What does that say about me?"

"It doesn't change who you are."

"Doesn't it?"

He took her hands into his and stared into her eyes. "It's not going to end until you put a stop to it."

"I wish it was that easy," she whispered into the wind.

"It is."

She shook her head. "If it was, I wouldn't have all these questions."

"That's something you have to work out for yourself. Pray about it."

Lorie stood on suddenly restless feet. "I have prayed, but I have no answers, only more questions."

"Don't go looking for the devil, Lorie," Jonah quoted.

But she wasn't looking for trouble or temptation. She just needed some firm ground to set her feet upon.

"How's this going to look for your baptism instruction?"

"How can I continue to learn if I don't know who I am anymore?"

"You're Lorie Kauffman. You always have been. You always will be."

She shook her head and began to pace. Jonah's hand snaked out and captured her arm in his warm grasp. His touch should have been reassuring and comforting, but it only made her sad.

"I don't want to hurt you," she said. "Never ever, do I want to hurt you."

"Then don't go."

"Please," she cried. "This is something I have to do. Please try to understand."

His posture deflated like a week-old balloon. "I'm trying," he said.

"That's all I can ask."

Two days later, Lorie managed to get off from the restaurant. She made up a story about her and some friends going to the pond to swim, and her *mamm* readily believed her. Lorie had a moment of remorse at the easy lie, but she reminded herself that Maddie was keeping secrets from her and had been for some time. If she wouldn't share what she knew about the situation, then Lorie had no choice but to find out on her own.

She snuck down to the end of the lane where their house sat and breathed a quick sigh of relief when she saw Luke was there and driving the little orange car that belonged to her father.

He waved at her when she got close. She smiled and waved in return, her footsteps quickening until she was almost running by the time she reached the car.

"So it works?" she asked, opening the door and folding herself into the passenger's seat.

"It runs great. Your father must have taken really good care if it."

"That sounds like him." The thought made her smile. That was the father she knew, the one who went the extra mile to make things right. He never cut corners or took the easy way out. He dedicated his entire self to whatever he was involved in whether it was singing in church or basic maintenance at the restaurant.

"You don't mind that I drove it here?"

"I love it."

Luke returned her grin and started the car down the road.

"It drives different than your car," she said after a time.

"Huh?" He looked over toward her, then used the shift stick in the center between them to slow the car as they merged onto the highway. "Oh, it's a four speed."

She raised her brows. He laughed.

"That means that the transmission doesn't automatically change gears. The driver has to do that." He turned back to monitor her expression. "Never mind."

She didn't understand the first thing about cars. Some of the members of their district, boys and girls alike, knew how to drive tractors. Oklahoma had rocky soil that took machinery to successfully farm. So many of her *freinden* had learned to drive out of necessity. Well, a tractor at least. But Lorie's family owned a restaurant and did no more farming than most *Englischers*. She didn't know the first thing about steering, trans-whatevers, and gears.

"Are you going to wear that into the home?" He nodded toward her dress.

Lorie ran her fingers over her prayer *kapp* remembering the distress it caused Betty the last time she had been there. "I don't suppose I should." But as she said the words, her fingers started to tremble.

"Hey."

She jerked her gaze back to Luke.

"It's not like you're jumping the fence. You're still in *rumspringa* . . . sort of."

But the tremor in her hands continued.

"I guess I'm not the best one to give advice, but it seems to me that in order for you to remain in the church, you need answers to these questions. The only way to get those is to talk to her."

"And the only way to talk to her is dressed as an *Englischer*." Whether she just needed a little time to get used to the idea or his words actually calmed her nerves, she didn't know. But the shaking inside her stopped and her hands grew steady as she removed the pins that held her *kapp* in place.

Luke let out a small cough and kept his eyes trained on the road as if she were half-naked beside him. For an Amish girl, being seen without a head covering qualified as partially clothed. "What about your dress?"

She inhaled as her hands flew to the fasteners of her *frack*.

A flush of red stained his face and neck. He cleared his throat. "I mean, maybe we should find something else for you to wear."

She swallowed hard and nodded. She hadn't thought about this when she was planning this trip. She only wanted to go visit her grandmother one last time. Find out a little more about her father. Then her mind would be free and she could concentrate on her baptism instruction and joining the church. "I don't have any other clothes."

"Of course not." He seemed to mull over her dilemma as he maneuvered through the growing traffic. They would be in Tulsa soon. "Sissy's a lot shorter than you, so her clothes wouldn't work. I know." He snapped his fingers and changed lanes.

Fifteen minutes later, he pulled to a stop in front of a secondhand store.

"Everything in here should be pretty cheap. A pair of jeans, maybe a T-shirt."

She had never worn jeans. Not even in the height of her run-around time. But she got a thrill from looking through them. She was tired of wearing the ugly black dress of mourning. Her father had lived a bright and happy life. Wouldn't it be better to honor his memory with the bold colors that he preferred?

"Do you know what size you are?" Luke asked.

She shook her head and continued flipping through the jeans.

"I guess you'll just have to pick out a couple of pairs and

try them on." He helped her decide, pulling a few hangers from the rack and handing them to her. "Here. Go try on these and I'll look for you a shirt."

The worn cotton was soft against her skin. The first pair was too big, then the second too small. The third pair fit okay. Well, at least she thought they did. She wasn't entirely sure how they should fit.

With her dress bunched around her waist, she studied her reflection in the mirror. The blue denim made her legs look long and her waist tiny.

"Here," Luke said from outside the door. "Try these." He dangled four hangers with shirts on them over the door.

Lorie hung them on a nearby hook and pulled her dress over her head. The red shirt caught her attention. It had a black-and-silver design on the front with swirls and rhinestones. Whether it was the embellishments or the taboo of wearing red, she bypassed the others and slipped it over her head.

"Are you okay in there?"

"*Jah.*" Disappointment filled her. The shirt was too little. It fit too close to her body, showing every curve and dip she had.

"Come out and let me see," Luke urged.

"This shirt is too small."

"Let me see."

Reluctantly she stepped out into the shop.

Luke smiled at her. "It's perfect."

She plucked at the fabric. "It's supposed to fit like this?"

He nodded.

How was she supposed to know? She never paid much attention to the clothes the *Englisch* girls wore. "I don't know, Luke."

"I've got an idea. Wait right here." His cane clicked as he made his way over to the rack of women's shirts and started flipping through them. Occasionally he would pull one out, look at it, then with a shake of his head, placed it back on the rack. "This one," he said triumphantly. He brought the garment over to her. "Put this over the top of the red one."

She eyed the stripey shirt with doubt but took it from him. It was sort of pretty. Plaid, she thought they called it, in colors of red and gray and white. It matched the T-shirt well enough. And the snaps on the front were pretty, some kind of pearly material that changed color in the light.

"Leave it open and roll the sleeves. Just a little," he instructed as Lorie carried out his commands.

"Are you sure about this?" She turned to once again eye herself in the mirror. She certainly wouldn't be fooling anyone into believing she was *Englisch*. Not if they looked at her closely. Her face was devoid of makeup, her hair pulled back in a knot with the part in the middle and the twists on either side at her temples.

"Positive. How about shoes?" he asked as she bundled up her dress in her arms.

"These are fine." She didn't want to spend any more of Luke's money. She would pay him back as soon as they returned to Wells Landing, but she hated being in debt, even for a little bit.

He shrugged, most probably figuring he had pushed her enough for one day, and together they started out of the store. They were halfway to the cash register when something sitting high on the top shelf of the women's section caught her attention.

"Oh," she gasped, stopping in her tracks as she stared at the shoes. They were flats like many of the Amish women wore for special occasions, but instead of being plain black or white they were an animal print. Leopard.

Luke took three steps without her before he realized she wasn't at his side and he doubled back to her. "Do you like those?"

She shook her head. "They're probably not my size."

"They look about right. Why don't you try them on?"

She shouldn't. She really shouldn't. But she wanted to so badly. Something about the shoes called to her. As if they knew her name and they were waiting there just for her. She shook her head again, this time to clear it of her fanciful thoughts. They were shoes. Nothing more.

"Go ahead." Luke reached for her dress and waited patiently while she removed her shoes and socks and slipped her feet into the fancy shoes. They fit perfectly.

"We're getting those," he said.

She opened her mouth to protest but no words would come. She wasn't sure what was so special about the shoes, but there was something. Something indeed. She gave Luke a small nod and followed him to the counter.

Walking out of the dressing room she had felt self-conscious, like everyone was staring at the Amish girl in *Englisch* clothes. But now she felt different. She couldn't quite explain it. Just different. Like maybe she could belong.

She pushed that thought away. Like Luke said, it wasn't as if she was leaving the Amish forever. This was just to pay one last visit to her grandmother and see if she could find out any more information about her *dat*.

The cashier bagged Lorie's Amish clothes and helped her cut the tags off her new ones. Then she and Luke walked back out to the car. They climbed inside and without another word, he drove them to Sundale.

He pulled into a parking space, cut off the engine, and turned to face her. "Are you ready for this?"

"I think so, *jah*." As she reached for the door handle, she thought back to the first time she had come here. She hadn't known what to expect then, but today she had a better idea. Today would be different, she could just feel it.

She stepped from the car and shut the door, catching a glimpse of her reflection in the glass window. "Wait a minute," she said, then pulled the pins from her hair.

"You're going to wear it down?" Even Luke looked shocked by the notion.

"*Nay, nay.*" She combed her fingers through the waist-length tresses feeling like a rebel. But this was perhaps the wildest thing she had ever done. When she had been running around, she had worked at the restaurant and helped with the younger kids. She didn't have as much time as most for getting into mischief. She hadn't gone to any of the wild parties that were always floating about in the rumors. She didn't drink alcohol or dress in *Englisch* clothes. So if someone found fault in her releasing her hair in public, so be it.

Satisfied she had pulled the stern middle part from her hair, she pulled it into a bun and pinned it at her nape.

So it wasn't the most forward of hairstyles, but it wasn't Amish and for today that was all that mattered. She looked at herself in the mirror, pleased with the transformation. She'd just have to remember not to send up prayers until she got her *kapp* firmly back in place.

"You're coming in, right?" Lorie asked him.

"Of course." Luke limped along behind her as they made their way to the door of the home.

Amber and Carol sat behind the desk just as they had during her first disastrous visit.

Amber looked up doing a double take as she recognized the two of them. Perhaps her change wasn't as altering as she had thought.

"Lorie, right?" She smiled at them and shot the other woman a satisfied look. "I told you she'd be back."

"I almost didn't recognize you," Carol said. "You look great."

Lorie's cheeks filled with heat. "I thought it would be best to come in *Eng*—regular clothes."

"You're probably right." Carol stood. "Miss Betty is in the rec room for arts and crafts, but I'm sure she'd love some company. I'll walk you down there."

Arts and crafts? She wouldn't be able to ask any questions about her father. How was she supposed to find out more about the car and everything else that he'd kept a secret from his family?

But she didn't protest—couldn't protest—as she followed Carol to the rec room. She'd just have to bide her time and hope for the best.

Chapter Seven

So far he'd made forty-seven planes, two coffee mugs, sixteen ashtrays (who even used ashtrays these days?), and countless coasters. But still no sign of Lorie.

Finals were over, graduation done, and now he had the daunting task of finding his grown-up job. But he was distracted—plain and simple—by a blond-haired girl who hadn't given him the time of day. Maybe he should just chalk his obsession up to working too hard and let it go.

"Can you help with this?" Betty Mathis held the small plastic loom toward him. The colorful rubber bands were a tangled mess instead of looking like they formed an item.

"Sure. What is it? A necklace or a bracelet?"

"A bracelet. Yes. We're making these bracelets to take to the VA hospital."

"The children's hospital," Stan grumped. "Why would a grown man want a rubber-band bracelet?"

Zach smiled at the idea of a wounded vet wearing rainbow-colored jewelry. Then again, maybe it would be a good idea after all.

He started to unravel the mess that Miss Betty had created

with her green and purple rubber bands. She had thrown in a red one every so often and the effect was . . . unique.

His attention shifted as the door to the rec room opened, and Amber stepped inside followed by . . .

"Lorie."

He almost didn't recognize her in regular clothing. But she looked amazing. He half-stood as she came near.

Surprise lit her brown eyes as her gaze landed on him. "Hi."

"Lorie has come to help with the crafts today." Amber's tone was that of a kindergarten teacher. Zach liked the woman okay, but he hated that she talked to the seniors like they were children.

Fern pushed her glasses a little higher up the bridge of her nose and studied the newcomer. "I've seen you. You came a couple of weeks ago to visit with Betty."

Betty raised her gaze from the knitting she had picked up the minute Zach started working on the bracelet. "Oh, Fern, you must be mistaken. I've never seen her before in my life."

Fern let her glasses slip back into place and turned her attention to the loom on the table in front of her. "Uh-huh."

For once Zach was glad that she didn't argue the point with her next-door neighbor. The two were like old hens when they started. But problems arose when Betty's confusion deepened and Fern insisted.

"Will you help me with this, dear?" Betty pushed the loom across the table in front of the empty chair next to Linda.

Lorie's smile was stunning.

"I think I'll go fill up the car."

For the first time Zach noticed the dark-haired guy who'd been with Lorie the time before. Were they a couple? Did it matter? It might. She was dressed in normal clothes.

Wait, that wasn't fair. The clothes she had on the other times he had seen her were normal for her, but he didn't know how to refer to her change in attire.

Lorie looked panicked for a moment, then pulled out the chair and nodded.

Zach wasn't sure if she was more concerned about being left alone with strangers or the thought of helping Betty with the bracelet. Heaven knew he'd made a bigger mess of it than the sweet lady had.

"My name is Lorie," she said to the table at large.

"Of course it is, dear." Betty smiled at her. "You have your father's nose."

She covered that nose with one hand and blinked a couple of times as if trying to decide how to answer and coming up short. She looked to Zach for direction, but he could only shrug. Who knew if Betty was truly remembering something or just making up her own reality? She had a tendency to do both regularly.

"You remember my father?" she asked. Her tone was offhand, like the answer didn't matter either way. But the tremble in her hands as she unwound the mess in the loom spoke of the emotions she was controlling.

"Of course, dear." Betty handed her a handful of red rubber bands. "Put these every so often. It makes a nice color contrast, don't you think?"

"Very much so." She sounded disappointed.

"He was my only child, Hank."

"Hank?"

Betty nodded. "That's what I called him. Me and his father. Everyone else called him Henry."

Lorie swallowed hard, tears misting her eyes.

Thankfully the rest of the seniors seated around them grew quiet as Betty continued to talk. "I have some letters that Hank wrote me years ago, I'm not sure why." A frown puckered her brow as she separated out the bright green rubber bands from the darker green ones. "But since he's your father, you might want to read them."

"*Jah,*" Lorie said. "I mean yes. Yes, I would. Very much so."

Betty smiled and patted her hand. "You just wait right here, dear, and I'll go get them."

"Do you want me to go with you?" Zach asked. Sometimes Betty had a tendency to get sidetracked. She could come back immediately with the promised letters or sometime next week. It was anybody's guess.

"Oh no, dear. You stay here and visit with your new girl."

He opened his mouth to protest, but got distracted by the pink flush staining Lorie's cheeks.

Linda put aside her bracelet loom and stood. "I'll go."

"Thanks," Lorie and Zach said at the same time.

Somehow the moment felt intimate, them both saying the same word simultaneously. Or maybe he needed to get some sleep, a new hobby, his head examined.

"She will come back, *jah?*" Lorie asked, looking around the table at the seniors.

"Linda will make sure she does," Eugene said. He pushed his loom away and shook his head. "I give up. Someone without arthritis needs to do these."

"You know anyone here without old Arty as a constant companion, you let me know," Stan said.

"There's an easier way to do this." Lorie's quiet words drew everyone's attention. She seemed uncomfortable with all eyes on her, but to Zach she looked cuter than ever.

"Show me." Eugene nudged his loom closer to Lorie. "Please."

"Sure."

Lorie took the loom from him and started unwinding the rubber bands. In no time at all she had a completed bracelet. Betty hadn't even returned from her room with the letters she had promised.

Lorie removed the bracelet from the loom and handed it to Eugene.

"Well, I'll be." He turned the piece this way and that examining it from all angles.

"Where'd you learn how to do that?" Zach asked. The Amish didn't wear jewelry. Did they? Then again, it wasn't like she was dressed particularly Amish today.

She shrugged one shoulder. "My sister makes them to sell to the tourists. She keeps a basket of them up by the register at the restaurant."

The seniors continued to admire her handiwork. Zach leaned in close. "That guy you're with. Is he your boyfriend?"

"Just a friend."

He gave a nod toward her. "And your clothes. Why were you wearing that dress at the auction and jeans today?" He asked his mother a ton of questions on the way home from Wells Landing. What she couldn't answer he'd looked up online. One thing was certain: the Amish were an interesting lot.

She looked a little panicked, and he realized his tone was a bit harsh.

"I was just wondering," he tried again.

"I'm not turning *Englisch* if that's what you mean. I think I confused Betty the other day."

He wasn't sure what turning English meant, but he could understand confusing Betty.

He didn't have time to ask anything else as Betty and Linda returned.

"Here you go, dear." Betty set a shoe box on the table at Lorie's elbow.

Zach wasn't sure if she was going to open it or toss it in the trash. From the look on her face, he'd think it was full of snakes instead of letters from her father.

"He died, you know." Betty sighed. "Well, that's what the therapist said. He told me that my granddaughter came by to tell me. Oh, how wonderful would it be if the two of you could meet!" Betty clapped her hands excitedly. "Maybe she'll come by again, and you can meet her then."

Lorie snagged his gaze again. "Maybe," they both said at the same time.

"They're serving lunch soon. Can you stay?" he asked her.

She shook her head. "I should get back."

"Lunch!" Betty seemed equally excited by the thought of it and her granddaughter. "Oh, I do hope we have leprechaun pudding today."

"There's no such thing as leprechaun pudding," Stan groused.

"You've never lived until you've eaten leprechaun pudding," Betty continued as if he hadn't spoken. "I wonder why we never have it."

Stan and Eugene shook their heads in unison.

Lorie pushed herself to her feet. "*Danki* for the letters. I mean, thank you."

"Is that German?" Linda asked.

"Pennsylvania Dutch," Lorie said.

"Well that explains it," Fern added.

"Explains what?" Betty asked.

"Why she was dressed Amish when she came last time," Fern explained.

Betty's brow wrinkled into a delicate frown. "Vickie?"

"Lorie," she corrected.

"She's never been here before."

Fern shook her head. She knew better than to argue with Betty when she got like this.

"Have you, dear?" Betty asked.

Lorie looked to Zach. All he could do was shrug. Who knew how Betty would react when faced with the truth. Sometimes she was calm as a kitten murmuring her standard, "of course" while other times she would argue until lights out.

"I have," she said gently. "But it's been a couple of weeks."

"Of course," Betty murmured, then her eyes brightened. "When you come back, will you bring me some leprechaun pudding? They never seem to have it here."

Lorie picked up the box of letters, its weight reassuring and stressful all at the same time. She wanted to rip it open and search through the contents to make sure it really contained the promised correspondence from her father. Betty was flighty at best. For all Lorie knew the box could contain useless scraps of paper.

She wanted to say a small prayer that it contained the words of Henry Kauffman—or Hank Mathis, whichever was his true name. Her stomach fell at the thought that she might not have even known her father's real name. Her head swam with the notion, and her feet tripped over themselves.

"Whoa, there." Zach reached out a steadying hand.

His fingers were warm and strong. Just what she needed at the moment, and she had to resist the urge to lean into him and gather some of that warmth and strength for her own. What would he think of her then? she wondered. Maybe nothing at all. English girls were more forward. But he knew she wasn't English.

Before she could give in to her weakness he released her. "I'll walk you out."

Lorie smiled, thankful to have him at her side. "I didn't have the heart to tell her that I have no idea what leprechaun pudding is."

"None of us do. I even searched on the Internet. Nada. We've decided that it has to be something she dreamed up in her head. One of the cooks even made vanilla pudding and colored it green with food dye, but she said that wasn't it."

"Poor thing." Lorie didn't know what else to say.

They made their way down the hall toward the front of the center. "What time is your friend picking you up?"

"I don't know. He's probably waiting in the car."

"He should have come back in."

"He thinks you like me." Lorie slapped one hand over her mouth. These *Englisch* clothes must be getting to her. Why else would she say something so forward to a man who was practically a stranger to her?

Zach stopped, forcing Lorie to do the same. His eyes deepened until they were as blue as the twilight sky. "He's a smart guy."

"W-what?"

"I do like you, you know."

"*Nay.* I didn't." Well, she had sort of hoped, but then realized the futility of that wish. Why did it matter if he liked her? She was going back to Wells Landing. This was her last visit to the center. She would spend the rest of the summer attending her baptism instruction and doing everything in her power to go forward with her life.

"Well, I do."

Her breath lodged in her throat. "I've got to go." She didn't know if Luke was even in the parking lot waiting for her, but she had to get out of there. She turned on the heel of her sassy new shoes and hurried toward the door.

"Lorie, wait."

His footsteps sounded behind her, increasing the speed of her steps.

"Lorie!" He caught her at the door.

"Zach, I—" She gulped.

He turned as a small cough sounded behind him.

Carol and Amber were watching their exchange with interested eyes.

"Come on." He clasped his hand around hers and pulled her out into the warm midday sun.

"Where are we going?" she asked as he tugged her through the rows of cars.

"Someplace where we can talk for a minute."

She planted her feet and refused to go any further. She might not be knowledgeable in the ways of the *Englisch* world, but she knew better than to get in the car with a man she barely knew. "No."

He must have sensed her fear or maybe it was the determined slant of her jaw. Whatever it was, he stopped. He released her hand and shoved his fingers into the back pockets of his jeans. "I just wanted to talk to you for a minute. I'm sorry. I didn't mean to scare you. It would be cooler in my car. I could start the air conditioner."

She shook her head.

He muttered something under his breath that sounded suspiciously like a curse, then he shook his head. "You don't need to be afraid of me."

"I'm not scared," she said. "It's just . . . I'm not coming back here."

"Because of what I said?"

"Because my place is in Wells Landing. I'm joining the church this year. I'm getting married soon."

"Married?"

"Yes."

He nodded. "Well, I guess that's that then."

She bobbed her head in return. "I guess." A horn sounded, and Lorie turned just as Luke pulled the little orange car into the parking lot. "I've got to go."

"Don't stay away from your grandmother because of me and my big mouth," Zach said.

"I'm not. But I can't keep coming here. I'm not sure how the bishop would feel about that. And I think I confuse Betty more than anything."

"She's your grandmother."

"I lived without her for twenty-three years," Lorie said,

ignoring the ache in her heart. "I'll send the letters back to her when I've looked through them. I just need some answers."

A confused frown puckered his brow, and Lorie realized he didn't know anything about her father's deception. There was no merit in telling him now. "Okay," Zach said. "But do me one favor. If you ever want to come back, let me know, I can come get you. No strings." He paused. "That means I won't expect anything in return."

She hid her smile. "I know." She glanced toward the car where Luke waited. She was torn between the two. She needed to leave. She wanted to stay if even for just a little bit longer. The thought of never coming again filled her with a deep sadness.

"Wait right here, okay?"

She started to protest.

"Please." He was so handsome that she couldn't resist. What was a couple more minutes anyway?

"*Jah,* okay."

"Stay right here." He walked backward a couple of steps, then turned and jogged toward the doors of Sundale.

"Are you coming?" Luke called from the car.

"In a minute."

He nodded, his smile smug and knowing, but she didn't have time to say anything in return. Zach came back out of the center.

"Here." He held out a little card of paper like the ones her father had made for the restaurant.

"What is this?" she asked as she took it from him.

"My number. You know, just in case you ever want to come visit and don't have a ride. I can come get you." He stumbled over his words. "No strings."

She turned the card over. The information for the Sundale Center was on one side. A phone number was written in scrawling numbers across the back. "I don't think I—"

"I get it. But just in case. You never have to use it. But I want you to have it. She is your grandmother after all."

Lorie nodded and tucked the card into the back pocket of her jeans. Just like them, she would take the card home and hide it from the world. She couldn't risk her entire life on a woman who could barely remember her name and a boy she'd just met.

Chapter Eight

Lorie managed to keep the box closed all the way back to Wells Landing. She stashed it in the storeroom behind her paintings and along with the box the police had given Maddie and the clothes she had bought at the secondhand store. She had taken them straightaway to burn them, but something about them—or maybe it was the shoes—kept her from destroying that one link with the *Englisch* world.

It was two days before she managed to sneak into the storeroom again. She sat cross-legged on the floor and pulled the shoe box stuffed with letters toward her, staring at it, wondering if she really wanted to open it. This entire situation seemed to be growing. She wanted one last visit to talk to her grandmother and instead she got a box of letters and who knew what else.

She sucked in a deep breath and reached for the lid. She wasn't sure what to expect, but the letters were there just as promised along with other mementos tucked between the pages. Ribbons, fancy napkins, even a few pressed flowers. She pulled out the envelope closest to the edge and checked the postmark against the one behind it. It seemed the letters were in no particular order, just stuffed inside, waiting for eyes to read them once again.

She unfolded the paper, realizing as she did that the letter wasn't in order. Immediately she recognized her father's spidery handwriting.

*I can hardly believe that Belinda has been gone
a year. I'd like to think she is still with us in spirit.
I know I see her whenever I look at Lorie.*

*She seems to be adjusting well. That's the beauty
of youth. She will bounce back a lot quicker, but it
saddens me to know that she won't remember her
mother.*

Tears filled Lorie's eyes. She dashed them away and continued to read.

*I wish I could bring her for a visit, but I'm afraid
it will only confuse her. Maybe one day she'll
understand that I did this for her. Until then, I've
enclosed a photograph. It's not the best, but the
Amish don't allow for their picture to be taken. I had
to sneak it when no one was looking. But I wanted
you to see how much she's grown.*

*I must go for now. Know that I love you and miss
you. Oh, how I wish things could be different. Maybe
one day they can.*

> *Your loving son,*
> *Hank*

Any doubts she had were dashed in that moment. Or maybe they were hopes that all of this was a terrible mistake. But the proof was there, in her father's own hand.

She flipped through the other pages of the letter. There wasn't much else of great importance, but she enjoyed reading her father's words despite their lack of answers. But her search dislodged the promised photo.

He was right. It wasn't the best picture, taken at an odd angle and grainy as if through some sort of screen.

She didn't recognize anything about the photo except her own face. The porch where she stood and the other surroundings were a complete mystery, though it did appear that they were somewhere in the country. She looked no more than four, if even that. Her hair was in pigtails like she had seen many Amish women style their young daughters' hair. She was a little old for the style. Perhaps her father did it out of necessity. Dads were no good at fixing their daughters' hair. Or maybe she'd had a haircut that made her locks too short to pull back in a bun. She wore a sage-green dress and a black *schlupp schotzli,* a pinafore worn by very young Amish girls. Her feet were bare, her smile broad. Despite everything, she looked happy.

One phrase kept playing over and over again in her head. *I did this for her.*

Did what? Convert to Amish?

That was possible. Perhaps her father had simply wanted to raise her in the close-knit community. He'd decided the best way to fit in was to convert. But why the secrecy? Why did he feel the need to lie to her about her grandmother and owning a car? If converted, why didn't he convert all the way?

As much as she wanted it to be true, the theory had too many holes in it to hold water.

She wanted to sit there all night and examine each letter, but the one she read had been so emotionally draining, she thought it might be days before she could look at another one.

She should paint.

The thought popped into her head like an exploding piece of popcorn. She should paint, get all these emotions out and onto the canvas. Surely that would help her move on.

She pushed herself to her feet, dusted off her dress, and fetched her painting garb. Painting was the one sure thing to get her mind off everything else.

* * *

"Where have you been?"

Lorie shrugged one shoulder and managed not to give an answer as Maddie continued to bark orders. "Get a serving apron on and wash your hands. There's too many people in here for you to lollygag about."

A bus had come in from Tulsa bringing with it a load of tourists clamoring for authentic Amish food. Like what Plain people ate was so much different than anyone else, Lorie thought as she tied a clean apron around her middle. She immediately regretted her rudeness, even if it was only in her head. She used to love the busloads of people coming in and the excitement it brought to the restaurant. To the entire town.

"Where have you been?" Sadie sidled up beside her and whispered out of the corner of her mouth. "She has been stomping around here for almost an hour."

"I lost track of time," Lorie explained, which truly wasn't an explanation at all. But she surely couldn't say, "I lost myself painting a picture of the grandmother I never knew I had."

Even with Betty Mathis's face floating on the canvas it was Zach's that kept invading her thoughts. Why had he given her his phone number? She had said that she wasn't coming back. Her visits would only confuse Betty, and Lorie herself lived too far away to make the trip regularly. Though according to Amber and Carol it seemed that her father had made it quite often. *But he had a car,* the voice inside her whispered. *He had a driver's license and means to get to Sundale whenever he wanted.*

"Yoo-hoo. Lorie." Sadie snapped her fingers in front of Lorie's face.

She started and turned to her sister. "*Jah?*"

"Wherever you went, it's time to come back."

Her eyes widened and her heart gave a hard pound. "I haven't been anywhere." How did Sadie find out?

"I didn't mean literally. You just seemed to be off somewhere in your own head."

"Oh, *jah*." Lorie gave a nervous laugh. "Sorry."

Sadie flashed her a small smile and patted her hand. "It's *allrecht*. Just try not to give *Mamm* a heart attack. What's that?" Sadie pointed to a smudge of paint on the back of her hand.

Lorie pulled her hand away and shoved it into her apron pocket. "Nothing. Just some dirt, I guess."

"Green dirt?"

"*Jah.*" She turned on her heel and started toward the table the passing couple had just vacated. "Time to get to work," she tossed over her shoulder. And with any luck, by the time the work was done, her sister would have forgotten all about the telltale paint.

He was being ridiculous.

"Why are we here again?" Cameron asked. Zach and Cameron Thompson had been best friends since their freshman year at OSU, even in spite of their three-year age difference.

"We came to eat authentic Amish food."

"Uh-huh." Cameron dragged out the word until it seemed like it lasted for days.

"Really." He reached for the door to the Kauffman Family Restaurant. "People do this all the time." At least that was the truth, but Cameron wasn't convinced. Zach wasn't even fooling himself. He had come to see Lorie. Like a fool he had given her his phone number, then realized the Amish didn't have phones. At least that was what the Internet said. How could she call him if she didn't have a phone? Or maybe she wasn't Amish any longer since she was dressed like half the girls he went to school with.

He wanted to ask her. Why she was wearing jeans and saying she was going to join the church? Was she really getting married? She was no older than he was, and Zach was nowhere near ready to settle down.

The bell at the door rang out to signal their entrance. A young Amish girl met them there. She had dark hair, fair skin, and hazel eyes. "Two?" She grabbed menus and looked at each of them in turn.

Cameron nodded.

"This way." She led them toward a booth, placing their rolled bundles of silverware by their menus. "Today's special is meat loaf, mashed potatoes, and locally grown, fresh green beans. I'll be back with a couple of waters to start you off, and I'll take your order then."

Cameron opened his menu and snorted. "Authentic Amish food."

"What? The Amish can't eat meat loaf?"

"Face it. It doesn't sound all that Amish."

"Whatever." He really hadn't come for the food. Though it would be good to have a home-cooked meal. His mother had been working double shifts at the retirement center. He'd been reduced to SpaghettiOs and ramen noodles. More often than not, ramen won out. He was so tired of not having a "real" job. His mother told him to be patient. The right job would come along. God had a plan and it would be revealed when the time was right.

He wanted to believe all that was true, but honestly he didn't have quite the faith his mother had. Sometimes he even wondered how she managed to keep hers intact after all that she had been through.

"You're buying, right?" Cameron asked.

Zach nodded. "But don't go crazy." It was Cameron's

consolation prize for traveling all the way from Tulsa to Wells Landing on his only day off in two weeks.

"I won't, I won't." Cameron waved a hand and buried his face back in the menu. "You know Dad will get you a job working with us."

The last thing he wanted was a "got for me" job. He wanted to earn his right to be at a workplace. That was why he couldn't accept Cameron's father's offer. Well, that and the fact that he wasn't qualified to pour concrete. "What's the difference between working at the center and what you do?" Neither one was in his chosen field of business.

"About eight dollars an hour."

Zach didn't have time to respond as the dark-haired girl came to their table again. "Are you ready to order now?"

"I'll have the meat loaf." He handed the menu back to her. As Cameron ordered the oven-fried chicken, Zach weighed the merits of asking the girl about Lorie. He kept quiet. He wasn't sure what it was, but something inside said he should wait a little longer before revealing his true reason for being in Wells Landing.

"And to drink?" she asked.

"Iced tea," they both said.

She marked it on her notepad. "I'll be right back with your drinks."

"So this girl," Cameron asked after their waitress had moved on, "she works here?"

"Her family owns the restaurant."

Their waitress appeared again with their glasses of fresh tea.

Zach took a sip, nodding his approval.

"Your meals will be out shortly," the waitress said, and moved away once again.

"So is she around?" Cameron scanned the restaurant as if he would be able to find her.

"I don't see her."

"So ask."

Zach shook his head. "I think I should wait."

"Why?"

"I dunno. She said she was joining the church and getting married. Seems like maybe I shouldn't—"

"She's getting married? You are so lucky you're buying lunch. Drag me to nowhere to see a girl who's getting married . . . to someone else!"

"Shhh! There she is." Zach nodded toward the door to the kitchen. Lorie pushed through looking so much like she had the very first time he had seen her at the auction. She looked so very Amish that he almost had trouble remembering how she looked in her plaid Western shirt and faded jeans.

"That's your girl?" Cameron's tone was heavy with disbelief. "She's Amish."

"I told you that."

"Maybe I didn't believe you."

She caught sight of Zach and stopped, her mouth falling open for a moment before she recovered. She turned away as if she hadn't seen him there.

Her reaction was obvious. She didn't want to talk to him. Or at least she didn't want to talk to him here where her family could see.

She kept her back to him as she started filling the army of pitchers with ice and fresh tea.

"Here you go." The young girl who had seated them slid their plates off the tray and onto the table in front of them. "Can I get you anything else?"

"I think we're good for now," Zach said, ready for her to be gone so he could see Lorie again.

She nodded her head. "I'll be back in a bit with some more tea."

"She's Amish," Cameron said again once they were alone.

"She's beautiful."

"How can you tell? She's got on all that . . ." He waved a hand around instead of finishing.

"You can't see past all that?" Zach shook his head. "Never mind. I'm glad you can't see it."

"Chicken's good though," Cameron said around a mouthful. "Really good."

Zach scooped up his own bite. The food was better than really good. It was the best he'd had in a long time.

He glanced back to the waitress station, but Lorie was gone. So much for his big plans to have another chance to talk to her. He didn't understand this obsession he had with her. It was almost as if the whole thing was out of his control. He just had to see her one more time.

"You've seen her. Now what?"

"Just eat," Zach grumbled. He glanced back to the waitress station. Lorie had appeared again and was heading their way with a pitcher of tea in one hand and one of water in the other. "How do I look?" he asked as she wound her way through the tables filling glasses as she drew closer to them. "I don't have sauce on my chin or anything, do I?"

Cameron grinned, tossing down his napkin with a shake of his head. "Man, do you have it bad."

Before he could even push his hair off his forehead and back into place or take one last swipe at any lingering sauce, Lorie was standing beside their table.

"Hi," she said. Her voice held a breathless quality.

"Hi," he returned.

She nodded toward his tea glass.

He pushed it closer to her.

"I didn't expect to see you," she said, her chin tucked close to her chest. Zach couldn't decide if she was being demure or if she was trying to keep everyone around from seeing the blush that rose to her cheeks.

"Obviously." This from Cameron.

She turned toward him as if she had just then realized he was there.

He gave her a wave.

"Sorry." Zach sat back in his seat. "Lorie, this is my friend Cameron. Cameron, Lorie."

"It's *gut* to meet you." She dipped her chin in his direction, then filled his tea glass as well.

"I was hoping that you would come back to the center and visit with Miss Betty."

Her mouth twisted into a small frown. "I can't. I don't want to confuse her. I told you I would send the letters back when I'd finished reading them."

"This isn't about the letters, and I don't think you confuse her any more than brushing her teeth or making balsa wood airplanes do."

"I have work to do here at the restaurant."

"Surely you get a day off."

"It's too far."

"I'll come get you." His words stepped all over hers, and he exhaled, trying to catch his breath and slow himself. "I'm sorry. I just think this is important."

She bit her lip and cast a quick look over her shoulder. Zach had the strangest feeling that she was checking to see where her family members were in relation to them. "I'm off next Thursday."

A ray of sunshine burst in his chest. "Great. Tell me what time and where you live, and I'll come by and get you."

She shook her head. "Out on Colton Road, there is a four-way stop with a little shack off to one side. I'll be there at ten." She gave him quick directions on how to get there. "Is that okay?"

Zach smiled. "That's perfect."

* * *

"How about we have a pond day on Thursday?" Jonah asked Sunday afternoon after the church service. The young people had all gathered to play softball and socialize.

"Th-Thursday?" Lorie jerked her attention in his direction. They were seated on the ground waiting on their turn to either bat or go back out in the field. Lorie loved playing softball on Sunday afternoons though today the sun seemed especially brutal as it seared through her black dress.

"*Jah.* My family is taking the day to go down to the pond, have a picnic, and just relax for the day."

"On a weekday?" she squeaked.

Jonah frowned. "What's wrong with you?"

"Nothing." She shook her head.

"So you'll come?"

"I can't. I already made other plans." *Please don't ask me what they are.*

"What are they?"

Lorie's heart sank into her stomach, which churned and flipped. She opened her mouth to respond, but there was no lie waiting to cover her planned trip to Tulsa. "I . . . I . . ."

"Hey, Jonah," Danny Fitch called from home plate. "You're up."

Thank goodness.

"I'm coming," Jonah called in return. He pushed to his feet and dusted off the seat of his pants. For a moment she was afraid he was going to demand an answer before his turn at bat.

Then he chose his bat and sauntered toward the thick piece of cardboard that served as home plate.

Lorie breathed a sigh of relief. With any luck, Jonah would forget all about his question, and she wouldn't have to come up with a plausible excuse as to why she was planning a trip to see her grandmother with an *Englischer* who made her heart pound in her chest and her mouth grow dry.

Chapter Nine

Lorie clutched the canvas bag containing her *Englisch* clothes to her chest and willed her heart to beat a little slower. She had no idea what kind of car Zach drove. And she couldn't risk being seen waiting for him. She peeked out the door of the old phone shanty, but there was no one around. It had to be getting close to ten, but she wasn't sure how close. She took a calming breath. He'd be here soon.

She had finally told Jonah that she had promised her day off to Caroline. She just hoped that no one asked Caroline about it. She didn't want her friend to lie for her. But she felt such an urgency to return to Tulsa at least one more time. She wanted to see Betty again. She remembered the clear look in her eyes when she'd told Lorie that her father had left letters. Lorie had read some of them, though they were filled with everyday occurrences like adding a new item to the restaurant menu and even all the time he spent securing the loan to open the restaurant.

Of the ten or so letters she had found the time to read, only the first one contained any information on her father, and even then, it only gave her more questions. What had her father done for her own good? And did it have anything to do with the lies he'd told everyone else?

Only one person had the answers. That was why Lorie agreed to meet Zach again. It had nothing to do with the sweet dimples he had on either side of his mouth or that squared-off chin and sky-blue eyes.

In reality, she wasn't even convincing herself, but it was better than facing the truth. She wanted to get to know Zach a little better. What had he been doing at the living center? Had he come all the way to Wells Landing just to see her?

Maybe it was Zach, or maybe it was all the other questions she had floating around inside. Maybe after all was said and done, she would be no nearer the truth than she was right now. But she had to try. Something in her wouldn't let it go. If the truth was out there, she had to find it.

With or without Zach.

She peered out the phone shanty door again. A small gray car inched along the road, driving no faster than a buggy. She'd recognize that dark head anywhere. Her heart gave another hard pound as she stepped from the small shack and waved.

He returned it and pulled to the side of the road. "Hi," he said, getting out of the car though leaving it running. He walked around the car and opened the door for her.

"Hi." Lorie tamped down the thrill that ran through her. No one had ever opened a car door for her. Okay, so that wasn't saying much. But no one had ever opened a buggy door for her either. Didn't the *Englisch* say that was the mark of a gentleman? She smiled at Zach and slid into the car.

"I wasn't sure what to expect." He climbed into the driver's side and gave her another smile.

"Me either." She glanced down to the bag she held in her lap. Her fingers twisted the fabric as she ducked her head.

He set the car into gear and then headed down the road. "Do you want to stop somewhere and change clothes? I mean, I assume that's what's in your bag."

"*Jah*. Yes. Maybe a gas station or something."

"I know just the place." He smiled, and her heart soared a bit.

This was bad. No matter how handsome he was—or sweet or good with her grandmother—the truth would never change: she was Amish, and he was *Englisch*.

"Zach," she started, completely unsure of how to say what needed to be said. How could she ask what she needed to know? "Is this a date?"

"Do you want it to be a date?"

What did she want? She managed to keep her shoulders from shrugging. She didn't know what she wanted. She hadn't given it any thought beyond wanting the answers to the questions that kept rising to the surface.

What was she thinking? This couldn't be a date. Soon she would finish her baptism classes and next year, maybe even in the fall, she and Jonah would get married like they had always talked about.

"I'm engaged." She said the words, but couldn't bring herself to look at Zach.

"Okay."

She couldn't tell how he was feeling from the one word, so she chanced a glance in his direction. He looked no different than he had before she had spoken. So she turned her attention back to the front. They were on the highway now, heading toward Tulsa.

"Betty's been asking about you," Zach finally said with a small shrug. "I'm just trying to help."

"I am thankful."

"I'm not gonna lie." He checked the mirrors and changed lanes. "I find you . . . intriguing."

She shook her head. "It's the prayer *kapp*." She reached up and pulled the pins that held it in place.

"I'm not sure I understand."

"*Englisch* guys see it as sort of a challenge."

He sent a perplexed look in her direction. "I don't know what you mean."

She thought about it a minute, trying to find the right words for her response. She had seen it so many times. An Amish girl falling in love with an *Englisch* guy. He promised the moon, then didn't deliver, leaving the poor *maedel* heartbroken and alone. She couldn't have that happen to her. And it wasn't going to. She had a future all lined out. All this with her father, it was nothing more than a detour to her well-set plans. "*Englisch* boys . . ." she tried again.

"Never mind. I think I understand." He took the exit off the highway and turned onto the main street before finishing. "You're getting married. I get it. And you think I just want—" He broke off before finishing and for that she was grateful. She couldn't imagine saying something like that out loud. Apparently he felt the same.

Instead of speaking, he pulled into a gas station and cut the engine. "They have a public restroom. You can go change."

She hesitated.

"I'll wait here. Okay?"

She nodded, then grabbed her bag and headed into the brightly lit store. People milled around, getting food and drinks, buying gas, and otherwise going about their daily lives.

Lorie hustled into the restroom and into one of the many bathroom stalls. She still held her prayer *kapp* in her hands. She hated just placing it in the bag to get crushed so she hung it on the back of the bathroom door while she stripped out of her Amish clothes and quickly pulled on the *Englisch* clothes she had bought with Luke.

They felt the same as they had that day, strange and wonderful, a little mischievous and somehow like she had been missing something for such a long time.

She folded her *frack* and apron as neatly as she could and

tucked them back into the canvas bag. Then she removed her clunky black walking shoes and slipped into the cute leopard-print flats she'd picked out at the secondhand store.

She stepped from the stall and stood in front of the mirror, for the first time getting a good look at the transformation the clothes brought to her. She felt different. She looked different, but in her eyes, she was the same. Or maybe it was because from the neck up she still looked Plain. Well, Plain minus the prayer *kapp*.

Pulling the pins from her hair, she wished she'd thought to bring a brush. She shook out the long tresses.

"Wow," the girl standing next to her at the line of sinks exclaimed. "Your hair is so long."

"I s'pose." Lorie hadn't thought about it all that much. Hair simply was. The Amish didn't cut it so everyone she knew had long hair, though it was always put up, wound into a bun and tucked under a prayer *kapp*.

"I wish my hair was that long." She wistfully stared at the ends of Lorie's hair.

"All you have to do is not cut it."

"That's easier said than done." The girl turned back to the mirror and swiped some shiny stuff on her lips.

Lorie had never used anything other than lip balm, but this was glossy and smelled like peaches. "You go in for a trim, and they cut three inches off. Dead ends, they always say. Whatever." She rolled her eyes.

Dead ends? Lorie had no idea what she was talking about. She pulled up the ends of her hair. It was uneven at best, a little like the mane of a horse. But not bad. She looked back to the young girl's sleek brown hair. It came to just below her shoulders but was smooth and even. Suddenly, even despite the coveted length, Lorie wished her hair was a bit more polished. Maybe she should get a trim, as the girl called it.

What was she saying? She wasn't cutting her hair. Her *mamm* would have a fit. All her life, she had been told time and time again: a woman's hair was her glory and all glory was to God. How could she give the glory to God if it was lying on the floor of some hair salon?

She wound her hair back into a knot at the nape of her neck though this time, like the time before, she released her middle part. The result was a little less Amish for sure.

It wasn't like she was leaving the Amish. She was visiting her grandmother and nothing more. Cutting her hair was completely out of the question.

She grabbed the handles of her bag and started for the door.

"It was nice talking to you," the girl said, pausing in her efforts of powdering her cheeks to catch Lorie's attention in the mirror.

Lorie nodded her head, but kept her feet moving. "*Jah*," she said. "You, too." Though more than anything, she found the conversation strangely unsettling.

As promised, Zach was waiting in the car when she stepped out of the store. She tried not to notice how his eyes lit up when he spotted her. Or the smile that spread across his face. Why did he have to be so cute? Or maybe the question was, why did he have to be so *Englisch?*

"Listen," he said as she slid into the passenger's seat. "I understand. Really. And I totally get it. I'm not ready for anything serious either. I just graduated from college." He shook his head. "I've got to find a job. Move out of my mother's house."

As Lorie watched him, the corners of his mouth turned down, and he got the same look on his face as her fun-loving father had whenever he paid the restaurant bills.

He started the car and pulled it onto the busy Tulsa street. Lorie grabbed the door handle as another car pulled up beside them too quickly. Just another reason why she could never make it in the *Englisch* world. The cars moved way too fast for her tastes. How did her father do it?

"It's okay," she said in return, talking as much to herself as she was to him. "It's just . . ." She tried to find the words, but failed. "Complicated," she finally finished.

"It always is."

They drove in silence for several minutes before he spoke again.

"Why did you have me pick you up in the middle of nowhere?"

How did she answer that? "I'm not sure my *mamm* would approve of me coming to Tulsa. And then there are my baptism classes."

He pulled into a parking space in the Sundale parking lot, then turned toward her. "Classes? What does that mean exactly?"

"All Amish go through instruction before they can join the church."

"And that's what you're doing now?"

"Yes."

"That sounds like a good thing. It is, right?"

"Of course. It's just that . . ." She bit her lip. "Well, the district, they watch the youth very closely. I can't mess up."

"Mess up?"

"Being seen sneaking off to Tulsa with an *Englisch bu* would surely count as messing up."

"But you came anyway."

"You said my grandmother asked about me."

He nodded, but swallowed hard. "Yeah."

"How could I not come to see her?"

He nodded. "So baptism classes, then what?"

"I join the church. Then Jonah and I can get married."

"I see."

She wilted with relief. She liked Zach and he was so handsome, but her place was with her family. In Wells Landing. "I'm so glad."

He nodded again, but didn't speak.

"Are we going in?" She nodded toward the big glass doors.

"Yeah, sure." He stirred as if he'd been deep in thought. Then he opened his car door and got out, immediately coming around to open hers. "So does this change everything?" he asked, as she stood there in the open car door so close to him she could smell the shampoo he'd used to wash his hair and the aftershave he'd put on that morning. The effect was nearly irresistible. Or maybe that was just Zach.

"This is all it has ever been," she said, wondering how many more lies she would tell before this day was through.

"Can we be friends?" he asked, closing the door behind her with a small thud. He took her elbow to lead her toward the living center, but apparently thought better of the decision and released her. She immediately missed his touch, though she knew it was for the best.

"Friends . . ." She smiled at him. "Thanks, Zach with an *h*. I'd like that very much."

He had only wanted to see her again. He hadn't thought about the consequences, how it would affect her. He'd only thought of her bottomless brown eyes and getting to know her better.

Now he felt lower than dirt. Man, did she have guys pegged. Well, English guys anyway. He had to wonder if he fell in that category. Had to be or she wouldn't have said anything to him. But if he was English what did that make Mick Jagger?

He shook his head and held the door open for her.

She smiled at him again, and the effect was nearly tangible. He felt the gesture all the way to his toes, the tips of his fingers, and all spots in between.

"Hi, Zach," Amber said as they made their way across the tiled foyer. "Lorie." Surprise lit in her eyes before she quickly covered it up again. He wondered if it was because of Lorie's clothes or the fact that she was with him. Then again, she had worn these very same clothes the last time she'd come to visit. "You're not scheduled today."

"No, I'm here on other business." Let her make of that what she would. He'd told Lorie that he would help her and that's exactly what he would do.

"Most of the residents are in the rec room for a little craft time before lunch," Carol explained.

He signed the visitors' log and waited for Lorie to do the same.

"Thanks." He nodded to each of the ladies in turn and gently guided Lorie toward the rec room. Oh, the talk he would have to face tomorrow when his shift started, but whatever. Lorie was a nice girl who found herself in a unique situation. It was his civic duty to help her. He almost snorted at his own thoughts.

Just keep thinking that, Calhoun. Delusion-ville was a nice place to visit but he couldn't afford to live there forever.

"Look, Zach is here." He didn't know who called out to him, but he waved a hand toward the occupants of table eight and started in their direction.

"And Leslie." Betty Mathis glanced up from her knitting, flashing each of them a quick smile.

"Lorie," she corrected.

"Of course," Betty murmured, but she had already buried her attention back into the yarn she held.

"I thought you were off today." This from Eugene. He lifted the sun catcher toward the light and squinted critically. "Should I add some green?"

Linda shook her head. "I told you that was too much orange."

"No such thing as too much orange."

Zach smiled. "That's because you graduated from OSU."

"You got that right." Eugene smiled and pushed his glasses back up onto the bridge of this nose. "'Course back then we were A&M."

"And the last class of Aggies. Yes, we know." Linda rolled her eyes. They were the perfect Oklahoma house divided. Eugene was a "Cowboy" and Linda was a "Sooner" through and through.

Typical for the pair, a good-natured, though heated, argument broke out between the siblings. "National championship" was tossed in along with "Football has nothing to do with academics" and other digs.

Lorie looked to him for guidance. Zach leaned in and whispered, "It'll be okay, just don't come for the Bedlam game." Then he realized who he was talking to and added, "That's when the two universities play one another."

She nodded, but still looked confused. Zach wondered how crazy she thought they were, arguing over which was the best school when according to the Internet the Amish didn't go to school past the eighth grade.

Was that possible?

He watched as she went around the table and somehow managed to completely calm the argument. She smiled at Eugene and then toward Linda. Helping each pick a new color to add to their sun catchers.

"We're taking these over to the nursing home," Stan said. For once Betty didn't try to correct him.

"What's a nursing home?" Lorie frowned and looked from Eugene to Zach.

How could she not know what a nursing home was?

"It's a place where they stash old cronies that no one wants around anymore," Eugene said.

"I'll call and see if your room is ready." Linda made to dial on her cell phone. Stan laughed while Eugene scowled at his sister.

Betty's mouth twisted into a frown, but her eyes sparkled. "Those two." She glanced over to Lorie. "Are you staying for lunch, dear?"

Lorie looked to him.

Zach shrugged. "Whatever you want to do is fine with me."

"I'd love to, *danki*—I mean, thanks."

"I do hope they have leprechaun pudding today," Betty said. "I haven't had it in forever."

Stan shook his head. "Nobody but you even knows what that is."

"Of course they do."

Stan looked to Zach as if searching for backup.

"Don't look at me." Zach held up his hands in surrender. He'd been caught in between these geriatric duelers too many times to get involved this time.

"But you don't know what it is," Stan prodded.

"Oh, leave her alone." Fern lightly smacked his hand in reprimand. "Just because you've never heard of it doesn't mean it's not real."

"Thank you, dear." Betty flashed her neighbor a smile. "And you," she said, frowning at Stan, "if you keep this up I'll have to take you off my Christmas list."

He seemed about to say something, but Linda elbowed him and shot him a stern look. He cleared his throat. "Well, I wouldn't want that, Betty."

"Very good." Betty folded her knitting and tucked it into her plastic shopping bag. "Should we go down there now?"

Eugene checked his watch. "I guess it's close enough."

The group stood and started putting away their crafts.

Zach chanced a quick look at Lorie who was helping them put the lids back on their jars of paints. A wistful look covered her face, but before he could ask about it, she hid it from view.

"Everyone ready?" Linda asked.

There were nods all around.

"Oh, I do hope they have leprechaun pudding," Betty said as the others groaned.

Zach just smiled and walked beside Lorie. It was a good place to be.

Chapter Ten

Leprechaun pudding. Why did that sound familiar? Lorie followed behind the table eight group as they led her and Zach toward the cafeteria.

Maybe because she had heard Betty ask about it before, the last time Lorie had come to visit.

She shook her head. It didn't matter. This was it. Her last time to come and visit.

Betty's mental state was a series of steep hills and who knew how she would react today. But Lorie had to give it a try.

They all grabbed trays and went through the line. Betty, of course, asked about leprechaun pudding. The young worker behind the counter said the coveted dish wasn't on today's menu while Eugene snorted. Linda elbowed him in the ribs, and Lorie hid her smile.

The *Englisch* may put their elderly in homes, but there were still those who cared for them both physically and emotionally. Her grandmother was in a good place, one that took care of her, provided her with food—even if there was no leprechaun pudding—and housed many friends to fill her days. Lorie couldn't ask for more.

They found seats, Lorie sitting across from Betty and

Zach. Everyone started to eat. Lorie wanted to pray, but having her head covered was so deeply ingrained, she refrained. What was worse? To pray without a head covering or not to pray at all? She picked up her fork and pushed the thoughts away. She'd ask for forgiveness later.

She waited until the first observations about today's lunch were complete before asking, "Tell me about your son, Betty."

Betty scooped up a bite of macaroni and cheese, her brow furrowed. "What do you want to know?"

Lorie shrugged. "Whatever you want to tell me. What did he like to do? Where did he live? Things like that."

"Oh, he was a good boy, my Hank. I called him Hank, but no one else did. They all called him Henry."

She had told Lorie that very thing last time she had visited, but she didn't say as much. Her grandmother seemed to be warming up to the subject, and she didn't want to interrupt Betty in case she shared something important.

"Where did he live?" she asked, her mouth growing dry. How much did Betty know of her son's double life?

"Oh, out in the country. That's why he couldn't come to visit more than twice a month. Well, that and the restaurant. That place kept him really busy."

"Did he ever mention his family?"

A frown once again appeared across Betty's wrinkled brow. "He talked about his children quite a bit, but I never got to meet them. Lovely children."

"How—"

Betty patted her hand. "He sent me pictures, you know. But I gave you all I had last time you were here."

"*Ja*—Yes, but I was wondering if there was something else. Something more."

"No, dear. Nothing more." But a darkness clouded Betty's pretty blue eyes blocking out the sparkle usually there.

Lorie swallowed hard and wondered if she had pushed too

hard. But this was her only chance. Unless she came back once again. What was the harm in that truly? It wasn't like she was going out to drive a car or worse. She was only finding out about the family she never knew she had.

Maybe she would come back. It would be *gut* to see Zach again. Ride in his car. Hear stories about her father. With Betty's mental limitations, it was almost impossible to determine how she would react and what she would share from day to day. Perhaps she should come again, just a time or two. What was wrong with asking a couple of questions and spending time with a sweet lady? Surely not even the sour-faced deacon could find fault with that.

She had to, as clearly as she had to dress in *Englisch* clothes. It was a part of her plan.

Yes, it was all clear now. Coming back. Just a time or two more. That was exactly what she needed to do. Now all she had to figure out was how to get there.

"Did you have a good time today?" Zach asked as they headed toward Wells Landing.

"*Jah,* I had a real *gut* time."

He smiled, and Lorie thought it might be the handsomest thing she had ever seen.

Then guilt swamped her. She wasn't supposed to care about the superficial. Okay, so Jonah was handsome to a fault as well, but in different ways than Zach. Jonah was tall and lanky, he had eyes the color of maple syrup and hair the same shade as wheat at harvest time.

"I guess you need to change clothes before you get home."

She looked down at herself. She had almost forgotten that she wasn't wearing her normal Amish clothing. What did that say about her that after two wearings her new *Englisch* clothes felt as comfortable as the *fracks* she had worn her entire life? "Yes . . . *jah.*"

He pulled into the parking lot of the next gas station they came to. Lorie grabbed her bag from behind the seat and hurried inside to change back into her regular clothes.

The bathroom was empty as she let herself into the stall and took her clothes from the bag. She shook her dress out, hoping some of the wrinkles would fall from the fabric before she ran into anyone she knew. Thankfully the black fabric hid a lot of the creases. With a sigh, she stripped out of her jeans and T-shirt and pulled her dress over her head. Her shoes were next, and she pulled on the black walking shoes and tucked her cute flats back into the bag. Then she let herself out of the stall and released the pins from her hair.

What would it be like to have it cut? She shook her head, thinking she needed to put a brush and a comb in her bag for future visits. Wait. What was she thinking?

She couldn't come back. She may not have found out anything about her father, but she couldn't risk another trip to Tulsa. There would be no need for anything else to be stored in her bag. In fact, the bag needed to disappear as soon as possible. Regardless of all her plans from earlier, she needed to put a stop to her deceit.

She separated her hair into the best middle part she could and pulled it into a knot. She secured it with the bobby pins, then reached into her bag for her prayer *kapp*.

But it wasn't there.

That had to be a mistake.

She set the bag on the floor and pulled out her clothes. She looked under her shoes. No prayer *kapp*.

With her eyes closed, she sat back on her heels and tried to think. Was it in the car? Where had she seen it last? Then she remembered. She'd hung it on the little hook on the back of the bathroom door. But not here. In the first bathroom on the way into Tulsa.

How could she have been so careless? An Amish girl's

prayer *kapp* was near sacred. How could she have been so irresponsible as to leave it somewhere?

She shoved her clothes back into her bag and tried to think. She stood and stared at her reflection. This would be all right. It had to be *allrecht*.

She would be home around two. Daniel's bus wouldn't arrive for another hour and a half. Cora Ann would walk from the schoolhouse directly to the restaurant where the rest of the Kauffman girls would be working. Lorie would be alone.

She sucked in a deep breath. It was going to be okay.

"Where's your cap thing?" Zach asked when she got back into the car.

Ignoring the hard thump of apprehension in her chest, she stored her bag behind the passenger's seat and gave a small shrug. "I guess I left it in the other bathroom."

"Is that okay?"

It has to be.

"Do you want me to take you back there to look for it? It might still be there."

Or it might not be. If she took too much time trying to find it she would get home at the same time everyone else did. And that wouldn't be *gut* at all.

"It'll be all right." Now if she could just convince herself.

Zach gave a quick nod, then pulled his car back onto the road. "Do you want me to take you home or back into town?"

"You can drop me off where you picked me up this morning. Is that okay?"

"You know that goes against everything my mother ever taught me about how to treat a lady."

"I'm sorry."

"Don't apologize. It's just . . ."

"What?" she asked.

"I hope you don't get in trouble for coming with me."

There was more of a danger of that now than there had ever been.

"It'll be fine, but . . ."

"But what?" He glanced toward her, taking his gaze from the road only briefly before turning it back again.

"I can't do this again."

"Okay," he said slowly. "Is this something I did?"

"Oh, no. No. But my family wouldn't understand."

"I see. And did you get all the answers you wanted about your father?"

"I—no, but I have to be satisfied with what I discovered."

He pulled the car to the side of the road. Lorie realized then that they had reached their deserted phone shanty at the four-way stop on Colton Road. She was almost home.

"I understand." He turned in his seat to face her. "It's probably better this way."

She nodded. "I appreciate you coming to get me and taking me to see my grandmother."

He smiled. "You're welcome."

"What do I owe you for the ride?"

A frown replaced his smile. "Owe me? You don't owe me anything."

"But you took me all the way to Tulsa and—"

"I offered to come and get you. I don't expect you to pay me."

"Are you sure? I don't mind paying you."

"Stop," he said. "I enjoyed myself. I don't want your money."

"Okay." She gave him a stiff nod. "Will you . . . will you explain to Betty, if she asks why I don't come back?"

"Of course."

At the sound of her grandmother's favorite phrase, Lorie's smile broke. She reached for the car door and fumbled to open it. Finally she released the handle and escaped before the tears that threatened started to fall.

There was no reason for her to cry. So why did she feel like bawling like a baby?

"Lorie?" Zach stood by his car, concern creasing his brow. "Are you going to be okay?"

She nodded, swallowing back the uncharacteristic tears. "Thanks again," she said. "For everything."

"Sure." He seemed reluctant, but he slid back into his car and started down the road.

Lorie watched him go for a few moments, then turned toward home.

Now all she had to do was get to the house without anyone seeing her bare head.

She was glad for the half-mile walk from the phone shanty to her house. It gave her the time to compose herself.

It wouldn't be long before Daniel's bus brought him home, and it wouldn't do for her eyes to be red-rimmed and filled with tears. He might be considered "special needs" by most, but he was smart in ways Lorie couldn't even begin to understand.

She let herself into the house, thankful to be home and at the same time sad. She would miss her grandmother, but she had her own future to think about. Her future with Jonah.

"Lorie! What are you doing here? Where's your prayer *kapp?*"

She gasped and whirled around coming face-to-face with Sadie. Lorie pressed one hand to her chest as she struggled to bring her heartbeat under control. "What are you doing here?"

Sadie crossed her arms and eyed her. "Daniel wasn't feeling good at school. They called and wanted someone to meet him here."

"Daniel's here?"

"He's resting."

"And he's okay?"

Her sister nodded. "Where's your prayer *kapp?*" Sadie asked again.

Lorie's hands flew to her bare head. There had to be an answer. One that Sadie would find acceptable.

"It's uh, well . . ." She had told so many lies in the last few weeks, it was as if her brain couldn't think of another one.

"It's that *Englisch* boy. You've been out with him."

Lorie wilted. If only it were that simple. "I'm not going again."

"Lorie." Sadie grabbed her hand and dragged Lorie up the stairs and into their shared bedroom. She pushed her down onto the bed and started rummaging through their closet. "All you have is your waterproof *kapp* until we can make you a new one. It'll be better than nothing at all, *jah?* But try not to get too close to *Mamm.*"

"Sadie, I—" She wanted to tell her sister everything, all about the box of her father's belongings, his tattoo, and her grandmother living in Tulsa.

"Lorie, promise me." Sadie turned toward her, the prayer *kapp* clutched close to her heart. "Promise me you won't go anywhere with this boy again."

She had already made that promise to herself. So why was she having such a hard time saying those words to her *shveshtah?* "Sadie, you won't say anything, will you?"

Her sister shook her head. "As long as you promise not to go meet him again."

"I promise," Lorie said. And she meant it, every word.

"Lorie, it's your turn."

Lorie stirred herself from her thoughts and stood.

"It's the tenth frame," Hannah Miller, Jonah's sister, continued. "Make it good. We're only five pins behind the boys."

Wednesday night was bowling night for the four couples. Tonight it was girls against boys. Lorie, Sadie, Hannah, and Hannah's cousin, Ruthie, against Jonah, Chris, William, and Mark. They had all been dating since their run-around years—Chris and Sadie, William and Hannah, Ruthie and Mark. As Lorie dried her hands on the air blower, she glanced around at all of them. She was the only one who hadn't joined the church.

"We're waiting," Jonah said.

Waiting.

She picked up her ball and headed for the lane.

It was best to get everything back to normal as soon as possible.

She lined up the pins and rolled her ball toward the end of the polished lane.

As promised, Sadie kept Lorie's secret, and *Mamm* hadn't noticed her change in prayer *kapp*. Lorie had stayed up that night sewing a new one. It was a small penance to pay for her transgressions. She wasn't about to call them sins. She hadn't done anything wrong. Not really. Well, aside from the white lies that she'd told, but she had asked for forgiveness. Now it was time to go forward.

"We creamed you tonight," Jonah said as he led her toward the tractor he'd parked at the edge of the lot.

"Three pins is not creamed," Lorie returned.

Jonah smiled. "Still more than the girls knocked down."

"You got me there."

They climbed into the tractor and started down the road toward her house.

"You seem different, Lorie."

"Different?" She had worked so hard these last few days to let all of her questions die unanswered. She had to face the facts; the more she found out the more questions she had. And none of the answers would change the core of what she knew to be true. She was Amish, her father was a good man, and Wells Landing is where she belonged. Oh, and Jonah. She would finish her classes, join the church, and marry Jonah.

"Good different," he said. "Happier somehow."

Her hard work was paying off. "Of course I'm happy."

And she hardly thought about her grandmother or the letters she had given her, the same ones Lorie had hidden upstairs in the storeroom. Or her paintings, some complete, others just outlines of unrealized ideas. Or Zach. She hardly ever thought about Zach.

She almost believed that.

"You seemed to have such a hard time after your father died," Jonah commented as they chugged down the darkened road. Above them in the deep blue sky a million stars twinkled and sparkled like unfulfilled dreams. Or unanswered questions.

"It was a difficult time," Lorie said. More difficult than he would ever know. But it wasn't time to rehash all the details. It was the time for moving forward.

How many times had she told herself that? It didn't matter. She would keep telling herself until she believed it.

Jonah pulled the tractor into the Kauffmans' drive. Several lights burned in the house, most of them downstairs. The younger children were most likely in bed. It was the one thing she disliked about bowling night. She wasn't able to get the sweet good-night kisses from precious Daniel.

"Would you like to come in and see if *Mamm* has any pie left?"

Jonah pulled the tractor to a stop, but kept the engine running. "Sorry. As tempting as that sounds, I've got a big day tomorrow."

She gave him a nod, then swung down from the cab to land lightly on her feet.

"Lorie."

She hadn't heard him join her over the rumble of the engine. "*Jah.*"

"Are we okay?"

"*Jah.*" Were they?

"I mean, sometimes I feel like you're a thousand miles away. And other times, everything *seems* fine." He shrugged. "It's sort of confusing."

"I'm sorry." She didn't know what else to say. She was sorry. And she had vowed to do everything in her power to make it right from now until they laid her to rest.

"I know all of this has been hard on you. And I can't pretend to understand. But as long as we're okay, I'm happy."

"*Jah.*"

He reached out and touched her cheek, trailing his fingers across her jaw. "Good night."

She tried to smile. "Good night."

Then he swung back into the cab of his tractor and with a small wave, backed out of the drive.

She watched him go with swirling emotions—thankfulness that he hadn't kissed her, sadness that nothing was going to change, and guilt that she felt that way at all.

Once he pulled onto the road, she climbed the porch steps and let herself into the house.

Mamm was seated at the kitchen table.

"Are you waiting up for me?" Lorie teased.

Mamm looked at her with serious eyes. "Should I be?"

"*Nay.* Of course not."

"I do want to talk to you."

That sounded serious. Lorie pulled out a chair and sat across from her *mamm*. She instructed her heart not to beat so fast. Sounded serious didn't mean it had to be serious.

"I just wanted to say that I'm proud of you. I was worried for a while after your father died. But I think you've finally come to realize—some secrets are better left secrets, *jah?*"

Lorie nodded. "*Jah,*" she said. "Is that all?"

Maddie nodded.

Good, Lorie thought. Now if she only believed it herself.

Chapter Eleven

Something was wrong.

Jonah glanced over to where Lorie sat next to Caroline and Emily, her best friends. Church seemed particularly long today. Whether it was because Dan Troyer, the minister, was preaching or the fact that Jonah had something special planned for Lorie that afternoon, he wasn't sure. But the service seemed to drone on and on, giving him more time than he needed to think about Lorie and the changes he had seen in her in the weeks since her father died. He couldn't decide exactly what it was, but it was there all the same. Jonah felt like she was slipping away. They had always had a rocky relationship. That much he couldn't deny. But this was different. He didn't know how he knew, he just did. More and more every day, he felt them drifting apart.

He looked to his brother, but Jonathan had his eyes straight ahead, back stiff and hands clasped between his knees. Jonah knew that position well. It was his "keep awake" pose saved especially for days when Dan Troyer was in the pulpit.

They had already been there three hours. The congregation had sung, listened to preaching, and prayed. Surely it was about time to go eat.

Finally the minister called for one last prayer, and they were dismissed.

The day had turned out beautiful. The men grabbed their meals and settled on one side of the yard as the women made the plates for the children, then filled their own.

Jonah hung back toward the end, waiting for Lorie to finish helping pour glasses of lemonade. He should have taken his plate and settled down with Andrew Fitch to eat. But he wanted to make sure Lorie remembered her promise to spend the afternoon with him.

"Hey," he said, coming up beside her.

She started as if she had been so engrossed in her own thoughts that she hadn't heard him approach. "Jonah," she breathed.

He loved the way she said his name. "After we eat, we're still heading out for our big surprise, *jah?*"

"Today?"

She had forgotten. Another sign that things were changing. They may have had a rocky relationship, but Lorie never forgot agreeing to a date. "*Jah.* Today." He tried to keep his anger from his voice, it wouldn't help matters any.

"I promised Daniel and Cora Ann I would take them to the park."

"Can't you do that next week?"

She shook her head. "They are meeting some of their *Englisch* friends there for an ice-cream picnic."

"Lorie." He had made so many plans. He'd managed to talk his *bruders* into taking care of all his chores this afternoon so he could take her to Skiatook Lake, where the *Englisch* kids went on sunny Sunday afternoons. He'd even hired a driver and now she was telling him she couldn't go?

"What?" She got that edge in her voice. The one that said a fight was brewing.

"Can't Sadie take them? I made a lot of plans for us today. Big surprise, remember?"

She shook her head. "You told me that was next week."

"It is this week."

"You know I always take the two of them to the park after church." She closed her eyes for a moment, then opened them with a sigh. "I don't want to argue with you."

"I don't want to argue with you either. I just want to spend time with you."

"Then come to the park with us."

"Alone. I want to spend some time with you alone." He leaned in a little closer so he could breathe in the sweet scent of the baby lotion she used to smooth the sides of her hair and the vanilla and spice that seemed to simply be a part of her. "Every time we go somewhere there's always someone tagging along. If it's not our friends, it's one of our siblings. I'm worn out by it, that's all." The instant the words left his mouth he regretted them. They sounded petty and small. He resisted the urge to fling his hat to the ground and run his agitated fingers through his hair. "Is it too much to want to spend a little time alone with you?"

"It is if it hurts a little boy in the process."

"I see." He braced his hands on his hips, his nostrils flared. Amish were taught to be peace-loving and docile, but she could make him madder than a wet hen in six seconds flat. "Just forget it."

"What is that supposed to mean?"

"It means I'll find someone else to drive to the lake and spend the afternoon with."

She glared at him, her normally warm, brown eyes snapping fire. "You do that," she snarled. "Just do it." She stormed away without a backward glance.

Jonah was left wondering if Jonathan had any plans. No one wanted to go to the lake alone.

* * *

This time she was not going to make the first move toward forgiveness. Oh, she forgave Jonah, but that didn't mean she had to be the one to say it first.

"Do you want to talk about it?"

Lorie glanced toward her sister as they pushed their younger siblings on the swings in the park. Normally, she loved coming here. The park held so many good memories for her. The days when she, Caroline, and Emily met at the picnic tables to eat lunch together. Talking with Emily after the death of her father. All the times she brought Daniel and Cora Ann here to play.

But today she had a sour taste in her mouth, and she would do almost anything to wash it away.

"This isn't about that *Englisch* boy, is it?" Sadie's voice dropped to a near whisper when she said *Englisch* as if it was a word not fit to be spoken at a normal volume. Or maybe it was the little ears they had so near. Daniel wouldn't say anything. He was too young to give much notice to what the adults around him said, but Cora Ann was on the line between girl and woman. She tended to absorb any and everything she could.

"*Nay.*" She said the words with as much conviction as she could scrape together. This didn't have anything to do with Zach. This was about her and Jonah and his unrealistic demands on her time.

"Are you sure? Because you've been . . ."

"I've been what, Sister?"

Sadie shook her head. "You've just been different is all. *Mamm* is worried about you. We all are."

"There's no need." Lorie smiled a little at Daniel's squeal when his swing soared even higher. She had lost her focus for a time, but Jonah or no Jonah she was staying right where she was. In Wells Landing and with her family was exactly where she belonged.

* * *

"Will you take this bowl of salad to table four?" Sadie pushed the heaping bowl full of Watergate salad toward Lorie, not waiting for her answer before turning away to finish plating someone else's dinner.

She picked up the bowl of pale green pudding mixed with pecans, pineapple, and baby marshmallows. "Why do they call it salad anyway? It's really pistachio pudding and—"

"And what?" Sadie asked.

"N-nothing." Lorie turned and started toward table four, her mind going in a hundred different directions. Could this be the leprechaun pudding that Betty was talking about? It could very well be. It was green and had been part of the Kauffman Family Restaurant's menu since they had opened. Maybe Betty meant to say Watergate and said leprechaun instead.

It was a long shot for sure, but Lorie couldn't help but feel she was onto something.

"Why do they call it Watergate? What's a Watergate anyway?" Sadie asked.

But Lorie didn't know the answer to that question either.

Lorie pulled the card from her apron pocket and turned it over. On the back just as it had been before was Zach's phone number. Should she call him and tell him that she might have figured out what leprechaun pudding was? It was the only nice thing to do. *Jah,* she would. She would do it for all the people who worked at the assisted living home and for Zach and Betty as well. How much easier would her life be if Betty could put a name to the dish she had requested for years.

She flipped the card over again and propped her feet against the stool inside the phone shanty. The small shacks that housed the Amish telephones on the roadsides were not made for comfort. After all, phone calls should be about emergency, not the fact that she hadn't heard Zach's voice in days and days, and she wanted to hear it once again.

She picked up the receiver and dialed before she could change her mind. She would call him and tell him that she had figured out the leprechaun mystery. She would ask how he was doing. How her grandmother was and then ask about the others she'd met there at the center. Then she would tell him bye, and that would be that. No more, maybe even less.

The phone rang three times on the other end before he picked up. "Hello?"

It was ridiculous to be so excited to hear him, but she was. "Zach?"

"Lorie?" His voice was incredulous. "Hi, uh, how are you?"

"I'm fine."

The moment stretched across the line, but Lorie couldn't think of anything to say. An awkward silence fell between them.

"How's Betty?" she finally asked.

"She's fine. But you know Betty. She and Stan got in an argument yesterday over the best color for panda bears."

"Let me guess, she thought they should have been blue and yellow."

"Turquoise and orange."

Lorie laughed. "Even better."

"So . . ." He dragged out the word until it would reach from her house all the way to the highway that led into town. "I'm glad you called."

"Me too."

"Do you need something?"

She shook her head. "I just wanted to tell you that—" *I miss you. I wish I could see you. I wish . . .* "That I found something I think might be leprechaun pudding."

"Really?"

"Watergate salad. You know with the pudding and marsh-mallows."

"You might be onto something."

Lorie flushed with pride. "You think?"

"Sure, the cook makes that for the holidays. And that would mean that she hadn't had it in a long time. I think you've figured it out."

Lorie smiled and silence fell across the line. "Well," she finally said. "I just wanted to tell you that so you could uh . . ."

"I'm glad you did."

"I suppose I should hang up now."

"Wait," he said. "How are your classes going?"

"Fine. Just a few more weeks now."

"That's good."

"It was really nice talking to you, Zach."

"You too, Lorie." Another long silence stretched between them. "If you'd like you could call again next week. That way I can tell you if the Watergate salad worked. I mean, you can call anytime you feel like it, but if you call next week then maybe I'll know."

"I understand." She sucked in a deep breath needing to end this conversation and this crazy desire she had to sit there all afternoon with him on the other end of the line. "Good-bye, Zach."

Then she hung up the phone.

Zach stared down at his phone screen. *Call ended.* She was gone.

He resisted the urge to say something ugly and pitch the phone against the wall. None of that would help. They were simply from two different worlds. He could never be a part of hers, and she wasn't coming to live in his. She was practically engaged. That was something he'd do well to remember.

"Bye, Lorie."

"Who are you talking to?" His mother picked that exact moment to carry a basket of clean clothes from the laundry room.

"No one."

"This doesn't have anything to do with that girl, does it?" She set the basket on the floor between them and settled herself into the armchair to fold.

He shook his head.

"Uh-huh." His mother didn't sound convinced. "That's not what Stan says."

"Stan has a big mouth."

"Seems to me that Eugene might have mentioned it once or twice as well. What I want to know is when I get to meet her?"

Zach tucked his phone into his pocket and tried not to frown. "You don't."

His mother stopped folding a towel and looked at him. Really looked at him with those mother's eyes that seemed to see straight through everything to the heart of the matter. "Did you two have an argument?"

"Nothing like that."

"I guess I don't understand."

"You have met her." There. Let her make what she would of that.

"I have?"

"She's Betty's granddaughter."

"Betty Mathis? Wait . . . the Amish girl?"

"Yeah."

She stopped folding clothes to give him another of those looks. "Then I really don't understand."

"There's nothing to understand. I think she's beautiful and funny. She's sweet and kind." He sighed. "In fact, she may be the best person I've ever met. But she's joining the church and getting married."

His mother's eyes lit with recognition. "She's the reason you asked me all those questions about the Amish on the way home from the auction."

He gave her a wry smile. "Yeah. That was the first time I met her. I never thought I would see her again, then one day I turn around at the center, and there she is."

"And it felt a lot like fate." His mother understood more than she realized. How could it not be fate or the hand of God that brought them together? How in this big ol' world had they found each other not once but twice? And if their meeting did have something to do with a higher power, then why did any further relationship seem as distant as the stars?

He didn't have those answers.

He shook those thoughts away and stood. "I think I'll go to the gym." Maybe a good run on the treadmill would help him clear his head.

"You don't want to stay and help with the laundry?" She flashed him a teasing smile.

"But you fold clothes so much better than I ever could." He leaned down and kissed her on the cheek.

"Charmer."

Didn't he wish. Maybe then he could convince Lorie to come to Tulsa one more time. With a shake of his head he grabbed his keys and headed for the door.

She wasn't going to call him. She wasn't going to call him. As much as she wanted to know if the Watergate salad was Betty's mystery leprechaun pudding, what difference did it make really? It wasn't like she had any other ideas. It wasn't like anything had changed between her and Zach. A phone call would only muddy the waters, and she was just about able to see the bottom.

She tucked her hand into her pocket and fingered the card that Zach had given her. It was creased and bent, even smudged in a few places because she had it with her at all times. She told herself it was to keep anyone else from finding it. But she knew the truth. She wanted a piece of him to keep with her.

She rolled her eyes at her own foolish thoughts. She should be ashamed of herself. More than ashamed. Her prayers tonight would be lengthy. Except when she started to pray, her mind went blank. She couldn't remember one thing that she needed to confess, one thing she needed to ask for. All she could manage were small prayers for her family and a request for peace. So far that prayer had been unanswered.

"I'm going down to the post office." She grabbed up the letters sitting by the cash register and fanned herself with them.

"Fred Conrad should be by any minute to get them," *Mamm* said with a frown.

"I could use the fresh air," Lorie explained, hoping *Mamm* wouldn't protest further. The walls were closing in on her. She just needed to get out for a minute or two before the early dinner crowd started to arrive.

"It's okay." Sadie shot *Mamm* a hard look. "We've got everything under control here."

"*Jah.* Okay," *Mamm* said. Another look passed between stepmother and daughter.

Lorie had the feeling they had been talking about her. The thought set uncomfortably in her craw. "I'll be back in a little bit."

She felt their eyes on her back as she headed for the door, but she refused to turn around and examine their expressions. Whatever secret they were keeping . . . well, she would let them have it in order to keep her own.

The sun was bright and hot, typical late June weather in Oklahoma. Lorie resisted the urge to twirl around in her skirt to cool herself. Twirling was not exactly a mourning activity. Instead she fanned herself with the letters as she made her way to the post office.

Wells Landing was in full swing. Buggies and cars alike inched along the streets. The market was open for business. Farms and vendors sold their wares next to the crafters and quilters. Sometimes Lorie envied the people who worked the market. They seemed to have so much more freedom than she enjoyed. Or maybe it was being outside that she envied. Then again it could be something entirely different.

Whatever it was, a longing rose up inside her. She tried to press it back down, but it kept rising like the ocean she had seen on the TV at the hardware store. A hurricane they had called it, with waves taller than a house. But unlike the hurricane, she should be able to ignore this longing, this whatever it was and go on. Was she the only one who felt this way? Did all the other Amish folks go through this? Whether they did or they didn't, it was something Lorie had never heard anyone discuss. That was the thing about Amish. They were a private people. Private even as individuals.

"Excuse me." She had been so buried in her thoughts that she ran smack into a man standing in front of the hardware store. "Oh, hi, Merv."

He smiled at her, revealing his white, white teeth. Secretly Lorie thought he used some of the whitener she had seen at the drugstore, but that would be vain and for an Amish man, not appropriate.

"Well, hello yourself, Lorie Kauffman. *Wie geht?*"

"*Gut, gut,*" she said. It wasn't really a lie. And it wasn't like she could tell this man her doubts and fears.

"Getting ready to join the church, I see."

She nodded.

"When it gets to be too much for you, come out and see me."

"I'm sorry?" Did she hear him right?

"The classes and the pressure. The trying to decide what to do. When all that becomes too much, come out to the house and see me."

"But—" she protested, not finishing the thought. *How do you know? What do you mean?*

He smiled at her again. "We'll talk then." He turned on his heel and sauntered away.

Lorie watched him go, confusion paralyzing her feet. How long she stood there watching him walk away she didn't know. She watched him until she couldn't see him any longer, then she kept watching just in case.

Merv King was a different soul. He kept to himself, making coffins that the Amish were buried in. He didn't have a wife that anyone knew of. And according to the talk at the sewing circles, he'd just appeared one day and that was that. Somehow over the years he'd become part of the community, yet he always seemed a little to the outside. Like he was one of them, but not. Somehow separate.

Of course if he went around telling people things like he'd just told her, she could see why everyone thought he was a little strange. Still, there was something about the man. She just didn't know what it was.

She pushed the thought away and walked on toward the post office.

Chapter Twelve

Was she out of her mind for coming here?

She set the brake on the buggy and tied the horse to a nearby hitching post.

Most probably. But here she was. Merv King's house.

In her defense, she hadn't planned on coming here. She had started off down the road to Bacon Dan's house. The Kauffman hens were having trouble laying right now. A coyote or bobcat was bothering them at night, and they seemed agitated and ruffled. Bacon Dan sold eggs in his roadside stand, and since he was their closest neighbor, she had set off to his house to collect some eggs.

The eggs were in the back of the buggy waiting for her to return home, but first . . .

It was only another mile out to Merv King's house. She started toward the workshop off to one side of the house. The whine of the gas-powered saws met her ears as she walked.

He had said to come by if she needed to talk. How did he know she needed to talk? Did he know what it was about?

These were only a few of the questions she hoped he would answer for her.

She snorted, then covered her mouth with one hand. She was being ridiculous. Her *mamm* was waiting for the eggs.

They were making pies for Esther and Abe Fitch. Lorie thought it was sort of dumb to make pies for the bakery shop owner, but a table fell on Abe in his workshop, and he had to have surgery on his ankle. Since he was laid up, it was customary for the community to help in providing food and assistance. Lorie would have thought a pot roast would have been a fine contribution, but *Mamm* had insisted on pies.

Secretly Lorie thought Maddie fancied her crusts better than those of the longtime baker. There had been something of a competition between Esther and Maddie for many years now. Of course, it didn't help that *Mamm* confronted Esther concerning her relationship with Abe Fitch back before they got married. Lorie had been horrified that her stepmother could be so bold, but that was Maddie.

The noise of the saws grew louder as she drew closer to the outbuilding. The air was tinted with the scent of freshly cut pine and the exhaust from the engine.

Why had she come here again? Oh, *jah,* because she was *ab im kopp*. Off in the head. She reached the door, then changed her mind. She shouldn't have come here. Merv's words were just the ramblings of a crazy old man. Except that he wasn't really crazy. Or old. She turned to leave, but his greeting stopped her in her tracks.

"*Oi!* Lorie Kauffman, where are you going? You just got here."

She stopped in her tracks as a red hound dog came from under the porch to growl at her.

"Don't mind her. She's just cranky. Harmless, but cranky."

Lorie turned around slowly, twisting one of the strings of her prayer *kapp* around a finger. She was hesitant to present her back to the dog, but she did as she gathered her response to Merv King. "Hi," she said. Not exactly the smartest thing she'd ever said. But honestly she had no idea why she had come here other than Merv seemed to know something about her that no one else did. How he knew it was anyone's guess.

"Come to talk, did you?" he called over the grind of the saw. He shut off the power and lifted his yellow safety glasses to rest on the top of his head. The cranky dog must have sensed that Lorie was welcome for the mutt crawled back into the cool shade under the porch, leaving the two of them and a handful of ducks in the yard.

Merv looked the same as he did all the other times she had seen him, except today he had headphones in his ears and a small silver rectangle clipped to the waistband of his trousers. An *Englisch* music player.

"I just happened to be out this way." Lorie released her prayer *kapp* string to twist her fingers in the folds of her black apron.

"Uh-huh." He lifted the board he'd been cutting and set it off to one side. Lorie took a step closer stopping just short of entering the shed altogether.

Coffins were lined up across the back of the room. All were the plain-looking pine boxes like her father was buried in. Even more were stacked to one side. Two half-finished ones rested end to end on two heavy wooden tables.

"Do you make the coffins for the entire district?"

"*Jah.* For the entire settlement even."

"That means . . ."

"I made your father's coffin."

"I miss him," Lorie said, finally stepping across the threshold. The scent of wood was even stronger inside and wasn't unpleasant even mixed with the odor of burnt motor oil. At least that's what she thought the smell was.

"Of course you do." He pulled the little bud things from his ears and tucked them under the edge of his suspenders. "You won't tell anyone about it, will you?"

She shook her head.

"Good. It'll be our little secret."

"So what do you listen to?"

He smiled. "All sorts of things. I have the Bible on here."

Lorie blinked and pointed to the tiny device. "On there?" It was so small.

"*Jah,* the whole thing. Someone reads it, and I listen." Then he winked. "But sometimes I listen to music. Rock and roll." His face grew dreamy. "Nothing like the Rolling Stones."

She smiled, though she had no idea what he was talking about. The line of coffins snagged her attention. She allowed her gaze to stick in one place all the while not really seeing what was before her.

"It's okay, you know."

She stirred and focused on him once again. "What's okay?"

"The *Englisch* world."

"I . . . I don't understand."

Merv leaned one hip against the worktable behind him and crossed his arms as if settling in for a long chat. "The bishops all talk about the perils of the *Englisch* world. Technology is bad, some books are a sin. Music is too much of a temptation. But it can't all be bad, *jah?*"

She wasn't sure how to answer so she kept quiet and waited for him to continue.

"There are parts of the *Englisch* world that are good. What would we do without *Englisch* drivers? Or *Englisch* doctors?"

She thought of Daniel and his *Englisch* school. "*Jah.* I s'pose."

"And then there are *Englisch* friends."

Her attention snapped back to him once again. "*Freinden?*"

He gave her a quick nod, then picked up another board.

"Why so many coffins?" she asked. Wells Landing wasn't that big of a town. Yet there had to be ten, maybe twelve coffins there in various stages of completion.

Merv looked around at his handiwork. "I'm going on vacation."

"Really?" Being in the restaurant business didn't leave much time for such things. Lorie had never taken a vacation in her life.

"I'm heading down to Pinecraft for a week."

Pinecraft was a truly Beachy Amish settlement in Florida. Because of their use of tractors, many called the residents of Wells Landing Beachy though they weren't as liberal as the Amish who lived in Pinecraft.

"Florida," she whispered.

"Oh, *jah.* I may even stay longer if I meet someone."

"You're looking to get married?"

He smiled in that way he had that made her feel stupid and sheltered all in the same instance.

"Not necessarily."

"Oh."

"You know what they say."

She didn't.

He chuckled. "What happens in Pinecraft stays in Pinecraft."

Nor did she know what that meant. "I hope you have a *gut* time." She turned and started back out of the workshop wondering why she had even come out here.

"Lorie."

She turned back toward him.

"It is possible to enjoy your life and live Biblically."

"*Jah.*" She gave him a small wave. "*Danki,* Merv King."

His words spun round inside her head as she drove back to the house. They were so simple. It was possible to live Biblically and still enjoy life. God didn't want his followers miserable. She knew that as surely as she knew her name. Her father had taught her that. She had seen him, loving the Lord every day, smiling, cooking food for the good people of Wells Landing. He enjoyed his life. And he lived Biblically.

Yes, she could say that. She had seen him pray. She had attended church with him for all the years of her life. He had helped his neighbor in the Amish way and though he had his secrets, when all was brought forth, it was his mother he was visiting. He was a faithful husband, a wonderful father, and a *gut* Amish man.

Whatever reasons he had for lying he had taken with him to the grave.

"Whoa." She pulled her buggy to the side of the road. Just ahead was a phone shanty. She didn't want to waste any more time. Merv King was right. She could live and love God. And she would start by calling Zach.

She hobbled the horse and let herself into the shanty.

Please answer. Please answer. Please answer.

The phone rang three times on the other end before he answered. "Hello?"

"Zach? It's me, Lorie."

"Lorie." He sounded happy to hear from her. "I didn't think you were going to call."

"I . . . I wasn't," she admitted.

"What made you change your mind?"

Merv's face popped into her mind's vision. "It's sort of a long story."

He laughed. "No matter. I'm just glad that you did."

"Me too."

They both fell silent though unlike the other times, this break in the conversation seemed natural.

"Did Betty like the Watergate salad?"

"She did. But it wasn't her leprechaun pudding."

"It was more of a guess than anything." She settled onto the small wooden bench and wondered how long she had before her family wondered if she was coming back with the eggs or if she had jumped the fence.

"But it was sweet of you to think about her."

"How is she doing?"

"If I tell you that she asks for you every day, will you come to visit?" He sighed. "That wasn't fair. I'm sorry."

"No. It's okay. In fact . . ." She couldn't bring herself to be so forward as to ask outright.

"What?"

She wound the phone cord around her finger until the tip turned white. Then she freed it, watching as the pink rushed back into the digit. "I've been thinking about coming back for a visit."

"Really?"

She exhaled, realizing only then that she had been holding her breath. "That would be okay?"

"Of course."

She smiled at his use of her grandmother's favorite phrase. "I'm off next Thursday. Would that be all right?"

"Yeah. Yes."

But they had yet to discuss the real issue at hand. It hid just below the surface, waiting for someone to notice it.

"Listen," he started. "I know you've got plans for your life, but we agreed to be friends. Right?"

She wilted with relief and smiled in spite of herself. "Friends, *jah*. I'd like that very much."

"Pick you up Thursday? Same time, same place?"

"*Jah,*" she said. "I'll be there."

"Lorie!" Eugene exclaimed as Zach and Lorie made their way into the living center. A group of the seniors were waiting in the seating area just to the right of the front desk. "We didn't think you'd ever come back."

"I knew she would." Betty smiled in that blankly understanding way she had that made Lorie wonder if she really knew what the conversation was about or if she was just speaking in order to keep from feeling left out.

"I missed you all," Lorie said as they took turns hugging

her. Normally the Amish weren't touchy sorts of people. But she loved the affection she received from this mixed group of senior citizens.

"We're going to the mall today," Stan said, using his cane to point to the minibus waiting outside the center's doors. They had passed it coming in, but she hadn't given it a second thought. Buses like that were commonplace in Wells Landing.

"If the driver ever gets here," Linda groused.

"The mall?" Lorie didn't bother to ask how the bus got in front of the center if there was no driver.

"Yes, dear." Betty took her knitting from her big plastic bag and spread it across her lap.

"Do you want to go?" Zach asked.

"To the mall?"

He nodded.

Strangely enough she did. Maybe the mall wasn't what drew her in, but the company she would keep. She loved spending time with the group from table eight. And then there was Zach. She loved spending time with him, too.

She and Jonah might have argued—they might even be broken up—but that didn't mean she could have anything other than friendship with Zach. If that was all she could have, she wanted it.

Enjoy life and live Biblically. That's what she was going to do. Have *Englisch* friends and visit them when she wanted and not worry about the gossiping tongues of others.

"There she is." Linda nodded toward the woman coming toward the bus. She had tan-colored pants and a royal blue shirt with three little buttons and a soft collar like the ones Lorie had seen men wear into the restaurant.

"Let's go then." Stan tried to pull himself out of the couch, but the cushions had settled, leaving him stranded. "Can someone pull me up?"

Tiny little Fern moved in front of him and held her arms out for him to take.

If she was going to pull on Stan, who was going to pull on her?

"Let me." Zach gently urged Fern aside and hoisted Stan to his feet.

The old man slapped him on the arm in thanks and shuffled toward the bus.

Fifteen minutes later they were on their way to Woodland Hills Mall.

Lorie swayed in her seat bumping knees and shoulders with Zach as they bounced along.

"Have you ever been to the mall?" Zach leaned in close so only she could hear.

"*Nay.*" She had never been to the mall. She had barely been out of Wells Landing. And up until just a couple of months ago, she had never thought to. Now she enjoyed the measure of freedom more than she cared to admit.

The bus driver let them out at the large glass doors. Stan had a scooter to help him get along while the others chose to walk.

"War injury, you know." He climbed aboard the motorized cart as Linda rolled her eyes.

The sheer size of the mall took Lorie's breath away. Nothing on the outside prepared her for the two-story building.

"What do you think?" Zach asked.

"I think it's beautiful." She resisted the urge to spin around in a circle to take it in from all angles.

He smiled as if she'd just handed him a present. "Come on." He grabbed her hand and led her farther into the building. "Let's see what we can get into."

The seniors had their own list of things they wanted to look at.

"Will she be okay?" Lorie asked, watching her grandmother walk away with the others. It was strange to Lorie that she had only known Betty for a short while yet she felt so responsible for her. Maybe because she reminded Lorie so much of Daniel.

"Stan won't let anything happen to her."

"Okay." Reluctantly she turned around and allowed Zach to steer her through the walkways. Music blared from inside the bright and colorful shops. Some had mannequins wearing tiny *Englisch* swim clothes while others promoted what they called "back to school clothes." And there was a shoe store.

Lorie had to still her feet to keep from moving closer and closer to the store windows. She wanted to press her nose to the glass and take in all the wonderful shoes. Cowboy boots and boots that looked like they were made out of raincoats sat side by side with cute beaded sandals and brightly colored sneakers. There were even some that looked like they were built for torture with impossibly high heels and pointed toes.

"I think he likes her."

"What?" She peeled her attention away from the colorful array of shoes and back to Zach.

"Stan," he explained. "I think Stan is sweet on Betty."

"*Jah?* How do you know?"

"He always sits by her at meals and craft time. And today, did you see the way he managed to ride next to her on the shuttle bus?"

Exactly the way he had done with her. Did that mean that Zach was sweet on her?

"Do you like them?"

Did he mean—? "The shoes? *Jah.* Well, most of them."

"Which are your favorites?"

"I like the boots. The brown ones."

He smiled. "Me too. Wanna try them on?"

She shook her head. "Oh, no. Thanks."

He seemed about to protest, then he gave a small bow and hooked an arm through hers. "As you wish." He grinned, apparently very pleased with himself. Then his expression fell a bit. "It's from a movie."

"Oh."

"Where would you like to go?" he asked.

"I don't know."

"Is it against the rules for you to try on clothes and shoes and such?"

She shook her head. "Not really, but . . ."

"But what?"

"It's complicated." How could she explain that "against the rules" was a bit too strong? But it would be frowned upon. And then there was the part of her that loved to wear the *Englisch* clothes, loved to spend time with Zach. That part of her made it necessary to refrain from dabbling too much in the *Englisch* world, lest she not want to leave it at all.

"I get it. I won't press, but promise me this. If you see something you'd like to try on or something you want to do, you'll tell me. Okay?"

"Deal."

They started through the mall arm in arm, looking through the windows of the many shops and watching the array of people as they walked by.

"There you two are." The sound of whirring motors met them before they turned and found Stan on his scooter with Betty on a matching one, riding by his side.

"Where did you get that?" Zach asked. The corners of his mouth twitched as if he was suppressing a smile.

"Customer service desk." Stan patted the front of Betty's scooter. "She's a beauty, yeah?"

"She sure is."

Lorie wasn't sure how to respond so she merely nodded.

"Where are y'all headed?" Zach asked.

"To the salon. I want to get a haircut. Wanna come along?"

Zach ran his fingers through his dark hair. "I guess I could use a trim." He turned toward Lorie. "Is that okay with you?"

"Sure."

So together the four of them made their way through the department store and down to the salon. It smelled in there, like the stink bomb Jonah and his brothers had set off in the schoolhouse when they were younger. She smiled at the memory even as she wondered if some young boy as trouble-some as Jonah had set off a bomb inside the hair salon.

A girl dressed all in black stood behind the counter. Lorie almost asked if she was in mourning, but then she noticed all the ladies cutting hair were dressed in black.

The pictures on the walls were gigantic and featured people with crazy hairstyles in a rainbow of colors. She really needed to get out more. She had never seen anything like this in tiny Wells Landing. Not that she wanted blue or purple hair, but it was interesting to know that other people did.

"What about you, hun?" The girl behind the counter popped her gum and waited for Lorie to answer. Her large, round earrings swung from side to side with the motion of her gum chewing.

"Me?"

"You want me to put you down for a haircut? I've still got one stylist open."

Lorie started to shake her head, then she remembered the girl from the gas station. She had envied Lorie's long hair, but Lorie had loved the look of the blunt cut the girl had. "Can you cut it straight across?"

"Hun, we can do anything."

Lorie glanced toward the picture of the man with one stripe of purple hair smack down the middle of his head. *Jah,* she supposed they could. "Then I would like a haircut." As she said the words her heart started to pound.

"I'll wait here," Betty said, settling herself down in one of the chairs in the waiting area while the girl escorted them back and introduced them to the people who would be cutting their hair.

Zach caught the woman before she could leave. "The lady out there. She's a wonderful lady, but she gets sort of confused. Will you keep an eye on her? We can't have her wandering off."

"Sure thing, hun."

With Betty taken care of, the stylists led Stan and Zach away. Lorie started after them, but the man who was supposed to cut her hair grabbed her arm to stop her.

"Women this way." He smiled.

Lorie cast one last look to where Zach and Stan walked away, then allowed him to lead her in the opposite direction.

He sat her in one of the many chairs that lined the room. Most were facing a long, long mirror, though some were turned in the opposite direction. "What are we going to do today?" the man asked. Brad, she thought the woman had said his name was. Brad shook out a length of slick black material and wrapped it around her so that the only thing showing was her head.

"I want it cut straight across the bottom. Can you do that?"

"Of course." As he spoke he pulled the pins from her hair, rubbing his fingers against her scalp.

She had never had another person touch her head that way and the sensation, though pleasing, was a bit unnerving as well.

"Oh, my," Brad breathed. "Honey, have you ever had a haircut?"

"No."

"It's almost touching the floor."

Lorie grabbed ahold of the arms of the chair as he somehow pumped her seat into a higher position.

"Is that a problem?" she asked.

"Not anymore." He spun her to face away from the mirror. Lorie held on for her life. These chairs were the craziest thing she had ever seen.

Then Brad lifted the counter behind her and exposed a shiny black sink. She watched him in the opposite mirror as he turned on the water and adjusted the temperature. Then he gathered her hair and trailed it into the sink.

"Now lean back."

Like she had much of a choice. His magic chair tipped backward, and she had no choice but to do the same.

The warm water washed over her scalp. The sensation wasn't at all unpleasant, but it was unexpected.

What did you think he was going to do?

"Loosen up," Brad said from above her. "This is supposed to be fun."

Loosen up.

Lorie closed her eyes and tried to relax.

Brad continued to wet her hair as he massaged her scalp and helped relieve some of her tension. Then the smell of the stink bomb was replaced with the sweet scent of apples. He washed her hair, put some sort of conditioner in it that smelled exactly like the shampoo. He wrapped it in a towel and spun her around to face the mirror again.

"And you just want the ends cut off?" He gently toweled her hair dry and started to comb through the thick mass. "No long layers?" His eyes met hers in the mirror.

She shook her head. She wasn't exactly sure what long layers were but she was pretty sure she didn't want them. She wanted the straight, even cut at the bottom of her hair just like the girl at the gas station.

"You can cut a little more off of it." Her mouth went dry as she said the words. But it wasn't like anyone would know. She wore her hair up every day. As long as she didn't cut bangs or any short pieces, who would know but her? The idea was strangely thrilling.

"How short?" He pulled the long strands over her shoulders. Using his comb, he measured how short she wanted to go.

Normally she could sit on her hair when it was unbound. But the idea of having it shorter was strangely appealing. Yet it would have to be long enough to make her normal knot under her prayer *kapp* or her family might start to get suspicious.

"Longer," she said as Brad used the comb to show her where he'd cut. He moved the comb again. "Longer."

He moved the comb down three more times before she was satisfied that she would have a different look without anyone in Wells Landing being any the wiser.

"You know if you cut at least a foot off of it, you can donate the hair to Locks of Love."

"What's that?"

Brad explained how the organization took real hair donated by people to make wigs for cancer patients who had lost theirs during treatment.

"That would put your hair right about here."

"*Jah*. Okay." She sucked in a gulp of air and squeezed her eyes shut tight. "I want to do that."

Chapter Thirteen

Zach flipped through the wrinkled magazine in the salon's waiting area. He had tipped the receptionist ten dollars for watching after Betty. Now she and Stan had headed to the coffee shop for a snack while he waited for Lorie. He wasn't sure how much longer she would be, but he was starting to get antsy. He tossed that magazine back onto the low table and reached for another.

"Well, what do you think?"

He turned toward the most beautiful girl he had ever seen.

"Lorie? Wow." He stood, never once taking his gaze from her. The magazine hit the floor with a *plop*. He bent to retrieve it, then straightened to stare at her once again. "I had no idea your hair was that long."

It had to reach all the way to the middle of her back if not a little below that. Parted in the middle, the pale blond tresses framed her face like silk curtains.

"You like it?"

"I love it." And that was the truth.

She smiled at the compliment while he scrambled to keep his wits. He had promised to be her friend, nothing more. And that was all they could be, just friends. But he had to admit that she had never looked better.

They paid for their cuts then left the salon for the main mall.

"What now?" he asked. Getting a haircut was a completely spur-of-the-moment idea. He had come today for the seniors, but it seemed like this would end up being a great trip for Lorie as well.

"Could we maybe . . . go back into that store and try on those shoes?"

"We can do anything you want." He checked his watch. "We have another hour and a half before the shuttle leaves."

She smiled and a little piece of Zach's heart became hers.

For the next hour, Zach watched as Lorie tried on shoes, jeans, and skirts. He smiled as she came out of the dressing room wearing a flouncy little flowered dress and the boots she'd bought at the shoe store.

"Does this look okay?" Her hair swung behind her, a spun gold mass of silk. She looked better than okay. She looked amazing.

But he had promised to be her friend. Nothing more. And a friend he would be. "Sure. Yeah. That looks really good."

"Like a real *Englisch* girl?"

He swallowed hard, but managed to keep his voice even. "As real as it gets."

Lorie floated along for the rest of the day. She couldn't believe what a great time she had just walking around the mall with Zach, Stan, and Betty.

Once they were back on the shuttle bus, all the seniors complimented her haircut. They told her how pretty she looked. She knew she was blushing, but she appreciated their kind words more than they would ever know.

And she wasn't about to feel guilty about the money she had spent. She'd never in her life spent so much in one afternoon, but the money had been the cash her father had in his wallet. She only spent about half, and she vowed to use the rest to buy surprises for the younger children.

"Thanks for the great time today."

Zach pulled just to the other side of the phone shanty. They had stopped on the way home and she had changed back into her Amish clothes. Thankfully, she had remembered to put her prayer *kapp* in a safe place this time. It now covered her recently cut and shampooed hair, though even the changes there were too subtle to be noticed. All in all there was no evidence of her day of visiting with her grandmother and otherwise acting like an *Englisch* girl. Further proof of the harmlessness of what she was doing.

She and Zach had talked it out and had agreed to be friends. They both knew enough to understand that things between them couldn't be any more than that. Her grandmother wouldn't expect anything from her except the occasional visit. It wasn't like Lorie was leaving the faith, she reminded herself. So what was the harm in spending a little time with her friends?

"I had a good time too." He smiled, but she noticed he leaned against the car door as if he needed to be as far away from her as possible. "I'm glad you came today."

"What about next week?" she asked, hoping she wasn't being too forward. Now that she better understood her relationship with Zach, both of them should be able to enjoy each other's company.

"Next week?" he asked.

"I thought maybe . . . I mean, I know gas costs money. I could give you some money for gas. That is, if you'll come get me again and take me to Sundale." She wound to a stop, then shook her head. "I'm sorry. I'm expecting too much. I'll hire a driver."

She couldn't hire a driver, and she knew it. But if what she was doing wasn't wrong, then why couldn't she hire someone to take her to Tulsa? *Why are you having to hide?* that little voice asked.

Because right or wrong *Mamm* would never understand.

Lorie reached for the door handle to let herself out of his car. It was time she got home.

He laid a hand on her arm to stop her flight. "It's not that. It's not the money or . . . or anything. I was just surprised. I didn't expect you to want to come back so soon."

"I had fun."

"Your family will be okay with this?"

Not really, but she had just found her grandmother and she still had a lot of questions that she wanted answered.

Like you asked questions of Betty today.

She pushed down that little voice once again.

"It'll be fine." It wasn't like anyone would find out.

"All right then. Same time, same place?"

"If you don't mind coming to get me."

He smiled then, that grin that would melt all the ice from the restaurant's ice machine. "Not at all. What are friends for?"

Her Amish clothes felt confining and stiff as she made her way back to the house. This was her life, and she needed to remember that. Not the sassy little boots and flowing dress she'd bought today.

She'd tucked her new purchases along with her old clothes into the canvas bag and left them in the shanty. She secreted them under the bench seat. Even if someone came along, they wouldn't be able to see her hidden treasures unless they knew where to look for them. If she bought any more, she would have to get a bigger bag. But that wasn't something she was going to do. Today was a special day. One that couldn't be repeated again.

She let herself into the house as Daniel came flying out of

the kitchen. A smear of chocolate painted one cheek. Her oldest sister followed close behind, her cooking apron dusted with flour. He and Sadie must have been making cookies.

"Lorie, Lorie, Lorie!" he cried, stopping just short of crashing into her. "I missed you today."

She scooped him into her arms, loving the warm weight of him as he hugged her close. "I missed you, too, Daniel. What did you do today?"

She set him back on his feet, smiling as he recounted his day of coloring, alphabet tracing, and number flashcards.

"What did you do?" he asked in return.

She hated lying to him, but she had no choice. It wasn't like she could tell him the truth.

"I went to visit some friends." That wasn't so much of a lie.

"How is Caroline?" Sadie asked.

Lorie's stomach fell at her tone. *She knows.* Ridiculous. "*Gut.* She's really *gut.*"

"That's great, because she looked very happy when I saw her in the market today."

Lorie straightened and met her sister's gaze. She couldn't tell if Sadie was mad or concerned. One thing was certain though. She had figured out where Lorie had been. "Daniel, why don't you go on up to your room now?"

"But the cookies."

"I'll call you when they're done. You can have some then."

"With a big glass of milk?" He looked at each of his sisters in turn.

"Of course," Lorie said.

"*Jah,* okay." He dragged his feet as he headed for the stairs. He might not learn as fast as other children, but he could sense emotions like no other. And the emotions flying around the room were thick as their *dat's* leftover chili.

Sadie waited until Daniel was completely out of sight before she spoke. "I thought you weren't going back."

"I wasn't."

"But you did."

"It's not that simple."

"Then tell me." She crossed her arms waiting for an answer.

"He was our *dat.* And she's our *grossmammi.*" Sadie may not have been Henry Kauffman's child by birth, but she was his daughter in every way that mattered.

"I cannot believe you."

Something rose up inside of Lorie. "I can't believe *you.* You should feel like I do."

"And how is that?"

"Like you've been cheated out of something." Until she said the words, she hadn't understood her own feelings. "Something big. Something important."

"And this has nothing to do with the boy."

Her heart gave a hard pound. "No," she scoffed. "Not at all." The lie almost choked her. Why was that one harder than the rest?

Sadie wilted with relief. "I know this has been hard on you."

Lorie nodded. "No harder than it's been on you and everyone else in the family."

"Everybody handles death differently. Who is to say if one way is better than the other?"

"*Danki,* Sadie."

Her sister pulled her close and wrapped her in a hug. Lorie realized then how few times her family touched one another. Oh, Daniel was different. He hugged everyone and in turn everyone hugged him back. But the Kauffmans tended to keep an arm's length between them at all times. But not her father. He had been a hugger, and she missed that something terrible. Everyone at the living center was a hugger, and she loved those touches.

She held her sister close, absorbing the warmth and love that Sadie represented.

"I'm just worried about you," Sadie finally said.

"I know."

Sadie pulled back, her hands braced on Lorie's shoulders. "Promise me you won't go again."

With baptism classes and everything else Lorie had at stake, it was the smartest decision. But what harm was there in going to visit *Englisch* friends? Yet she didn't want to lie to Sadie. Not again. "Sadie, I—"

"Promise me."

"I promise," she said, hating the lie all the more for the relief it brought her sister.

"You seem unusually happy tonight." His mother took a bite of the casserole she'd made and waited for his answer.

What did she want him to say? That even though they could be nothing more than friends, he was still giddy over the prospect of any sort of relationship with Lorie Kauffman. Or was it Mathis? Did it matter?

Giddy. *Oh, if my friends could see me now.*

"I just had a good day."

"I heard you went to the mall with some of the residents today."

"I did."

"And a certain granddaughter."

So that's what this was about. "Yes." He set down his fork and waited for her to continue. "Go ahead. Spill whatever it is."

His mother shook her head, the light catching the strands of silver nestled in the brown. When had his mother started turning gray? And why hadn't he noticed? "It's just . . . well, she's Amish."

"I'm aware."

"But you don't get it. She's Amish." She said the last word until it sounded more like a disease than a religious belief. "You don't know enough about them. She won't leave the faith. And you seem to like her so much. I don't want you to get hurt."

He shook his head. "It's not like that."

His mother shot him that look, the one she saved for instances like this where he was only kidding himself.

"Okay, so maybe it is," he conceded. "But I know she has plans that don't include me. We've talked about it and agreed to just be friends."

That was supposed to wipe the look off her face, but it didn't. "Some of the best and worst relationships in the world started out as just friends. Just look at me and your dad."

Zach shook his head. "I don't want to talk about him." Too many bad memories. And Lorie thought her dad had kept secrets.

"I know." She stood and gathered her plate to take to the kitchen even though she was only half finished with dinner. "I'm headed back to the living center."

"Working a double today?" He hadn't heard her mention anything about that.

"Yeah. Then I start second shift tomorrow night."

"Okay then, I'll see you when you get home."

She started for the kitchen, then stopped halfway to the door and turned back to him. "Your father . . . I know he did some bad things, but he loved you. Please don't ever forget that."

He wanted to believe her. He really did. But when his mom had to work double shifts and swing shifts and way too much in order to make ends meet, Zach had to ask, if he loved them so much, why did he lie?

* * *

Lorie let herself into the storeroom and cautiously closed the door behind her. She hadn't been up here in weeks, but the urge to paint grew so strong she had to give in. She uncovered the last canvas she had been working on and stared at the painting. She didn't know why she did this. Her paintings didn't look like what she had painted. More like a bright, childlike version with thick swatches of paint and slightly off dimensions.

Yet as horrible as they were, she still had the urge, the uncontrollable drive to sneak away from all that she knew to be good and true to come up here and create. She supposed in that way she was a lot like Daniel and a thousand other children who couldn't reproduce an exact image of what they drew and instead did the best they could. Their parents and teachers oohed and aahed over their efforts and that was that.

She retrieved the cutting board she used to hold her paints and the shirt she wore to protect her clothes.

So if she had no true talent, why did she feel it necessary to make all these pictures? Why did God give her the desire to paint if the effort would only hurt those around her?

Maybe this desire wasn't from God but from the devil himself.

No. She didn't believe that. She couldn't believe that.

And then there were the letters. Just another reason she had avoided the storeroom as long as possible. As much as she wanted to read every word her father had left for her, she couldn't. She had read the first ten or so letters, then put them aside. She hadn't discovered her grandmother's and her father's secrets. But if he would keep those from her what wouldn't he hide? What if Caroline and Emily were right? She couldn't go back and forget everything she had found out already but she could stop herself from learning more. Betty held the key to the secrets, but with her mixed up thoughts,

Lorie didn't know whether what she said was the truth or the truth only in her mind.

And leprechaun pudding.

Lorie dipped her flat, broad brush into the green paint and added it to the canvas. Why did it seem so familiar?

Maybe it was something she and her father had before her mother died. Maybe the recipe was in among the letters her father had sent Betty.

Lorie looked toward the box. She said she wasn't going to go through them all. What good would it do anyway? Of the letters she'd read, only one of them had any significance and even that was vague at best.

But if it held the secret to leprechaun pudding, she could pass the information along to the head cook at the center. And Betty would be so happy. If she truly remembered what leprechaun pudding was. Who knew? Leprechaun pudding could be something she had made up entirely in her own head.

Lorie stepped back from the painting and studied it with a critical eye. It was bright, as bright as the sun catchers the seniors were making on one of her visits. Splashes of green, royal blue, and orange made up the angled lines of his face. Zach.

She shook her head. A bad remembrance of Zach, but even if she could paint like *Englisch* photographs she would never be able to capture the mischievous gleam in his pale blue eyes or the handsome slant of his chin. It was probably better this way. She sighed and looked back to the box of letters.

Maybe there was something beneficial in there. A recipe. A photograph. A mention of something that would lead her down the right path.

She rinsed out her paintbrush in the jar of solvent and glanced back over to the box.

What would it hurt if she read a couple more? After all,

she had promised to take them back to Betty once she had finished reading them. If she wasn't going to read them, then they needed to go.

She wiped her hands on an old rag and looked back to the painting. She had a little while before it would be dry enough to hide away.

She gave the painting one last look, then sat on the floor and pulled the box into her lap. Just a few wouldn't hurt anything. Lorie pulled a letter from the stack and started to read.

Chapter Fourteen

"I think I know what it is," Lorie said as she slid into the passenger's seat of Zach's car.

"Hello to you, too."

"Sorry. I'm just excited."

"I can tell." There was that smile again, the one that made her heart flutter even though it shouldn't.

"Hi, Zach. I think I know what leprechaun pudding is."

"Really?" He put the car into gear and started down the road.

Lorie wasted no time pulling off her prayer *kapp* and carefully laying it in the backseat. No sense in having a repeat of the prayer *kapp* debacle. She pulled the pins from her hair and ran her fingers through it to pull out the crimps.

The car slowed and she turned to Zach. "Everything okay?"

He swallowed hard and nodded. "Sure." The car sped back up to a normal speed, and they were on their way.

"So what is leprechaun pudding?"

She turned in her seat to look at him as he drove them down the highway. "I looked through some of the letters that my father sent to Betty, and I found a recipe for a lime and mint breakfast pudding."

He made a face. "Lime and mint pudding?"

"It's better than you think."

His frown deepened. "You've eaten this?"

"Of course."

He shook his head. "To each his own, I guess."

"Do you think the cook will make it for Betty?"

"I'm sure she will."

They drove to the gas station where she had changed clothes before. Zach waited in the car for her while she dressed in her *Englisch* clothes. Then she ran back out to meet him, and they were on their way again.

Carol and Amber at the front desk didn't bat an eye when they walked in together. Carol was on the phone and managed a quick smile and wave before turning her attention back to what the person on the other end of the line was saying. Amber smiled as well, as if she had a secret bigger than the one they had. Then she ducked her head and pretended to be filing papers.

"Everyone should be in the rec room," he said, leading her through the hallways.

She pulled him to a stop outside the rec room door. "Zach," she started, "I just wanted to thank you for bringing me. I mean, it is your day off."

"It's my pleasure."

"It still means a lot to me."

He nodded toward the group of seniors that gathered at table eight. "It means a lot to them, too."

The seniors caught sight of them and waved.

"Zach and Lorie are here," she heard someone exclaim. She thought it was Eugene.

"Come on." He grabbed her hand and led her into the room.

After a robust round of greetings, Zach and Lorie sat down and helped them make some sort of braided bracelets that he referred to as friendship bracelets.

"I don't know why they have us doing stuff like this. It's near impossible with my stiff fingers," Stan groused.

"Hush," Fern reprimanded. "It's good for your joints."

"I don't see how. Makes me feel like a durned fool."

"Amen to that," Eugene bellowed.

"Oh, don't you start in, too." Linda sighed heavily.

Lorie shot a smile at Zach. He returned it and went back to helping Betty with her purple-and-green creation.

"I think it should have some red, don't you, Billy?"

"Zach," he corrected.

"Of course." She released the string to pat her perfect hair back into place.

"What are we doing with these again?" Fern asked.

"Cancer hospital," Eugene hollered.

"That's a good idea," Betty said. "Then it definitely needs a splash of red. It's such a cheery color. Don't you think so, dear?" She looked to Lorie for backup.

She wasn't sure what to say. Red was one of those colors that the Amish didn't wear very often, if at all. Their colors tended more toward blues, purples, and greens, but she supposed red was a nice enough color.

She must have taken too long to answer for Betty shook her head. "You probably don't wear red, being Amish and all." She said the words as offhanded as one would comment about the weather.

Lorie looked to Zach. He merely shrugged and went back to his braiding, but she caught a small glimpse of his smile before he hid it from view.

Thankfully, no one said any more about the color red or being Amish.

"Are you ready to go to lunch?" Stan stood and looked around the table at his companions.

Lorie hadn't realized so much time had passed. But a

break for lunch would be the perfect time to ask the cook about the leprechaun pudding. "Sure."

They stood and started gathering up their craft supplies. Each one of them placed their bracelet in the basket of completed ones that would be taken to the cancer hospital and distributed among the younger patients.

Zach grabbed her hand before she could walk out with the others. "Just a sec," he said, turning her hand over in his.

She met his gaze as he took the bracelet he'd made and placed it around her wrist.

"This is for you," he said, looking away so he could tie the braided strings.

"For me?" Amish didn't wear bracelets. But he had made this especially for her. It was more about friendship and less about vanity. What could be the harm in that?

He finished tying the strings and released her hand. "You're supposed to wear it until it falls off, then you make a wish and it'll come true."

She looked at the bright bracelet and back to him. "Are you serious?"

"About wearing it until it falls off? Yes. About your wish coming true?" He shrugged. "That theory has never been proven either way."

She smiled. It might be a strange custom, but she liked it. Or maybe what she liked best was that he had made it for her.

"Come on," he said, taking her hand into his. "Let's go get in line before all the mac and cheese is gone."

Lorie and Zach got into line and waited to get their food and talk to the cook. Mabel, the head chef, promised to make the breakfast pudding for Betty. Of course, Lorie had to promise to bring Mabel a jar of the Kauffman sourdough starter and a starter of friendship bread.

"What's friendship bread?" Zach asked as they grabbed

their trays and headed for the table where the others had already gathered.

"It's a bread starter, like the sourdough but with yeast. And it's a sweet bread," she added. "It's passed on from person to person. I'll give her the starter, and she'll feed it for ten days."

"Feed it? How exactly does one feed bread?"

Lorie laughed. "She'll add ingredients for ten days, milk, flour, sugar."

He nodded as if he understood, so she continued.

"Then once she's reached her ten days, she'll separate the starter and share it with a friend."

"Who will feed her starter for ten days."

"Exactly."

He smiled and nodded. "That's a nice custom."

"Darn tootin'," Stan said. "It's some good bread, too."

"I imagine Mabel won't share since she has to feed so many of us," Linda mused.

Lorie hadn't thought of that. Maybe when she came back next week she would bring a couple of starters. That way they would have plenty.

The conversation died down a bit as everyone began to eat.

Lorie tried not to stare as Zach interacted with the seniors, helping them remember events of the past week, listening to their stories, and even cutting Stan's meat when he got frustrated with the dull knife he'd gotten.

"Don't know how anyone can expect a man to cut a piece of meat with a butter knife."

"It's not a butter knife," Fern countered.

"Might as well be," Stan groused. "I have to have someone cut my meat like a toddler."

"I don't think toddlers eat meat that needs to be cut," Linda countered.

"How do you know?" Eugene asked. "You never had any little ones."

"I cut your meat often enough," she countered.

Eugene snorted, but otherwise didn't comment.

Betty hid her smile and a snicker behind her hand. Zach kept on cutting Stan's meat without a pause. It was as if he was immune to their bickering. Or perhaps that was just part of his makeup, part of what made Zach Zach.

She braced her chin in her hand and gave him a long look.

"What?" he asked.

"You're not at all what I thought *Englisch* boys would be like."

"Oh yeah, how was that?"

"Self-centered and up to no good."

"Wow, there's a stereotype."

Her cheeks filled with heat. "In their defense, our *eldra* are just trying to protect us."

"Do you think you need protection from me?"

"*Nay,*" she said without hesitation.

His eyes darkened until they were almost the color of the twilight sky.

A thick moment passed between them, then he cleared his throat and looked away.

"I never asked you how you and I managed to have the same day off," she said, feeling a change in subject was in order.

He shot her a sheepish grin. "I traded with someone."

"You did?"

"Yeah."

If she wasn't mistaken, the pink color rising up his neck was a blush. The thought that he could be embarrassed over her. Well, it was thrilling.

She looked back to the helping of macaroni and cheese on her plate, aware that everyone had stopped eating to stare at the two of them.

She wanted to ask him how he felt coming to work when he

was off to allow her time to spend time with her grandmother. Even when he didn't get paid.

But she ducked her head over her plate and let the subject drop.

They stayed at the center through lunch. Afterward the seniors all begged off any more activities in favor of taking a nap.

Zach led Lorie through the center and out into the summer sun.

"What would you like to do?" he asked, walking her toward his car.

"I guess I thought I would go home." A small frown puckered her forehead. Zach longed to reach up and smooth it away. Not because he didn't like it, but he could use an excuse to touch her.

"It's still early," he said. "We could go over to the park and take a walk. We don't really have time for the aquarium or the zoo. How about a movie?"

"A movie?"

"Sure. Why not?"

She paused as if thinking it over.

"Have you ever been to a movie before?"

She shook her head, her hair swinging from side to side releasing its intoxicating fragrance.

Whoa. He had it bad. Not that he could do anything about it. Not that he *would* do anything about it. Friends. Just friends. That was what they'd agreed to. That was what they'd be.

"Is that against the rules?" he asked.

"Well, I mean," she stammered.

"I'll take that as a yes. Do you have anything that you'd like to do?"

"A walk sounds nice."

Zach smiled. "A walk it is."

Fifteen minutes later he parked his car near the Arkansas River and got out. Lorie followed suit and stared at the running water in front of them.

The Arkansas wasn't a big river, but it cut through Tulsa, lending its beauty to the town.

He took her hand and steered her down the asphalt path that ran through the park. "I used to love to come out here when I was younger," he said, wondering where the words had come from. He hadn't thought about all those years ago in a long time.

"With your *mamm?*"

"My dad."

She tilted her head to one side, and Zach couldn't help but see that it was the perfect angle for him to swoop in and steal a kiss. "You never mention your *dat.*"

He hated that he brought it up. There was nothing but painful memories. He shrugged it off. "It's a great place to ride a bike." As if to prove his statement, a biker whizzed past.

"I love to ride bikes."

"You do? That's not against the rules?"

"It's called the *Ordnung,* and no, it's not."

"Maybe we can bring our bikes here and ride one afternoon."

She smiled, and he swore the world grew a little brighter. "I would like that very much."

They made their way past the statue of the mountain lion and the hawk, then found a bench to rest a bit before heading back to the car.

"So the *Ordnung,*" he started, wanting to learn more about the rules that she followed. "It tells you everything?"

He knew he butchered the pronunciation of the word, but she didn't correct him.

"Not everything. Some things are understood."

"Like?"

"Wearing black when in mourning. Staying in mourning for a year. Which Sunday we go to church. Things like that."

"You don't go to church every Sunday?"

"Every other one."

"What about this Sunday?" he asked, an idea dawning.

"This is a non-church Sunday."

"Do you think you could come here?"

"To the park?"

"To Tulsa."

"I don't know," she started slowly. "Sometimes we go visiting."

"I understand. I just thought it would be fun. I thought maybe we could go to my church, then spend a little time with Betty. Or we could come back out here for a bike ride. Or catch a movie." Anything she wanted to do as long as she spent time with him.

She chewed on her bottom lip as indecision lit her brown eyes.

A big fist squeezed his heart. "I've put you in a bad position. I'm sorry."

"I want to. Really I do."

"But you can't."

She sighed. "I can. Of course I can."

His heart lifted. "Are you sure?"

"Very sure."

It would only be two more days until she got to see him again, but Lorie couldn't wait. Friday afternoon, when she got home from the restaurant, she snuck out to the phone shanty just down from their house. Unlike the one she hid in when she was meeting Zach, this one had a working phone. Three of her neighbors used it regularly, though most times her family called who they needed from the phone in the restaurant.

She held her breath as the phone rang on the other side of the line. She told herself it was all in the name of leprechaun pudding, but she knew better.

Still that would be her first topic of conversation when he picked up the phone instead of how badly she missed him.

"Lorie?" he answered, surprise coloring his voice.

"How did you know it was me?" She perched on the hard wooden bench as she waited for his answer.

"Caller ID."

She wasn't entirely sure what that was, but she wasn't about to ask. It really wasn't important how he knew it was her, rather that he seemed so pleased to be talking to her.

"How did the leprechaun pudding go over?"

"The lime-mint stuff?" He sucked in a breath. "Some liked it. Others not so much. But it wasn't Betty's leprechaun pudding."

"Too bad. I was hoping."

"Yeah," Zach said. "Me too."

"Did you try any of it?"

"Uh, no."

She could hear the smile in his voice. "Chicken," she teased.

"Oh yeah?"

"Yeah."

"Then maybe we should have a taste-off."

Lorie wrinkled her nose even though he couldn't see her. "What do you mean?"

"I'll try the mint-lime pudding thing if you try . . . sushi."

"Sushi? Isn't that raw fish?"

"It doesn't have to be raw."

"If you'll eat the lime and mint pudding and I don't have to eat raw fish, then I'll do it."

"You will?"

"*Jah.* Sure. Why not?" She was feeling particularly adventuresome.

"Sunday?"

"Deal."

"I'll see you then."

"I'm looking forward to it."

Lorie hung up the phone and tried not to float back home.

She had two more days before she saw Zach again. Two more days before she could take him up on his sushi dare.

Sushi. It seemed so sophisticated and stylish. So *Englisch.*

She wrapped her arms around her middle and gave herself a small hug of joy as she crossed the road and started up the drive. She wouldn't spoil her mood by trying to figure out exactly how she would get away on Sunday. She just would.

His buggy came into view first. She saw it before she saw him. But she had spent enough time in that buggy to know. Jonah had come calling.

She hadn't seen Jonah since their argument last week after church. She should feel bad that he had hardly crossed her mind since then, but they had argued so often she was used to the cross feelings by now. At least she thought she was. And it wasn't like they had broken up. Just had a disagreement. Jonah was busy helping his father on the farm these days while she was working at the restaurant and . . .

Running off to Tulsa with strange *Englisch* boys.

She pushed the thought away.

Jonah was her Jonah and nothing was going to change that. Not even walks in the park, sushi, and a long-lost grandmother.

He was sitting on the porch waiting for her, watching for her. He returned her wave and smiled.

She hadn't seen him in so long she'd forgotten how

handsome he was. Tall and slender with wheat-blond hair and eyes the color of sweet maple syrup.

"Hi," she said as she drew close enough that he could hear her.

"Hi." He stood, stretching out his pant legs and adjusting the suspender galluses over each shoulder. "I would have come sooner, but it's been pretty hectic at the house."

"I understand."

He tilted his head to one side and studied her. "What's going on with you, Lorie?"

Her hands flew to her knot of hair. Did she look different? Could he tell? No, he couldn't. Surely he couldn't. But she felt a little conspicuous as he continued to survey her with searching eyes. "*Nix*," she said. "Nothing." She patted the back of her prayer *kapp* as if checking to make sure it was in place, then slowly lowered her arms.

"What's that?" he asked.

"What?" Lorie looked down her front, afraid that she had forgotten part of her dress or that somehow Jonah would know that she had been dressing *Englisch* on her days off.

"That." Jonah pointed to the braided threads that made up her friendship bracelet.

"*Nix.*"

"Everything can't be nothing, Lorie."

"It's a friendship bracelet." Best to stick as close to the truth as possible. She wasn't doing anything wrong, not really. But that didn't mean Jonah would understand.

"I'm not going to ask where you got it or why. You've been having a hard time lately. I understand that. But I do need you to do one thing."

She managed not to wilt with relief. "What's that?"

"Talk to the bishop about your troubles."

"My troubles." It wasn't quite a question.

Jonah took her hands into his, lightly squeezing her fingers in reassurance. "Death is a natural part of life, but that doesn't mean it's easy to accept. I know how close you were to your *dat*."

She squeezed his fingers in return. "*Jah*. Okay, then." How could she refuse him? He was only worried about her. But Lorie didn't need to talk to the bishop. She just needed a little more time. Once she joined the church, it would be harder and harder to justify going to Tulsa with Zach. After she and Jonah married, it would be impossible.

Marrying Jonah. The thought didn't fill her with excitement like it once did. She was being ridiculous. She knew from early on that she would marry Jonah, despite all their arguments and differences of opinion. No couple got along all the time.

He leaned in and placed a sweet kiss on her forehead. "I love you."

"I love you, too." But the words felt thick and uncomfortable.

"I only want what's best for you." He rested his chin on her head, keeping her close, but not completely in the circle of his arms. That was Jonah. So traditional. He hadn't even kissed her lips, preferring instead to save that pleasure for when they were married.

"I know," she whispered in return.

"Walk with me?" He released her as she nodded and took her hand into his own.

Together they started off down the path toward the small stock pond behind the barn. The Kauffmans only kept their horses and a few chickens. The restaurant business didn't allow for a lot of time to care for livestock and the pond was a remnant of the previous owner.

They walked side by side and another walk popped into Lorie's mind. Her and Zach on the Riverwalk. Such a fun day. So different than this walk since there were people all around, some skating, others jogging or biking. It was like going for a walk with the entire city and not, all at the same time.

"I've been talking with *Dat*," Jonah said as they walked. "About where we will live after we're married."

She stumbled a bit, but recovered her footing quickly.

"Are you *allrecht?*"

"*Jah. Jah.*" She had not given any thought to *after* she and Jonah married. All of her plans had centered around the *getting* married.

"He thinks as the oldest, I should stay there at the house with him and *mamm*. That way I'll be close for the fall harvest and replanting."

It seemed logical enough. But living with Jonah and his *eldra* meant leaving her own family behind. Sadie, Melanie, Cora Ann, Daniel. The thought made her heart ache. But that was her duty. As Jonah's wife her place was at his side. The Bible was very clear on that. So why did the thought fill her with dread?

"You're quiet," he said as they reached the small pond.

A couple of plastic lawn chairs sat close to the water's edge, so Cora Ann and Daniel could easily fish with minimal effort.

"I'm sorry. I don't mean to be. It's just . . ."

"Go on," he urged.

"That's so soon," she said. "And so many changes. Maybe we should wait."

"I don't understand."

"Maybe we should wait until next year to get married."

He blew out a quick breath and released her hands to prop his on his hips. "I understand that. I don't get why you said it."

"It's been a hard year on my family. *Dat*'s gone. Everything is changing. Maybe too many changes in one year. I mean, Melanie is waiting until next year to marry. *Mamm* wants her to finish out her mourning before she joins her life with another."

"Did Maddie ask you to wait?"

Lorie shook her head. *Mamm* hadn't asked her to wait. And she hadn't questioned why until now. Why did Melanie have to postpone her marriage and Lorie didn't?

"So you're saying you don't want to get married." Hurt tainted his words.

"I'm not talking about never getting married. I'm just talking about not getting married this year."

"What's the difference?"

"A year," she said.

"Not funny, Lorie."

"I'm not trying to be."

"Then what are you doing? Breaking up with me?"

"I never said that." Anger rose inside her. Why couldn't he understand? He was as bad as *Mamm* wanting to forget everything the minute her father died and moving on like it was no big tragedy. Well, it was a tragedy, and it was important to her.

"I've been waiting so long for you to join the church so we could get married. I don't want to wait another year. I'm twenty-four years old. Most of my friends have two kids now and here we are just about getting married."

"This is life, Jonah. Not a competition."

"I feel like I compete. I compete with Daniel and the others for your time. I compete with your father for your love and attention. I compete with anything and everything in your life because you keep putting it all ahead of me."

"I do not." He was wrong.

"You do." Did she?

She crossed her arms and squeezed, needing a hug in the worst way. "I don't mean to."

He blew out another breath, this one frustrated. "I feel like you're shutting me out, Lorie. I'm trying to give you time and space and whatever else it is you think you need. I've been more than patient, but it's wearing thin."

"What are you saying?"

"I want to get married this year, Lorie. I want to work on my father's farm and start a family with you. Is that so much to ask?"

"What about what I want?"

"I thought that's what you wanted too. I guess I was wrong." He turned to leave.

"Jonah, I—" she began, but she wasn't sure how to finish.

He pivoted around to face her once again. "I'm done waiting, Lorie. The longer you keep this up, the harder it's going to make it in the future."

"Are you saying the wedding is this year or not at all?"

His eyes clouded over with pain and regret. "*Jah*. So what's your answer?"

Tears stung the back of her throat. How could she explain? It wasn't that she didn't want to get married. She just didn't want to get married *now*. This year had brought so many changes, one more would make her crazy. It was too much. It made her heart pound and her mouth dry. Why couldn't he understand? Why couldn't they wait?

He gave a sad nod. "That's what I thought. Good-bye, Lorie." He turned and left her standing by the pond. She was numb with grief and something else, something she couldn't name.

She watched him go, wishing Zach was there. He'd know what to do.

Chapter Fifteen

"You're awfully quiet. Are you sure everything's okay?"

They were halfway to Tulsa, and so far, Lorie had barely said a word.

"I'm fine."

"You want to talk about it?"

"Jonah and I broke up."

He was nearly embarrassed at the surge his heart gave, and he was certainly glad she couldn't read his mind. *Down, boy.* The fact that she was no longer promised to another didn't mean jack. They were still from two different worlds. Worlds that had no overlap. "I'm sorry," he murmured.

"For good this time. I mean, we've broken up before over the years, but this time he meant it."

"This didn't have anything to do with me, did it? Or the trips to Tulsa?"

"No. Sort of." She laid a hand on his arm. Her touch warmed and comforted, but after a second it was gone. "It's not your fault. It's no one's fault."

"You sure about that?"

She smiled then, that sunshine smile that brightened even the cloudiest of days. "Positive."

After her confession, she seemed more at ease. Zach was

grateful. He enjoyed her company more than she would ever know.

They stopped for her to change. He loved it when she wore her flower-print dress and cowboy boots, her hair loose and free.

"I almost forgot," she said as she got back into the car. "I brought you something." She held out a small container filled with something green.

"Is that what I think it is?"

"Lime and mint breakfast pudding." She shot him a sweet smile like it was the best thing in the world. Or maybe that grin was devious.

"Are you sure I have to try this?"

"Only if you want me to eat raw fish."

He cleared his throat and prepared to pull back into traffic. "I said you didn't have to eat raw. What I usually get is cooked."

"We had a deal. You try this, and I'll eat sushi."

He sighed. "Fine." After all, how bad could it be?

Lorie wasn't sure what to expect from an *Englisch* church. She had passed by them, seen the ones in Wells Landing with their big white steeples with crosses on top that reached toward the sky. But she had never actually been inside one.

Zach parked his car and walked hand in hand with her to the front of the church. She told herself that he was only being supportive, but she enjoyed the feel of his strong fingers wrapped around hers.

"Hi, Zach." The man standing at the door shook Zach's hand and gave him a bright yellow paper. It was folded in half, and Zach didn't bother to look at it. Lorie wondered if they passed notes like this every Sunday. "Good to see you today. Who's this?"

"Pastor Bennett, this is my friend, Lorie."

Pastor Bennett shook her hand and gave her the same yellow paper that he had given Zach. "Glad to have you visiting today. Do you have a regular church home?"

"Yes," she said. "Of course."

The pastor smiled. "Good, good. Hope you enjoy the service."

She nodded and stepped into the church. It was beautiful, this house dedicated to one purpose. The Amish believed that having church in the home reinforced the importance of family and togetherness, but she felt like God was watching her as she looked around His house.

The building was trimmed in beautiful oak wood with a smooth finish to rival the work of Abe Fitch. Mossy green carpet covered the floor and long benches lined each side. Stained glass windows graced the outside wall, letting in shards of colored light. A dove, an ark, even the three crosses of Galilee were depicted.

"What do you think?" Zach asked as he led the way down the center aisle.

"It's amazing. Beautiful." Maybe even the prettiest building she had ever seen.

"Here." He stepped aside and waited for her to make her way down the bench, then he followed behind her.

Her eyes grew wide, but she tried her best to hide her confusion. "You're sitting here with me?"

"Of course." The warmth of him filled the space next to her. "Do Amish men and women not sit together at church?"

She shook her head.

"That's a shame. How can you share the Word together if you're not side by side?"

"I don't know." She had never thought about it before. And she had never asked. The men sat on one side and the women on the other, and that was just the way it was.

He grabbed her hand and squeezed her fingers. She loved the intimacy of his hand over hers. Zach was much more open with touches. Most *Englisch* were, she had heard, but she loved it. Instead of making her uncomfortable, it made her feel special, cared about. She wanted to go on holding his hand for as long as possible.

He let go of her hand as a man in a dress shirt and slacks stood behind the tall desk up front. "That's the music director," Zach explained. He pulled a book from the slats in the back of the seats in front of them and handed it to her.

"Now, if you will all turn to page one sixty-eight."

A woman started playing a piano and another a similar instrument that seemed to magnify every sound she played. The people all around them began to sing. Lorie tried to follow along and soon got the hang of it, reading the words and singing as she read.

So many differences. So many things alike. She loved having music in church and being able to sing along to it. And she especially loved sitting next to Zach during the service. If the preacher said something particularly interesting, he squeezed her hand to let her know how he felt about it. This unspoken communication was new to her and intriguing.

They prayed out loud, which was different for Lorie, but she liked having someone put those words to God. And they stood while doing so, which seemed odd, but natural all the same. About an hour into the service, they sang another song, passed a couple of plates around to collect money, then the preacher led one last prayer and dismissed them.

The congregation rustled around collecting their things.

"That's it?" Lorie asked, hesitant to get her bag in case it was not really time to go.

"Yeah." Zach shook the hand of the man in front of them, then grabbed his Bible. "Are you ready to get something to eat?"

"Just an hour?" Lorie looked around. Everyone seemed serious enough. The preacher had taken up his position at the door once again and was shaking people's hands as they left. The children came back into the church from who knew where. Lorie hadn't realized there were no kids at the service until they came back.

"How long is Amish church?" Zach asked.

"Three hours. At least."

Zach whistled under his breath. "I guess if you add in Sunday and Wednesday nights it's about the same amount of time." He took her elbow and led her toward the church exit. "But I wouldn't want to sit in one place for that long each week."

"Every other week," Lorie reminded him.

"That's right."

They shook the preacher's hand. He invited Lorie to come back anytime and the two of them walked through the parking lot toward his car. People waved good-bye, made lunch plans, even shook one another's hands as they prepared to leave. All in all, it was an uplifting experience and not at all like she thought it would be.

Terrible. Worse than terrible. Lime-mint pudding was as close to poison as Zach had ever eaten. He swallowed the bite as quickly as he could, nearly choking as it slid down his throat. They were seated in the sushi restaurant, waiting on their orders to be delivered to their table. Lorie had insisted that he try the pudding while they waited.

He managed to hide his grimace.

"Do you like it?"

"It's good," he managed. "Real good." *Lord, please don't strike me down for lying.*

She laughed. "No, it's not. It's terrible."

"Wait. What?" He took a quick drink of water to wash the rest of the pudding from his mouth.

"It's awful."

"But you said you liked it."

"No," she said slowly. "I said it was better than you think."

"But—"

"I never said I liked it."

"If it's so terrible, why did you make me eat it?"

She smiled. "I dunno. Just to see if you would, I guess."

"That was a mean trick, Lorie Kauffman."

"But funny." She laughed, and he decided he liked the sound. He hadn't heard her laugh much. He supposed losing a father and finding a long-lost grandmother could do that to a person. As terrible as the lime-mint pudding was, he would gladly eat it again if it would make her happy.

"What is this one again?" Lorie used the chopsticks to pick up a piece of the sushi roll. She was getting the hang of this eating with sticks. This time she didn't even drop it.

"California roll," he replied.

He had ordered them two variety platters that had different kinds of sushi for her to try. It was fun to eat something so exotic, though everyone in the restaurant looked just like her. Did that make her exotic too? "I think I like it best," she said after she swallowed the bite.

"Everyone does. Did you try the volcano rolls?" He pointed to the piece with one chopstick. "Those are my favorite."

She shook her head. "That one's too spicy."

"Good," he said, popping a piece into his mouth. "More for me."

Sushi wasn't half bad, she decided. She picked out another piece. Nirvana roll she thought he'd said.

"So," he asked, "What do you think?"

"I like it." It was surprising. Sushi was so different than anything she had ever eaten. Her family's favorite place to eat—aside from their own restaurant—was a fast-food chicken place in Pryor. But they only ate there when they took someone to the doctor. Even then, *Mamm* would protest until Daniel joined in the persuasion. She always gave in to him.

"Now don't you feel bad for giving me that green poison?"

Lorie took another bite of the sushi and savored the many flavors bursting on her tongue. She acted like she was thinking about her answer. "No," she finally said.

Zach acted like he was mad.

Lorie laughed. How many times had she laughed since her father died? Once? Twice?

"You should laugh more often," Zach said, his eyes suddenly serious.

Lorie ducked her head. The moment between them quickly turned more intense than any one before.

"Sorry." He flashed her a sheepish grin. "It's just you're so pretty when you laugh."

He thought she was pretty? No one had ever said sweeter words to her before.

She would surely be cackling like a hen if she spent much more time with Zach. Being with him made her happier than she had ever been before.

The fact was frightening as well as thrilling all at the same time.

Lorie floated around all day Wednesday. Only one more day and she would see Zach again.

Despite the lightness in her heart, she had to control her giddiness. Word had gotten around the district that she and Jonah had called an end to their relationship. To appear too carefree would raise suspicions and send tongues to wagging. Nor would it show the conflicts in her heart. She loved Jonah, but it was hard to concentrate on those feelings with all the other things going on in her life. Had they already been married, their bond would have survived. But having to support their relationship, worry about joining the church, and deal with all the revelations this summer had brought . . . well, it was just too much.

She tripped around the restaurant, filling the napkin holders and trying to not appear as if she was falling in love. Because the person who filled her thoughts was not the man for her. "Lorie," Sadie called from the kitchen entrance. "Phone's for you."

Phone? She never had phone calls at the restaurant. Most everyone she knew was close enough to walk down and talk if they needed something. She hoped nothing was wrong with Caroline or the kids. Or Emily.

Flashbacks from the police calling to tell them that her father had been in an accident whizzed through her mind as she wound her way around the tables back to where her sister waited.

Sadie frowned, but Lorie couldn't tell if it was from confusion or consternation. Maybe it was sadness.

Her mouth went dry as she took the receiver and pressed it to her ear. "*Jah?*"

"Lorie?"

"Zach." She hadn't meant her voice to be so loud. "Zach?" she whispered.

Sadie's frown deepened.

"I'm sorry to call you at the restaurant. I hope that doesn't cause problems with your family."

She turned away from Sadie's hard stare. "No, it's fine. Is everything okay?" *Lord, please don't let it be Betty.*

"My car won't start. I took it to the shop. They think it's the alternator." He gave a small chuckle. "That doesn't mean anything to you, does it?"

"Not a thing."

"Don't feel bad. Most regular girls don't know what that

means either." He paused. "That didn't come out like I meant it. Not regular girls. Non-Amish, I mean."

"*Englisch,*" she supplied, hiding her smile.

"Oh, okay. Anyway, I won't be able to come get you. My mom needs her car, and my sister's husband is out of town."

"I didn't know you had a sister." Just one of the many things they never got around to talking about.

"Yeah. She's a lot older than me. Married, kid, the whole shebang. But I'm sorry about tomorrow. I was looking forward to seeing you."

She wasn't going to lie. "Me too."

"Hopefully, my car will be ready by next week. I wish I had another way to come get you."

A whole week without seeing Zach. She hated the idea. Maybe she could call Luke, and he would come get her and—"You can borrow my car."

"You have a car?"

"*Jah.* I mean, yeah. It was my *dat*'s."

"I don't know, Lorie."

"I do. It's the perfect idea. It's at my friend Luke's house. I'll call him and have him bring it to the living center."

"If you're sure . . ."

"I'm positive." She did her best to contain her smile, but she was just so happy. She was seeing Zach tomorrow and that was all that mattered.

He really wasn't sure about this.

Zach stood in front of the living center and waited for Lorie's friend Luke. He had the feeling this was the same guy he had seen her with that very first time she had come to Tulsa. She'd said they were only friends, yet he couldn't help but wonder.

He pushed that thought away. Like it mattered. Lorie and Luke could be long-lost lovers or really "just friends" and either way Zach's relationship with her would remain the same. Friends. Only friends.

A flash of light drew his attention to the turnoff for the center. An odd-looking orange car pulled in and drove toward him. A vintage Volkswagen Karmann Ghia. He loved those cars. Mainly because there weren't many of them around any longer. At least not around here.

The car putted toward him and parked in the first available space after the handicap spots. A dark-haired man got out and started toward him.

"Luke?" he asked.

He nodded. "Zach."

"I appreciate you bringing the car to me."

"Anything for Lorie."

He wasn't sure how to respond to that.

"There's a half tank of gas. That should get you through until your car is repaired."

Zach waited as Luke turned the keys over in his hand. A large letter *B* made up the decorative key ring. He briefly wondered if it stood for Betty, then thought he remembered someone saying that Lorie's mother's name was Belinda. "Do you need me to drop you off someplace?"

Luke shook his head. "There's my ride."

A pretty blond-haired girl pulled up in a brand-new Mustang convertible. Any doubts Zach had about the relationship between Luke and Lorie were laid to rest as the girl waggled her fingers toward the other man. Definitely something going on between the two of them.

Luke held up the keys. Zach reached out, but he didn't release them. "One more thing," Luke said. "Lorie is one of the nicest people I know. She's not used to guys like you. *Englisch buwe*. If you hurt her, I will find you."

"I—" He stopped, not sure what to say next. *There's nothing more than friendship between us. I wouldn't hurt her for anything in the world. She's too special to me.* But nothing sounded strong enough to convey his true feelings for Lorie. In another life, one where the both of them weren't from such different backgrounds, he'd do everything in his power to make her fall in love with him. Given half the chance, he thought she might return those feelings. But in reality they were just two people connected by a love of the seniors and a weird twist of fate. And that's all it could ever be without breaking the hearts of the people they loved the most.

Lorie smiled as she spotted the familiar orange car poking down the road toward the phone shanty. Luke hadn't hesitated when she asked him to take her father's car to Sundale and leave it for Zach. She'd have to remember to bring Luke up a big batch of his favorite cookies next time she visited.

She slung her bag of clothes over her shoulder and shut the shanty door behind her. She had to temper her smile at the sight of Zach driving her father's car. Or maybe it was Zach waiting for her that thrilled her so.

"Hey." She slid into the car next to him, the action as natural as breathing, though she didn't take the time to examine it.

"Hey." He smiled, and it nearly took her breath away. Maybe this friends thing wasn't such a good idea. But the thought of never hanging out with Zach again made her stomach drop into her lap.

He put the car in gear, and they were off.

"You want to listen to the radio?"

"Sure."

He flipped it on and tuned it to a station. Lorie liked the music. It was upbeat and catchy, but she didn't know anything about it, other than it was very different from the music at church.

Zach smiled and turned it up a notch more, singing along about a girl named Brandy. Lorie settled down in her seat and enjoyed the ride and watching him when he wasn't looking.

Once the song ended, he turned the music down. "I'm confused. Tell me why you have a car again."

Lorie recounted the tale. That it was her father's car. No one in the family knew about it except her stepmother, and Maddie preferred to pretend it didn't exist. "So you can drive it as long as you need to."

"That's a generous offer, but—"

"No buts," she said. "It's the least I can do. It's not like I know how to drive it or anything."

"What? You mean you don't know how to drive your own car?"

"It's not really mine. I mean, I guess it is now. Sort of. But it isn't like Amish kids are taught to drive."

"You could always learn."

She shook her head. "Don't you have to have a license for that?"

"So you get a license." He shrugged like it was the easiest thing to do.

Lorie shook her head. "In just a few weeks, my baptism classes will be over. "There's no sense doing all that to drive for like two days. Besides . . ."

"Besides what?" He glanced at her from the corner of his eye.

"I don't think the bishop would approve."

"Probably not."

But the bishop wouldn't approve of her running around Tulsa in *Englisch* clothes with an *Englisch bu* in her father's car. *Jah,* there would be a lot of questions to answer on that one. So many that having a driver's license might be over-looked in the mix. She shook her head to clear those thoughts.

"You could still learn to drive it. If you want. I mean, I could teach you."

"It doesn't require a special teacher?"

"Only if you don't have someone to teach you."

Learning to drive would be interesting. And what would

be the harm. She already owned the car. At least until Luke sold it for her. Plus, so many of the residents of Wells Landing knew how to drive a tractor and treated them like cars, putting around town with their rubber tires. "Did you have someone to teach you?"

"I went to Driver's Ed." He smiled in remembrance. "My mom tried to teach me, but she got too nervous with me behind the wheel."

"You're a great driver." At least she thought he was. He had gotten her all over the place without crashing.

"I wasn't always. But that's part of learning, I suppose."

"So what about your father. Did he not want to teach you?"

"No." He shook his head and changed lanes. Somehow Lorie got the impression that he was uncomfortable with the topic.

"You've never mentioned your dad."

"I don't want to talk about him, okay?"

"Okay," Lorie agreed, but she saw the flash of pain in his eyes as he spoke.

Chapter Sixteen

"I'm telling you no one uses these durned things anymore. I don't know why we're even making them." Stan pushed the wooden loom aside and wiped his forehead like he had been plowing a field instead of making a woven-yarn hot pad for the women at the domestic violence prevention center.

"That's not the point," Fern said.

"I know. I know. It's all about working the fingers."

"And helping those young girls get back on their feet," Linda reminded him.

"Some of them are men, you know." Betty stopped to count her stitches, then started knitting once again.

Lorie was glad to get to spend some time with her grandmother. Betty seemed to be having a good day. She was focused and well-spoken. Lorie hadn't even heard her say her standard "of course" more than once or twice since she and Zach had arrived.

Stan harrumphed, but didn't say anything. Lorie was grateful. Linda looked ready to give him a tongue lashing if he disputed the facts of their conversation.

Zach took over Stan's loom, helping him to finish winding the yarn. Then he tied the loose ends and clipped it from the frame. "There." He pulled the mat into place and showed it to Stan.

"It's lovely," Fern said.

"Very," Lorie agreed. Of course it didn't hurt that it was in her favorite shades of blue.

"Maybe you should keep it. At least I know it'll get used."

"That's sweet of you, I can't keep it. It's going to someone who needs it." Maybe they didn't need the actual item, but they needed to know that someone was thinking about them.

"Pah." Stan waved a hand around as if to erase her words from the air. "You've made one and that would be an extra. Put yours in the box and take mine with you."

The gesture warmed her heart. These seniors had become so important to her over the last few weeks. Not just Betty, but all of them—grumpy Stan and cantankerous Eugene. She would miss them terribly when she stopped coming here.

Why stop?

Why couldn't she come here even after she joined the church? What harm was there in visiting with her grandmother and helping the seniors with their craft projects? She enjoyed them and they seemed to like her just fine. Why did she have to choose between the church and them?

Zach.

How long could she pretend that every day she didn't like him more?

"Lorie?"

She shook herself from her thoughts, realizing that the others had put away their crafts and were preparing to go to lunch. "Sorry." She stood and made her way to where they waited.

It was the truth. Every day she liked Zach more. At this rate she would be completely in love with him before the end of the summer. And where would that leave her? Joining the church and living in Wells Landing while her heart was in Tulsa with Zach. How would she survive that?

"Are you coming, dear?" Betty asked.

Lorie nodded as they followed behind the others to the cafeteria.

"Oh, I do hope they have leprechaun pudding today. They haven't served it in forever."

Lunch consisted of roasted chicken with mashed potatoes and gravy, green beans, and salad, with red gelatin for dessert.

Lorie sat across from Zach and tried not to think about how handsome and sweet he was and how much she would miss him when she joined the church. She still had weeks to go before that happened. After that . . . well, she would deal with that when the time came.

"What are you doing?" Lorie asked, mouth open as she stared at Stan. He had tipped his dessert plate toward his mouth and was sucking the gelatin straight from it.

"I'm eating," he said around his mouthful.

"You shouldn't eat dessert before your meal." She hadn't meant to sound stern, but she couldn't imagine eating the sweets before the main foods. *Mamm* would not have stood for it.

"We're old. We always eat dessert first," Eugene boomed, scooping up his own dessert.

The others nodded.

They were just so sweet and honest, Lorie couldn't help but smile. Truly what was the problem with eating dessert first? Her heart warmed, and she smiled at Stan. "Next time I'll bring you one of Esther Lapp's buttermilk pies."

Stan's expression turned dreamy. "Yum. Buttermilk pie is my favorite."

"It'd surely be better than this." Linda took another bite of the gelatin.

"If they can serve this, I don't know why we can't have leprechaun pudding," Betty said.

"Maybe because it doesn't exist," Stan grumbled, his earlier happiness vanishing in an instant.

"I thought we went over this." Fern shot him a stern look. "Just because you don't know what it is doesn't mean it doesn't exist."

"Maybe we could help you get some if you would tell us what it is." Zach looked to Betty and lifted a fork loaded with mashed potatoes. "What about these?"

She shook her head. "Mashed potatoes? Why on earth would mashed potatoes be leprechaun pudding?"

"Potatoes . . . Irish . . . leprechauns." He shrugged.

"I'm sorry, dear, but that's just plain silly."

"I'll tell you what's silly," Stan started. "Ow." He frowned at Linda who shot him an innocent look.

Lorie suspected she had kicked him under the table. "Maybe if you would tell us what it is, we'd have an easier time finding it for you."

Betty turned clear blue eyes to her. "You don't know? Why, dear, you were the one who named it that."

"Me?"

Her grandmother nodded. "Yes, indeed. That means you already know what it is. Now all you have to do is remember."

The conversation around her turned to other things, but Lorie was stuck on Betty's last words. She had named leprechaun pudding? But how was that possible? She must have been three or four at the time. How was she supposed to remember something from twenty years ago when she was just a toddler?

Everyone finished their lunch and started planning out their afternoon.

"Are you ready to go?" Zach asked.

Betty and the women were gathering in Linda's room to watch *The Price Is Right* while the men decided to take naps.

"Yeah, sure."

Together, the group walked back through the hallways. Each went to their own rooms.

"Will you come back next week?" Betty asked Lorie.

She looked to Zach who gave a quick nod. "Of course I will." She hated relying on him to come get her, but she enjoyed the time she spent with him and with the seniors. And he didn't seem to mind. "I'll see you then." She leaned in and gave her grandmother a quick hug, then pulled away with tears stinging the back of her eyes. What was wrong with her? She had been so emotional lately. She supposed that was to be expected, but the Amish didn't show so much emotion in public.

She turned away, but Betty caught her arm before she could leave. "Lorie, dear. You know that your father was a good man. Remember that about him."

Was Betty having a clear moment when the past and present separated and she knew who was president and what day it was? "I will."

"Don't just say that to humor an old woman. I know sometimes I say crazy things." She chuckled. "But right now I'm telling you the honest truth. The things your father did . . . it was only because he loved you. He wasn't trying to cause you pain or give you doubts. He only wanted to protect you."

Hadn't she said something very similar a few short weeks ago? "Protect me from what?"

Betty shook her head. "You haven't read the letters."

"No." She had only read a dozen or so of them and quit. Her pain had been too raw so close after her father's death, and she'd started to doubt she would find anything of use. Or maybe she had started to worry that whatever she discovered, her view of her father would be changed forever. She would rather remember him laughing and cooking, enjoying his life and his family rather than sneaking away to Tulsa and living a life no one else in the family knew about.

"You need to. It's important you hear this from him. You read the letters and I'll answer your questions then, okay?"

"Okay."

"What do you suppose she meant by that?" Zach asked as they headed down the highway toward Wells Landing.

"I don't know. Do you think her mind was clear?"

"It seemed so to me, but sometimes it's hard to tell."

They rode in silence a while before Zach spoke again. "Are you going to read the rest of the letters?"

"I suppose I have to if I want to know the truth."

"Or you can just let it go and not worry about it."

That was, as the *Englisch* said, *easier said than done.* "I can't. I wish I could, but I just can't."

"I understand." He didn't take his eyes from the road, but his jaw tightened as if he was clenching his teeth.

"Does this have something to do with your *dat?*"

"I really don't want to talk about him."

The edge in his voice made her drop the subject quick. But he had helped her so much. She just wanted to do the same for him. "Yeah, okay. But if you ever change your mind."

His fingers tightened on the steering wheel, but otherwise his demeanor remained the same. "Thanks," he said. "But I won't."

Zach breathed a small sigh of relief that she dropped the subject of his dad without further comment. He supposed she understood better than most how the secrets a person kept could ruin the lives of everyone around them. And his father had secrets. Oh, boy, did that man have secrets. Another woman, two children, and an apartment in the south side. But what hurt the most was when all was said and done, his father chose his other family over Zach and his mom. Lorie didn't know how good she had it. As far as secrets went, Henry Mathis/Kauffman's were tame in comparison.

"Can we listen to the radio again?" Lorie asked.

"Sure." He showed her how to turn the knob to find a different station. The car was old, before the push buttons, preset stations, and cassette players.

She fiddled with the knob, turning over some pretty good songs, but he wanted her to pick what she liked. He'd have the radio all the way back home, but once she got out of the car, she was faced with a life without music. He didn't know how she could stand it.

"Is there anything by the Rolling Stones on here?"

"Maybe. Wait. How do you know about the Rolling Stones?"

She shrugged. "A friend of mine said he liked them."

"Luke?"

"No. Merv King. He's the coffin maker for the district."

"I see." He didn't. He'd never given much thought to coffins, Amish or otherwise. "How does he hear them?"

"He has one of those music players with the things you put in your ears."

He smiled, thinking of an Amish man, full-on beard, listening to the Rolling Stones. Yessiree, the Amish were much different than he'd originally thought. "Isn't that against the rules?"

"Yeah, but sometimes . . ."

He waited for her to continue.

"Sometimes it's a dumb rule and needs to be broken." She slapped a hand over her mouth and turned pink from her fingers up. "I didn't say that."

"Oh, yeah you did," he teased.

"I think you're having a bad influence on me."

He couldn't tell from her tone whether she was joking or serious. He took a chance to study her face for a minute. Kidding, he decided. But he wanted to give her a real answer. "Maybe, but you're definitely having a good influence on me."

Friday brought another busload of tourists into Wells Landing that made Saturday's business look pitiful. Lorie was both thankful and resentful of the distraction. She wanted to climb up into the storeroom and get out the box of letters that Betty had given her. But she knew once she did, she would want to paint a little as well. She had managed to squelch that desire for almost two weeks, but she knew eventually that it would overtake her. It always did.

But for now, she settled herself to the mindless task of her restaurant chores—filling up the ice bins, rolling silverware, and cleaning the waitress station. Lorie was wiping down the counter when *Mamm* approached.

She frowned at the string tied around her wrist. Like Jonah, she preferred to pretend it wasn't there, but Lorie knew it was bothering her all the same.

"You will not wear that to church," Maddie said during a lull in Saturday's diners.

"I don't see anything wrong with it." She tried to keep her voice steady and even, but she could hear the edge of defiance in it.

Mamm's frown deepened. "You are attending classes. You'd best keep that in mind. I'm sure you wouldn't want the embarrassment of your vote not being approved."

"No. *Nay.* Of course not," she murmured, instantly regretting her tone. It was the last thing she wanted. But she remembered the look on Zach's face when he tied the string to her wrist. She knew it was silly, but she wanted to wear it until it fell off. She wanted to make that wish and see if it came true.

But if she took it off, all that would be nothing but words. She wouldn't. It was as simple as that. She would wrap a bandage around her arm and say that one of the chickens pecked her when she went out to gather eggs. Or that she'd burned her arm on the fryer.

She shook away the little voice that said she was being deceitful and concentrated on the absurd rules that the Amish made up. It was a piece of string. Not gold or pearls. She wasn't wearing it in vanity. The whole thing was ridiculous.

Mamm moved away satisfied that she had done her duty in keeping Lorie on the straight and narrow path to baptism. Sadie sidled up with a tray holding three iced teas. "Can you take these to table four for me? I've got to go to the bathroom."

"Too much water at lunch?"

"*Jah.*" Sadie nodded, her prayer *kapp* strings dancing across her shoulders.

Lorie would take the drinks to the table, then she would take a little break. She deserved it. And maybe if she went to the storeroom when she knew she had to get back to work, she could resist the urge to paint.

It was another hour before Lorie managed to slip away from the restaurant and up to the storeroom. She didn't have much left on her shift, but she had to take the opportunity when she had it.

The storeroom was a little warm so she removed her apron and fanned herself with a piece of cardboard from one of the boxes.

Lord, please let this answer my questions. Let Betty be right about my dat. *Amen.*

It wasn't a lot to ask. Her faith in her father had been bruised, but not destroyed. He was gone now, and she would love to have that confidence back. The confidence that Betty had when she told Lorie that her father was a good man.

She did her best to ignore the call of her paintings and instead sat cross-legged on the floor next to the box of letters.

The first one she pulled out must have been written long after her father married Maddie. He talked about Cora Ann as a baby and even sent a picture of her sweet, toothless grin.

The following four or five that she read were along the same lines, just a letter to catch Betty up on all that she had missed not being in their lives. But why had her father separated the two parts of his family? What would make him take the people that he loved the most and push them far from each other?

Betty said her father was a good man, and she was holding on to that with everything she had.

Dear Mom—

I hope this letter finds you well. I would just call, but I'm not sure how far spread the power of the Prescotts extends. I may be a bit paranoid, but I can't allow them to know my plans.

The attorneys have advised me against this, but I don't know what else to do. I don't stand a chance against Belinda's parents. They have too much wealth and power, and I am quickly running out of money to fight them. I don't even know why they want Lorie so bad. They never come to see her, haven't seen her even once since she was born. But I guess they think she can replace Belinda in their lives. I shudder to think what they would turn her into. She's a loving, sweet child. In their hands, she would come out like the rest of B's family. How Belinda escaped being a narcissistic basket case is anybody's guess.

I won't tell you when or where I'm going. That way if anyone asks, you can honestly say you don't know.

Don't worry yourself. I made sure your bills and everything are paid up until the end of the year.

*Surely by then I can get the two of us settled. With
any luck and God on our side, the Prescotts will give
up and leave us alone.*

Your loving son,
Hank

Her mother's parents had wanted her? Did that mean they
were planning on taking her away from her father? She
checked the date on the letter. She would have been three
then. It was June, which meant her mother could have only
been gone for six months or less. How could anyone want to
take a child from their remaining parent so soon after the
other's death? She couldn't wrap her mind around it. A
strange feeling stole over her, and her skin started to itch.
What kind of family did her mother have?

She folded the letter and slipped it back into its envelope.

Suddenly she was more uncomfortable than she had ever
been. Her head was sweating, and she thought she might be
sick. Her hair was pulled too tight against her scalp. She
couldn't take it any longer. She took off her prayer *kapp*
and set it to one side, then released the pins securing her hair.
The feel of the tresses tumbling down her back was like the
taste of freedom.

She breathed a quick sigh of relief and reached for the
next letter. She still had so many unanswered questions. So
many things that she still didn't know. Did this mean her
father only turned Amish to hide out from her mother's
family? Is that what everyone meant when they said he just
did it to protect her?

The next letter she unfolded shed no more light on these
mysteries as she scanned the words he had written. He talked
of Daniel and his love for his only son. This was surely what
her grandmother meant when she said he was a good man.
Everything Henry Kauffman did, he did in love. In love for
her and the rest of his family.

But if he wasn't Amish then when did he convert? When had he said his vows in front of the church and God? And why hadn't Maddie mentioned it before? Why had her father never mentioned it? Something like that wouldn't have been a secret. Or maybe it *shouldn't* have been a secret.

Lorie took out another letter and started to read.

Dear Mom,

Well, we did it. We've moved into hiding I guess you could say. But that sounds so much like a bad spy movie. I've got Lorie with me and she's safe. That has been my goal all along. I know eventually the Prescotts will grow bored with the search and another pet project will take the place of them wanting Lorie. We'll just have to wait it out. I won't tell you exactly where we are. Not yet anyway. But I will say that we are in a small town, the kind of place where everybody knows everyone else. This will be the perfect place to allow Lorie to grow up untainted by the wealth that nearly destroyed Belinda. I am so grateful to God for leading us here. We've started to go to church and do our best to become a part of the community. You would love it here. The air is fresh and clean, and you can see a billion stars at night.

But for now, I know this way is best. Soon, I'll bring you here, and you can live with us. I know you would be happy here, just as we are. I can't wait for that day.

Your loving son,
Hank

He didn't name the town nor did he say anything specific that would identify the place, but it sure sounded like Wells Landing. But when he talked about church was he talking about the Amish or someplace else? There was no way of knowing. He could have been anywhere in eastern Oklahoma. The area was dotted with tiny towns like Wells Landing.

Yet one thing was certain. He had moved wherever to protect her, and she couldn't find fault in that.

She reached for another letter.

My Dearest Mother,

It broke my heart nearly in two when I got the call about your stroke. The doctors tell me it's a mild one and that you should recover nicely, though you might have some memory loss and problems in the future. I am grateful that you are so strong. But I regret that I have not been to see you in the last year.

Lorie stopped reading and checked the date. It was over a year since the one she read before. He had moved to the small country town and then kept himself in town instead of going to Tulsa to visit with his mother. Why?

I have been courting a woman here. (How old-fashioned does that sound?) I think I'm going to ask her to marry me. I know, it may seem sort of sudden, but she is a fine woman. She has a daughter who is just a couple of years younger than Lorie. We get along well, and I think we could have a good marriage. In the years to come, Lorie will need a mother and Sadie (that's her daughter's name) will need a father.

I hadn't meant to stay here this long, but I love the gentle ways of the Amish. I love the rituals and beliefs. The slow pace of their everyday life. Though I have to say that the restaurant business isn't always as easygoing as some of the other jobs here in town. I'm even getting used to my beard.

*I had wanted to bring you here to live with us, but
I can see that you would be better off where you are
right now. Maybe after you are back on your feet. My
main concern is your health and Lorie's happiness. I
trust in the Lord that if those two things are secured,
then everything else will fall into place.*

*I will try to come see you soon. It's hard to get
away, and I know that you need lots of rest. But know
that I am thinking about you and praying that you
will have a speedy recovery. Remember with God all
things are possible.*

> *Your loving son,*
> *Hank*

If she had any doubts before, they were gone now. Her
father had moved to an Amish community and just became
one of the residents.

She supposed that was entirely possible. The Amish were
a very trusting people. They wouldn't question a man and
small daughter who came to live among them. Just look at
what happened with Caroline and Emma. She had just shown
up one day alone and pregnant. The residents of Wells Landing had taken her in and treated her like one of their own.
They had assumed she was a widow and from there Caroline's secret began. Why would they not accept two other
wandering souls into their midst?

But her father had moved here from Tulsa. That meant he
was *Englisch*. And if he was *Englisch*, what did that make
Lorie?

Really, really confused.

Chapter Seventeen

Lorie awoke with a start surprised that she had been asleep. Her heart pounded in her chest as she looked around at her strange surroundings. She wasn't at home in her bed, but lying on the floor in a room. The storeroom. It started coming back to her. She was in the storeroom above the restaurant. She had come up here to read some of the letters that her father had sent to her grandmother. Her father was really *Englisch* and had only been pretending to be Amish all of these years.

She pushed herself into a sitting position and struggled to wipe the cobwebs from her brain. She must have fallen asleep.

Soon it would be time to open the restaurant. No, not today. Today was Sunday. Soon it would be time for church.

Church!

She was awake in an instant. She had to get out of here and home. It was morning time, that much was certain, but how late was anybody's guess. She had to get home and pray all the way there that she hadn't missed any of the service. But given the bright light pounding through the windows she was already too late.

She pushed to her feet, scooping the letters together and

stuffing them back into the box as she stood. She had to get home. She had to get to church. She had to get dressed.

She wrapped her apron around her waist and haphazardly tied it in the back. But there was nothing she could do about her hair. The pins she had removed the night before were nowhere to be seen. Her only choice was to grab her prayer *kapp* and get out of there as quickly as she could.

The sun was bright and high in the sky when she tripped down the stairs. She didn't wear a watch, but it was late. Really, really late. And there was no excuse for her tardiness. How could she explain why she missed church? Her baptism classes.

She dropped onto the bottom step, her head in her hands. She might be able to explain away why she was late for church and wasn't wearing her prayer *kapp,* but there was no excuse for missing her baptism class.

Slowly, she pushed herself to her feet. There was no sense in hurrying now. The damage was done. Dejected and dreading what was to come, she started toward home.

She was sitting at the table when everyone arrived back home from church. She'd had enough time to walk all the way home, change her clothes, and pull her hair back before they arrived back. She felt a little better now that her prayer *kapp* was in place once again. But she knew it was a false sense of security.

Her sisters were laughing and talking as they came into the house, but all joy ceased the minute they saw her there.

"Sadie, take Daniel upstairs and help him change his clothes."

"But—"

"Now, Sadie."

Her sister took Daniel by the hand and led him toward the stairs. He looked back at her, his eyes sad behind his wire-rimmed glasses. Lorie shot him a reassuring smile. He returned it, but in that moment between them, they both knew. Life would not be the same.

"Let's go check on the kittens." Melanie took Cora Ann by the arm and led her toward the front door.

Mamm's steady gaze never wavered from Lorie. A reckoning was near.

Then they were alone.

Maddie continued to look at her. Just look at her.

"I'm sorry," Lorie finally said. The words sounded hollow and couldn't hold the meaning she felt in her heart.

"I don't know what to say, Lorie." *Mamm* crossed her arms and took a deep breath. Lorie hated the pain and disappointment on her stepmother's face. "What was so important that you didn't come home last night? That you missed church and your baptism class this morning?"

How could she explain? How could she make *Mamm* understand without revealing all her lies? All the deceptions, trips to Tulsa. Her paintings. The letters. Everything would come out. What was the use in spreading all that pain around? "I'd rather not say." It would only bring more disappointment, more hurt, and more heartache.

For a moment she thought *Mamm* might completely lose her composure. She recovered, though her cheeks were stained red from her suppressed emotions. "You'd rather not say?" The words were cold, hard, and flat.

"I don't think you would understand." It was the gentlest way she could say it.

"Is this about the tattoo?"

"I can't believe that it means so little to you."

"Maybe you are the one who doesn't understand." *Mamm* pulled out the chair opposite Lorie and sat down. Or rather collapsed into it as if her legs couldn't hold her up any longer.

"Then tell me," Lorie begged.

She took a deep breath. "When I met your father, he was

the greatest man I had ever known. Funny, smart, and a hard worker. I was just coming out of mourning and trying to raise Sadie all on my own." She twisted her hands together on the tabletop and stared at her fingers as if they held all the answers. "I was thrilled when he showed an interest in me. Then on our wedding night . . . well, I saw the tattoo."

"Did he explain it to you?"

"He told me he got it on his *rumspringa*."

"So you just let it go?"

"I chose to not pursue an answer."

Lorie started to protest, but *Mamm* continued.

"What good would it do? We were already married. It was my duty as his wife to believe him. You have to let this go, Lorie. I'll talk to the bishop, try to explain why you missed the class. Maybe he'll have mercy on you and give you the instruction himself. But you have to let this drop."

"I can't promise that." Tears stung her eyes and scalded her cheeks as they slid down her face. There was still so much she hadn't found out. Like what leprechaun pudding really was and if her mother's family was as bad as her father had thought.

Her mother's family. She had an entire side to her family tree that she had never met before. She had never even thought about it. But of course her mother came from somewhere. That meant a grandmother, a grandfather, maybe even aunts and uncles, cousins and more. Lorie deserved the chance to meet them, get to know them.

"You have no choice." Once again *Mamm*'s voice grew hard and stern, a sure sign she wasn't backing down. "You will either let this go, or you will not remain here."

"What?"

"If you are going to continue this investigation, or whatever you want to call it, then you cannot live here."

"I just want to know the truth."

"And we are just trying to move forward. You are upsetting

the other children. You are either a part of this family or not. You have to choose."

"When?"

"Now."

Her breath caught in her throat. Her heart stopped. How could she choose? This was the exact reason why she had kept everything a secret. To Maddie Kauffman it was all cut and dried, black and white. There was no space in between. But that space was where she now lived. "I won't choose."

"Then you will leave. And never come back."

Zach pulled his phone from his pocket and checked the caller ID. Lorie. He hadn't expected to talk to her today. What a great surprise. "Hello?"

"Zach?" Her voice was thick and rusty like she had been crying.

"Are you okay?"

"No," she sobbed. "I'm not. I"—she hiccupped—"have to leave."

He sat down on the couch just as his sister walked back into the room. He had come to visit her after church and now this.

"Who is it?" Ashtyn asked.

He held up a hand to stay her words and turned his attention back to Lorie. "Leave? What do you mean leave?"

"Can you come get me?"

"Of course." He stood.

"Who is it?" Ashtyn asked again.

He shushed her. Then to Lorie he said, "I'll be right there."

"Thank you." On the other end of the line he heard her breath catch on another sob. "I'm going to the restaurant to get a couple of things. Can you meet me there?"

"I'll be there in twenty minutes."

"It may take me longer than that to get there."

"I'll wait for you."

"Okay. Bye." And then she was gone.

Zach ended the call and shoved his phone back into his pocket.

"Who was that?"

"Lorie." He didn't have time to explain or debate, discuss, or even lightly talk about this. Lorie needed him, and he had to get to her.

"Your Amish girlfriend?"

"She's not my girlfriend." He said the words, but they tasted bitter on his tongue. As much as they were the truth, he hated them all the more because of it.

"Uh-huh. You've been driving her car for the last three days."

"That doesn't mean anything."

"Whatever." His sister rolled her eyes. "I see how your face lights up when you talk about her."

That might be true, but it didn't push their relationship into the we-can-work-this-out category. So much stood in their way, things that could never be brought to terms. "I'm going to get her. Find out what's happened."

"Is she okay?"

"I think so." But he hated hearing her cry. It broke his heart as if he were the one responsible.

Ashtyn nodded, then kissed his cheek. "Be careful. And bring her by if you have a minute, I would love to meet her."

He nodded, though he had no intentions of bringing Lorie to Ashtyn's house. He would never hear the end of it from his only sibling.

Zach palmed his keys and headed out the door.

Lorie moved farther onto the side of the road when she heard the sound of a horse and buggy coming up behind her.

She had gotten her clothes from their hiding place in their

barn, then stopped at the phone shanty only long enough to call Zach. She had left the house without saying good-bye to any of her siblings. She couldn't. Especially not Daniel. She didn't want to have to explain why she was leaving. Or how their mother had made her choose between the two separate parts of her life. It was better to just leave. Or at least that's what she kept telling herself.

Her tears had dried up, no longer did they fall so freely. Zach's vow to wait for her was like a bandage to her heart. The last person she had met in her life was the one willing to stand by her side. She wasn't walking away from her family. She was walking toward him.

"Lorie!" Sadie called over the rattle of the rig. "Where are you going?"

She shook her head and kept walking. There was no explanation that wouldn't bring them all more pain.

But Sadie was persistent. She pulled the buggy ahead of her and stopped in the road, blocking Lorie's path. She hopped down and rushed toward her. "What is going on? *Mamm* won't talk, but is slamming around the house. All she would say was that you were gone. What does that mean, gone?"

"I'm leaving." She moved to go around her sister, but Sadie was fast and sidestepped in front of her once again.

"Does this have anything to do with you missing church?"

"Don't get involved, Sadie. Just let it go."

"I am involved, and I can't let it go. You're my sister. And I love you."

Lorie stumbled, her stiff disposition crumbling a bit before she pulled herself back together. She moved around Sadie, and this time her sister let her go.

"Where are you going?" Sadie called after her. Footsteps sounded behind her as Sadie followed.

"I told Zach I would meet him at the restaurant."

"Zach?" Sadie got ahead of her once again, stopping and blocking her path. "The *Englisch bu?*"

"Yes."

Sadie's expression dissolved into pure hurt. "You said you weren't seeing him any longer. You promised."

"I lied." Her words were stiff and callous, and she hated them. But at least they were the truth. She had been lying to herself and her family for so long, at least now she was telling the truth.

Sadie grabbed both of her arms and stopped her in her tracks. "I don't understand, and I'm not going to pretend I do. But above everything else, you are my sister. Get in the buggy, and I'll take you into town."

Lorie wanted to protest, keep marching down the road, but she was hot and tired. Her tears had drained a lot of her energy. She wanted nothing more than to sit down on the roadside and talk to her sister. Just talk before she had to leave and never see her again. *Mamm* had been clear about that. It was all or nothing. Lorie could live by neither.

But her pride kept her going.

"Please, Lorie."

She stopped. What harm would there be in riding into town with her sister? What foul in enjoying her company one more time? "Okay."

Sadie wilted in relief, then led her back to the buggy.

In silence, they climbed on board and started for the restaurant.

"You could change your mind, you know," Sadie said a few minutes later when they pulled in front of the restaurant. Like many of the businesses in town it was closed on Sundays, preferring to uphold their religious beliefs and not bow to the demands of the tourist trade.

Lorie shook her head. "I can't." Too many hurtful words had been said. Too many secrets had been kept. How could she pretend now that she didn't know they existed? Was this what Caroline and Emily had warned her about? Could all of this heartache been avoided?

Suddenly she was angry with her father. If he had never held these secrets to begin with, then none of this would have happened. But he had, and there was no going back.

"Thanks for the ride, Sadie. Now go home." She started up the stairs that led to the storage room. She had to get the letters to take with her. There were a few more left in the box that she hadn't read. Maybe they would give her more insight into her father's thoughts. Maybe they would take away this anger she now felt toward him.

"Lorie." Sadie tied the horse to the hitching post and ran up the stairs behind her. "Please."

But she had to see this through. She didn't want to leave and never see her brother and sisters again. But she didn't want to stay and pretend that nothing had happened, that her father hadn't lied to them all for twenty years or more. It was something she just couldn't do.

She let herself into the storeroom and wound her way through the supplies until she reached the little area she had pared out for herself. She wanted to take her painting supplies but she wasn't sure if they would fit into the car. She could take her box of paints, the box of letters, and a few of her completed works. Her easel and the rest of her paintings would have to stay for another day, if she ever came back for them at all.

"What are all these?" Sadie stared at the canvases like she had never seen anything like them before.

"Paintings."

"But where did they come from?"

"I painted them."

"You?" The one word was whispered and incredulous, like

the entire concept was more than Sadie could comprehend. "You've been painting. A lot."

Lorie stacked the paintings to one side and gathered up the rest of her things. It would take several trips to get everything downstairs. What did she have now but time? She pushed past Sadie and trudged down the stairs.

Zach still hadn't made it to the restaurant. Lorie stacked her possessions to one side of the buggy. She left her bag of clothes beside the box of paints and headed back up the stairs.

Sadie was standing right where she left her, gaze still holding on the brightly colored paintings. "I don't understand."

She tried to harden her heart. Not for her sake, but for her sister's. What good would it do to tell all of her father's secrets but to damage how Sadie forever viewed the only man she knew as a *dat?* But she couldn't stand the lost expression on her sister's face. She supposed that was how she had looked when she had first seen the tattoo. When she had looked into the box the police had brought to them. The box of her father's possessions.

"*Dat* wasn't Amish." There was no sugarcoating this one.

"Wh-what do you mean?"

"I mean he was *Englisch.* When he moved here, he was *Englisch,* and he only pretended to be Amish to hide me from my mother's family."

Sadie shook her head. "That can't be true. I saw him. I saw him pray and dress like an Amish man. I saw him live every day as an Amish man."

But did that truly make him Amish?

Lorie shook her head. "I only know what I know."

Sadie slumped against one of the boxes and watched as Lorie continued to sort through the paintings. One part of her wanted to take them all while another wanted to just walk away.

She grabbed the first five on the top and started for the door. She had to get out before she lost her nerve.

"Lorie, please." Sadie stirred herself and stumbled behind her toward the door. "Lorie."

"I've got to go, Sadie. I don't expect you to understand."

"Lorie."

"What's going on here?" Zach stood just outside of the storeroom on the tiny landing. "Lorie?"

She managed not to let her tears fall as she saw him. "Here." She thrust the paintings into his hands and brushed past him and down the stairs.

He followed behind her as Sadie sat down on the top step of the stairs. Lorie refused to break as her sister lowered her head into her hands. Sobs shook her shoulders. Lorie had to be strong for all of them.

"Lorie?" Zach loaded the paintings into the trunk of her father's car.

She slid into the passenger's seat and closed her eyes against the maelstrom of emotions. "Please," she whispered. "Just get me out of here."

Chapter Eighteen

They drove in silence for most of the trip back to Tulsa.

"Do you want to talk about it?" Zach asked as they sped along. She had been sitting there, head back, eyes closed. So quiet he was starting to worry.

He never once thought to question why she had called him and what had happened. She needed him, and he was there.

"Not yet," she whispered. "Maybe when we stop."

"Okay," he returned. Though he had no idea where they would stop. He hadn't given the where a second thought as he loaded her possessions into the little orange car and sped off while her sister sat on the steps and sobbed. Something bad had happened. He just didn't know what. Lorie needed him. It was enough for now.

He would take her home. His mother could help them. Whatever Lorie had gotten herself into, his mother could help. She could think clearly while they were too close to see a solution.

He didn't say anything more as he maneuvered the Tulsa streets. He had a gut feeling that Lorie was fighting demons in her own mind. That required silence to accomplish.

Fifteen minutes later, he pulled the Ghia into his drive and cut the engine.

"We're here."

She turned her head toward him and opened her eyes. "Thank you," she whispered.

Then to his dismay, her brown eyes filled with tears.

"Don't cry." It had been hard enough to hear her sobs through the phone lines, but in person, it was almost more than he could bear.

But her tears kept coming.

He wrapped his arms around her as tightly as the console between them would allow. She was warm and soft and so very sad.

He just held her, giving her time to cry it out. There would be a time for talking later. She could tell him what happened then. Right now, it was all about her and the comfort she needed.

After several minutes of holding her close, she sniffed and pulled away. She let out a teary chuckle. "I got you all wet."

He looked down. The front of his shirt was damp. "No worries," he said. "Are you ready to go in?"

"Is there anyone else here?"

"My mom might be home by now. Are you up for that?"

"I guess I have to be. We're here, aren't we?"

"We can sit here as long as you like. Or go somewhere else." He had no idea where.

"Thank you," she said with a smile, but reached for the door handle and got out of the car.

Zach followed suit, leaving all her things in the car for later. It wasn't like they were going anyplace. And he didn't know what Lorie's plans were or even if she had any.

She reached into the backseat and grabbed a familiar canvas bag. He had seen it enough to know that it held her English clothes. Evidently she was staying for a while.

Together they walked to the front door. He used his key and let himself in. "Mom?" he called, tossing his keys onto the table by the door. "Mom?"

"In here," she returned from the kitchen. "Did you have a nice visit with Ashtyn?"

"Yeah." He stood there, not really sure how to respond. How did a guy tell his mother that he'd brought an Amish girl home? He was saved having to find an answer.

His mother came out of the kitchen, wiping her hands on a dishtowel. "I'm glad I—hi."

"Mom, you remember Lorie. She's Betty's granddaughter."

His mother didn't miss a beat, though he could tell that another place setting for supper was the last thing she had expected. "Yes, of course. How are you, Lorie?"

"Fine, thank you." Though her red-rimmed eyes and tear-stained face belied her words.

His mother's eyes asked questions he had no answers for. But maybe they could work through it later. "Uh, Lorie, would you like to change clothes? Or take a shower?" he asked.

She swung those big brown eyes toward him. "What?"

"If you want to freshen up or whatever . . ."

She glanced from him to his mother and back again. "Okay. *Jah*. Yes. Okay."

She had to be in some sort of shock. He just wished he knew more about what happened. His mother wanted answers as well, and he sure wouldn't be able to give them to her. They would just have to wait until Lorie was ready to talk.

Lorie stepped from the shower feeling a little refreshed though still emotionally bruised. Life could change in an instant, she had quickly learned. Her life had taken several of those changes in the last couple of months.

She toweled herself dry and wiped the steam from the mirror. She barely recognized the face staring back at her. The skin under her eyes was purple. Her hair hung damp and lank around her face. Everything she had loved had been taken away, but the same brown eyes stared balefully back at her.

She finished her toiletries and pulled on her clothes, then started combing the tangles from her hair. Halfway through, she cracked open the bathroom door.

Voices floated in to her from the living room.

"You don't want her here?"

"Zachary Wayne. That is not what I said, and you know it. But she doesn't belong here."

She heard Zach scoff. "Do any of us belong here?"

"I knew I should have never let you take philosophy."

"Really, Mother, she has as much right as anyone else to happiness and a good life."

"So you're saying she didn't have a good life with the Amish?"

"Ugh! Would you stop putting words in my mouth?" Zach growled, sounding so much like the cranky dog at Merv King's house that it brought a smile to her face. Even if they were talking about her like she was a lost kitten. "She left. That's all I know. I don't know for how long or why. But I do know that if she wanted to get out of there, then she deserves the chance."

"I'm just afraid—"

"That I'll get hurt. I know. I know. But this isn't about me. It's about her."

Lorie's heart soared in her chest. Of all the people she had met, Zach understood better than anyone, *Englisch* or Amish.

"I hope you know what you're doing." His mother sighed.

"I do." His words were so confident, they made her feel like everything was going to be just fine.

Oh, how she prayed that it was.

Dinner was ready by the time Lorie stepped from the

bathroom. Zach and his mother must have been talking while she cooked.

"Let's eat," Mrs. Calhoun said. "Then we can talk."

"If you want to," Zach added.

His mother shot him a look so familiar Lorie almost laughed. Almost.

"We can talk then, yes," Lori replied.

Zach had driven out to Wells Landing to get her right after she had called. His mother had taken her in and was about to feed her like one of her own. The least Lorie could do would be to explain what had happened.

Everyone gathered around the table. Zach's mother said a quick prayer thanking God for their food and the beautiful day. Lorie hated saying a prayer without her head covered, but she was in a different world now. Surely God would understand. So she said an extra prayer for wisdom and courage to get her through the coming days and for forgiveness for praying with her head bare. She hoped the prayers reached their destination.

"Do you want to tell me what's going on before we have to face the firing squad?" Zach asked, handing Lorie a rinsed plate to load into the dishwashing machine. It was smaller, but not too terribly different than the one they had at the restaurant. It didn't take her long to figure out the proper way to load it.

"I overslept this morning."

He shrugged, clearly not understanding the seriousness of what she had told him.

"I went up to the storeroom—"

"Where you were today?"

"Yes. I put the letters that Betty gave me up there."

"And a few other things as well." He was obviously talking about her paintings.

"I went up to the storeroom last night," she started again. "But I fell asleep there, and when I woke up, I had missed church."

He made a commiserating face.

"And my baptism class."

"I take it this is not a good thing."

She shook her head. "It is not done. And certainly not because a person fell asleep while reading letters her possibly *Englisch* father sent her definitely *Englisch* grandmother."

"I get it. Go on."

"I woke up and walked home."

"You walked to your house all the way from the restaurant?"

"I had no other way to get home."

He nodded, but didn't interrupt again.

"When my family arrived back home from church . . . my *mamm* told me that I had to give up trying to find out the truth or leave."

"So you left." It was almost a question.

She shook her head, not in answer but to try to clear her thoughts. It did not work. "I didn't know what to do, but I can't give up reading the letters and learning the truth about my father. The things I read last night . . ." Again she shook her head. "There's so much. So many questions. Every time I read another letter, I have more and more questions."

"Then you deserve more and more answers." He said it so simply she wanted to trust his word, but she had walked away from everything she knew. She was having trouble believing she deserved anything at all. "Hey." He touched the back of his fingers to the side of her face and trailed them across her cheek. She closed her eyes against the tingles the feel of his skin on hers produced. "You'll get through this."

She opened her eyes and looked into his. "Will I? Everything I've known is gone."

He grabbed her hand and led her through to the living room. His mother was waiting there, sitting in an armchair, flipping through a magazine like she didn't have a care in the world.

Zach walked her over to the sofa and sat down beside Lorie. Strange, but she almost felt as if they were a team. The two of them against the world.

Mrs. Calhoun shut her magazine and set it to one side. She turned kind eyes toward Lorie. "Would you like to tell us what happened today?"

Zach took Lorie's hand into his own, lacing their fingers together as he spoke. "Lorie had a disagreement with her family and can't go home."

A frown wrinkled Mrs. Calhoun's smooth brow. "Zach, I'm not going to stand on ceremony here. Tell me what happened, and what we do from here."

He started to speak again, but Lorie stopped him, laying her other hand on top of their intertwined fingers. "I can't go home," she started, then recounted the story to Zach's mother. When she was done, she stopped and waited for Mrs. Calhoun's response.

"What do we do now?" she asked, looking from one to the other.

"I don't know," Zach said. "I was hoping that you would have some ideas."

"Well, it's pretty obvious that she can't stay here." She nodded toward their clasped hands. Lorie tried to pull away but Zach refused to let her go.

"Are you saying that you don't trust us?" Zach asked.

Lorie's cheeks flamed hot enough she was sure her hair was singed.

"I'm saying that there's no need to expose yourself to temptation."

Zach rolled his eyes at his mother, but agreed. "Okay. So where do we keep her?"

"I'm right here," Lorie protested.

"She's not a puppy," his mother added.

"Okay, sorry." Zach released her hand to hold his up in surrender.

She immediately missed the warmth. But it was better this way. She needed to learn to stand on her feet if she was going to survive out here in the *Englisch* world.

His mother picked up the phone and dialed a number from memory. She looked at them and flashed a smile that Lorie suspected was meant to be reassuring, but seemed a bit pained all the same. "Ashtyn, we have a favor to ask of you."

"Are you sure this is okay?" Lorie asked.

"Of course," Ashtyn said brightly. Almost too brightly and Lorie had to wonder if she was really all right with Lorie staying with her. Or maybe Lorie was feeling a bit unwanted, shuffled around. Lost.

"You'll have this room all to yourself. Well, at least for a week or two. My son is with his dad." She made a face so much like Zach and their mother that Lorie almost laughed out loud. The stress of the day must be getting to her.

She didn't want to stay here. She didn't want to go home. She didn't want to go back to Zach's house, even though she would sleep in the car if that meant she could remain at his side.

Maybe she should have just had Caroline or Emily come to get her. But Caroline had a new baby to tend to and Emily was the bishop's daughter and pregnant herself. It wouldn't look good for her to be harboring an Amish fugitive.

"Thank you," Lorie said, not asking what she was supposed to do when Ashtyn's son returned from his father's. That was one problem that didn't have to be solved tonight. When stacked up against all the ones that she couldn't solve . . . Well, it was easily pushed aside to worry about another day.

"You're going to be fine here, okay?" Zach said. He took her hands into his and squeezed them as if it would give her the courage to make it through the night.

"Okay," she whispered in return.

"I'll just be . . ." Ashtyn backed out of the door and disappeared down the hall.

"Tomorrow I'll come get you, and we can talk. Make some plans."

Figure out what an Amish girl did in the *Englisch* world. "Okay."

"I'm just a phone call away if you need me. Just use Ashtyn's phone and call, okay? No matter what time it is."

"I'm fine." If only she believed it. She squared her shoulders and pasted on a brave expression. She might not be fine now, but she would be. She wasn't the only Amish girl to leave. Somehow she would figure out everything. "So I'll see you tomorrow?"

"I promise."

She smiled, and Zach squeezed her hands one last time. Then he turned on his heel and left her standing in the middle of a room filled with dinosaurs.

There were all colors of the beasts painted on the pale blue walls. Red, dark blue, and green. A dinosaur lamp sat next to a bed with a dinosaur coverlet. Even the sheets were covered with the beasts.

She sighed, already missing the room she shared with

Sadie. Oh, her sister. What must she be thinking? The image of Sadie crumpled on the top step, her shoulders shaking, would be forever etched in Lorie's mind. She hadn't wanted to hurt her sister. She hadn't wanted to hurt anyone in her family. As much as she loved her father this was all his fault, but she was too drained to even get angry about it. All she felt was weary, like she had used up all the emotions she had in one day.

She moved to the door and started to close it, but not before she heard Ashtyn say, "When I told you to bring her by to meet me, this was not what I had in mind."

Lorie shut the door and made her way to the tiny little bed, doing her best to keep the fresh tears from falling.

"I know what I'm doing," Zach said for the umpteenth time. "And bringing her here wasn't even my idea."

"Sure, Mom called, but you had a hand in this."

"Oh, I suppose you would have handled this differently."

Ashtyn collapsed into the sofa and stared at him with eyes just like their mother's, soft, green, and knowing. Sometimes when he was with the both of them at the same time he felt like a stranger in a familiar land. "I don't know," she finally said. "Is she going to be able to survive out here? You know, without her people?"

"I don't even know if she wants to stay here."

She gave him a wise stare. "But you want her to."

"She's amazing." No sense in denying the truth. He could never hide anything from Ashtyn the same as his mom. "Beautiful, sweet, caring."

"You love her."

He scoffed. "I've barely even held her hand."

"You think that's what it takes to figure out if you love

someone?" She shook her head. "Like I can tell you about love. Two failed marriages."

"Don't be so hard on yourself."

"Just be careful."

"Now you're starting to sound like Mom."

"If we're both saying the same thing, maybe it's advice you should listen to."

He nodded. But when he thought about the girl sleeping in his nephew's room, he wondered if it wasn't already too late.

Chapter Nineteen

For the second time in two days, Lorie woke up in a strange room. It took a few minutes of taking in her surroundings before she realized where she was and what had happened the day before. She had left her home in Wells Landing, left the Amish to come to Tulsa, to stay with Zach's sister in this room filled with dinosaurs.

She sighed and threw back the covers, stretched and yawned, then pulled them back into place.

No sense in lollygagging around. Putting off the inevitable was not going to change a thing. She pulled on her jeans and a T-shirt, ran her fingers through her hair, then stepped out into the hall.

Following the smell of fresh coffee, she made her way to the kitchen. Ashtyn was there, wearing a T-shirt, pajama pants, and a faded pink robe. Her dark hair was pulled into a messy ponytail near the top of her head. She turned as Lorie came into the room. "Coffee will be ready in a minute. Zach has already called. He'll be here soon."

"This early?"

"It's already eight."

Eight o'clock? She had never slept so late in her life. If she were home, she would have already fixed breakfast for the family, put Daniel on the school bus, and sent Cora Ann out to gather eggs. Or down to Bacon Dan's if the hens weren't laying.

But she wasn't at home.

Ashtyn raised the coffee urn in question.

Lorie nodded and sat at the table while Zach's sister poured them a cup and slid in across from her.

"I've only got about fifteen minutes, then I gotta scoot."

"You have to go to work?"

"I drew first shift for this week."

"Oh?" She tried her best to appear interested and knowledgeable, but Ashtyn saw through her in a second.

"I'm a trauma nurse," she explained. Then shot Lorie a smile. "That means I work in the emergency room helping people."

"Like your mother."

She cupped her hands around her mug and gave Lorie a small smile. "Sort of. Yeah."

"What about your *dat?* Zach started to tell me something about him the other day, but then he sort of shut down."

"If you want to know something about our father, then you're going to have to ask him. Sorry. You're close enough. When he wants you to know, he'll tell you."

"There's nothing going on between the two of us."

"Funny, but that's exactly what he says too."

Lorie frowned. "Why is that funny?"

"Funny strange," Ashtyn said, taking a small sip of her coffee. "Not funny, ha ha."

"Why is that strange?" she persisted. If she was going to survive in this world, she would have to figure out what these people were talking about.

Ashtyn shrugged. "Seems to me that the two of you spend an awful lot of time making sure everybody knows that there's nothing going on."

"But there's not."

"Protesting only makes everyone see that there could be. Or maybe that y'all want there to be."

She wanted to protest, but she was struck dumb by the thought. Something more between her and Zach. The thought sent a little shiver down her spine. But she shoved away the thrill and concentrated on reality.

Ashtyn stood and took her coffee mug to the sink. "I'm going to get ready. Zach should be here any minute." Just then the doorbell rang. "That'll be him now. Can you let him in?"

Lorie nodded, and Ashtyn made her way down the hall.

Zach looked even better first thing in the morning. His hair was still damp and nearly black. And he smelled good, like a mixture of shampoo, toothpaste, and fabric softener.

"Hi." He flashed her a grin as he stepped into the house.

"Hi," she said as she stepped aside and returned his smile.

He shoved his hands into his pockets and just stood there, looking at her. "Did you sleep okay?"

"Yes. You?"

"I wasn't in a strange bed in a strange house."

"Surrounded by dinosaurs," she added.

He chuckled. "Not that either."

"Dinosaurs aside, I heard what Ashtyn said last night."

"About?"

He was stalling. "Are you really going to make me say it?" she asked. "She doesn't want me here."

His mouth pulled down at the corners. "I'll talk to her."

"Please, don't. I don't want to be a burden."

"I don't want you to feel like you're a burden."

"She didn't make me feel anything but welcome. But I know that my being here is causing her . . . distress."

He shook his head. "Ashtyn is very protective of her privacy since the divorce. She never said as much, but I think her last husband was controlling. She doesn't like to answer to anyone."

Last husband? How many had there been? "This is her house. She deserves to have it the way she wants it to be."

Zach wrapped his hands around her upper arms and rubbed his thumbs against the tender skin on the underside. "Owen—that's her son—won't be home for another ten days. You are welcome to stay here until then."

"What happens after that?"

"We can figure that out when the time comes."

She hated the uncertainty. It was bad enough that she had no idea what tomorrow would bring. She had left everything she had ever known and loved behind. She had no money except for the little bit she had found in her *dat*'s wallet. She had no idea how long that would last. Or how she would get more. How she would survive. How she would make it there in the *Englisch* world.

She shook her head. "I should have never come here. This was a mistake." She needed to get out of there. Leave. Go back to where she belonged before too much damage had been done.

"Hold on," he said, his grip tightening just enough to hold her in place. He took a deep breath. "I won't keep you here if you really want to leave. But I thought you wanted to find out more about your father."

"My mother's family," she whispered.

"Your mother?" His eyebrows shot nearly into his hair. "You've never mentioned your mother before."

"I guess she's kind of like your father."

Zach's shoulders slumped just a bit, before he recovered. "I think we need to sit down and talk before this goes any further."

They settled around the kitchen table as Ashtyn came out of the back in those pajama-looking outfits that Lorie knew medical people preferred. "I'm out," she told them, walking through the kitchen and grabbing her purse from a table by the back door. "Lock up when you leave, 'kay?"

"Sure. Have fun at work."

She shot him a sideways look that was both cross and strangely humorous all at the same time. "Yes, because my job is so full of laughs. See you tonight, Lorie." She rattled her keys and let herself out the back way.

"See? I told you she didn't mind your being here," Zach said.

"Okay," Lorie replied, but she wasn't sure. She didn't have anywhere else to go. She would stay right where she was. For now.

"What time do you have to go to work today?" she asked. "You do have to work, right? It is Monday."

He shook his head. "I took the day off. Job interview." He made a face that let her know he wasn't looking forward to it.

"Why are you looking for another job? Don't you like working at the living center?"

"Well, yeah." He stood and pointed to the coffeepot. "Is that fresh?"

"She made it this morning."

He poured himself a cup and returned to the table. "I just need more, you know?"

"Sorry." She shook her head. "That's not something I understand."

"But you want more for your life."

"I s'pose."

"I do too."

"But you're so good with the seniors, and they seem to love you so."

"That's true, but I want to buy a house, get married some-day. I can't do that on what I make there."

"Of course you can. Look at the Amish. We raise our children on farms with barely any income."

"I wish it was that simple."

"It is."

He shook his head. "Not out here."

"It should be. Maybe then more people would be happy."

He smiled. "You might just be right about that."

She grinned in return. "I know I am."

Zach wished he had Lorie's confidence as he walked out of the downtown office building three hours later. He had taken Lorie to the living center to visit with the seniors while he went to the interview. But the "we'll be in touch" left him wishing she was waiting in the car to tell him that everything was going to be fine.

He let himself into the Ghia. What were they going to do for the rest of the day? Make clay ashtrays? He snorted, started the engine, and headed back across town.

Twenty minutes later, he pulled in front of the living center and parked the Ghia in the employee parking spaces. Just a few more minutes and he would see Lorie again. It shouldn't have, but his heart pounded a little harder at the thought.

He found her in the rec room with the seniors. Not just table eight, but all of them who had craft time before lunch. Some were standing, others sitting, but all had some sort of easel in front of them with large paper propped up for them to paint. Some were using brushes, but others had rags and sponges, while still others were using nothing but their hands. All of them, even Stan and Eugene, had smiles on their faces.

He looked around for Betty. Instead of knitting, which was her preference to the usual craft of the day, she had what looked to be the cut end of a bottom of romaine lettuce. She dipped it into the paint and pressed it to the paper creating a geometric rose print.

She squealed. "Look, Leslie! I did it."

Lorie smiled, but didn't correct her grandmother. Betty

might not always get their names right, but she remembered them and that was something.

Then Lorie caught sight of him and smiled. "How'd it go?"

He shrugged, not really wanting to talk about it. He moved farther into the room, closer to her. "What are y'all doing?"

Her entire face lit up like nothing he had ever seen. "Painting."

"I can see that." He had almost forgotten about the paintings that he'd stashed in the trunk when they left Wells Landing yesterday afternoon. He wished now that he'd gotten a closer look. If she could have the seniors painting such a variety of types of works, he wanted a closer look at her own paintings.

"Well, when we first started working on crafts everyone seemed . . . disinterested. So I asked Carol and Amber if we could paint."

The joy on her face was infectious. It spread around her like a beautiful fog, weaving in and out of the people in the room and touching everyone along the way.

"Everyone seems to be having a really great time."

Her grin widened as her gaze wandered around the room. "You really think so?"

"Absolutely."

"I've had a good time too." She turned her attention back to the seniors. "Okay, everyone. It's almost time for lunch. Time to finish up."

Several groans went up around the room.

"Maybe we can paint again tomorrow," Zach suggested.

"Can we finish our paintings then?" someone asked.

"Yeah, I wanted to hang mine in my room."

"I was going to give mine to my granddaughter."

"If you don't finish them tomorrow, then I'll make sure you get a chance later in the week," Zach said.

A round of agreement went up around the room. The

seniors started cleaning up their painting supplies, while Lorie gathered her own.

"Have you been painting long?" Zach asked.

She stopped putting the lids on her paints. "I guess." She seemed to think about it. "I can't remember a time when I didn't want to paint."

"How did you know that?"

"There are these pictures in my head, but the Amish frown on art and paintings."

He looked at the paper in front of her. It appeared to be mostly done, an Amish boy wearing glasses. The child was turned to the side, his hat shading part of his face. But somehow she had captured the energy that simmered just beneath the surface. His blue shirt and suspenders were typically Amish, but the painting was anything but average.

"My brother," she explained.

"It's beautiful."

She tilted her head and studied the work as if she had never seen it before. "You really think so?"

"You can't see the talent you have?"

"It's not like it really looks like him. Like a photograph, I mean."

"Not all paintings have to look exactly like the real thing. Have you never seen a Picasso or a Van Gogh?"

She frowned.

"I guess not. But trust me on this one. These paintings are really, really good. And even more than that, the seniors look like they enjoyed their craft time more than ever before."

"It was fun for me, too."

"Thanks for that, missy," one senior said on the way out the door. "Best craft hour we've had in three years." He smiled, then hobbled out of the room.

Zack leaned in close, smelling apple shampoo and the moisturizer that his sister preferred. "Just so you know, he's only been here three years."

She laughed, the sound near musical.

"Are you two coming?" Stan thunked his cane against the floor as if that would help them make up their minds and get a move on.

"Be right there," Lorie called.

"You go on ahead," Betty said to Stan. "I'll wait on them."

"I hope you're not hoping for leprechaun pudding today," he grumbled. Apparently his good mood over painting could only last so long.

Betty shook her head. "I'm not worried about that. Not as long as I get to eat with my granddaughter."

"How does a person go about finding someone?" Lorie cut her gaze to Zach as he drove the little orange car toward his sister's house.

"Internet, I guess."

"Like on the computer?"

"Exactly like the computer."

"Can you help me?"

He pulled the car into his sister's drive and turned to face her. "Who do you want to find?"

"My mother's family. I figure if I'm going to be here, then I should at least try to find them." She chewed on her lip as the doubts surfaced. "Do you think that's a bad idea?"

"Only if you don't want to find them."

"Will you be serious?"

"Sorry." He shot her a sheepish grin. "If you want to find them, then I think you should."

"I don't know." Lorie laid her head back on the seat rest and closed her eyes. "I don't know what to do."

"Are you staying?" he asked. "Here, I mean. In Tulsa. Away from the Amish."

She rolled her head toward him and opened her eyes. "I don't know."

The clear blue of his eyes grew cloudy. "That's something you'll have to decide."

"It's complicated, huh?"

"Very."

"What do I do?" Why were there so many decisions to be made? She wasn't sure how long she could stay in Tulsa, with Zach. She didn't want to leave him, but could she adjust like Luke had to *Englisch* living? Did she want to? She missed her family. But she couldn't go home without the answers she needed. The only way to get those answers would be to talk to her mother's family. And there was only one way to do that. "Will you help me find them?"

"Of course."

She smiled in what she hoped was confidence. But she prayed that she was making the right decision.

It took everything Zach had not to try to persuade Lorie to stay. It was selfish and unfair, but he wanted to all the same. If he was being honest with himself—not at all like he had been with Ashtyn—he was falling in love with Lorie. There. He'd admitted it. And that was the first step to recovery. But did that only count against addiction? What did one do to get over an impossible love?

He sat down at his sister's kitchen table and booted up his laptop.

"Are you certain this will work?" Lorie asked.

"I am. Are you certain you want to do this?"

She sighed. "Just because I look them up doesn't mean I have to go visit them."

"That's right."

"Then let's do it."

It wasn't hard to find the affluent Prescotts of Dallas, Texas.

"That's my family?" Lorie asked, her eyes wide as she stared at the pictures of the mansion on the computer screen.

Zach couldn't imagine how she was feeling. She came from a humble background. The images before her were anything but.

"How does one family get so much?" she whispered.

He scrolled down, though her eyes remained transfixed on the screen. "It says here they dabbled in ranching and then found oil on their property. Looks like they sold everything off and now they dabble in anything that will make them more money." He couldn't imagine the sweet woman at his side coming from such a materialistic family.

No. He needed to be fair. Just because the Internet claimed they were only concerned with the bottom line didn't mean it was true. Everyone deserved a chance to counter what was written about them.

"Well, there they are."

She nodded. "Okay."

"I doubt they're going anywhere. You have all the time in the world to decide if you want to visit them or not."

"I wish that were true."

He turned away from the screen and took her hands into his own. "Lorie, I've been debating on whether or not I should say this. So I'm just going to put it out there. You can stay here. Not at Ashtyn's maybe, but here in Tulsa. We can find you a place to live, a job. If you want to, that is."

She stared down at their hands. "I don't know what I want." She shook her head. "That's not true. I want to visit with the seniors every day and have you teach me to drive. I like wearing jeans and leaving my hair down. But if I stay, then I can't return to Wells Landing."

"Is that one of those rules?"

"That's one of my *mamm's* rules. She doesn't want me to come back and influence the other children into following my steps."

"So if you stay here, this is all you have?" He stood, suddenly full of too much energy.

"Basically. Yes."

"And if you return, you have to give up everything that you've been doing here."

She nodded.

"And painting?"

"Painting is definitely not approved. What should I do?"

He reached out again and pulled her to her feet. "I don't have any advice to give you, Lorie." The sadness on her face was almost more than he could bear. Why did she have to choose? Why did it have to be one or the other? He trailed his fingers down her cheek, loving the feel of her skin under his.

"I know," she whispered. Her eyes fluttered closed, and he knew she was feeling it, the same as he was. That pulling attraction. But was it the lure of the forbidden or truly something special happening between them?

He should stop the madness before it went too far. He'd told his sister that he couldn't fall in love with Lorie because he hadn't even kissed her. So he shouldn't kiss her now. That was just heading into dangerous territory. Yet he was powerless to stop himself. Or maybe he simply didn't want to.

He pulled her closer, lowered his head, and touched his lips to hers.

She was everything he had dreamed about and more. Full of innocence and wonder, adventure and sweetness. And he wanted the kiss to never end. Did that mean he was in love?

Love was such a strong word. It was a kiss. That was all. Any red-blooded American man would do the same. Kiss her and see what she tasted like, what she felt like in his arms. Test her warmth in his embrace. But that didn't mean love. It was attraction, chemistry, a little too much life-stress. Stress, yeah, that was it.

She sighed as his mouth moved over hers. A sweet innocent sigh that made him think of things not so innocent. He had to put a stop to this and quickly. She wasn't like the other girls he'd dated. She wasn't versed in the ways of the world.

He would punch anyone who took advantage of her. He had to stop before he needed to take a swing at himself.

He released her and set her back, a little away from him. "I'm not going to apologize. I've wanted to do that since the very first time I saw you."

She pressed the back of one hand to her lips. Her eyes were dark and unreadable. She looked as shocked as he felt. Maybe that was a good thing. He hoped it was.

"I don't want you to apologize."

He nearly slumped in relief. To say he was sorry would take away all the spectacular delight in what just happened.

"Whew, what a day! I'm thinking pizza for supper." Ashtyn came through the back door, stopping just inside at the sight of them standing there. She set her purse on the cabinet and looked at each of them in turn.

There was no hiding what had happened between them. The look on Lorie's face was enough to tell the truth. And he had the feeling that his expression was just as dumbfounded.

Something else had happened, something more than a kiss. Something deep and mysterious, as old as time itself. Was that love?

"Are you staying for supper, Zach?"

"Huh?" He turned his attention back to his sister only realizing then that he had been staring at Lorie once again. "Supper, yeah, sure."

"Can I talk to you for a minute?" Ashtyn asked. "Alone." She wrapped her hand around his arm and pulled him from the room. For the first time since they were kids, he let his big sister push him around. She shoved him into the tiny hall bathroom and shut the door behind them. She leaned back against the door and crossed her arms. "Explanation, please."

"Explain what?" He was stalling; it was apparent to both of them. But he needed a little more time to figure out what he was feeling before he started telling his sister about it.

"What I just walked in on in my own house."

"Certainly not what you're thinking you interrupted. It was just a kiss." *Liar.*

"So there is something going on between the two of you."

Zach shook his head and breathed a heavy sigh. Finally he got enough air into his lungs that his brain was functioning properly once again. "A kiss," he said again. "I kissed her. That's all."

But his sister was nothing if not shrewd. "That must have been some kiss. You look like you've been hit by a train."

He stepped in front of the mirror to look at himself. He did look a bit ragged. But finding out that he might possibly be in love with an Amish girl whose family was one of the wealthiest in east Texas and then kissing that girl until the breath caught in his lungs . . . well, that tended to show on a guy's face.

"Whatever," he said.

"Don't whatever me. I haven't been married twice without seeing that look before. Just be careful," she said. "This situation . . . well, it looks like it would be too easy to hurt or get hurt. And I don't want that for either one of you."

He nodded. "I will." But he feared it was already too late.

He had fallen in love with an Amish girl.

Chapter Twenty

Lorie managed to keep herself together all through dinner and the marathon of sitcoms that Zach and Ashtyn insisted on watching. In truth, she enjoyed the zany antics of the two girls and one guy who shared an apartment. She didn't get all of the jokes, but she had fun watching the two of them laugh together.

But when Zach finally said good night and let himself out, Lorie said she was going to bed too. In the privacy of the little dinosaur room, she relived every moment of Zach's kiss.

To say she had been caught off guard could not express how she really felt. And the fact that she had never been kissed before . . .

She collapsed into the bed and stared up at the ceiling. It was just dark enough that the glow-in-the-dark stars there were starting to show. She tried to concentrate on them, but all she could think about was Zach.

What was she doing? He was *Englisch*. A kiss from him was not as special as from an Amish boy. Oh, it felt special. It made her stomach flutter and her knees shake. She wanted it to never end.

But she had to keep things in perspective. Zach was

handsome and worldly. He probably went along kissing girls willy-nilly. She wasn't fooling herself. She couldn't compare to the *Englisch* girls with all their sophistication and knowledge about such things. She had to protect her heart before she lost it completely.

She rolled to one side, thinking about how he cradled her against him. Longing and guilt swamped her at the same time. Was this where she belonged? Was she destined to go home to Wells Landing? Could she live without the closeness of her siblings? Could she survive in the *Englisch* world? Could she walk away from Zach and his brilliant smile?

The stars grew clearer as she shifted once again, her focus changing from Zach to the ceiling above her. Something tangible, solid. Daniel would love to have something like the stars on his ceiling. If *Mamm* would allow it. Lorie didn't know how Maddie would react to such a decoration, but if she had to guess she'd say that her stepmother would allow it for Daniel.

Tears stung her eyes. Daniel would be in bed now, sleeping and waiting for the new day to start. She wondered what Maddie told him about where she was and why she hadn't come home. Daniel was simple in his mind. He would believe anything *Mamm* told him. Lorie only hoped that Maddie's anger and disappointment hadn't gotten the better of her and poisoned whatever she said to the young boy. Lorie couldn't bear to go back and have Daniel hate her.

But was she going back? Once again her thoughts had gone in a complete circle. No closer to an answer than she was before, Lorie thought to pray. She wanted to, but she had left her *kapp* in the car. She gathered the small blanket from the bottom of the bed and draped it over her head. It wasn't quite the same, but she hoped God would understand. She closed her eyes and started to pray.

* * *

"Have you decided what you want to do about your family?" Zach asked.

They were sitting at lunch the next day, eating with the seniors as had become their custom. Lorie had helped them finish their paintings. They had left them in the rec room to dry. As they headed off to the cafeteria, one of the other workers had asked her about the painting. Lorie was thrilled to be consulted about the artwork and gladly told the employee what they had done.

Now all of table eight was gathered around, but there was no leprechaun pudding in sight.

"My mom's family?" she asked, not quite understanding. Maybe because she'd had such a tough night trying to figure out where to go from here.

"Yeah."

Lorie shrugged. "I came this far. It seems useless if I don't continue on. Don't you think?"

"I say that's completely up to you."

Lorie had spent what seemed like hours with the blanket on her head praying for wisdom and more. She needed guidance. She trusted God. She knew He wouldn't lead her astray. But she wanted answers now. The one time she needed her father the most, he wasn't there.

"Again, up to you." Zach studied her face and suddenly Lorie was reliving that kiss all over again. Heat rose into her cheeks. Was he thinking the same thing? "This sacrifice has been yours. You make of it what you will. No one here will judge you."

She looked around at the seniors all sitting at the lunch table. They had come to mean so much to her. No. They wouldn't judge her. But the good Amish people of Wells Landing would weigh in on the merits of chasing down her mother's wealthy family.

"I want to go see them, but I don't know how I will get there."

"I'll take you. We can go down and get a hotel. Then drive back the next day."

"In the orange car?"

He shook his head. "We'll borrow my mom's car. It's more reliable."

"That's asking a lot."

Zach's eyes turned suddenly serious. "I promised I would help you find your mother's family, and I will. Even if it means driving to Dallas."

Betty leaned close to Lorie and whispered, "That sounds like love to me."

But Lorie wasn't sure if she was clearheaded or being typical Betty.

"Hush," Stan said. "If a man wants to take her to Dallas, then he should. And women shouldn't be reading too much into it. That's the problem with girls today."

"Like you know what girls are like today. How long has it been since you had a date?" Linda said.

"It's been since you had one."

Betty blushed.

"What are you arguing about?" Fern asked.

"Women," Eugene joined in. "We're *discussing* women."

"Now why does that sound derogatory?" Linda asked. "Oh, because you said it."

Zach caught Lorie's attention and smiled.

She returned it, then ducked her head, the kiss coming back once again.

"Well, I think a man should be able to take a woman to Dallas for an overnight trip without everyone making too big a deal of it," Stan said.

"Here, here," Eugene added.

"After all, it's the twenty-first century. Why can't two

people go out of town together without everyone thinking that there's more going on?"

"Are you saying that a guy could take a girl out of town and not expect anything more from her?" Linda asked, eyes wide.

Stan nudged Zach in the ribs. "What is it with women these days? Do all the girls think boys only want . . ." He raised his eyebrows suggestively.

Zach shrugged, but his cheeks seemed a tad bit pinker.

"Lorie?"

She jerked to attention as Fern spoke her name. "Huh?"

"What do you think boys have on their minds these days?"

"I couldn't begin to guess." Her own cheeks filled with heat.

"So you're saying that Zach should be able to take Lorie to Dallas to find her mother's family, and she won't have to worry about him thinking too much about the trip," Linda asked.

"That's exactly what I'm saying," Stan said with a nod.

"Lorie, dear," Betty started. "I think you should go."

A chorus of "me toos" went up around their table.

"It's all settled then," Eugene said. "Zach and Lorie are going to Dallas."

The seniors from table eight smiled in approval.

Lorie looked to Zach. He was smiling to himself and shaking his head. That's when she knew: they had been set up, though neither of them had seen it coming.

Spending four hours in the car with Zach should have made her at least a little uncomfortable, but Lorie was relaxed and happy as they drove along. Well, she was nervous and anxious about seeing her mother's family. Zach had worked whatever magic he had over the Internet and found a phone number. The Prescotts had been surprised to hear from her, but welcomed her visit with more enthusiasm than she had ever expected.

Despite all her crazy feelings, she was happy, content even, to be by Zach's side riding along.

Dallas traffic was unlike anything Lorie had ever seen. It looked as if billions of people were driving their cars as fast as they could, trying to get someplace before it was too late. She wanted to close her eyes, but it made her dizzy so she opened them again.

"All the road construction has put us behind. I think we should call the hotel and tell them we'll be late checking in. Then we can grab something to eat and get ready to meet your family tomorrow. Sound good?"

"Good enough for me."

He gave her instructions on how to look up the number for the hotel on his cell phone and had her dial. She hung up the phone looking at it with awe. "I have got to get me one of these."

Zach chuckled. "We'll do that next."

Lorie hardly slept a wink that night. Aside from knowing that Zach was sleeping so close, on the other side of the wall of their adjoining rooms, she tossed and turned worrying over what was to come. Yes, her mother's family had agreed to have her come and visit, but it didn't mean anything beyond that. What if they didn't like her? Or thought she was weird because she had been raised differently? This was the grandmother who threatened to take her from her father. Had she made a mistake in coming here?

"Wow, you look . . . tired," Zach said over breakfast the next morning.

She shot him a look and reached for the coffee.

They ate in silence, then checked out of the hotel.

Zach was quiet as he drove the busy Dallas streets. He'd

even turned off the radio. It was as if he knew she needed silence to prepare herself for what was to come.

Soon they were pulling through a neighborhood with houses bigger than she had ever seen.

"One family lives there?" she asked, pointing to a large brick structure with three stories and a porch that looked bigger than their barn.

Zach nodded. "Awesome, huh?"

She turned toward him. "It's . . . excessive. Wasteful."

He cleared his throat. "I guess I never thought about it that way. Most people dream of living in a house like these."

"What about you?" She hadn't meant for her question to sound so stern or judgmental, but there it was. "I'm sorry. It's just . . . is that why you want to have a better job than the one you have at the living center? A house like that?"

"Well," he started, then stuttered a bit as he continued, "it doesn't have to be that big. But I want my own house and—"

"What good is a house that big? Especially if there are only a couple of people living in it."

"I guess I never thought about it. What's that house number up there?"

"Four sixty-eight," she replied, though she suspected he had purposely changed the subject. She would allow him this. She hadn't meant to criticize him and his goals for his life. They were his own. And if he wanted to work at a job he might not like in order to get an overlarge house, who was she to say otherwise?

"Then it should be that one up there." He pointed up the street.

She might be mistaken, but the sandstone and brick structure looked to be the largest house on the street. Was her mother's family really that wealthy?

The house looked even bigger in person than it did in the pictures Zach had shown her on his computer.

Zach drove his mother's car toward the closed gate and pressed a button of some sort.

"Yes?" a cultured voice drawled.

"My name is Zach Calhoun. I'm here with Lorie Kauffman. Uh, Mathis."

"Come right in." A buzz sounded and the gate slid open without a sound.

"Are you ready for this?" he asked.

"No." Her voice trembled.

"We can still turn around and leave if you want to."

Lorie swallowed hard.

"Sir?" The same voice that greeted them from the box on the side of the gate spoke again. "It's safe to drive in now."

Still Zach waited for her response.

"We're already here. Might as well," she finally said.

"Let's do this." He nodded, then put the car in gear.

Minutes later he pulled the car onto a circular drive, which curved around a fountain that rivaled the ones she had seen at the park in Tulsa.

He had barely shut off the engine when the front door opened and a woman in a plain gray dress stood in the doorway waiting for them.

"Right this way," she said, leading them down a marble-floored hallway.

She opened a door halfway down and stepped aside so they could enter. "Mrs. Prescott, Lorie Mathis and Zach . . ."

"Calhoun," he supplied.

She stared at him as if the sound of his name was offensive. But she didn't say anything. She merely closed the door behind them leaving Lorie and Zach alone with the three women in the room.

To Lorie their relationship seemed obvious—grandmother, mother, and daughter.

"Oh, my." The eldest woman stood. Her skin turned ghostly

pale. "Oh, my dear," she whispered, vaguely reminding Lorie of Betty. "I had given up hope of ever seeing you again." She clasped one of Lorie's hands and pulled her farther into the room.

"Who are you?" Lorie asked, keeping a hold of Zach as she followed the woman. She had been intent on trying to keep as composed as possible without completely losing her mind. She supposed Zach's touch, his hand on hers calmed her nerves enough that she could speak in complete sentences.

"I'm your grandmother. Ellie Prescott."

"You're my grandmother," Lorie repeated in awe. She had never thought this day would come, never even dreamt it a possibility until a few short weeks ago.

Tears rose in the older woman's eyes. "Yes. And this is Gina, your aunt, and Taylor, your cousin." The two other women remained seated.

She had an aunt and a cousin. Maybe more. An uncle. More cousins. "It's so good to meet you." Lorie said the words though the air in the room was brittle. The two younger women seemed hostile toward her, but she had done nothing to them. Maybe she was mistaken. "Are you my mother's sister?" she asked Gina.

"I'm her brother's wife." Her red lips smiled, but the action didn't reach her hard green eyes.

"I have an uncle?" she asked.

"Had," Gina corrected. "He died in a boating accident a couple of years back."

"I'm sorry," Lorie murmured, confused by Gina's callous attitude and cold words.

"Come. Sit," Ellie said, making way for the two of them on the small couch opposite where Gina and Taylor lounged like they hadn't a care in the world. Even then, a tension hung about them that belied their dismissive demeanor.

"What about the other family members?" Lorie asked. She had come all this way. She wanted to meet everyone she could.

"My husband, your grandfather, died last year. Heart attack. God rest his soul." She made some sign over the front of her chest that to Lorie looked almost like a cross. "It's just Gina, Taylor, and me these days."

"How interesting that you came here now," Gina said, looking from Lorie to Ellie and back again.

Ellie smiled, but to Lorie the action looked forced. "We're not going into that right now."

Gina shrugged.

"Tell us, dear, where you've been all these years." Ellie squeezed her hand and smiled reassuringly. This one lit up her entire face.

Lorie started slowly, but managed to tell the story of her father, his death, and what she had been doing for the last twenty years.

Ellie shook her head. "I've made so many mistakes over the years, but none so big as threatening to take you from your father. I want you to know that my intentions were pure. I only wanted to give you everything you deserved."

Gina snorted. At least Lorie thought she did. When she turned her attention to the other woman, Gina looked off into the distance as if staring out a faraway window.

"I've had a good life," Lorie said, focusing once again on her grandmother.

"Tell me," Gina said, leaning forward as if preparing to listen to a riveting tale. "How long did it take you after the news release before you decided to come here?"

"Gina. We are not going to do this today." Ellie pressed her lips together as if she wanted to say more, but needed to temper the words.

"When would be a good time then?" Her voice dripped

with a poison Lorie could not name. "You have two months to live. Three, if you're lucky. And then here comes Princess Belinda's only child to claim her part of the Prescott fortune. How convenient for you." She turned her venom on Lorie.

Zach stood and pulled Lorie to her feet. "I think we should go."

"Please don't." Ellie was standing in a heartbeat.

Lorie bit her lip, unsure of what to do. The woman, her grandmother, was dying. Lorie wanted to console her, spend all the time she could with her, and then what? In the end, she would be heartbroken having lost another person so dear to her. She didn't think she could bear it.

"He's right," Lorie said. "I never meant to upset your family."

"A little while longer," Ellie pleaded. "Just the three of us."

Gina scoffed, but it seemed she knew when she had pushed beyond the boundaries and didn't say any more.

Lorie looked to Zach.

"It's up to you," he said.

"Okay." Lorie gave a quick nod.

Ellie slumped with relief. "Let's go out on the north veranda. It's nice out there this time of day."

Lorie didn't look back even once as Ellie led her and Zach down a wide hall and into an open space in the house. She thought the *Englisch* called it an atrium, but she wasn't sure. One thing was certain, she had never seen anything like it before.

"Right this way." She pointed toward the floor to second-story ceiling windows. Lorie realized that one of them was a door. Outside a table waited with cushioned chairs and a large brown-and-white umbrella overhead.

She sat down opposite Zach. At the door she heard Ellie say, "Can you bring some refreshments to the north veranda,

Helga? We need enough for three. My granddaughter, her boyfriend, and myself."

Boyfriend? Lorie looked to Zach, but he acted like nothing momentous had been said. Is that what they were? Boyfriend and girlfriend?

Ellie was smiling as she took her place at the table. "Helga will be here shortly with some refreshments. In the meantime, tell me everything you can remember."

"Everything?" Lorie asked.

Ellie's smile grew wider. "Well, I don't have a long time left on this earth, so I can make do with whatever's on your mind today."

Lorie started telling stories about her life with the Amish. How her father had taken her there to live. She told Ellie about the restaurant and church, her friends, and Esther's bakery down the street from Kauffman's.

"Miss Ellie, it's time for you to rest."

Ellie stirred herself as Helga came onto the veranda. "Just a little longer," she said.

But the large woman was insistent. "I've let you stay out here an hour past what I thought was healthy. Now it's time to rest." She turned her attention to Lorie and Zach. "I'm sorry, but she really needs to rest."

Zach stood as Lorie pushed herself to her feet. "We understand," he said.

Ellie's face fell with disappointment, but she rose and together the three of them made their way toward the front door.

Lorie wasn't sure what to say. "I'll pray for you," didn't seem like quite enough for someone who knew they were about to die. But she would pray for Ellie, that she found the peace she deserved.

"I wish I had come sooner," she said. In the hard light of the foyer, she could see the dark circles under Ellie's eyes and the strain of worry on either side of her mouth. She hid it well, but the woman was ill.

"We all wish a lot of things, sweet Lorie, but I'll make it right." She touched her fingers to Lorie's cheek and smiled. "I promise you. I'll make it right."

Lorie hugged the fragile woman, then she and Zach made their way back to the car.

"What do you suppose she meant by that?" Lorie asked.

Zach shook his head. "I have no idea."

The trip back to Tulsa was quiet. Zach knew that Lorie had a lot on her mind. He'd told her several times that if she needed him, he was there for her. He hoped now that she remembered. It was one thing to find a grandmother you had never known and quite another to discover that the long-lost relative was terminal.

"Did I do the right thing, Zach?"

"By going to Dallas?"

She nodded.

"I think so, yeah. I'm glad you got to spend a little time with Ellie. And I think she enjoyed the visit too."

"I didn't make it worse?"

He took his eyes from the road for a brief second. "Definitely not. I'm just sorry that you two will never get the chance to know each other better."

"Me too." She laid her head against the window and fell silent once more.

"But you had today. And you still have Betty. Well, most of the time."

She chuckled, the exact reaction he was hoping for.

"I lost my grandparents a long time ago."

"You did? I mean, you're so great with the seniors. I guess I thought . . ."

"That I had grandparents lined up waiting on visits?"

Another chuckle. Good.

"I love the elderly," he continued. "I always have."

"They love you, too."

"No more than you," he said. "I've never seen them happier than when they were painting."

She shrugged. "It was only because it was something new."

"Maybe." But he knew the truth.

They rode in silence for a bit, then Lorie turned to him once again. "What now?"

"What do you want?"

"Me?"

He had a feeling she had never been asked that before. "You have to decide what's next. But I figure finding a job. Working on a place to live. I can work something out with Ashtyn, but she can be a little covetous of her time alone. So don't take it personally."

"I won't."

"If you're staying, that is." Okay, so he was out and out fishing for answers. He wasn't trying to push her either way, but the more time he spent with her, the more time he wanted to spend with her. If she entertained any thoughts about staying, she needed to make some plans.

"Find a job," she repeated.

"Sure. You have restaurant experience. You could make decent money as a waitress."

She nodded. "What about a place to stay?"

He didn't want to go into the complexities of credit apps and security deposits. "Why don't you plan on staying put for now, and we can figure that out after you find yourself a job."

"If you're sure," she said.

"I'm sure. You just leave Ashtyn to me."

Chapter Twenty-One

Finding a job in the *Englisch* world was not nearly as easy as it sounded. It might have been if she had been looking for work in or around Wells Landing. But the managers and owners of all the various stores and restaurants didn't understand why she had only attended school until the eighth grade, why she had no Social Security card, and why reliable transportation to work might be more difficult than it sounded.

In the end, she managed to find work as a short order cook at a small diner within walking distance of Ashtyn's house. She took the rest of the money she had saved and bought a couple pairs of jeans from the secondhand store along with some T-shirts and a pair of pink pajamas with a cartoon kitten scattered all over them. If nothing else, the sleepwear made her smile at the end of a hard and confusing day.

The worst part was not seeing Zach. He came over when his schedule allowed. But since he had joined the National Guard in order to help pay for his school, he had to go "play war," as he said, for two weeks, leaving her to fend for herself.

"I'm sorry. I wouldn't leave if I didn't have to."

"I know."

They were sitting on the back porch at his sister's house, watching as the sun set over the tops of the neighbor's trees.

"Ashtyn and Mom will help you with anything you need."

She nodded, but Zach's family were the last people she wanted to accept more help from. They seemed to like her well enough, but Lorie had the feeling that their acceptance of her had more to do with their love of Zach rather than any warm feelings they might have toward her.

"It's only for two weeks," he said. "Then I'll be back."

She nodded.

It was probably for the best, she told herself. Things between them were more confusing than the Tulsa Transit bus schedule.

He had only kissed her that one time, though she relived it every night. Yet he still continued to hold her at arm's length. Everything she had been told about *Englisch* boys didn't apply to Zach. He was caring and polite and seemed to respect her conservative upbringing. Well, either that or she was a really bad kisser.

That was it. Or maybe he just didn't like her the way she liked him. He was smarter in the ways of the world. He knew more about men and women. Had probably kissed a dozen girls. She would never be able to compete with that. The thought of having to contend for his attention made her want to hide under the covers.

It was the hardest two weeks of her life. She had thought the Amish way of life was hard. Walking to work every day in the summer heat, even without the mourning black, had her guzzling water to and from work. But she got no reprieve behind the grill. The restaurant was small and confined, the heat from the kitchen seeping into her pores. As much as she loved the feel of her hair against her back, she had to wear it up, off her neck, to help keep cool. She didn't remember working at Kauffman's being this difficult. Or maybe it was being surrounded by people who loved her and who she loved in return that made any tough situations more bearable.

That didn't even take into account her pay. Even working forty hours a week, minimum wage was barely enough to cover her living expenses. And she was still staying with Ashtyn.

Ashtyn's son had come home from his dad's. A cuter five-year-old Lorie had never seen. He had dark hair like his mother's but tawny brown eyes that must have been a legacy from his father. Owen Williams was sweet and fun, but of course he wanted his dinosaur room back. Lorie could understand that, and sleeping on the couch wasn't much different than sleeping in his narrow bed, but at least inside the room she had a little privacy. In the room she didn't feel like such a charity case.

She mopped her forehead and trudged down the street on what was the hottest day on record for the year. That was all everyone entering the diner had talked about all day. What it meant for the crops and livestock. She would have thought city dwellers would have a different conversation topic than the folks in Wells Landing, but it seemed that what affected the farmers and ranchers affected them all.

A car pulled up behind her and slowed. She didn't turn around. Didn't need to in order to know who was behind her. The same three guys had been harassing her for days. Who knew why they were out every day just waiting for her to leave work. Or how they knew she was vulnerable to the *Englisch* world. Somehow they just did. Giving her a hard time gave them some kind of weird pleasure she would never understand. But today she wasn't in the mood.

She kept walking as they pulled up even with her.

Don't even look at them.

"Hey, gorgeous. Wanna ride?"

She whirled around at the sound of the familiar voice. "Zach?"

He was sitting behind the wheel of his little gray-colored car looking like one of the soldiers she had seen on TV.

His grin was broad and catching. Despite the heat and the fact that she was bone weary, despite the hardships of the past two weeks, she smiled in return.

"Come on. Get in."

She slid into the passenger's seat, sinking into the cool interior with a small sigh of pleasure.

He pulled the car back onto the street. "How 'bout we catch a movie?"

"Right now?" She was so tired all she wanted to do was sink into a warm bath—after she cooled off, that was—then get into her cutie pajamas and pretend her life had come out just the way she had always dreamed.

But her plans to marry Jonah and live out her days working at the restaurant in Wells Landing seemed as far away as the moon.

"No, tonight."

"Okay, sure." She loved the idea of going to the movie with him, just the two of them, alone in the dark. The thought was thrilling. Oh, how she missed him these past two weeks.

Weariness forgotten, she hopped out of the car when they got to Ashtyn's. "Are you coming in?"

He plucked at his uniform jacket. "I need a shower. Pick you up at six thirty?"

"Perfect." She smiled and waved him away, then ran into the house to shower and change.

Zach was nothing if not punctual. He arrived at six thirty on the dot. "Are y'all ready to go?"

"Y'all?" she asked.

"Here he is." Ashtyn herded Owen from his bedroom. He was decked out in some sort of costume. Lorie thought the

Englisch called them superheroes. Though she wasn't sure what was so heroic about being bitten by a spider. Everyone she knew had been bitten once or twice.

"Owen is going with us?" She hoped her voice didn't sound too disappointed. She loved the little boy, but she was looking forward to spending time alone with Zach.

"Tonight's the premiere of the latest Spider-Man movie. The little man and I have a standing date for them. Right, buddy?"

Owen grinned, showing his missing front teeth. He'd lost a tooth while Zach had been gone.

His uncle made all the proper exclamations of joy over the recent loss and Lorie's annoyance melted away. Zach was a good uncle. He loved Owen as he would one of his own. Poor Owen didn't have a dad around all the time, and Zach seemed to have made it his mission to make sure that Owen missed out on nothing because of it.

While Zach examined the gold dollar the tooth fairy had left in place of the tooth, Lorie's thoughts filled up with Daniel. She missed her brother so. She missed them all. She had told herself that it was better to cut ties completely. She couldn't go back and forth and try to visit. It would be too confusing for Daniel. But suddenly she wanted to see him so bad she could taste it. She needed to go back, even if for only one last time to see her brother and sisters. She needed to explain to them what had happened. But she knew Maddie would never allow that. Only one of her children didn't share a blood relationship with Betty Mathis and that was Sadie. But to the rest of the children, Betty was their paternal grandmother.

"Lorie? Are you ready to go?"

She shook herself out of her thoughts, realizing that Zach must have been trying to get her attention for a while. "Sorry," she mumbled. "I'm ready." She grabbed her purse and headed out the door.

* * *

"Are you avoiding me?" Sunday afternoon after hamburgers and baked beans at his mother's house Lorie finally got up enough courage to ask Zach directly.

She had worked the day before at the diner, but Zach had promised them a fun evening.

His eyes widened in surprise. "No. Of course not," he scoffed. "Yes."

"The answer can't be both."

"Then yes," he said with a heavy sigh. "I'm avoiding you. Well, not you, but yes."

"Zach, would you please make sense?" His doublespeak was making her head hurt. Why was the *Englisch* world so confusing?

He took her by the hand and led her out to the gazebo his mother had built in the yard. It was a pretty structure, painted white with vines growing all around it. It looked wonderful and romantic like something out of an *Englisch* fairy tale. Despite the beauty of the surroundings, Lorie had the feeling that she wasn't going to like the topic of the conversation. But she had asked and now she had to see it through.

He sat her down on the built-in bench on one side of the gazebo while he sat on the other. He wasn't more than three feet from her, but she felt like it was a chasm.

"I want you to know that I care about you very much."

Her heart sank to her toes. Every breakup between her and Jonah had begun in a similar way. Not that she and Zach had a relationship. At least he had never said anything of the kind.

And you're the idiot who went and fell in love with him.

"But you don't love me."

He braced his elbows on his knees and ran his fingers into his hair. "I don't know. Life is just really confusing right now. For both of us."

She nodded.

He sat back. "I think maybe we should take this a bit slower. That's all. It's not you—"

"It's me," she finished for him. She had heard the line in one of the romance movies that Ashtyn liked to watch. Though she never thought she would hear those words for herself.

"Okay, that was trite. But I don't want you to think that you're not a fabulous person. You are."

Suddenly, she understood. That was why he didn't call their trip to the movies a date. And why he brought Owen along. The pair might always go see the superhero movies on opening weekend, but she had a feeling it had more to do with her and less to do with Spider-Man.

"I . . . well . . ." She wasn't used to talking about such matters, and the words wouldn't come. Certainly not the words she wanted to say. He was the reason that held her here. His bright eyes and charming smile. But if there was no future in them . . . No, that was thinking like an Amish girl. What would an *Englisch* girl say? She was an *Englisch* girl now. Or was she just ex-Amish? Never to completely fit in with either world. "Whatever," she finally managed.

He muttered something under his breath, then he blew out a frustrated sigh. "I've hurt you. I never meant to hurt you."

"It's fine," she said, though her heart was breaking. "It's not like I'm falling in love with you or anything."

"That's not what I mean."

"Then what do you mean?"

"I just think we should take a break."

"From each other?"

He shook his head. "I'm trying to find a job, and you're supposed to be learning how to drive. We've got work and the seniors. There just seems to be so much going on right now. I don't want you to get overwhelmed."

"You're overwhelmed."

"Yeah, maybe. Yeah."

She jumped to her feet. "Would you stop answering my every question with multiple answers? How am I supposed to know which one to believe?"

He was on his feet in an instant beside her. "This is exactly what I'm talking about. We're both stretched so thin right now, neither one of us has any more energy to give a relationship."

"Whatever," she said again. It was one word that could successfully hide her broken heart. She started out of the gazebo, but he caught her arm before she could make her escape.

"Lorie, I—"

"It's okay, Zach. I understand. I may be Amish, but I'm not a child." She pulled away from him and stalked toward the house.

She didn't hear from Zach at all on Monday. As if living with his sister wasn't awkward enough, now he was truly avoiding her. There was no denying it. She had only seen him twice in two weeks. Normally, he would come to his sister's for supper or pick up Lorie and take her to his mom's for the evening meal. But this night he didn't even call.

Lorie tried to pretend that everything was as it should be, but she knew that Ashtyn had picked up on the change. Zach's sister kept glancing toward her as they watched TV. She would turn her gaze from the set to look at Lorie, then the clock, the phone, and back to the TV. A few minutes later she would start the process all over again.

"Did you and Zach have an argument?" she finally asked. Owen had gone to bed, and Lorie wondered if Ashtyn had waited to question her until the little ears were out of the room.

"No. Yes." Great. Now he had her doing it. Lorie shook her head trying to clear her thoughts and come up with a good answer. She owed Ashtyn that much. "He thinks everything is moving too fast between us." So different than Jonah who wanted to get married and have children right away.

She hadn't thought of Jonah in weeks, and suddenly she missed him like she missed her own family. With Jonah she had known where she stood. She knew what their relationship was about. He didn't have to go looking for a job or play war for money. Jonah knew where his place was in the world. He had been waiting for Lorie to find hers.

"That's male for 'I'm scared.'"

"Scared of what?"

"Love. Commitment. How you make him feel."

"No, that's not it at all." Scared of love. She had never heard such a thing. Maybe Zach didn't want to get married. Maybe he thought she did. Maybe he was scared of love. Why did *Englischers* make everything so complicated?

"Just think about it, okay? Men can be weird sometimes. And you just have to give them space to work it out. Not that it ever worked for me. But Zach is different. He's a good guy. It's just he's got a lot on his plate right now. Once things settle down, he'll be right back to the same ol' Zach." She patted Lorie's knee and stood. "I've got a big day tomorrow. Think I'll go on to bed. Don't stay up too late."

But sleep was a long time coming.

Lorie waited until Owen and Ashtyn left for the day before she picked up the phone and called the diner. "I won't be in today. In fact, I'm going to have to quit," she told her boss. She couldn't make it on the money she made there. Not even if she worked twice as many hours.

He was furious, threatening her to get her to come to work. Just another part of the *Englisch* world she didn't understand.

She straightened up, did the breakfast dishes, and vacuumed the carpet so Ashtyn could come home to a clean house. She made their beds and gathered her things. But she couldn't just leave.

She sat down at the kitchen table with a piece of paper and a pen.

Dear Ashtyn,
    First of all, I want to say thank you for opening your home to me. Not many would do that for a stranger, and I am grateful.
    I'm sorry I am leaving so suddenly, but after last night, I realized that it's time for me to go back to where I know I belong.

As she wrote the words, a crushing sadness settled over her. She didn't want to leave, but she knew she couldn't stay. She'd felt the same when she walked out of Wells Landing. She didn't belong either place any longer, but it was better to go back to where she had come from than to try to force her place in this new world.

    I enjoyed my time I spent with you. If I can ever return the favor to you, I most definitely will. Please tell Owen good-bye for me.
    I wish you all the best.
                                    Yours,
                                    Lorie Kauffman

She folded the paper to rights and propped it against the saltshaker in the center of the kitchen table. Then she took out another piece of paper and started a letter for Zach. She made three attempts before she wadded up them all and pitched them in the trash. He would understand soon enough, when he saw that she was gone. And he wouldn't have to worry about her anymore. He wouldn't have to second-guess any of his decisions or wonder if he had done the right thing by coming to get her and bringing her into his world.

She pushed to her feet and reached for the phone. One phone call and she would be on her way home. She dialed the number from memory, then cut the friendship bracelet off her wrist, her heart numb as she laid it to the side. She changed into her Amish clothes, wound her hair at the back of her head, and pinned her prayer *kapp* firmly into place. Then she gathered her things and waited for Luke to come get her once again.

Zach dug his phone out of his pocket and checked the screen to see who was calling. His sister. He had been at work all day. It was almost six o'clock and time to go home. What could his sister want?

"Hi, Ash."

"She's gone."

"What? Who?"

"Lorie. Lorie is gone."

He stopped. He had to have heard wrong. "What do you mean *gone*?"

"Is there a part of *gone* that isn't clear?"

He took a deep breath. Ashtyn had to be mistaken. Lorie must have been called into work. Or gone to the store. She hadn't stopped to say good-bye. Surely she wouldn't go without saying good-bye. Why would she leave?

He hadn't realized he'd asked the question out loud until Ashtyn answered. "Her note said she needed to go back where she belonged."

She belonged here, didn't she?

Evidently she didn't feel that way. He tried to make her understand. Maybe it was better this way. He was falling for her hard and fast with no way to support her or even himself if their relationship went further. There was no future for them, and Lorie deserved a future filled with everything she wanted. Right now he couldn't give her that.

"Zach?"

"I'm here."

"Are you okay?"

He smiled, though the motion felt grim on his lips. "Yeah. It's better this way."

Wasn't it?

Chapter Twenty-Two

"Home or to the restaurant?" Luke asked as they neared Wells Landing.

"Home," she said without hesitation. Just in case there was a scene, she would rather that happen in private instead of their place of business.

It was two o'clock in the afternoon. No one would be home this time of day in the middle of the week. Daniel would be at school and everyone else would be at the restaurant. No one would come back to the house until about four when Daniel got off the bus. That would give her plenty of time to prepare herself for what was to come. Not that she had any idea how *Mamm* would react. Her *mamm* might be upset now, but the forgiveness would come. It might take a while, but it was the Amish way.

"Are you going to be okay?" Luke asked as he turned down the road that led from the highway to the Kauffmans' house.

"*Jah.*" She gave a reinforcing nod.

"You look a little brokenhearted."

"Nah." She tried to look like she thought he was crazy,

but her face felt a little more like a scary Halloween mask instead.

"I've seen that look too many times to buy that load, but if you don't want to talk about it, fine. But when you're ready, if you need someone, you know where to find me."

"Can you do me a favor?" she asked as he pulled into her drive.

"Anything. You know that."

"Will you go get my *dat*'s car from Zach's house?"

He nodded.

"*Danki.*"

"Do you still want to sell it?"

The thought broke another little piece off her heart. But what choice did she have? She didn't need a car in Wells Landing. "*Jah.*" She opened the door and got out.

"You want me to stay until someone comes home?"

"*Nay,*" she said. "This is something I have to do on my own."

A little after three thirty, Lorie sat down at the table to wait on whatever was to come. She didn't have long to fret over it. Shortly after she settled in, Sadie arrived back at the house.

"Lorie?" She stopped just inside the door, surprised by her sister's presence.

"Hi."

Tears filled Sadie's eyes as she flew across the room to wrap Lorie in a warm hug. "Please tell me you've come home to stay."

"I'm here to stay." The words tasted bitter on her tongue. But there they were. She was back in Wells Landing. Back to stay. Back where she belonged.

She tried to smile, tried to look happy, but the joy

wouldn't come. Thankfully Sadie had enough bliss for the both of them and didn't notice her lack of enthusiasm.

They sat down at the table with a plate of Sadie's peanut butter cookies and tall glasses of milk. The memories of all the times they had done the same stung Lorie's eyes, and she had to blink back tears of her own. But she said she wasn't going to cry. She had made up her mind what needed to be done and she was going to do it. There should be no crying. She managed to push the tears back and keep them at bay.

"Does *Mamm* know you're back? Of course she doesn't. What about Jonah? Oh!" Sadie clapped her hands together. "He is going to be so happy to see you."

"I doubt that very much." She had broken Jonah's trust long before she missed her baptism classes. "He's probably already seeing someone else."

"Nope." Sadie smiled, self-satisfied with her *Englisch* ways.

"That still doesn't mean that he will forgive me for what I put him through."

"I think you might be surprised by what a man like Jonah could forgive." She cocked her head to one side as if listening to a faraway sound. "That's Daniel's bus."

Lorie pushed to her feet. "I'll walk down and meet him."

Sadie nodded, somehow sensing that Lorie wanted to see him alone.

She stood on the side of the road as the bus driver pulled to a stop and Daniel climbed down. He caught sight of her and his eyes grew wide. A grin spread across his face and the sunlight reflected off his glasses as he started to run toward her.

"Lorie, Lorie, Lorie!" he cried, his arms outstretched. "You're home! You're home!"

"I'm home." She scooped him into her arms, backpack and all, and hugged him close. She breathed in the scent that was little boy as the tears started to fall. It had been so hard leaving him behind. How did she ever think she could go for the rest of her life without seeing him?

Cora Ann and Melanie were equally happy to see her when they arrived home from the restaurant. Cora Ann took one of Lorie's hands into her own and refused to let it go as they sat at the table and caught up with each other. There was a new teacher starting at the school. Their cousin Rachel had been selected to instruct the scholars in the upcoming school year. Melanie chatted on and on about her wedding. *Mamm* was no longer making her wait until her year of mourning was over before she got married. They had already gone to the fabric store and picked out the bolt of material she would use for the dresses, but she was sure they could order more so Lorie could have a dress as well.

Lorie mustered a smile at her sister's happiness. The world had gone on without her in it, just as the *Englisch* world would too. Still she wondered if Zach knew she was gone. Was he sad? Would he call? She should have tried harder to write him a letter explaining how she felt, but it was so hard to tell him that without revealing the love she felt for him.

Sooner or later she would have to explain. It was the least she could do. But for now, she would enjoy her family and worry about reasoning tomorrow.

"Where's *Mamm?*" she asked as the conversation wound down.

"She was waiting on the supply truck." Cora Ann rose to her feet and started toward the kitchen. "I guess I'll start supper."

"I'll help." Lorie followed behind her needing something to do to keep busy. She wasn't worried about the paintings in the storeroom. Sadie knew they were there. She had probably told *Mamm* about them the day Lorie left. Besides, she was turning her back on the *Englisch* world like she should have done so long ago. They were a part of her past and she couldn't be concerned with what happened to them now. Though the thought of them being thrown out or destroyed made her stomach sick.

The sisters worked together to finish dinner. Lorie did her best to appear happy and content to be with the family. She was happy to see them all again and her smile was genuine as long as she didn't think about staying forever and never again seeing Betty and the gang of seniors at table eight in the Sundale rec room. Or never seeing Zach again.

But this is the way it had to be.

Lorie was just pulling the bread from the oven when *Mamm* came into the house. Daniel flung himself at her hollering, "Lorie's home! Lorie's home! Lorie's home!" He grabbed *Mamm*'s hand and jumped up and down for joy and emphasis.

Lorie set the pan of biscuits on the table. Sadie stopped pouring glasses of water and tea and waited to hear what was next.

Then Cora Ann dried her hands on a dishtowel and started out the door. She loved the horses almost as much as the restaurant. Most times she was the one to unhitch them and take them to the barn.

"Don't brush her too long, Cora Ann. It looks like your sister has dinner about ready."

"*Jah, Mamm.*"

Lorie took that as a good sign. Her shoulders relaxed, and the air in the room lost most of its tension. Everything wasn't completely back to normal, but it would get there eventually. *Mamm* had never been the emotional type. Lorie had no call to think she would be any different now.

"It's *gut* you are home, Lorie Jane." A ghost of a smile whispered across her lips.

For now that was enough.

* * *

Daniel went to bed early. He'd worn himself out in his excitement. Lorie took him upstairs and helped him get ready for bed, combing his hair and helping him brush his teeth.

Once he was in his sleep shirt, Lorie tucked him into bed and read him a story. It was about a little *Englisch* boy who misbehaved and got sent to his room to have grand adventures, returning to find that his mother had saved his supper for him. Lorie didn't think Daniel understood the story so much, but he loved the softly colored pictures of the monsters and other creatures on the pages.

The book didn't appear to be something the Amish would approve of, but yet *Mamm* let him have it. Was it a result of her doting on Daniel or could it be that Maddie Kauffman didn't always follow the *Ordnung* to the letter?

Once Daniel drifted off, Lorie made her way back downstairs. The rest of her family was waiting there. *Mamm* read the Bible aloud while the others listened, each doing something else as well. Melanie was embroidering a design onto a handkerchief, Cora Ann was making a get-well card for someone in the church, and Sadie was sewing up a hole in a pair of Daniel's britches.

Lorie wasn't sure how to take the fact that they had started the reading without her. But most probably it was *Mamm*'s way of letting her know that forgiveness didn't mean she didn't have consequences. She had left the family and now she had to work her way back into it.

"Do not love the world or the things in the world," *Mamm* read from the book of 1 John. "If anyone loves the world, the love of the Father is not in him. For all that is in the world— the desires of the flesh and the desires of the eyes and pride in possessions—is not from the Father but is from the world. And the world is passing away along with its desires, but whoever does the will of God abides forever."

Lorie settled onto the couch next to Sadie. *Mamm*'s

choice of verses was directly aimed at Lorie and everyone
knew it. She supposed she deserved a lecture on the perils of
the world. But she had been out there in it. She had seen
many godly people, many *Englischers* doing good deeds and
loving those around them. The postman came into the diner
every day and ordered a hamburger to go. One day Lorie had
seen him giving it to a dirty little boy sitting on the curb. The
child looked hungry and old despite the fact he was only
about eight. She'd had people pay the bill for the diners
behind them and others leave tips that were bigger than their
checks. Not everyone in the *Englisch* world was only interested in finding pleasures and sins.

Zach showed her that by going with her all those Thursdays
to let her visit her grandmother. He might have changed his
mind about the two of them, but he was a good person inside.
She had known that from the first time she had seen him. She
just didn't understand how good until she spent some time
getting to know him.

But how well did she know him really? He never would
tell her about his dad or the problems they had. She only
knew that it had to be bad for Zach to hide it from the world.

After *Mamm* finished her Bible reading, they prayed together as a family and everyone started for their rooms. She
and her sisters climbed the stairs one after another. She and
Sadie shared one bedroom while Melanie and Cora Ann slept
in another. Daniel was the only one with a room to himself.
Tonight Lorie was glad she would have her sister close. She
had missed those talks late into the night. Wondering when
they would get married and to who. Both of them had
thought they would be married by the time they were twenty.
But here they were, both of them over that age and unmar-
ried. At least Sadie had joined the church and was ready if
the right man happened along. Rumor around was that Chris
Flaud was sweet on Sadie, but Lorie had her doubts. She had

seen that look in Chris's eyes. That faraway look of a dreamer.

Lorie unpinned her prayer *kapp* and set it on the top of the dresser. She released her hair and started undoing the fasteners on her *frack*.

Behind her, Sadie gasped. "You cut your hair," she whispered, though from her tone Lorie couldn't tell if she was impressed or horrified.

She shot her sister a rueful smile. "Yeah. Sort of a whim." Still she didn't regret it. She pulled her nightgown over her head, then perched on the edge of her bed and brushed through the long tresses. She already missed her soft kitty pajamas, but how could she embrace life back with the Amish if she held on to parts of the *Englisch* world? That was the very same reason why she couldn't go back to visit Betty and the rest of the seniors at Sundale.

"Does *Mamm* know?"

"No, and I plan to keep it that way. I'm home now."

Sadie nodded. "Best to let your transgressions die a quiet death."

"Do you think the church will be really hard on me?"

Her sister dropped onto her bed and sat cross-legged in the middle. Methodically, she began to brush her hair. "I don't know. I mean, you aren't baptized."

"But I missed two baptism classes."

"*Jah,* for sure Bishop Treger was not happy when he came to talk to *Mamm*."

Lorie winced, imagining how that conversation went.

"*Mamm* tried to explain to him that you had taken *Dat's* death hard and probably should have waited until next year before beginning classes. She even told him that she had pressured you to join the church before you were ready."

"She said that?"

"It's the honest truth."

Lorie knew her sister spoke the truth, but she was still

surprised that her *mamm* understood. "I suppose that I will
have to wait until next year to join the church." It wasn't all
cut and dried, but it surely would have been easier if it was.

"What about Jonah?"

"Were you telling the truth when you said he wasn't
seeing anyone else?"

"Of course." Sadie set her brush to one side and pulled her
hair together at her nape and started to braid it. "I think he's
been waiting for you to return. I heard that Sarah Yoder was
hoping that once you left, he would notice her, but Jonah has
never had feelings for anyone but you."

But could he get over her leaving? Did she ever want
him to?

Sadie tied a handkerchief around the top of her hair and
waited for Lorie to follow suit. "Are you ready to turn out the
light?"

She nodded. She was exhausted. The day had been long
and stressful and for now all she wanted to do was sleep.
Surely when she was asleep she'd have fewer opportunities
to think about Zach and everything she'd left behind.

Sadie turned off the battery-operated lantern, and the girls
crawled into their beds. Lorie had forgotten how quiet and
dark it was in Amish country. There were no shining street-
lights or cars zooming past. If she listened very closely, she
could just hear the hum of the traffic on the highway, but
the sound was so faint it was more like the hum of Ashtyn's
refrigerator than the roar of traffic.

"I kept the rest of your paintings," Sadie said quietly. "The
ones you left in the storeroom."

"Why didn't you throw them away?" Lorie asked across
the darkness. It would have been easier not to see them ever
again. But she was thrilled nonetheless.

Sadie's bedsprings squeaked as she turned to face Lorie.
"I couldn't have put them in the garbage. They are a part of
you. And quite beautiful, I might add."

"You think so? I mean, you don't think they are sinful?"

"How could something so lovely be a sin, *Shveshtah?*"

Lorie had asked that very same thing more times than she could count. How could she have these pictures in her head? Were they not from God? She had the ability to paint, and though they weren't very good in her eyes, they were as necessary as breathing. She had a burning inside her to create these pictures. Was it from God? How could she believe that it came from anywhere else? "You really think they're good?"

"*Jah,* I do." Silence fell between them and for a moment Lorie wondered if her sister had drifted off to sleep. "There's something special about your paintings," she said. "I'm not sure what, but when I saw them, I could just tell. After you left I went to the library and looked at this book filled with photographs of these paintings by great *Englisch* artists. They were so beautiful and amazing, even though they don't look like the real object that was painted."

"Picasso and Van Gogh?"

Sadie sat up in her bed. "How did you know?"

"Zach said something about it." It was the first time she had said his name since Luke had dropped her off.

"I don't know if yours are as good as theirs. I'm just an Amish girl, but your paintings gave me the same feelings that theirs did. Does that makes sense?"

"I think so."

"They were good feelings. Happy feelings. How can that be bad, Lorie?"

She didn't have the answer and didn't try to give one. She didn't understand it either, but somewhere along the way, some bishop or church leader decided that painting was vanity or false gods and idols, something that made it a sin for the Amish people. Lorie wasn't about to question their judgment now. She had already done that and look where it had gotten her.

"We all struggle in some way, Lorie. The secret is learning to keep the balance."

When had her sister gotten so wise?

Keep the balance. That was exactly what Lorie intended to do.

"I was afraid of this."

Zach looked up from his plate to study his mother's expression. "Afraid of what?"

"That she would leave and you would be brokenhearted."

He scoffed. "My heart's not broken." He took a bite of his casserole as if to prove his point.

Mom wiped her mouth and gave him that look.

She didn't understand. Zach couldn't be brokenhearted. He would have to love Lorie for something like that to be true. He enjoyed the time he had spent with her, but he didn't love her. Not really. How could he? They'd only shared one kiss. Love took a lot more than that to grow.

"What?" he asked as she continued to monitor him.

"Are you going to tell me why she left?"

He shrugged. "You know all there is to know. The letter she left for Ashtyn said that it was time to go back to where she belongs." It still rankled that Lorie left an explanation for Ashtyn, but not one word for him. He thought they were better friends than that.

More than friends, the tiny voice inside him whispered.

Yeah, maybe more than friends. Or at least they could have been if they'd been given a little more time. Or if she hadn't run out.

"I don't understand," Mom said. "She seemed to like it here well enough."

He didn't either, but he had stopped trying to figure out females in elementary school. "I guess being away from her family was too hard on her." He shrugged. "I don't know." He wished he did.

He refused to believe that telling her they needed to slow things down between them was the reason she left. She said she'd understood. She said she wasn't a child. But what if she didn't? What if she said that just to save face?

She might look like an English girl, but that didn't mean she was. She was still Amish at heart, raised by conservative beliefs and strict rules. Suddenly, he felt as if he had just made the biggest mistake of his life.

Chapter Twenty-Three

Lorie's first day back at the restaurant was both comforting and sad. Most of the diners were tourists and didn't know that she had just returned from the *Englisch* world, but a few were long-standing members of the community both *Englisch* and Amish. Their response to her ranged from utter joy that she was back to thinly veiled uncertainty as to whether or not she would stay.

But her own heart soared as the afternoon neared. Caroline and Emily walked in.

"There you are!" Caroline exclaimed, rushing over to wrap Lorie in a warm hug. Lorie closed her eyes against the happiness she felt at seeing her friends again.

"Can you sit with us?" Caroline asked, once Emily had taken her turn hugging the breath from Lorie.

She turned toward Sadie who waved her away with one hand. "I can handle it if you want to take a break."

Lorie smiled at her in gratitude, then the three of them found a booth. The lunch crowd had trickled down to a couple of diners and the dinner crowd wasn't due for a couple more hours. By then Lorie would be at home getting Daniel off the bus, but for now she wanted to catch up with her friends.

"Are you going to tell us what happened?" Caroline asked. "Or are you going to make us guess?"

"You mean I haven't been the talk of the sewing circle?"

"Oh, you have been," Emily assured her. "We just weren't sure how much of it was true."

Lorie started at the beginning, recounting her tale from the time she fell asleep in the storeroom till her arrival back in Wells Landing the day before.

Caroline sat up straight in the booth, her eyes wide. "That's some story."

"I'll say," Emily agreed. "I can't believe that you met your grandmother."

"Both of them," Caroline said.

"I'm not sure I would believe it either if I hadn't lived it myself."

"I knew that box was going to lead to trouble." Emily shook her head.

But it wasn't the box, but how Lorie had reacted to it. She thought she could keep a foot in both worlds, but that proved impossible. As much as she enjoyed all things *Englisch,* how could she stay there without a decent-paying job, without her family, without Zach caring for her as much as she had him?

"I'm glad I found out about my family," Lorie said. "I learned a lot while I was away." In those short weeks she had learned that the *Englisch* world was hard to live in and the Amish were ill prepared to survive there on their own. Her first clue should have been the transition house that Luke had moved into shortly after he left. It was a rental that the owners saved for ex-Amish who wanted to leave their church. No one stayed at the house for very long, but all were young men who wanted to get a fresh start in the *Englisch* world.

"Now you're back," Caroline said. "And planning to stay?" It was more of a question than an observation.

"*Jah,*" Lorie said. "Of course." She had said the words so many times in the last two days that they were getting easier and easier to say. But she understood what the words said that no one else did. That she would never see Zach or Betty again. She would never wear her jeans or little animal-print shoes or even find out what leprechaun pudding was. But that was a small price to pay to stay with her family. She couldn't live without her friends and her siblings. Every time the Amish way of life got too stifling, she would remember that she had returned for them. Always for them.

"Have you seen Jonah?" Emily asked.

Lorie shook her head. "You're as bad as Sadie."

"Well, he isn't seeing anyone yet."

"Caroline," Lorie pleaded.

"It's true," Emily added. "Well, except for Sarah Yoder. She started coming around just after you left."

"Sadie said she had a thing for Jonah."

"I don't think he has a thing for her," Caroline said.

"I wouldn't be so sure," Emily countered. "I heard they went out twice already."

"That's only because he didn't think Lorie was coming back."

Lorie swung her gaze from friend to friend as Emily and Caroline discussed the potentially budding relationship between Sarah and Jonah.

Emily sat back in the booth and crossed her arms. "I say now that Lorie is back, Jonah will drop Sarah like a hot potato, and that will be that."

"I hope not." Lorie wasn't sure how she felt about that. She cared for Jonah. She truly did, but after having such a sweet relationship with Zach, she wasn't sure she wanted to go back to the arguments and tension she shared with her onetime love. Then again, look how her time with Zach turned out. Their time together might have been more evenly tempered, but it sure didn't mean much to him.

"Well, are you?" Caroline asked.

Lorie pulled herself from her thoughts and focused on her friend. "Am I what?"

"Going to see him before church," Caroline repeated.

Lorie shook her head. "I don't think so."

"You know church is at their house this week."

Great. Sunday was a church day. She had lost track of the count when she was in Tulsa. So much for delaying her talk with Jonah. It wasn't that she didn't want to talk to him. She just didn't know how to explain. Zach's excuse of "it's not you; it's me" came to mind, but this time it really applied. Jonah hadn't done anything wrong. It wasn't his fault that her father died, that she discovered his tattoo and that led her to a web of deceit.

"Saturday, we're planning a buddy bunch day. Can you come?" Emily asked.

"I don't see why not." Other than the fact that it would put her a day closer to a confrontation with Jonah. He was part of their buddy bunch. If she was lucky, he would have other plans and couldn't attend.

"We're taking a picnic to Millers' Pond to swim," Caroline added.

So much for that idea. Maybe she should get it over with and talk to him then. Or maybe she should be really brave and go talk to him tomorrow. *Jah,* that would be best. Whatever they decided they could show everyone at the picnic, instead of having a public confrontation as their first meeting since her return.

"Can you bring some chips and drinks?" Emily asked. "That wouldn't be hard to get together between now and then."

"Sure, *jah.*"

Caroline clapped her hands together in excitement. "It'll be just like old times," she gushed. "I can hardly wait."

* * *

Lorie put off talking to Jonah until Friday before their buddy day.

She stood at the door of his house, trying to get the courage up to knock. "Chicken," she muttered to herself, and raised her hand to knock.

Gertie Miller answered the door on the second knock. She dried her hands on a dishtowel and other than raising her brows in question, she didn't appear to be overly surprised that Lorie was there.

"I was wondering when you would come by." Short and round, Gertie Miller was the exact opposite of her son, though she did lend him her wheat-blond hair and tawny eyes.

"Hello, Gertie Miller. Is Jonah home?"

"*Jah.* He's in the barn with his *dat.*"

"*Danki.*" She gave a small nod to Jonah's mother and turned to go to the barn and talk to her longtime suitor.

"Lorie."

She turned as Gertie called her name. "*Jah?*"

"We're glad you're home."

She gave Jonah's mother a grateful smile, but it felt like one she had seen on the mouth of a plastic doll. She wished she was as happy about being home as everyone else seemed to be.

"Give it some time," she muttered to herself as she headed for the barn. This year had been filled with too many changes. Things had to settle down soon, maybe after Melanie's wedding. That was the next big change the Kauffmans faced. Maybe after that, everything would return to normal. Or as normal as it could be considering all they had been through this year.

The interior of the barn was cool and dark as she stepped inside away from the bright rays of the summer sun.

"Jonah?" she called.

"Back here," he called, followed by, "Lorie, is that you?"

"*Jah.*" She followed the sound of his voice until she found him, tending to a mare who was about to foal.

"What are you doing here?" Not *it's good to see you again.* Or *when did you get back?*

"I came to talk to you, but . . ." She took a step backward. "I can see you're busy. We can do this later."

"Jonathan," he called, giving the mare one last reassuring pat on the neck.

His brother appeared from the tack room holding a harness in one hand. "*Jah?*" Then he caught sight of Lorie and stiffened. "Hi, Lorie."

She dipped her chin in response.

"Can you keep an eye on Joni? I think she has a couple of hours yet, but just in case."

"*Jah,* sure." Jonathan hung the leather on a hook by the door.

"Take a walk with me?" Jonah asked.

Lorie made her way to the door of the barn with Jonah right behind her. Together they stepped into the bright sun. Lorie shaded her eyes as Jonah motioned for them to take the path through the cornfields, the one that led to the pond.

"Caroline and Emily told me there was a buddy day tomorrow," she said as they walked.

"And you're thinking about coming?"

"It is my buddy group too."

He sighed. "You're right. Of course."

"I just thought it best that we figure out how we want to handle the situation before we are actually in it."

"And what do you suggest we do?"

"That depends on you," she said.

They had reached the crop of trees that surrounded the pond. Lorie wound through the big oaks and pines that made up the oasis in the middle of the Miller cornfield. Jonah was quiet as he followed behind her.

Haphazard rays of sun made their way through the

branches of the trees and sparkled off the water. Lorie loved coming to the pond. Loved swimming here and the time spent picnicking and just relaxing on the banks.

She settled down on a fallen log, waiting for him to answer. He remained standing, looking as if he was about to start pacing at any moment.

"I don't know how to act, Lorie. I don't know what to do about any of this."

She nodded. "I never meant to hurt you."

"It shouldn't have bothered me so much," he said, sitting on the ground beside her. She could reach out and touch him, but he seemed so far away. "We were broken up when you left. But it did." He picked up a rock and skimmed it across the water. It skipped three times before sinking.

"I hurt a lot of people," she said. "Though that was never my intention." She shook her head, trying to get all her thoughts in one place. "I just had so many questions."

"And now?" He pitched another stone into the pond.

Zach's face appeared in her mind. "I realize finding those answers wasn't worth hurting the people I care about the most." *Or breaking my own heart in the process.*

He stopped collecting rocks to skip and looked at her. It was the first time he had done that since she arrived at his house. "You're different now."

"That's crazy."

"*Nay,* it's not. I can't tell you what it is, but somehow you're different."

Lorie grabbed a stone off the pile he had collected and flung it toward the water. She got two skips before it sank.

"If you don't want to talk about it, I understand."

"There's nothing to talk about." Two skips and her second rock dropped to the bottom.

Jonah pushed to his feet and took a rock of his own. "Like this." He threw it side-armed, the rock skipping four times before disappearing under the water's surface.

"Impressive." She mimicked his throw, but only managed three skips.

"Yeah, but I can't get more than four."

"That's better than I'm doing." She tossed another one, but lost her form. The rock sank like a leaky boat.

He pitched another. "Everyone is going to be watching us tomorrow."

"I know."

"How are we going to respond?"

She didn't know why everyone would make a big deal out of it, only that they would. "We've known each other too long to be hostile to each other."

"I agree."

"Even if we aren't getting married."

"But we could change our minds about that later. Right?"

Surprised, she swung her gaze to him. Surely he was kidding with her, but his expression was as serious as a funeral. "*Jah.* I suppose so."

He flashed her a ghost of a smile.

"It will be next year before I can join the church."

"Didn't your *eldra* tell you that the right person is worth waiting for?"

"Are you saying I'm the right girl?"

"I'm saying that you were for a long time, and I'm not ruling it out yet." He stopped. "Unless you want me to."

Her heart thumped hard in her chest. She didn't know what she wanted except for Zach and that wasn't possible. She cared for Jonah. She always had. He would make a *gut* husband and father. "Can we just take things slow and see where they go from there?"

For a moment she thought he would tell her no. Then he gave her a small nod. "*Jah.* Sure. And tomorrow?"

She knew what he was asking. Most everyone in their buddy bunch had gotten married to another member of the group. Caroline and Emily were the exceptions. Lorie knew they were coming, which meant they would bring their spouses. It was very possible that she and Jonah might be the only two single people there.

"We can hang out with each other, can't we?"

"*Jah,* but everyone is going to think there's more."

"I'm so tired of worrying what everyone else is thinking." She sighed, heavy and long.

"I understand. After you left—" He shook his head and didn't finish. He didn't have to. She knew what he was going to say. After she left everyone was talking about her, him, and the two of them. She had escaped those rumors until the day she came back, but Jonah hadn't had it that easy. He'd had to endure the sad looks and whispers behind his back.

"People are going to talk regardless. How about we please ourselves and not worry about them?" she said.

"And if they ask?"

"What do you want to tell them?"

Jonah thought about it a minute, then smiled. "How about we tell them that if they want to know more, they'll have to wait and see."

As far as Lorie was concerned, it was the perfect answer.

Jonah let go of the knotted rope and plunged into the water. He surfaced and tossed his hair out of his eyes before moving to the side so Andrew could have his turn.

So far, so good. No one had said anything to him about Lorie and her presence at their buddy day, but he knew it was only a matter of time. He'd caught their looks when they thought he wasn't paying attention.

Andrew splashed into the pond next to him and surfaced seconds later, laughing and sputtering as he did so. Jonah liked Andrew. He'd arrived in Wells Landing a few years back with a broken heart. Who knew he'd end up married to another newcomer in their district and that love would heal both their hearts.

But it was Andrew's cousin Danny who swam over to him and said, "So what's going on?"

Jonah looked at the canopy of trees and sunshine above them. "It's a *gut* day for a picnic."

"That's not what I mean, and you know it."

He did, but he'd been hoping to get out of actually answering.

"So?" Danny asked. "What's going on between you and Lorie Kauffman?"

"*Nix,*" he said. "We're just *freinden.*"

Danny laughed. "Uh-huh."

Jonah had known it would be like this, but as he said the words, he wondered how honest they really were. Was there truly nothing going on between him and Lorie? They had been a couple so long; could they go back and be less? With everything that had happened this summer, could they ever be more?

"I don't expect you to understand," he finally said.

"Julie's cousin, Sarah, really likes you, you know."

He did know. But that didn't change things. Jonah had to work out whatever still lingered between him and Lorie before he could go on with his life. Much less start anything new with someone else. "We're talking things through," he finally said. "Taking it slow and seeing where it goes from there."

Danny shook his head. "Do you really think she's going to stay here after living with the *Englisch* for almost three weeks?"

"Why should I think anything different?"

"Love truly is blind."

"What?" Jonah asked.

"Just something I read on an *Englisch* greeting card." Danny flipped over onto his back and swam away.

Was this how it was going to be now? Was everyone going to question their motivations and the sincerity of their love?

Lorie may have left to go live with the *Englisch*. He tried to understand her reasoning, but he couldn't. He couldn't put himself in her place and figure out what he would do in the same situation. He had tried on several occasions. But the situation was so bizarre. He couldn't imagine finding out that his father had a secret life among the *Englisch*, or that despite everything he'd been told in his life he was not really Amish.

He swam toward shore and grabbed his towel from a low-hanging tree branch. He shook the water out of his ears and wiped the excess moisture from his hair. Despite his efforts, the water dripped from his hair to slide down his back.

Lorie waved him over to the blanket where she sat with Caroline. "Are you ready for a sandwich?" she asked. "Or some cheese and crackers?"

He dropped down beside them on the quilt. "Where's Andrew?"

Caroline pointed toward the rope swing where Andrew appeared to be gearing up for the jump of the day.

Raised in the conservative Swartzentruber district in Tennessee, Caroline wore a dress even for swimming. Jonah had heard Andrew teasing his wife a little when they'd first arrived, but he knew that it was all in love. Caroline wasn't the only one there who felt more comfortable keeping with traditional dress, while Lorie and some of the others wore one piece *Englisch* swimsuits with T-shirts and shorts over top of them.

Lorie smiled and handed him a glass of lemonade. She seemed happy enough, but still she was different than the girl she had been. Sad. That was it. She seemed a little bit sad. As if she had left a chunk of her heart with the *Englisch*. Or maybe the problem was losing her beloved father. He couldn't imagine what that felt like. The Amish talked of God's will and acceptance of what came, but he knew that if he'd lost his father he would have a tough time moving on. At least for a while. For Lorie it had only been a few months. She just needed space to heal. Surely that's all it was.

He was glad they were taking it slow. Maybe then he would have time to understand. Bring back the happiness that once shone in her eyes. Regardless of their differences and all the arguments and breakups over the years, he loved her with all his heart and he always had.

Chapter Twenty-Four

"I still don't understand," Stan said as he and the rest of table eight worked on their latest craft. "Beaded key chains for the soldiers overseas," he grumbled. "What the heck does a man in a combat zone need with a key chain? And a beaded one at that."

"I'd much rather be painting," Linda agreed.

"Oh, yes, dear. Painting would be nice." Betty looked up from her knitting and gave them all a smile.

"And how is it that she gets out of making these blasted things?" Stan asked.

"I am knitting scarves for the soldiers," Betty explained. "Perhaps you should take up a yarn craft and you could do the same."

Stan shook his head. "Those men in the Middle East have about as much need for a wool scarf as they do a beaded key chain."

"And women," Linda added. "There are women there too."

"So when do we get to paint again?" Eugene boomed.

How did Zach explain? "Lorie was in charge of painting."

"Who?" Betty asked.

"Lorie," Zach said again. How many times were they

going to make him say her name and how many more times did he need to say it before the pain of her leaving lessened?

"Oh, nice girl," Betty said.

Her leaving had left a big hole in his heart. It wasn't like this was his first breakup. In fact, they hadn't been dating to start with. How could they break up if they had never been together? As far as non-breakups went, this one was the worst. Not only did his family—Owen included—ask him daily if he had talked to her, the seniors kept asking the same thing. They wanted to rehash every minute of every conversation he'd had with Lorie in order to find out what he did to make her leave. In the end he could only come up with one explanation. She missed her family and wanted to return home. But his theory nagged at him, made him toss and turn at night.

"Get her back," Eugene hollered.

Zach blinked away his thoughts. "What?"

"Get. Her. Back," Eugene said as if it was the simplest thing in the world.

Get her back.

"Lorie went back to her family in Wells Landing."

"Doesn't she know we like her?" Stan asked.

"Her family is there." It was the best explanation Zach had.

"She could still come visit." This from Betty.

"No." Zach shook his head. "Lorie's Amish and her family doesn't want her spending so much time out of their community."

"That doesn't make any sense," Linda said.

"She didn't look Amish to me," Stan said, holding up his key chain to inspect it closer.

She didn't to Zach either. It was easy to forget what she looked like in her Amish garb when he preferred her in that floral dress and cowboy boots.

But he knew something that the seniors at table eight

didn't. Lorie had left all her English clothes at Ashtyn's house. She wasn't coming back.

"Are you going to be okay?" his mother asked that evening over dinner.

He didn't bother to ask her what she was talking about. Instead he gave her his best scoff. "Of course. Why wouldn't I be?"

She dunked a piece of her takeout chicken into its sauce. "I've never seen you act like this over a girl."

"I'm fine. Just nervous about the interview tomorrow." He had a job interview the next day at ConocoPhillips in Bartlesville about an hour north of Tulsa. But the idea of moving that far away didn't settle well. Or maybe it was the thought of starting over. He would be low man on the totem pole, stuck in a cubicle for the first few years. Somehow that seemed more like a prison sentence than a starting point of his life.

"You'll do fine."

She was his mother. Of course she thought that. But if Zach was being honest with himself, he didn't really care how he did. For some reason it didn't seem as important now as it had a couple of months ago.

He dragged a couple of fries through his ketchup puddle and stuffed them into his mouth. Change was always hard. Starting a new job, a new career were no exception. He would miss the seniors, especially the seniors at table eight. In the span of a few short weeks, they would lose Lorie and Zach. But he couldn't worry about that. The seniors had suffered loss before. They would recover. Zach wasn't so sure about himself.

* * *

He wouldn't say he bombed the interview, but he could have done better. He tried, maybe too hard, to show enthusiasm for accounting in the main offices of a major oil company, but something was missing. And it wasn't just Lorie.

Yes, he finally admitted it to himself. He missed Lorie. He might even be in love with her, but what good would it do either of them. What was he supposed to do? Go after her? Convince her to come back to Tulsa with him?

He shook his head and pulled his gym bag from the backseat of the Ghia. Lorie's friend Luke would be by to pick it up later. For now, Zach had to get inside and clock in. He had pushed it a little close, but if he hurried he'd still have time to change out of his interview clothes and into his regular work attire of jeans and a black T-shirt like the rest of the nonmedical employees wore.

He stepped into the cool lobby, blinking several times to clear the sunspots from his vision.

"There you are." He heard Carol rather than saw her. "Mr. Anderson, this is Zach Calhoun, Sandy Calhoun's son."

"It's good to meet you." The man grabbed Zach's hand and gave it a strong shake before Zach even registered who he was. Frank Anderson was the owner of this living center and three others spread between Tulsa and Oklahoma City.

"You too, sir." What did the owner want with him?

"I came by for a visit today and got quite an earful from some of the residents."

He knew just which ones.

"Can you tell me about this?" He held up the painting that Lorie had done of her brother.

"My friend, Lorie Kauffman, painted that." She was his friend, right?

"Do you think she would be interested in painting a few more like this for us to hang here in the center?"

He thought of her telling him how painting wasn't allowed among the Amish. "I don't think so."

"Is it a matter of money? I'll pay her a fair price. All of my residents would love to have paintings like these to look at instead of that sort of thing." He waved a hand at the geometric abstract print hanging above the reception area couch. There was nothing wrong with it, but even Zach could see that it didn't have the same energy as Lorie's painting. Her colors were brighter, yet somehow soothing and peaceful. They held both an innocence and a sophistication just like the artist herself.

"She's gone back to live with her family."

A frown marred Mr. Anderson's brow, but he didn't pry. Instead he pulled a card from his breast pocket and handed it to Zach. "If you talk to her, will you tell her I'm interested?"

"Of course." Like he was going to talk to Lorie ever again.

Frank Anderson thanked him and left the center.

Zach checked his watch ten minutes later, and he still had to change clothes.

"Calhoun."

Luke Lambright, Lorie's ex-Amish friend, strolled into the center. Zach wasn't sure, but from the look on Luke's face, his threat to make Zach pay if he broke her heart wasn't a bluff. But Zach had done nothing of the sort. Had he?

"Here are the keys. I filled it up with gas."

"Cool," Luke said. "Thanks."

Zach shrugged. "It was the least I could do," he said, even though Luke taking the car meant Zach would have to catch a ride home with his mother.

"You leave anything in the car?"

He had meant to clean everything out of it last night, but he managed to talk himself out of it until it was too late. But he hadn't left anything in the car. He'd only driven it twice since Lorie had left and only then in the best interest of the battery. At least that was what he told himself.

"Wait. I think I might have something in the trunk." He

turned to Carol. "I know I'm late, but can you give me a couple of minutes?"

Carol smiled. "Of course. I would say take your time, but the group that always sits at the one table together have come out three times to ask where you are."

"I won't be long."

He followed Luke out to the car and raised the front hood. There they were—his basketball shoes, right next to the paintings Lorie had stashed there when she'd called him to come get her from Wells Landing.

"Do you think Lorie would want to sell her paintings?"

"Those?" Luke pointed to the canvases all stacked in one corner of the trunk. "Lorie painted these?" He pulled one out and examined it. It was a rendering of Betty, half in sunlight and half in shade. The picture was poignant and intriguing at the same time. And knowing both the artist and the subject made the painting even more special. The two sides of Betty.

"This is fantastic," Luke said, glancing at the next painting on the stack.

"I know. But do you think she'd want to sell them? The owner here at the center wants to purchase some of her work to hang in the homes."

"I don't know about selling them, but I could ask. I know she can't keep them once she joins the church."

And marries her fiancé.

He had been such a fool.

"Will you call her and ask? I can take care of everything from there, but if I call, she probably won't answer."

"Yeah, sure." Luke studied him, though Zach couldn't tell what he had on his mind. "I won't ask what happened between the two of you. But if I ever find out that you intentionally hurt her . . ."

Zach shook his head. "I wouldn't hurt her for anything in the world. I don't think she wanted to leave the Amish in the first place."

"A person doesn't leave the Amish on a whim. She has it in her somewhere or she never would have thought about it."

Zach wondered how much he knew about Lorie's father. But that wasn't his secret to tell.

"Here." Luke took the paintings from the trunk of the Ghia. He handed half of them to Zach and carried the rest of them inside the building. "I think these would be safer inside until we find out what Lorie wants to do."

Carol helped Zach find a place to store the paintings, then he changed his clothes and clocked in. Craft time was almost over when he finally made his way to the rec room. As far as days go, he was exhausted, and it hadn't even truly begun.

"We were beginning to think that you weren't coming in at all today," Stan grumbled as Zach made his way over to the table.

"I had a job interview this morning." As he said the words he realized how much he hated them. He didn't want to leave the living center and all of its eccentric residents. He loved them all. But he couldn't afford to keep working there forever. He had bills to pay. Plus, he was twenty-four years old. He had to move out on his own sometime. But this place had taken hold of his heart. Despite the fact that he had spent the last four years studying accounting and how to manage a company's fiscal needs, he would rather make beaded key chains with a bunch of senior citizens.

His mother would say that he was putting off the inevitable. That he was trying to hold on to life before graduation and the good times from then. But it was time to grow up. He knew that. Everyone had to eventually.

She was unusually quiet tonight. But if Jonah was being honest, Lorie had been unusually quiet since she had returned from the *Englisch*.

Oh, how he had hoped they could return to the life they

had before she left. Things were good. He thought they were good. Not perfect. But what in life was?

All he had wanted to do since he was eighteen was marry Lorie Kauffman and start a family. But he wondered if maybe he wanted that more than she did.

In the three weeks since her return, they had been together as friends, going to all the activities they had before as a couple. Bowling night, volleyball games, game nights with other couples. He had managed to keep their relationship on even ground, but he missed the old Lorie, the stubborn girl who argued with him. The one who had an opinion and wasn't afraid to share it. This person she had become was reserved and silent. She didn't argue with him or fuss when things didn't go the way she thought they should.

But was she different because of what happened to her while she was with the *Englisch* or because she never wanted to return in the first place?

"Why did you come back?" He hadn't meant to ask the question, but there it was out in the open as they drove home from yet another game night. This one with Emily and Elam.

Jonah had brought the tractor to pick up Lorie thinking she might prefer the faster transportation since she had spent three weeks riding around in cars.

"It's hard there."

He frowned at her too simple answer. "What do you mean?"

"To live." She turned toward him, and he could see the sadness in her eyes. "I don't know how Luke managed it." She shook her head and faced forward once again. "Everyone expects you to have more schooling. You have to learn to drive. I guess that wouldn't be so hard for you since you can drive this. But I don't know how. The only job I could find was making minimum wage. A person can't live on that. I was staying with Zach's sister. It's just hard."

He wished he hadn't asked. She didn't hate the people or how they treated her. She hated the fact that she didn't fit in. "If you could drive and had more education, would you have stayed?"

She tilted her head to one side. "I don't know. Maybe."

He really wished he hadn't started this conversation. Things were going fine between them. Maybe not great, but fine. So why did he have to go and ruin it?

"Are you going to stay here, Lorie?"

"*Jah,*" she said. But she hesitated before answering.

"If he came after you would you go?"

"Jonah."

"Would you?"

"Don't make me answer that."

"I need to know, Lorie. I need to know where we're headed."

"Can we just start from now and go forward from this point? Why do we have to go back?"

Because back was safe. Back was before her father died, and she discovered the secrets he'd kept. Before the fancy *Englischer* came into their lives and ruined everything. Before she left and returned a different person.

It was on the tip of his tongue to ask her if she loved him. If she loved Zach the *Englischer,* but he managed to bite it back. Some things he was better off not knowing.

"*Jah,*" he said. "Forward it is." At least then they would be together, and that was all he had ever wanted.

"Lorie." Sadie's voice drifted across their darkened room.

Lorie had thought her sister asleep when she had let herself in from her date with Jonah. She had been extra quiet as she changed into her nightclothes and climbed into bed. Not quiet enough that she didn't disturb her sister.

"*Jah?*"

She heard Sadie turn over in her bed. "Did you have fun tonight?"

"I s'pose."

"Are you going to marry Jonah? I mean, I know you're not supposed to tell and all, but I just want to know. Melanie's getting married in a few weeks. If you marry Jonah that will leave me and Cora Ann."

"I don't know," she answered truthfully. "We talked a little about it tonight."

"You did?" Sadie's voice was a mixture of happy and sad. "If you marry him, you'll stay, *jah?*"

"Of course." Wasn't that the whole point? Come back and start over as a good little Amish girl. Pretend that she had not lived among the *Englisch*. Or tasted the freedoms there. Pretend that her father had not lied to everyone. Keep the secrets he started.

Thinking about it pressed against her shoulders like the weight of the world.

"I want you to stay," Sadie started, "but I don't want you to get married and move out. I would miss you so."

Lorie turned to her side to face her sister even though she could barely make out her form in the dark. "Me too. But it'll be a while before that happens. I still have to join the church. If we get married, it'll have to be next year."

"I hadn't thought of that." Sadie gave another sigh. "I don't think I'll ever get married."

"Don't say that. Of course you will."

"*Nay.* I'm twenty years old. And Chris . . ." Her voice trailed off into the darkness between them.

"You never know what God has in store for you."

"I've told myself that for so long, I was almost starting to believe it. But now I realize God may have different plans for me."

"Like what?"

"I do not know, but I'm searching for signs."

Lorie smiled in the dark. Her sister was special. She always had been. She was kindhearted and sweet, the favorite cook and waitress at the restaurant by far. "What's wrong with wife and mother?"

"Have you not been listening to me?" Sadie asked without malice.

"I guess we will find out in His time."

"*Jah.*" Sadie grew quiet and for a time Lorie thought she had fallen asleep. "I don't know if I told you, but I'm really glad you're home."

"Me too," she said, hoping her sister didn't hear it for the lie that it was.

She had to be *ab im kopp* for coming here. Or maybe she was off in the head because she thought Merv King might have the answers she needed.

He was sitting on his porch when she pulled the team into his drive. Two glasses and a pitcher of lemonade sat on the small table next to him. He smiled and waved, then waited patiently for her to tether her horse. She wouldn't be there long enough to turn the mare out into the pasture. She shouldn't be there at all.

"*Oi,* there, Lorie Kauffman. It took you long enough to get here."

She wasn't sure how to respond so she gave him a quick hello in return and climbed onto the porch to sit in the chair next to him. "How was Pinecraft?" she asked.

"How was the *Englisch* world?" he countered. He poured them both a glass of lemonade. Lorie realized he was waiting for her to start her story, but she was at a loss. How was the *Englisch* world? Big? Scary? Hard to survive in?

But it was really none of those things.

"It was sad for me," she finally managed.

"Sad how?"

"Sad because I couldn't see everyone here. But I still liked it. I mean, it was hard and different, but it was an adventure, you know?"

"*Jah,*" he said. "I know." They sat in silence for a few moments. "Are you going back?" he asked.

"*Nay.*" She took a drink of the lemonade to ease her suddenly dry throat.

"Tell me," Merv said.

How did he do that? How did he know that she was holding back things she hadn't even admitted to herself? "The thought of never going back fills me with such sadness it makes my knees weak."

"And thoughts of leaving here?"

"Are the same." She stood and went to the porch railing, staring out toward the road. A few trees blocked her view, but she could still see a bit of the asphalt ahead, Merv's dented mailbox, and the rusty fence on the other side of the road.

"So you are trapped in between. The girl who wants to be in both places and belongs in neither."

"What do I do?" she asked into the wind.

"What do you want to do?" Merv asked in return.

She had no idea. "Why is this so hard?"

"Everything worthwhile always is," Merv said. "But you're a smart girl. If you want something bad enough, you'll find a way."

His words echoed in her head all the way back to her house. She unhitched the buggy and turned the mare out into the pasture. Then she wandered down past the old smokehouse to the bottom of the hill. There used to be a creek there, but it had long since dried up. Or had the water gotten tired of its home in those banks and just gone somewhere else?

She sat down in the tall grass and looked out over where

the creek used to run. Was it as simple as Merv King said? Was there an answer that she wasn't seeing?

She missed Zach, Betty, and the rest of the seniors at the living center. But if she left Wells Landing, she would miss her family, the restaurant, and the friends she had made over her lifetime.

Merv was right. She belonged neither place. So where should she stay?

The rumble of an engine sounded from the direction of the road. Daniel was home.

She pushed herself to her feet and brushed the dried grass from her skirt. Life without Zach or life without Daniel. The choice was clear. For now she was staying right where she was.

Chapter Twenty-Five

July faded into August and before Lorie realized it September turned to October. The atmosphere around the Kauffman household was happier than it had been in a long while. The closer they got to Melanie's wedding the more the air crackled with excitement. Lorie floated along doing her best to fit back into daily Amish life while trying not to miss Zach so much it hurt. Every day she had to stop herself from going to the phone shanty to call him or the Sundale Retirement and Assisted Living Center to find out how he was. How Betty was and how the rest of the seniors at the living center were doing. Had they figured out what leprechaun pudding was?

And painting. She missed painting so bad it left a metallic taste in her mouth. But staying Amish meant living by the Amish rules. Technically she was still in *rumspringa,* but it wouldn't be any easier to give up painting next year once she started her baptism instruction again.

She sighed and plunged her hands into the large bowl of biscuit dough. It was her turn to serve time in the kitchen. It wasn't so bad. She actually enjoyed her days of solitude when she was head cook. She didn't have to force a smile or pretend to enjoy chatting with *Englischers* who didn't know how lucky they had it. They weren't caught between two worlds. They didn't have to choose between the two things that made them the happiest.

She had finally come to terms with what happened between her and Zach. But she had to remove herself from him in order to see it. It was just another example of what happened when two people from two different backgrounds collided. Regardless of her feelings for him or any feelings he might have had for her, how were they supposed to overcome everything that stood between them? She was Amish, and they were expected to marry earlier. They looked for a mate, and she had projected those feelings onto Zach.

Lorie took out a handful of dough and patted it flat on the floured counter. She rolled it to less than an inch thick, then started cutting out biscuits for the dinner crowd.

"Can I talk to you?" *Mamm* stuck her head in the kitchen, her gaze settling on Lorie.

"*Jah.* Of course. Just let me finish these biscuits."

"Cora Ann can do that. Come on." She motioned Lorie toward the door.

Lorie washed her hands and dried them on a towel before following *Mamm* into the back offices of the restaurant. The space was cramped and filled with boxes filled with years of bookkeeping. She perched on the metal chair in front and waited on *Mamm* to scooch behind the desk. Lorie squirmed in her chair as her mother stared at her.

"What?"

"It's not easy," *Mamm* said, her mouth turning down at the corners. Lorie had never seen her look quite as old and tired as she did in that moment. And for the first time since her father's death, Lorie wondered how she was handling life without Henry Kauffman. "It's not easy for me to admit that I've been wrong."

To Lorie's dismay *Mamm*'s eyes filled with tears. "*Mamm,*

what's the matter?" She leaned forward in her chair and clasped Maddie's hands into her own.

Maddie shook her head. "Let me finish while I still can." She took a deep breath and squeezed Lorie's fingers. "When I told you that you had to choose, I thought I was doing what was right for everyone. But then you left. I prayed for you day and night. Daniel hardly ate anything while you were gone. Sadie cried herself to sleep every night. It was one of the hardest things I have ever had to live through. I don't want to go through that again."

"You won't," Lorie promised. "I never meant to worry you."

"You are worrying me still."

Lorie shook her head. "I don't mean to."

"You smile and act like everything is okay, but when you think no one is looking, I see the sadness in your eyes."

Lorie blinked back tears of her own. She released *Mamm*'s fingers to dash them away with the back of one hand.

"I should have never made you choose."

"You were only looking out for the family."

Maddie gave her a patient smile. "I was only looking out for myself." She shook her head. "When I first saw your father's tattoo, we were already married. I needed him. He needed me, so I chose to believe what he told me about it."

"That he got it during his *rumspringa*."

"I believed him because it was easier than facing the truth."

"Which was?" Lorie asked.

"That maybe he wasn't who he said he was."

"He wasn't," Lorie whispered.

"I know."

"But that doesn't mean he wasn't a good man."

"I realize that now, but at the time . . ." She sighed. "I'm only human."

"He was only trying to protect me." She told *Mamm* about

the letter she had read. All the things her father did to protect her from her mother's family's influence. And how Zach had taken her to Dallas to meet the Prescotts.

"Zach. That's the *Englisch bu* you've been seeing?"

"*Nay.* I mean, *jah.* Yes. But that's over now."

"He is the reason you are so sad."

Lorie nodded. "It's just . . . I don't think he cares about me the same way I care about him."

"Then he's more of a fool than most *Englisch.*"

Lorie smiled at *Mamm*'s motherly attitude. "It's all right." Her heart was broken, but one day soon it would be whole again. She hoped.

"So what now?" Maddie asked.

"Nothing, I guess. Help Melanie get married. See where things go with Jonah. Baptism classes next year."

"You don't want to return to the *Englisch?*"

"I didn't say that."

"So you do."

"I didn't say that either."

"Either you do or you don't, Lorie. It can't be both. What is it that you want?"

She wanted to be able to see her family, but she wanted to know who she might have been had her father made different choices all those years ago. She might not be the exact same person, but she would be different than she was now. She might have been a secretary in a big office building, a teacher for young children, or even an artist.

"There was a time when I wanted to see what was out there for me," she finally whispered. She stiffened her spine and waited for *Mamm* to redden with anger. But that didn't happen. Instead of frustration and ire, Maddie looked at her with love and hope.

"Then you should go back."

Lorie shook her head. "I don't have money or a job. No schooling to help me get a job." No Zach.

"You think you are the only Amish to ever leave?" Maddie asked. "If you want it bad enough, you will figure out how to get it."

Hadn't Merv King said almost those same words to her? The problem was she didn't know what she wanted. Well, she did. But she wanted both worlds and that was the one thing she couldn't have.

"This might help though." She extracted an envelope from the top drawer of the desk and pushed it across to her.

"It's open," Lorie said as she studied the return address. Sundale Retirement and Living Center. And it had arrived almost two months ago.

"I meant no harm." Maddie shrugged. "I only wanted to protect you."

Lorie pulled out the letter and unfolded it. Another piece of paper fluttered out and landed in her lap. It was a check for a thousand dollars! She scanned the letter, suddenly realizing why Luke had called and asked her what she wanted to do with her paintings. She told him that he could keep them. She had no idea he might have other plans.

"He sold my paintings?" She looked to *Mamm* for confirmation.

"I had no idea there were any paintings."

Heat filled Lorie's cheeks. She had kept so many secrets herself. "I was afraid of disappointing everyone."

"You seem to have a talent," *Mamm* said. "I can hardly find disappointment in that." She took a deep breath. "And I won't stop you."

"Are you saying I can go back to the *Englisch* world?" She had to have misunderstood.

"That's exactly what I am saying."

"What about the family?"

"If you are following your heart, I won't keep your siblings from you."

"You mean that?" Lorie could hardly believe her ears.

"More than I've ever meant anything in my life."

Lorie launched herself across the desk and wrapped her arms around her *mamm*. Not an expressive person, it was a few minutes before her arms came around and squeezed Lorie in return.

"Does this mean you are leaving?"

Lorie shook her head. "I don't know what I'm going to do. But when I decide you'll be the first to know."

It was the hardest decision Jonah had ever made in his life. He prayed about it, consulted with his father, even asked his mother what to do. In the end they told him that it was his decision whether or not to take his relationship with Lorie back to the level it had been before she left. It wasn't that he didn't love her. He'd loved her since he was eighteen years old. The question was should he put his heart on the line again. Was she happy back with the Amish or would she leave once more only to break his heart in two?

He swung down from his tractor and straightened his suspenders. He repositioned his hat, cleared his throat, and stared at the sky as he gathered his thoughts and his courage. He'd parked directly in front of the Kauffman Family Restaurant in hopes of talking to Lorie today. Settle this between them. Get both of their futures outlined and facing forward.

He stepped inside the restaurant, his gaze immediately seeking her out. It had always been that way between them. She captured his attention from the start. Always had.

She was standing by the ice machine. He caught her attention, sending a wave in her direction. Then she wiped her hands on a dishtowel and headed his way.

"I didn't expect to see you today."

Jonah tucked his hands into his pockets, suddenly more nervous than he had ever been. "Can I talk to you for a bit?"

"*Jah,* let me get Sadie to watch my table for me."

"I can wait."

"No need. I just have the one." She went back to the waitress station and spoke to her sister for a minute before joining him at the door once again. "Do you want a cup of coffee? Or an iced tea?"

He shook his head. "Can we walk for a bit?"

She frowned. "Sure."

Together they headed out the door and down the street toward the small city park that split Main Street down the middle. Despite the encroaching autumn, the sun beat down on his shoulders as he led her toward the park.

"Why do I have the feeling this isn't going to be good?" she asked.

"Is that how you want it to be, Lorie?"

She shook her head. "I don't want to fight with you. It's just been a long . . . day."

It had been a long summer.

They wandered over to a picnic table and sat on the table-top, their feet on the bench below. A few kids were playing on the swings while a couple more were at the slide, one trying to go down while the other crawled up the chute.

"When you left, I didn't know if you were ever coming back."

"I'm sorry." She clasped his hand in her own, squeezing his fingers. "I worried a lot of people and that was never my intention."

"I know that now." He turned her hand over in his and looked at the tiny creases lining her palms. "But at the time I was angry and hurt."

She nodded, but otherwise didn't respond.

"I've prayed even more since you came back."

"Why?"

"For understanding and wisdom. See, I didn't know what I should do. The girl I love has come back home, but we can't get married now."

"Because of the baptism instruction."

"*Jah*." He looked out over the playground. The wind blew a wayward kite across the ground. It tumbled and turned in the Oklahoma breeze. A young boy about eight years old chased after it, a chocolate Lab on his heels.

"But I also realized a lot of other things while you were away."

"You did?" she asked.

"I learned that it's not *gut* to take someone for granted."

"You think I took you for granted?" she asked.

"I think I took you for granted."

She tilted her head to one side, the strings from her prayer *kapp* brushing against their fingers. "What are you saying, Jonah?"

"I'm saying that I want to marry you, Lorie Kauffman. I have wanted nothing more since I was eighteen years old. But in all that time I never once asked you to be my wife." He moved down to the bench below her. He held one of her hands in his while she pressed the other one to her mouth. Her brown eyes were wide and filled with tears. He could only hope that was a *gut* sign. "Will you?" he asked. "Marry me, that is."

"Jonah, I—"

"Wait." He held up one hand. "Before you answer. I need to tell you something else."

She swallowed hard and nodded, dropping her hand into her lap as she waited for what he would say next.

"I talked to the bishop. He's a fair man." That was one thing about Bishop Ebersol, he was fair to a fault.

"You talked to the bishop about me?"

"I did. I told him that you had made some mistakes, but that you had a tough year. He understood with all the things you had learned about your father."

"Oh, Jonah, I didn't want all the secrets to get out."

He shook his head. "Do you really think the bishop is going to go around and tell everyone your family secrets?"

"*Nay.* I don't."

"But I thought the bishop should know so he could better understand what you have been going through."

"What did he say?"

"He said with secrets like that, it was a miracle you didn't go plum crazy."

Lorie laughed, the sweetest sound he had ever heard. All around them cars purred by, horse and buggies creaked and groaned as they rolled down the streets, and the birds in the trees chirped out the last of their summer songs.

"He and I agreed that giving you stability and a good foundation for the future was the best thing we could offer you. So he's agreed to give you special baptism classes in order for you to join the church this fall."

"But everyone has already been baptized for the year."

Jonah shrugged. "I guess he thinks it's more important to get you in the church than it is to follow a bunch of rules on how to do it." He reached for her other hand and held them tightly, absorbing her warmth as his own and gaining strength to ask the question that would change their lives forever.

"Lorie, will you marry me?" He sucked in another breath before continuing. "Bishop will give you classes and in two weeks, the church can take a vote. After that, you can be baptized, and we can be married."

"This year?" she squeaked.

"All you have to do is say the word. So what's it going to be, Lorie? Will you be my wife?"

"Did you go?"

Zach pasted on a bright smile and flashed it at all the seniors seated at table eight. Despite his efforts, no one believed him.

"That's a no," Stan said.

"If you won't do it for yourself, do it for us," Linda pleaded. "We're tired of these terrible crafts." She held up today's effort, some sort of origami he thought was supposed to be a fox but looked more like a wounded dog.

"Yeah," Eugene bellowed. "Every time I pass that picture of hers in the hallway I want to go see her myself."

"I wonder if we can get the shuttle to take us there," Linda mused.

"That's a great idea." Stan pushed to his feet. "I'm going to talk to Carol about it."

"Face it," Fern said, shooting Zach a stern look. "You messed up big-time with this one."

Zach knew they meant well, but every time he came to visit they brought up Lorie. How was he ever going to get over her if they wouldn't quit talking about her? "Okay, I'm going to say this one more time. She's Amish. She's gone back to live with her family." *And I should have never messed with her emotions.*

"Pshaw," Betty said, waving away his protests. "She was born into this world. Not theirs. She belongs here."

It was the age-old nurture versus nature debate. Maybe he should find Lorie and ask if she wanted to be a part of some scientific study on the matter.

"Speaking of," Eugene said. "When are you going to quit that day job of yours and come back here full-time?"

"Yes," Linda added. "We hardly ever see you anymore."

How could he tell them that he needed the money from his day job? It sounded so materialistic and heartless. Suddenly the conversation he had with Lorie when they were driving through the Dallas neighborhood came to mind. What was more important, being happy or money? Why couldn't a person have both?

"Wouldn't it be great if we can get the shuttle to go to Wells Landing?" Eugene said.

"You'd go with us, right?" Fern asked, pinning him with those sharp blue eyes. "That way you can see her and find out how she's doing."

"She's probably already married," Zach warned.

"Pshaw," Betty said again. "That girl was crazy about you."

He wanted to believe that it was true, but uncertainties plagued him. She had been gone from Tulsa for months. No doubt she had settled back into her previous life. The one without him.

Before Zach could respond, Stan hobbled back up, rubbing his hands together in apparent glee. "She said she would work on it, but I think it's a done deal. We're going to visit the Amish."

"Lorie," Betty added.

Same thing.

Chapter Twenty-Six

"This is it?" Stan pointed his cane in a circle encompassing all of what was Main Street, Wells Landing.

"Stan," Betty admonished. "This is a delightful town."

"Uh-huh," Stan replied.

"Do you want your scooter?" the driver asked.

"In this town? The mall is bigger than this place."

"Well, I think it's charming." Linda ducked so she wouldn't hit her head as she descended from the shuttle steps.

"It does have a real homey feel." Fern hooked her handbag over her arm and surveyed the place with a much less critical eye.

Of course, Zach thought it was charming as well, but this is where Lorie lived and that alone drew him to the place.

The bus driver poked his head out the doors and signaled for Zach. "I'm going to fill up for the trip back. Can you take care of everyone until I get back?"

"Of course."

The driver climbed back behind the wheel and backed the shuttle onto the road.

"Is that it there?" Eugene pointed one gnarled finger toward the Kauffman Family Restaurant.

"It is," Zach replied.

"Looks empty," Stan grumped.

"There's a note on the door, dear," Betty said. "What does it say?"

Zach crossed the street with Fern and Betty close behind.

Closed for Wedding. Reception at 3:30.

"Closed for a wedding?" Fern asked. "Who gets married on a Thursday?"

Only someone in a big hurry. Zach's heart fell. He was too late. He should have come months ago, right after she first left. He should have told her that he was scared. That he was falling for her too fast, and he wasn't sure what to do with such intense feelings for someone he had only known for a short time. But he had told himself that he needed to let her go. What a fool he had been.

"You don't think . . . ?" Betty asked, looking from the sign to him.

"I don't know," he whispered. But he had his suspicions even though every fiber of his being hoped and prayed that he was wrong.

"Betty, we're walking down to the bakery. You want to come with us?"

She shook her head. "I'm staying with Zach."

Leave it to Betty to have a day of clarity when he needed to be alone.

There was a small bench outside the restaurant. The two of them settled there and watched the town. Not much was happening today. A few of the non-Amish vendors had put up Halloween decorations, but for the most part the town showed signs of early fall. A few leaves stirred around in the wind. The sun shone, but the air held the promise of cooler weather.

"Please tell me that you aren't going to sit here until three thirty and wait for her."

Zach scoffed. "Of course not."

She patted him on the knee and gave him that typical Betty smile. "Then come on. If you don't want something yummy from the bakery the least you can do is take your mom back something."

"You're right." Coming here was the dumbest idea he had ever been talked into, but he was here and Lorie was getting married. Time to move forward. He stood and held his arm toward her. "Milady. Where would you like to visit first?"

Betty swung her gaze from one side of the street to the other. "And I can go anywhere I want?"

"But of course."

Lorie's grandmother smiled so big. "I want to go swing."

Three hours later, after swinging in the park, grabbing a sandwich from a place called The Cheese House, and looking at so many quilts Zach was starting to see the patterns even with his eyes closed, it was time to meet the shuttle that would take them back to Tulsa.

"This wasn't why I came here at all," Stan grumbled. "I wanted Zach to see Lorie."

"We all wanted Zach to see Lorie," Eugene boomed.

He shook his head. "You guys are the sweetest, but Lorie got married today."

A chorus of "What?" went up all around the group.

"She got married today." He patiently explained how Lorie had told him she was engaged when she left the Amish all those months ago.

"That doesn't mean this is her wedding they are talking about," Stan said.

"Why else would she return?" Whose wedding could it be if it wasn't hers?

"There could be a hundred reasons," Linda said.

He wanted to believe that, but he couldn't allow himself that much hope.

"Look." Betty grabbed his sleeve and pointed toward the door of the restaurant. A group of Amish women all dressed in the same color of blue were standing outside. Many more buggies and tractors were pulling into the parking lot behind the building.

"There she is." Stan swung his cane around toward the girls dressed in blue.

Zach almost didn't recognize her in her Amish clothing, but there she was.

He wanted to run to her and ask her to please tell him that she hadn't gotten married, but he couldn't embarrass himself that way. What good would it do anyway?

"Yoo-hoo, Lorie. Over here," Betty called out, and waved to her granddaughter.

Lorie turned toward them, her eyes wide as she took them all in. She said something to the girl standing closest to her, then crossed the street to where they waited.

"It's so good to see you." She hugged everyone in turn, then pulled away when she got to Zach. "W-what are you doing here?"

He shoved his hands into his pockets and shrugged. "The seniors wanted to take a trip out here and see the town."

"Oh," Lorie said. If he wasn't mistaken he thought he heard disappointment in her voice.

"It's a senior trip," Fern said. "Get it?"

Lorie smiled, but the action didn't quite reach her eyes. Zach had a feeling there was more to it than her just not understanding the joke.

"We didn't mean to crash your wedding," Zach said. "We were just about to go home anyway."

"You didn't," she said. "Wait. It's not *my* wedding."

"It's not?" Could he hope now? He squashed that thought.

Just because she wasn't the one who got married today didn't mean she wanted anything to do with him.

"My sister Melanie got married today."

"Your sister?" He had to stop repeating everything she said. "I mean, how nice for her."

"We're just about to open the restaurant for the reception. Would y'all like to join us?"

Betty moved to stand next to Lorie. She hooked one arm through her granddaughter's and gave her a smile. "I would love to meet your family. Especially your mother."

"She's my stepmother, really."

Betty nodded. "Of course."

And just like that Zach found himself in the middle of an Amish wedding reception.

There was enough food to feed half the town. Even though it hadn't been that long since he'd eaten, he accepted a plate of cake and milled around between all the Amish folk and tried not to feel like the odd man out. Was this how Lorie felt when she came to Tulsa to visit?

The seniors didn't seem to be having the same problem. Perhaps that was the beauty of growing old. A person could adapt better because they had lived through more. Or maybe like Stan most of them just didn't care anymore. Zach smiled at the thought and watched as Fern and Linda talked to a very round lady with sparkling brown eyes and a kindly smile. Eugene and Stan had slid into a booth and were eating cake like they would never be allowed to have it again. Thank goodness neither one of them was diabetic.

"Hi."

He turned, surprised to find Lorie standing there. He had hoped to get a moment alone to talk to her but had started to believe that it was a lost cause. "Hi."

"I was surprised to see you today." She laughed and stared out among the guests. "More than surprised, really."

"The seniors decided they wanted to take a trip, and here we are."

"All the way to Wells Landing?"

"You know how stubborn they can be."

She gave a small nod. "I do at that."

"Is that your stepmother?" Zach asked. "The one who keeps looking over here and scowling?"

Lorie chuckled. "That's not a scowl. She always looks like that."

"Wow, that must have been hard as a child."

"It wasn't always easy, but she has a good heart. Next to her is my sister Melanie."

"The one who got married today?"

"*Jah.* Yes. And the tall girl next to her is Sadie, my stepsister. Then Cora Ann and Daniel."

Such a sweet family who had recently lost their father and patriarch. No wonder it was so hard for Lorie to remain away from them. But why did she have to leave without a note?

"Why did you disappear?"

She sighed and stared off through the front window of the restaurant, but Zach had the feeling she was looking at something only her eyes could see. "I didn't mean to. I tried to write you a letter to explain, but I couldn't find the words."

"You could have come and talked to me."

She shook her head. "I was afraid that you would talk me into staying."

"Would that have been so bad? Don't answer that."

"Why did you come here, Zach?"

"The seniors talk about you every day. They want to see you and decided to make this one of their monthly outings."

"I know why they came. Why did you come?"

He sighed and pitched his half-eaten cake into the nearby trash. As good as it had been when he first started eating it, the flavor had somehow turned to chalk. "I guess I wanted to see for myself. See if you are happy and well." He paused. "Engaged."

"I'm not," she said. "I mean, I'm happy and well, but I'm not engaged."

His gaze snapped to hers. "You're not?"

She shook her head. "He asked me to marry him, but I had to tell him no."

"You had to?" His mouth turned to ash, and his heart thumped painfully in his chest.

"Had to." It seemed as if the words were coming harder for her. "You see, I think I might be in love with someone else."

Hope burst like fireworks in his chest. "You might be?"

She expelled a heavy sigh as if she had been waiting for him before she could continue. "I'm pretty sure," she said. "But I don't know how he feels about me."

He opened his mouth to tell her exactly how he felt when Betty rushed up, a plate of lime gelatin in her hand. "Look," she squealed. "Leprechaun pudding."

After Betty's revelation about the lime-flavored dessert, Lorie and Zach were separated. The next thing she knew she had to help clean up the mess and Zach and the seniors were gone. She hated the delay in talking to him, but she supposed someone else's wedding was not the best place to declare your love for someone.

"Is that him?"

Lorie tied up the trash bag and turned to face Jonah. They hadn't talked any since she had turned down his proposal. She knew he was hurt, that she had hurt him, but she hadn't meant to. Sometimes things just weren't meant to be. "Yes."

He nodded and shoved his hands into his pockets. "Does he love you?"

"I think so, *jah*." Zach hadn't had a chance to say the

words, but Lorie had to believe they were in his heart. He had come all the way to Wells Landing to see her after she left without an explanation to him. That had to mean something.

"Is he going to marry you?"

Lorie pulled the bag from the can, then Jonah was there taking over the task. "It's not like that with the *Englisch,*" she said, following him out to the Dumpster.

He pitched the bag inside, then dusted his hands as together they walked back inside the restaurant. "I wouldn't know."

"Jonah." Lorie laid a hand on his arm. "Please don't be bitter." She had seen what bitterness had done to her *mamm*.

"I don't know how else to be. I have loved you for so long."

"And I you, but sometimes love isn't enough."

He scoffed.

"Not when two people want different things from life."

"What is it that you want, Lorie Kauffman?"

"I want to paint," she said. "I want to volunteer at the living center. See my grandmother whenever I want. Visit the new friends that I've made."

He blew out a frustrated breath. "I've tried to understand. I truly have. But I don't see the lure of the *Englisch* world."

She touched her fingers to his cheek and gave him a small smile. "That's because you are truly Amish, but I am not."

"You were raised here. How can you not be Amish?"

She shook her head, unable to answer that. "There are *gut* things out there waiting for you, Jonah Miller. Don't let them pass you by because you are looking back at me."

"Lorie, this came for you yesterday, but with all the excitement, I forgot to give it to you." Sadie handed her a letter.

The wedding had gone off without a hitch. Melanie had

married Noah Treger, the son of the bishop in the next district over. It would be weird not attending church with Melanie on Sunday, but it would be the last week Lorie herself would be part of the Amish community.

She hadn't heard from Zach since the afternoon before. She had hoped that he would call and explain what his feelings for her were. But either way, she was headed to Tulsa. Luke had helped her get a place in a transition house. She had taken the money from the sale of her paintings and used it to get started in her new life. She still had to find a job, but she wasn't as concerned with that as she had been before. She knew that she was making the right decision and because of that everything would fall into place. She was learning how to drive a car and soon she would take her GED test. She was even thinking about going to college. But she knew that was a ways down the road for her. Still it was good to have dreams. Even if they didn't include Zach.

She had hoped that he would call, but he had disappeared. She supposed she deserved that considering how she left him before. But there was truly only one reason why he would walk out and not look back. He didn't feel the same way for her as she did for him.

Her first *Englisch* heartbreak.

She tried to tell herself that she would get over it, but she knew that healing would be a long time in coming.

"Thanks, Sadie," she said, turning the letter over in her hands. The writing was unfamiliar though the return address was Dallas. Her name was written in a flowing script that was thin and elegant.

Without looking up, she slid into a booth and tore open the seal.

My Dearest Lorie,
I'm writing this letter to you knowing that when you get it I will be gone. I know I am not long for

*this world, but I'm giving this letter to my attorney
to save until my will is read. See, I know how the
remainder of my family will react when they know
that I am leaving you part of the estate. But you are
a Prescott regardless of what name you use. My
blood runs through your veins, and you deserve a
part off all that I own.*

*That said, I am leaving you five hundred thousand
dollars. This is a pittance compared to the remainder
of the estate's worth, but if you are frugal and invest
well, you should be able to live comfortably for a
good long while. Long enough for you to decide
what you want to do with your life.*

*Lorie, I have so many regrets in my life, but none
so heavy as how I treated you and your father. Chalk
it up to a foolish and grieving woman who was
neither perfect nor forgiving. So strange what a few
years and terminal cancer can do to change what's
important in one's life.*

*I only wish that you and I had found each other
sooner, but I am grateful that we found each other
at all.*

*Please take care of yourself, dear granddaughter.
Know that if at all possible I am watching over you
from heaven.*

> *With love and regrets,*
> *Ellie Prescott*

Lorie wiped away her tears and tucked the letter and the
check back into the envelope.

"Are you okay, Sister?" Sadie slid into the booth opposite
Lorie.

She nodded. "*Jah*. My grandmother died."

"The lady that was here? The one who kept calling the gelatin dessert pudding?"

A small bark of laughter escaped Lorie, but she shook her head. "That's *Dat*'s *mudder*, this is my *mudder*'s *mudder*."

Sadie nodded.

"She left me a great deal of money," she said in awe.

"That's *gut, jah?*"

"*Jah*." She would never get to know Ellie Prescott, but Lorie wouldn't have to worry about anything for a long time.

"Lorie," *Mamm* called from the door to the kitchen. "There's a man on the phone. Said he was from the Sundale something or another home. Wants to talk to you about a job teaching the residents how to paint."

"Well, here you are," Luke said as he pulled her car in front of the Hillview Apartments.

"Aren't you coming in?" Lorie asked. Overwhelmed with the task of buying furniture and getting everything set up in the apartment, she hired a decorator to take care of the basics. It was a splurge, she knew, but the only one she'd indulged in since she had received her inheritance.

"Nah. Sissy is already waiting, and we've got to go meet her father at the track."

"Oh." Lorie did her best to hide the disappointment from her voice, but it was there all the same.

She supposed that was the way it would be. She was on her own now. Might as well get used to it. But alone didn't mean lonely. She was excited about the new adventure awaiting her. Tomorrow she would start her new job as art director at the Sundale Retirement and Assisted Living Center.

"Thanks for the ride."

Luke nodded. "I'll leave your car right here."

"For when I learn how to drive it."

"You'll learn soon enough."

Lorie dug her keys out of her purse and slung the strap over her shoulder.

"Call me if you need anything."

"Of course." She had a brand-new cell phone with all the important numbers plugged in for when she needed them.

She waved at Sissy and Luke as they sped off in her shiny convertible, then made her way down the sidewalk toward unit 6A.

She felt deliciously *Englisch* as she opened the door and let herself in.

The scent of roses met her as she dropped her purse in the chair by the door.

Large bouquets of flowers sat on every available surface, the coffee table, the end tables, the dining room table, even the kitchen cabinets. There were all colors from white to red and were mixed with other fragrant blooms. Ribbons, balloons, and a trail of petals led from the front door to the back of the apartment.

She was pretty certain she hadn't asked for any of this, but it had to be the decorator. No criminal would break in and leave flowers. Would they?

"Hello?"

"Hi." Zach came out of the kitchen wiping his hands on a dishtowel and wearing an apron. "I wasn't expecting you for another hour."

"What are you doing here?" She hadn't seen him since he had left her sister's wedding without a word. That had been three weeks ago.

"I'm welcoming you to your new home." He took off the apron and tossed it onto the counter behind him. "I've got dinner in the oven and a couple of surprises for you."

It was a surprise all right. "I don't know what to say."

"You don't have to say anything." He took her by the arm and led her toward the camel-colored sofa. All her furniture was plain and solid colors, but she wanted to be able to add her own personal touches to the place as she found things that made her heart beat a little faster.

"I like the picture," he said, nodding toward the canvas she had painted of him. Thankfully it had been in the stack of paintings that Lorie had left behind in Wells Landing, though now it hung in the greatest place of honor: above the fireplace mantel.

Heat filled Lorie's cheeks. "I didn't mean for you to see that."

He settled on the sofa and patted the cushion next to him. "I like it."

She eased down next to him and hid her trembling hands by tucking them under her legs. "Why are you here, Zach?" She wanted to believe that he had come because he loved her and wanted to give their relationship a second chance, but she couldn't allow those feelings to have their head.

"There are a few unresolved issues between us."

"Like?"

"My father for one."

Lorie managed to bite back the dozen or so questions that raced to the tip of her tongue. As patiently as she could, she waited for Zach to continue.

"I won't bore you with all the details of my childhood, but for the most part it was good enough. Until one day this stranger called the house. A woman. She sounded nice enough, but what she had to say . . ." He shook his head. "It seemed my father had two families, the one with me, Ashtyn, and Mom and another with this woman and three little girls."

Lorie inhaled sharply, searching for something to say. "How old were you?"

"Eight. Ashtyn was twelve." He took a deep breath as if gathering the courage he needed to continue. "Basically Mom told him he was going to have to choose, so he did. He chose them."

Her heart broke for him. "I'm so sorry."

"Yeah, me too. But it was a long time ago. I do my best to move on. Some days are easier than others, but the pain is always there."

"Is that why you didn't want to talk about it?"

He nodded. "I don't like digging up the past. I don't like trying to figure out why I wasn't good enough for him to stay."

"Oh, Zach." She scooted a little closer to him and laid one hand on his cheek.

He covered it with his own, then lowered them both to his lap. His dazzling smile shone through his hurt. "But I didn't come here to talk about him. I came to talk about us."

Lorie shook her head. "But I thought . . ."

"What?"

"I thought you wanted to take things slow."

He nodded. "It's best, don't you think? I mean you just moved here and have a lot on your plate. I think you deserve some time to adjust a little before getting married."

"W-what?" Had she heard him right?

"I don't want to rush you," he said. "That's why I waited."

"I don't understand." She wanted to.

"I love you, Lorie. I have since the first time I saw you. But I couldn't persuade you to come here. You had to make that decision on your own. Staying away from you these last few weeks has been harder than you will ever know."

He pushed to his feet and reached into his jeans pocket. Out came a little black box, and he was on his knee in a second.

Lorie sat there, stunned.

"I said I was going to do this after dinner, but I've waited three weeks for you to get here and all of my life to find you. No more waiting." He opened the box to reveal a thin gold band with a clear diamond sparkling in its center. "Will you marry me?"

Lorie's heart soared as Zach shifted to both knees and wrapped her in his arms. He lowered his head and captured her mouth in a kiss so full of promise her head swam.

How had she gotten so blessed to have everything come together so fully? How could she have everything she could ever want and more?

Zach lifted his head, kissed the tip of her nose, and rested his forehead against hers. "I'll take that as a yes."

"Yes," she breathed.

"We'll take our time, okay? Maybe get married this time next year."

"Okay." She pulled him close for another lingering kiss.

He laughed a little, stirring the breath that separated them. "Maybe the summer would be better."

Lorie nodded. "Summer," she repeated. "Summer would definitely be better."

Epilogue

"All right, everyone, grab the pop bottle and dip the bottom into your paint. The four points are going to be your flowers."

Zach watched as the room full of seniors did as Lorie instructed.

Oh, how she had blossomed in the last few weeks. Her confidence had grown, her eyes sparkled, and in general she looked like she was deeply in love.

And he was the man she dreamed about. How lucky could one guy get?

"I thought we were going to paint Christmas presents." Betty looked from the bottom of the bottle to the blank canvas, then back again.

"These are Christmas presents," Lorie explained. "Once we're done, you can gift them to whoever you want."

"But I wanted to paint a *present*." She frowned.

"How about next week?" Lorie asked. "We can use them to decorate the halls. For the holidays."

"Of course," Betty murmured.

"Betty, quit asking questions and paint," Stan grumbled.

"I was just wondering," she shot back.

Fern pinned Stan with a fierce look for a woman who barely weighed eighty pounds. "Quit fussing at her."

"Is there any orange paint?" Eugene looked skeptically at the pan of pink that sat between him and Linda. "I'd rather have orange."

"No orange," his sister said.

And the almost good-natured argument was under way.

Zach sent a small wave toward his fiancée and left the rec room. He could watch her paint all day, but for now he had a supply closet to organize and an order to put in. But soon he would join her and the rest of the seniors for lunch.

"Zach," Carol called from the front of the Sundale Retirement and Assisted Living Center. "Can you help me please?"

He found Carol on the stepladder doing her best stretches but still unable to reach the very top of the Christmas tree.

"Let me," Zach said, taking the top of the tree star from her as she descended the small ladder.

With ease, he clamped the star in place and stood back with Carol to admire the tree. Right after Lorie returned to Tulsa, Zach had quit his office job in favor of working at the living center and doing books on the side. So far his freelance venture had three steady clients—the Kauffman Family Restaurant, Sundale, and Cameron's father's concrete company. More clients were sure to come, but he was enjoying his full-time job at the living center more and more each day. Maybe because he could peek in and see his beautiful Lorie anytime he wanted.

"How's it look?" Carol asked, indicating the fully decorated tree with sparkling lights and deep red bows.

"Beautiful," he said, but not as gorgeous as the woman he would marry next year or the tree she had put up at her apartment. For a girl who had never celebrated Christmas this way before, she embraced the concept fully, putting up a tree so tall the very top was bent over from lack of room.

"Merry Christmas," Amber called as she walked through.

"Happy New Year," Carol returned.

And it was—a merry and happy time. He and Lorie would get married sometime next June. As newly converted to the English world, she wanted to follow the custom of a June wedding, though he doubted she would cave in to all the frills and pomp that Ashtyn was trying to convince her to use. Knowing Lorie, she would be in full wedding dress, her long, blond hair a beautiful halo around her face, and cowboy boots on her feet. She was one of a kind for sure.

One of a kind and all his.

He sent up a small prayer of thanks. How blessed could one guy be?

Please turn the page for an exciting sneak peek of

Amy Lillard's next Wells Landing Amish romance,

JUST PLAIN SADIE,

coming in April 2016!

"I have something I need to talk to you about."

At Chris's words, Sadie's heart pounded in her chest. Was this it? She had been waiting on this moment for a long, long time. Now it was about to happen on this cold but bright January day on his father's farm. She had known something was up when he'd asked her to take a walk, but she hadn't dreamed that today could be the day. Yet from the sound of his voice, Chris had something very important to say. As important as a marriage proposal? She could only hope.

Sure, she and Chris Flaud were nothing more than best friends who had been paired off in their buddy bunch like a true couple instead of just good pals. But what better person to marry than a best friend? She knew all his little habits, all his quirks, and shortcomings. So she didn't love him with that breathless wonder that the English novelists talked about. There was more to a marriage—more to life—than that.

"*Jah?*" The one word was a mere whisper upon her lips. She had wanted to come across as strong and true, yet all she sounded was anxious and fretful. But she was anxious and fretful.

More than anything in the world she wanted to get

married. That wasn't so much to ask, was it? Especially when everyone around them thought they were just being secretive when they claimed to be only friends. A couple of years ago Sadie gave up defending their friendship and let people believe what they wanted. They were doing that anyway. But somewhere along the road, she had started to think about marriage. Not in a silly romantic way, but in a strong steady kind of way. And she knew that one day Chris would be her husband. She just knew it.

Was today that day?

He took her hand into his own, turning it over and tracing the creases on her palm. "This is kinda hard to say." He glanced up at the sky, across the field where they sat next to a half-frozen pond. He looked at his lap, then back at their hands once again. "It's no secret that you're my best friend, right?"

"Of course." She did her best to sound confident, but she feared she had failed miserably.

"Best friends should be able to say anything to each other, right?" He seemed to be asking himself rather than her, so Sadie kept quiet and waited for him to continue. "It's just that . . ."

Her heart pounded even harder in her chest, so hard that she thought it might fly away on its own.

"What I'm about to tell you is just between the two of us, okay?"

She nodded, breathless as she waited for him to continue.

"I'm going to Europe."

Suddenly the world was swept out from underneath her. She took her hand from Chris's, using it to steady herself, though she was still sitting in the same place she had been before. Everything seemed tilted now, a little askew, not quite right. He was going to Europe?

Europe?

"Sadie? Are you okay?"

She cleared her throat and managed to nod. "*Jah,* of course." Her voice didn't sound like her own, and a sudden chill ran through her bones. She pulled her coat a little tighter around her. "I think my ears are playing tricks on me. I thought you said you were going to Europe. That can't be right." He was supposed to be proposing, stating his intentions of joining the church and making her his wife. Wasn't that what everyone thought would happen?

"That's what I said." His voice seemed small as if it was coming to her from down a long tunnel.

"Europe?" Thousands of thoughts flew through her head at once. Europe was so far away; was he asking her to go too? No, wait. He hadn't said anything about getting married, about joining the church, about the future they would have. Just Europe.

Sadie pushed to her feet, though the world still seemed to be spinning, her emotions a strange mixture of disappointment and relief.

"I told you how I wanted to travel." From behind her, Chris's voice held a damaged edge, as if somehow her reaction had wounded him.

"*Jah,* you did." She stifled a laugh and whirled back to face him. "A lot of us talk about the things that we want to do. But they're not things that we are really *going* to do."

"You thought I was just talking?"

He had talked for hours and hours about seeing the world and what it would be like and traveling and how it would feel to be on a boat, to be on a plane, to be in a car in the remote places he'd read about on the computer at the library. But that was all she thought it was—talk. Reluctantly, she nodded and wondered how the day had turned so wrong.

Chris pushed to his feet and came to stand by her side. He reached out as if he were going to touch her, then he seemed to change his mind and dropped his hands back to his sides once again. "I thought you would understand."

"I do." She wanted to. But how did she explain to him that searching for his dreams was killing hers? Was it so much to ask to want to be married? It was all she wanted from life. To work her job at the restaurant, get married to a nice man, have children, and live out her days in Wells Landing. They seemed like attainable dreams, but now they were as far away as the moon.

He expelled a heavy breath. "I'm not going yet," he said. "This summer. I talked to a travel agent, and he got me a good deal for June. Flights and all that."

Travel agent? "You're going to get on an airplane?" Of all the questions she had to ask, that one was perhaps the least important, but the one that jumped to her lips first. She turned to him then, searching his features for some sort of explanation as to what made him want to fly half the world away when as far as she could see everything she needed was right there in Wells Landing.

"That part makes me a little nervous." He chuckled. "But I'm looking forward to it. It's an adventure out there, Sadie. Don't you see?"

All she could see were her dreams slipping away, her best friend not joining the church, not staying in Wells Landing, and not being a part of her life for much longer.

"You're not coming back."

"Oh, Sadie, don't be like that. Of course I'm coming back. Airplanes are safe now. It's not like what you think."

Sadie shook her head. "I'm not worried about the plane, *it's you.*" Chris wasn't the only Amish man who wanted to see the world, who wanted to taste the pleasures that lay beyond the boundaries of their district. And all too often the people who left never came back. Luke Lambright, her sister Lorie, just to name a few. But Sadie had never understood the call of the English world. She was happy being Amish. She was happy right where she was. That might be simplistic or naïve, but that's just the way she was.

Chris was leaving; she was staying. It was as simple as that.

"I haven't told anyone else," he said.

"You told me."

"That's different. I knew you would understand."

Did she?

"You can't tell anyone," Chris continued. "No one. Not even Ruthie, Hannah, or Melanie. Not until I tell my parents."

"Okay," she agreed, albeit reluctantly. The one person she would want to talk to was gone. Her sister Lorie had left Wells Landing last year to move to Tulsa. That had been a hard time for Sadie. Their father had just passed away and Lorie had discovered he had a tattoo that no one else knew about. That made her search for more things. She uncovered a grandmother living in a nursing home in Tulsa and a whole secret life that her father had lived without anyone in Wells Landing knowing about. Even worse, Henry Kauffman hadn't been Amish nor had his last name been Kauffman. And Sadie had managed to keep all that to herself. What was one more secret?

Though she missed Lorie terribly, she knew her sister was happy now. She wasn't having to hide her paintings, or wonder about what her life would have been like had her father not made the choice to hide her out in the Amish community, pretending to be Amish himself as he raised her Plain. It had been two months since Lorie had left.

Two long months of waiting for her visits, waiting for phone calls at the restaurant, and envying the happiness that she had found. For not only was she living out her dream getting to know her grandmother and teaching painting to the senior citizens at the Sundale Living Center, she had met the handsome *Englischer*, Zach Calhoun. They were planning their wedding for some time this June. And now this.

June was going to be a very busy month.

"Chris, you should tell them." She had been walking around

with so many secrets inside, but this was different. It was one thing to hold her own secret from the community in order to not damage her father's memory within the district and quite another to keep someone else's secret from the people who loved him.

He nodded. "I know, I know. But I'm not ready to tell them yet. I don't think they'll handle it well."

"What would give you such an idea?"

"Sadie, really?"

"I'm just saying that their youngest son decides to travel off to Europe and not join the church. Why would they find any fault in that?" She wasn't about to apologize for her sarcasm. Maybe it would shake some sense into Chris, make him see how his choices were going to affect everyone around him.

"I never said anything about not joining the church. I can go to Europe. I'm still in my *rumspringa*. I can travel, come back, and take baptism classes next year. Bishop Treger let Lorie take his classes."

Sadie didn't point out that hadn't gone over very well, and she didn't think the bishop would allow that to happen again considering the fact that Lorie dropped out of the classes and moved away. Besides, if Chris really wanted to join the church he would just have to wait one more year. Bishop Ebersol might not be thrilled with him waiting until he was twenty-four, but she doubted Chris would be the oldest Amish man ever to join. If he joined.

"And my parents have Johnny," Chris continued. "He's taken over the farm. He's going to run everything. They don't need me for that. Why should I not live my life? Do the things I want to do."

"Can you hear yourself? How selfish you sound? Does that not bother you?"

Chris shoved his fingers through his hair knocking his hat to the cold ground. "This isn't about being selfish or not. It's about an opportunity. I've saved my money. I've worked hard. I don't see why I shouldn't be allowed to spend that money as I want. I can't get this out of my system any other way, Sadie—" He growled in frustration. "I thought you would understand."

Sadie blinked back tears. This was not how this conversation was supposed to turn out. Even if it hadn't been a marriage proposal the last thing she wanted to do was fight with Chris.

"I'm trying to. Really I am. But with *Dat* and Lorie . . ." She shook her head. "I'm sorry, Chris. I know you have to do what's right for you." Even if it meant her giving up her dreams. After all, she and Chris had been friends for so long everyone thought they would eventually get married. He hadn't tagged her for marriage, which was common for men who hadn't joined the church to do for young ladies who had. It was like a promise, so to speak, so when he joined the church they would be officially engaged.

Even though Chris hadn't made that promise to her, everyone just assumed that Sadie was Chris's girl, and no one came around courtin'. And so with Chris, all her dreams of marriage were flying off to Europe.

"Will you be happy for me?"

She nodded, her throat clogged with emotion. "I am."

"I can't ask you to wait for me."

Of course he wouldn't. Nor would she ask that promise of him. He didn't love her like that. *Jah,* if they were to marry, they would make a fine couple. But love would never be a big part of it. She couldn't ask him to promise to return, to promise to marry her, to promise not to turn English.

Despite his arguments otherwise, she knew that once he left, he'd never return.

She could only enjoy him for the time he would remain in Wells Landing, and after that . . . ? Well, she was glad that she had her job at the restaurant and her family. If nothing else those two things gave meaning to her life.

And that was more than some people had.

"I think it's over this way," Chris pointed down the long aisle of booths set up for the weekly farmers' market in Pryor.

Sadie looked down the walkway of vendors, shading her eyes against the noonday sun. "Are you sure?" Row and rows of booths were set up all looking just enough alike that Sadie was quickly turned around. They had passed the stand a bit ago, but Sadie wanted to wait until it was time for them to leave before she made her purchase.

"Why do you need buffalo meat again?" William asked.

They had all come out together, her little group of coupled-off friends: she and Chris, William and Hannah, Mark and Ruthie.

"It's bison meat," Sadie corrected. "And it's for Cora Ann." She shook her head. "*Mamm* said she could pick out some new recipes for the restaurant. And she chose something with bison meat."

Chris laughed. "What is she doing? Reading *Food and Wine* magazine again?"

Sadie returned his chuckle with one of her own. "What do you mean again? She never stopped."

Of all her siblings, Cora Ann was the most like their father. She had a love of food and restaurant work that made Sadie a little envious. Oh to know what you wanted out of life, and to be able to get it.

Sadie loved her work at the restaurant, she really did. But not like Cora Ann. At thirteen, her youngest sister was constantly pouring over food magazines and recipes. Sadie even caught her on the Internet checking out different recipes on the restaurant's computer. *Jah*, Sadie was certain that one day Kauffman's Family Restaurant would be in Cora Ann's capable hands.

Mark took a couple of more steps in the direction that Chris had indicated. "I think I see it." Then he grabbed Ruthie's hand and together they started in the opposite direction.

Sadie whirled around. "Where are you going?"

Mark turned and walked backward not bothering to let go of Ruthie's hand as they continued. "Just because you want to buy buffalo meat doesn't mean we do." He gave them a grin. "We'll meet you at the van."

"Bison meat," she corrected once again, then turned around just in time to see William and Hannah head off down another aisle. She didn't even bother to ask them where they were going. It was like that these days. Since she and Chris were the only couple in their bunch who hadn't gotten married, she felt like a third wheel, even when they were together.

Well, that wasn't exactly true. Lorie and Jonah had been a part of their group once upon a time and they hadn't gotten married. And she and Chris weren't a couple. Just best friends, sidekicks.

"I guess it's just me and you." Sadie sighed. The six of them had hired a driver to come to the market so they could shop and spend time together. So much for that.

Chris smiled. "Just the way I like it."

Last week, those words would have made her heart pound in her chest, but today they only made her sad. Her time with Chris was growing smaller each day.

Together they made their way through the milling shoppers. The market was a great place to find fresh produce and other ingredients for the restaurant. Normally, Sadie loved coming and wandering through the stalls and stands, learning of new foods and tools. A little of anything and everything could be found at the market.

"Are you serious about Europe?" She hadn't meant to ask the question, but it had been building inside her for days. Ever since Chris had told her about his plans.

"*Jah.* Of course."

She nodded.

"You haven't told anyone, have you?"

"No." And she wouldn't. Not until he broke the news to his parents.

Chris pointed up ahead. "There it is."

Sadie recognized the sign. HEIN FARMS, it read. EXOTIC MEATS AND ANIMALS. But the man standing at the booth was not the one who had been there earlier.

This man was . . .

She stumbled as he turned to face her.

The most handsome man she had ever seen.

And a Mennonite.

"Can I help you?" he asked. His voice was smooth, not too deep. Just right. In fact, everything about him was just right from his sun-streaked blond hair to his dark brown eyes.

He wore faded blue jeans like she had seen Zach Calhoun wear, an orange and white checkered shirt, and black suspenders. Suddenly she felt more than plain in her mourning black. Not that it mattered.

"*Jah*, I was here earlier talking to a guy about some bison meat."

"That was my friend. He was watching the booth for me. Ezra Hein," he said with a nod.

"Sadie Kauffman. Nice to meet you," she returned. "He gave me some quotes when we stopped by earlier. I have them here." She reached into her bag and pulled out the piece of paper with the price per pound that the friend had written down for her. Her hands were trembling as she handed it to Ezra.

"That's a lot of meat," he said.

"My family owns a restaurant in Wells Landing."

He nodded.

Was it just her or was this conversation awkward? Probably because instead of talking about meat and restaurants, she'd rather be talking about anything else with him.

He had to be the most intriguing man she had ever seen. Attractive, polite . . .

She pushed those thoughts away. He was a Mennonite, and she was Amish. He was handsome, and she was plain. What would a guy like him want with a girl like her?

"Do you get the meat locally?" she asked, trying to remember all the things *Mamm* had wanted her to ask.

"You could say that. We raise them ourselves, then send them to a butcher in Tulsa. He packages everything there and we pick it up when it's ready."

"Really?"

He smiled. "Yes. We also have ostriches and deer, if you're interested. All of our stock is organically fed. Even the camels."

Sadie was just drifting off into an Ezra-filled daydream when his last word brought her back to reality. "Camels? You don't eat them, do you?" She tried to not make a face. But camel meat?

Ezra laughed. "No, we keep them for milk."

"Camels, ostriches, bison, and deer? That sounds like quite a farm."

"You should come out and see it sometime."

She would like nothing more. And suddenly Chris going to Europe didn't seem like the end of her world. "I would like that." She smiled. "So can you supply us with that much bison?"

He nodded. "Of course. When would you like delivery?"

As he worked out the details of the order with Sadie, she had a hard time concentrating on what he was saying and not how he looked and smelled while he was saying it. And sh⌐

wondered when she might be able to get away to visit the Hein farm.

She signed the papers, handed him a business card for the restaurant, and shook his hand, loving the feel of his strong grip and his warm, calloused fingers.

What was wrong with her? She must have been out in the heat too long, though it was the prettiest day in late January that she could ever remember. Seventy degrees couldn't really be described as hot.

"Well, Sadie Kauffman. I'll be seeing you."

She smiled at his words. Was that promise she heard in his voice, or just wishful thinking on her part? *Please let it be promise.* She couldn't say what was so special about Ezra Hein, but it was there all the same. Suddenly the chasm between Amish and Mennonite didn't seem so impossible to cross.

"He's flirty," Chris commented as they turned to go. He wore a frown on his face, his brow wrinkled with disapproval.

Sadie had almost forgotten he was with her. "He's just nice," she said. No sense in getting her hopes up only to have them dashed to pieces.

"If you say so."

"I do." As they walked back down the aisle to find their friends, Sadie looked back at the stand.

Ezra was looking after them, her business card in one hand and a smile on his face. He caught her gaze and gave her a little wave.

Sadie returned it, then faced front, trying not to count down the days until she would see Ezra again.

More by Bestselling Author
Hannah Howell

__Highland Angel	978-1-4201-0864-4	$6.99US/$8.99CAN
__If He's Sinful	978-1-4201-0461-5	$6.99US/$8.99CAN
__Wild Conquest	978-1-4201-0464-6	$6.99US/$8.99CAN
__If He's Wicked	978-1-4201-0460-8	$6.99US/$8.49CAN
__My Lady Captor	978-0-8217-7430-4	$6.99US/$8.49CAN
__Highland Sinner	978-0-8217-8001-5	$6.99US/$8.49CAN
__Highland Captive	978-0-8217-8003-9	$6.99US/$8.49CAN
__Nature of the Beast	978-1-4201-0435-6	$6.99US/$8.49CAN
__Highland Fire	978-0-8217-7429-8	$6.99US/$8.49CAN
__Silver Flame	978-1-4201-0107-2	$6.99US/$8.49CAN
__Highland Wolf	978-0-8217-8000-8	$6.99US/$9.99CAN
__Highland Wedding	978-0-8217-8002-2	$4.99US/$6.99CAN
__Highland Destiny	978-1-4201-0259-8	$4.99US/$6.99CAN
__Only for You	978-0-8217-8151-7	$6.99US/$8.99CAN
__Highland Promise	978-1-4201-0261-1	$4.99US/$6.99CAN
__Highland Vow	978-1-4201-0260-4	$4.99US/$6.99CAN
__Highland Savage	978-0-8217-7999-6	$6.99US/$9.99CAN
__Beauty and the Beast	978-0-8217-8004-6	$4.99US/$6.99CAN
__Unconquered	978-0-8217-8088-6	$4.99US/$6.99CAN
__Highland Barbarian	978-0-8217-7998-9	$6.99US/$9.99CAN
__Highland Conqueror	978-0-8217-8148-7	$6.99US/$9.99CAN
__Conqueror's Kiss	978-0-8217-8005-3	$4.99US/$6.99CAN
__A Stockingful of Joy	978-1-4201-0018-1	$4.99US/$6.99CAN
__Highland Bride	978-0-8217-7995-8	$4.99US/$6.99CAN
__Highland Lover	978-0-8217-7759-6	$6.99US/$9.99CAN

Available Wherever Books Are Sold!

Check out our website at
http://www.kensingtonbooks.com